The Realm of the Hungry Ghosts

D1628452

Gary William Murning

GWM Publications

Contents © Gary William Murning 2012

The right of Gary William Murning to be identified as the author
of this work has be asserted in accordance with the
Copyright, Designs and Patent Act 1988.

British Library Cataloguing in Publication Data available.

ISBN 978-0-9570636-0-0

Cover designed by Gudrun Jobst
www.yotedesign.com

In memory of Jean Currie

Also by Gary William Murning

If I Never

Children of the Resolution

Chapter One

"Are you planning on staying in there all day?"

I looked up at her. Ashley Moore, my beautiful if sometimes rather apathetic wife – our sleepy two-year-old daughter Nadine Verity perched on her hip, head on her mother's comfortable chest. From my hole in the ground, at least four feet down, and with the sun behind her, she was an impressive figure. Actually a little on the short side, and with a carelessness about her that had once been attractive, my perspective imbued her with an elegance that quickly made me forget my irritation at being interrupted.

"You know me, love," I said. "I don't plan." This wasn't entirely true, and she knew it. I could actually be methodical to the point of fastidiousness when the mood took me – and whilst I may have rarely planned in any overt way, I was nevertheless inclined to think well ahead. With my work, if nothing else.

She gave me her best I'm-trying-to-be-patient look and lifted Nadine higher on her hip. "Yeah, whatever," she said. "But are you staying in there all day, or what? In case you've forgotten, a certain little lady is having a few friends round later and... well, let's just say I'd rather have that living grave of yours filled in before they come, if you don't mind."

We'd already had this conversation and she knew very well that filling in my hole at this early stage in the game was simply out of the question.

The day was warm – promising intense heat and high humidity – but it was cool where I was, and, briefly, I took solace in that. Closing my eyes and breathing in the damp, fibrous scent of soil and clay, I tried to remember what it was like to be autonomous, to never be answerable to anyone, alone, selfish and focused entirely on my own goals and obsessions. That had been the post-university bachelor me. An alien figure, it now seemed. And however annoying Ashley's nagging could be, I found I didn't truthfully envy that shadowy half-man.

And so, very calmly, I reminded myself just how lucky I was and said for the umpteenth time, "Darling, you know I can't fill the hole in. I haven't fixed the problem, yet."

Nadine had picked up on the tone of exaggerated patience in our voices. She glanced warily from her mother to me and back again. The fleeting suspicion I saw in my daughter's indigo eyes made me feel like a stranger. I wanted to smile at her, tell her that everything was going to be all right – but I just wouldn't have been convincing.

"There isn't a problem, though, *darling*," Ashley insisted. "So the lawn gets a little water-logged now and then. It's a lawn. It's not as if our foundations are filling with water or anything."

"I want the lawn to be nice."

"Because your dad always kept it nice. I know. And that's lovely, it really is, but how is a bloody big hole going to help."

I wasn't entirely sure, but I couldn't tell her that. The hole had been an impulse – something I'd felt I'd needed as much for the hole itself as for the solution I'd hoped it might provide. Some men collect beer mats or pornography, but I had discovered a love of holes – this hole in particular – and protecting my latest obsession required a little creative reasoning.

"Clay," I said, wondering if I'd perhaps inadvertently hit on something. "It... it holds water, you see. And there's an awful lot of it down here, which means that because this section is lower than the lawn it's not allowing the run-off to... well, run off."

I thought I saw a brief flicker of admiration pass behind her squinted eyes – but it was difficult to be sure of anything with the sun where it was and my neck beginning to ache from looking up at her.

"The clay holds it?"

"Indeed. The clay holds it."

"Cway," Nadine chuckled. I reached up and tickled her bare foot and she reflexively pulled it away, laughter hiccupping from her as she buried her face in Ashley's chest.

"I see," Ashley said, refusing to be distracted. "So what if there's clay under the lawn? You gonna dig that up, too?"

"I won't get it filled in today," I said sullenly. "But I'll make it

6

safe."

After I'd piled bags of sand and cement from the garage around the hole, and laid some old fence panels over it, I went inside to get washed up and changed.

Nadine was playing with a spatula on the kitchen floor whilst Ashley watched the portable television on the worktop in the corner as she ostensibly made eggy sandwiches for the "party". I stepped over Nadine and soaped my hands meticulously in the sink – scrubbing beneath my nails and ensuring that not a speck of dirt remained.

The woman on the telly said, "But Charley, I'm ready to forgive you", and Ashley snorted derisively.

"Anything interesting?" I asked, drying my hands on an inferior brand of kitchen roll.

"Just the usual brain-dead twonks subjecting themselves to superficial analysis," she said. "You're not wearing that T-shirt, I hope."

"I was planning on the white shirt with blue stripe."

"I thought you didn't plan." She knew I was still a little pissed off about the clay, so her tone was light and conciliatory. I was happy to meet her halfway. After all, whatever had been said, I still had my hole – if only for the time being. That had to be a kind of victory.

Grabbing her around the waist, I pulled her close – some mashed up egg flicking from the spoon she was holding and landing on the carpet tile nearest Nadine. Frowning at it and sniffing the air thoughtfully, Nadine swatted it like a fly with the spatula – gleefully grinding it into the carpet.

"You're a right smart arse today," I whispered in Ashley's ear. "But you knew that already, right?"

It had been difficult for Ashley and me recently, and we were both quick to acknowledge that. I couldn't recall the last time a day had passed without there being friction and badly concealed impatience between us – without either one or both of us finding something in the other to irritate and distract. For me, it was usually a mark of frustration – with Ashley and her couldn't-care-less attitude, with my work, with the waterlogged hole. For Ashley, I suspected her moods were more complex than that. She was a deep creature who had too much time to think, even with a two-year-old to run around after, and I couldn't help feeling that all it would take for her to find me a little less irritating would be for her to work a little harder around the house, get a part-time job, even.

Today, however, it felt different. As I pulled her to me, trying to ignore the stink of the hard-boiled eggs, I looked into her eyes – almost as rich a shade of blue as Nadine's – and saw something of what we had once been reflected there. The energy, the sublime sense that anything was possible – the overwhelming attraction and the heartfelt conviction that this brought with it. Life was a fairytale in which evil things happened, but good always prevailed. Love was real and enduring, something to be counted upon and which would always inspire the correct choices.

"One of the many things you love me for," Ashley whispered huskily. "Don't fight it." She put her free hand in the back pocket of my jeans and pressed me firmly to her – kissing me on the mouth. I felt her warmth – a supremely personal thing – and thought of the way the perspiration dribbled between her breasts on the really hot days.

"We have company," I said – reminding her that our inquisitive daughter was sitting on the floor not two feet away, quickly losing interest in the squashed piece of hardboiled egg.

"She'll be okay here for a short while. She can finish making the sandwiches." Ashley grinned, her perfect teeth somehow intimidating. She was joking, of course, but I couldn't help feeling that sometimes – *just sometimes* – she would gladly leave Nadine all alone, or dump her with a relative stranger, if it meant she could get a little instant gratification of one kind or another.

"She'd eat all the bread and mash the egg into the carpet," I said. "Nice thought, though. Maybe we can talk your mam into having her over the weekend – have a couple of evenings to ourselves."

Ashley pulled away and went back to making the sandwiches, shrugging. "Not exactly spontaneous, though, is it?" she asked.

"Spontaneity is what got us Nadine in the first place. Now that she's here, however, well, you know. We are parents first and foremost."

"Are we?"

"Yes."

8

"First and foremost?"

"I like to think so."

Looking at me over her shoulder, she was about to say more. Her breathing was slow and measured, her eyes fixed and unwavering. Someone on the telly was shouting about how his bitch should show him some respect, man, and I couldn't help feeling that that was the shape of things to come – for us all. Fame at any price, everyone the celebrity, the media validating antisocial behaviour, making it perversely respectable to wallow in the mire as long as you remembered not to talk into camera. Ashley enjoyed this daytime mish-mash of dirt and dysfunctionals, whatever she said to the contrary, and as she stared at me, her mouth open with a partially formed response, I half expected her to spout some suitably inane chat-psychology crap about mothers not losing themselves, how they needed "space" and an "identity" separate from the child. Thankfully, she was not quite so crass.

"Go get changed," she told me. "And take a shower first. You stink."

I stopped by my study on the way to the bathroom – just to see if the notes for my next novel had finished writing themselves while I'd been down in my hole – and read through what I had written earlier that morning, wondering where in the hell this was going and if it was destined to be as dire as the rest of my recent, as my agent would have it, unpublishable work.

Examine the possibilities of the Sorrow Street Asylum, I read. *Look in particular at ways in which it can be connected to the Cult of Elvis and, specifically, the* M' Boy, M' Boy *story.*

There were any number of problems that would need to be solved if this novel were to be viable – but I instinctively knew that that could only be achieved during the writing. It was largely true that, as I had said to Ashley, I didn't plan. Beyond a little preliminary research and a few rough ideas as a jumping off point, I preferred to solve the problems along the way – knowing from past experience that a plan in excess of a thousand words would kill the project stone dead for me. But it was a hair-raising way to work, and now I had my hole to occupy me, I couldn't see myself starting it for a week or two yet.

At the window, I peeled off my T-shirt and looked down onto the back garden. It had been my father's pride and joy before the car crash that had killed him and my mother five years before. It had always had a certain order that I couldn't quite fathom in Dad's day – a quintessential pattern that existed within the deceptively apparent chaos. Plants and flowers I couldn't name sprouted randomly, but never clashed or looked inappropriate. Rows of vegetables filled one corner – so crisp and succulent I now felt nostalgic for them. And the lawn... his lawn. It had possessed a certain simplicity, and yet had an obvious quality about it that came from hours of care and dedication. Precisely mowed contrasting rows of light and shade, consistent length no matter the time of year and never so much as a hint of a yellow patch – these were the things in which my father prided himself, and this pride had carried itself over into the rest of his life. An unassuming, gentle man, he had moved through life with generosity and grace. And all this had been typified by his little patch of garden – bought with the house from the council when I had been no more than a babe in arms, an "investment", Dad had always said, though I'd always suspected that money had been the last thing on his mind.

Now, looking down onto the lawn, something occurred to me. I sat down at my desk and stared at the skirting board, mulling over the anomaly as the screensaver – images of a very nearly naked Ashley and a mischievous Nadine – kicked in again. Nothing had changed since Dad's day – that was the first thing that occurred to me. The house was where it had always been, the garden was where it had always been – and the boundary fence hadn't been messed about with, as far as I could tell. So why the sudden drainage problem? For as long as I could remember, the lawn had been the epitome of perfection and however lovingly Dad may have tended it, I doubted that that would have been possible if he'd had to contend with the problems I now found myself facing. Could drainage problems develop spontaneously, I wondered.

I pondered this briefly as I took my shower, but quickly dismissed it.

I wasn't entirely sure what I was supposed to do in a room full of e-number high toddlers, so when I felt I'd made my toilet last as long as was reasonable and finally went downstairs, I was rather relieved to see that only a couple had thus far arrived.

Maggie, an old school friend of Ashley's had brought "Wee Mark" – a bruiser of a kid who had a habit of pinballing through the house with a maniacal air about him. He was trouble but I couldn't help but admire his rough-and-tumble resilience. Beside him, Nadine's other little friend, Veronique looked even more sickly then usual – sitting in the corner of the settee, hugging her knees and staring around the room with the biggest, brownest eyes I'd ever seen.

Nadine guarded her latest Action Man suspiciously, holding him tightly by the head whilst Molly, Veronique's mum, talked to her about Jesus.

Ashley rolled her eyes at me from the kitchen doorway and said, "Looks like there's a bug doing the rounds. The rest of them are either busy soiling themselves or trying keep out of its way."

"A right stinker, by all accounts," Maggie said. "If you'll pardon the pun." She giggled – and judging by the flush of her cheeks I guessed Ashley had already introduced her to the Vodka bottle (not that they weren't already well acquainted).

"Projectile vomiting, the lot," Ashley said – with rather too much enthusiasm for my liking. "Maybe getting Mum to have Nadine this weekend wasn't such a bad idea after all."

"Do you feel that's wise?" Molly – all slacks and sensible shoes – stood from her crouching position and her knees popped. Apparently her tales of crucifixion and resurrection when all done with for now.

"Why wouldn't I?" Ashley said.

"Oh, no reason," Molly replied – meaning she could think of plenty, at least half of them with a perfectly workable Jesus reference.

"Spit it out, Moll," Ashley said impatiently as Wee Mark shuffled off the edge of the settee and tried to stare down the blank television screen. It occurred to me that maybe I could have made my shower last a little longer – until the hot water had run out, perhaps.

"It's just that it strikes me as a little inconsiderate," Molly said artlessly. "Your parents aren't spring chickens anymore and to be possibly subjecting them to diarrhoea and projectile vomiting doesn't seem all that Christian to me, that's all."

11

"You're forgetting, I'm not a Christian," Ashley said. Maggie chuckled and helped herself to another vodka.

I pushed past Ashley into the kitchen, and then went out into the back garden – deciding that the best course of action was to just leave them to it. Ashley was more than a match for Molly's promise of perfection in Christ. She'd read enough to be able to pull Molly's favoured crutch right the fuck out from under her, if she so wished, but I didn't particularly want to witness it. Ten years ago, I would have ridiculed Molly for her belief – but no more. As ridiculous as it all so clearly was, a part of me envied her that conviction. No doubt, no questions that couldn't be answered with "the Lord moves in mysterious ways" – there was a kind of attraction in that.

I sat on the low wall beside the rockery, looking at Dad's lawn and sipping on a Stella I'd got from the garage. After a few minutes pondering afresh the conundrum of the waterlogged lawn, Maggie came out to join me – bringing her glass and the vodka bottle along with her.

Maggie and I had always got on. Conversation was easy, in spite of the fact that we'd once spent an entire weekend fucking each other's brains out at her mother's cottage in Wales – just weeks before my marriage to Ash. In retrospect, we both knew it had been foolish and relatively meaningless – but it was something we had shared, and I could only ever look on Maggie with fondness.

"Ashley's on about the fundamental differences between the biblical Jesus and the historic Jesus again," she said.

"Going to be a long afternoon, then."

"Looks that way."

We sat like that for a short while, neither of us saying anything – sipping at our drinks and staring at the garden. The sun was hot on the side of my face and I knew that if I didn't move soon I'd end up looking like a crude Bowie alter ego. I was tempted to go inside to see how it was going between Ash and Molly, but I got the strangest feeling there was something Maggie wanted to say to me. I waited a while longer and just when I'd finally managed to convince myself that I'd been mistaken, she said:

"Something weird's been happening to me, Sonny."

As a conversational opener, it wasn't all that unusual or

compelling – especially coming from Maggie. She was the kind of person who attracted weirdness the way some folk attract junk mail, and I maybe took a little too much pleasure in telling her this.

"This is different," she insisted. "I'm worried, Sonny. Worried for me and worried for Mark.... Since Jim... you know... since what happened I'm all that Mark's got, and I don't like what's happening. It threatens me and by default it threatens Wee Mark. That's just... I can't live with that."

Putting my bottle on the pavement by my feet, I twisted to get a better look at her. Since Jim's death from cancer a little over a year ago, time had started to take its toll on her. Her dark hair was now streaked through with grey and her mouth seemed shrunken – the lines radiating from her lips growing perceptibly deeper. There was a degree of sorrow behind her lacklustre eyes, but more than anything I thought I saw fear there – fear of being alone, of having to face whatever it was that was going on in her life without having someone to help, someone to say the right thing and watch out for her and Wee Mark. I didn't know if I was the right man for the job, but I did know that Ashley would be deeply disappointed in me if I didn't at least try.

And so, without giving myself time to reconsider, I said, "What is it, Mags?"

She took her time – that's what I noticed more than anything. It was so unlike her. Normally impulsive and a little dippy, she sat beside me and very methodically worked through the facts.

"It started about three weeks ago," she said, ever so calmly – the sweet, onion smell of the vodka carrying to me on her breath. "I thought it was just my imagination to begin with. You know what it's like when you live alone. Your mind works overtime. So I didn't pay much attention to it. I tried to forget all about it, get on with my life, but I still couldn't escape the overwhelming feeling that I was being watched. I couldn't see anyone, but that didn't mean they couldn't see me..." It was starting to get away from her. She paused and closed her eyes, taking a delicate sip of her vodka – a sigh escaping her before she continued. "Then the phone calls started. From a withheld number. Silence, at first, then... he watches me all the time, Sonny. That's what the phone calls are all about. He itemises my day – telling me what I've done, where I've been. It's... I can't see him, but it's as if he's with me all the time, inside my head. I swear he even knows when I masturbate." She seemed to feel that this last was more than I needed to hear, so moved on quickly. "The police weren't much help. They suggested I keep a journal, change my number and get back to them when I had an idea who it might be."

"Change your name to Catherine Zeta Jones," I suggested. "That might help."

She smiled sadly. "If only it were that simple. I'm scared, Sonny. I mentioned it to Ash and she said I should have a word with you. She said you'd know what to do."

It was nice to know my wife had such confidence in me. The truth was, however, I didn't have a clue where to start, or what to suggest, even. I was a poorly paid (not to mention piss-poor) novelist and, yes, I had a few people I could call upon when the chips were down – but this certainly wasn't something I was in any way prepared for.

"She said that?"

"I'm afraid so." Taking my hand, she gave it a firm squeeze. I remembered what it had been like to be with her. Hurried, frenetic – nothing even remotely resembling love. Purely physical and very wet. It was all so far removed from who we now were, and I suddenly wished it could have been different. I wished that my parents and Jim were still alive, I wished that I could have loved Maggie *and* Ashley, I wished that the world were not such a complicated place with its death and betrayal, its confusing blend of love and need.

"Don't look so worried," Maggie said, squeezing my hand again. "I know it's a tough one. I just thought... well, three heads are better than one, right?"

Something occurred to me. It wasn't exactly the most impressive thought I'd ever had in my life, but at least it was somewhere to start (and something that would show Maggie and Ash that I wasn't about to dismiss this out of hand). "You said he always knows where you've been, right?" I said.

"That's right, yes."

"Detailed and consistent?"

"Very."

"But you've never seen him."

"Not that I'm aware of."

I got quickly to my feet – kicking over the bottle of Stella in the process – and marched resolutely along the path at the side of the house and round to the front. I heard Maggie hurrying along behind me, breathy and concerned as her flip-flops shuffled and slapped. I smelt honeysuckle and the faintly ripe odour of the hedge that marked the front boundary of our property. If I'd had time to think about it I might have done it differently, but as it was I marched on through the gate and out onto Sorrow Street.

I don't know what I'd expected to see – some guy in dark glasses, perhaps, suspiciously lurking by the streetlamp, smoking and blowing rings into the air as he nonchalantly considered his next move. Maybe this was the moment he had been building up to all along; confrontation, the ultimate explanation. Weeks or months of steady surveillance followed by a formal introduction and... and what?

The street was deserted, of course – unusual in itself, but doubly so given that it was the height of summer and the kids were off school. I stepped out into the middle of the road, Maggie panting behind me as she rested against the gatepost, and turned full circle – scanning the full length of the road, looking at windows and cars parked in driveways, waiting for my eyes to lock with those of a stranger or, perhaps, someone I actually knew. A Tarantino moment would follow. Or perhaps not.

"Sonny?" Maggie said. "What?"

"I don't know," I answered. "I just thought it seemed logical." I shrugged. "It made sense to me," I added as I walked back towards her. "He knows where you've been so... guess it isn't that simple."

"And what if it had been?"

"Eh?"

"What if it had been that simple? What would you have done?"

Leaning against the other gatepost, I considered this for a moment – feeling my heart rate slow and the perspiration itch in the pits of my arms. The sour taste of beer in my mouth, I suddenly didn't want to think about the things that might have happened.

"I'd have given Ash a shout," I said.

Feeling rather foolish, I returned to the back garden with Maggie –

still considering her problem, but determined to do my best to find a more rational approach to a solution. I heard brittle, childish laughter as we walked along the path, and imagined myself lifting Nadine high into the air, spinning her around, covering her with kisses and blowing wet raspberries against her neck as she giggled with near-hysterical delight. Everything made sense because of her. She was the explanation and the cause and at unexpected moments like these I realised just how deeply connected we were.

When Maggie gasped, it took me a second or two to see what the problem was. She stopped and I almost walked into the back of her. Somewhere – far off, it seemed – I heard the word "Jesus" and understood that Ash and Molly were still arguing in the house, each as deeply entrenched and oblivious as the other. Maggie shuddered and reached behind her, blindly groping for my hand and pulling me level with her so that there could be no doubt that I was seeing what she was seeing.

It seemed that Wee Mark and Nadine had escaped the suffocating confines of the house and were now playing quite happily in the back garden – walking purposefully back and forth across the fence panels I'd placed over my hole, one of the sand bags split where they had apparently clambered over it. The panels bounced frighteningly as Wee Mark took his turn, singing the words "Billy Goat Gruff" over and over. The wood made a protracted creak and, as I ran forward to grab Mark whilst Maggie pulled Nadine away from the hole, I imagined it splintering – Mark's rough and tumble resilience finally getting the better of him.

Blessedly, I got to him before anything nasty could happen. Lifting him and holding him to me, Maggie doing the same with Nadine, we stood like that for what seemed like a very long time – each holding the other's child, neither wanting to acknowledge the things that might have been.

"We thought you and Maggie were out there!" Ashley insisted.

I held Nadine now, Maggie keeping a firm grip on a struggling Mark. Nadine smelt hot and sweet, and it was hard not to find this soothing. Veronique hadn't moved from her place on the settee and she looked up at us as if this were all the confirmation she needed that we adults were indeed an entirely different and extremely peculiar species. Nadine blew a saliva bubble and it popped against my cheek.

"And you didn't think to check first before you let them go wandering off?" I knew I was on shaky ground, but as, oblivious as Wee Mark to the dangers of the troll beneath his "bridge", I just kept right on going. "Jesus Christ, the two of you sit on your arses in here arguing about some bloke who's been dead for nigh on two thousand years and –"

"Jesus was not just some bloke," Molly said indignantly. "He was the Son of God and if anyone's to thank for Wee Mark and Nadine being safe, it's him and I really don't think you should –"

"Shut up, Molly," Maggie said.

"'Ut up, Molly," Nadine whispered.

I could see that Ashley was approaching critical. Her jaw was clenched and the vein in the centre of her forehead stood out. She looked as irritated by Molly as the rest of us – but I knew that when her fists finally released themselves, fingers uncurling like the petals of some carnivorous plant, I would be the one at whom her wrath would be directed.

I could see this very easily getting nasty. Ashley wasn't entirely in the wrong, here, maybe not even in the wrong at all – but I wanted to punish her for all the other times she'd been complacent, let her know that there was only so much I was willing to put up with. I remembered just the week before, coming downstairs in the middle of the afternoon after a long morning's work only to find Ashley asleep on the sofa whilst Nadine played quietly by herself. All the doors through to the back garden had been open – to freshen the stifling air and no doubt let a few flies and bees in – and I remembered controlling my anger, reasoning my way through it before waking Ash. I made excuses, pointed out to myself that Nadine wasn't the type for wandering far from her mother's side but, ultimately, it had been an irresponsible thing to do, and I'd wondered how many times it had happened before. In the end I had woken her gently and given her the benefit of the doubt (not in the mood for an argument), accepting her explanation and apology, but now that little episode came back with all its unclaimed force and I suddenly felt that Ashley and I were alone, that we were the only two people on the fragile face of the planet, and the urge to tell her what I thought of her was too strong to resist.

Very calmly, I took a step towards her – glancing down and noticing that her fists were still clenched. Wee Mark grumbled and whined, trying to escape his mother's grip, but even that faded to the distance. My ears filled with a whirling, swooshing liquid sound and I heard my own voice as if I were under water.

"Our daughter is not a toy to be discarded once you've tired of her," I said, a little menacingly. "She isn't just another of your whims – she's a precious little thing that needs looking after."

"You think I don't know that?"

"I think you forget it far too often."

I thought she would fight. Her hands remained clenched and she blinked rapidly, flushing with colour – her cheekbones becoming more prominent as emotion claimed her.

"I could never forget it," she told me, taking Nadine from me and kissing the confused child on the forehead. "I would never *want* to forget it. But sometimes it's hard. Harder than you'll ever know, Sonny. It's okay for you. You hide in your office or down your hole most of the day – and you think you're justified in doing that. And you are. To a point. But me... I get tired. I get scared and lonely."

"The burden of motherhood," Molly said.

"Shut up, Molly," Maggie and I said in unison.

"I'm only –" she started, but Ashley cut her off.

"I'll do anything to keep her safe," she said. "You know that, Sonny."

The danger had passed. I reached out and brushed my fingers over Ashley's cheek – seeing just how unfair I had been. Veronique watched us, her wet mouth hanging open, and I said, "Yes, I do."

Chapter Two

We'd planned to meet at our local – a pub just down the road from me that had a fine selection of specialist beers, a fairly respectable menu and a charming, eavesdropping waitress by the name of Polly – but my old friend Oliver Montgomery wasn't feeling particularly well. I'd therefore agreed to go round to his place and let him "bung something it the microwave" for us. It was not an arrangement I found all that attractive, but Oliver was a good mate and an excellent sounding board, so postponing just wasn't an option.

I got there at ten thirty, knowing that if we were going to do lunch the Oliver Montgomery way it would require a few warm up laps first. Before leaving, I'd promised Ashley that I wouldn't get too drunk – but we both knew that there was no such thing as "too drunk" where Olly was concerned and she'd said with a wry smile that she'd expect me when she saw me.

"We okay?" I'd asked before heading out of the door.

"Of course." It had come out a little hesitantly and she'd had to repeat herself – telling me that I'd been right, we both had, and she loved me all the more for caring as much as I did. Waiting for Oliver to return to his shit-heap of a living room, however, I couldn't help wondering just how "okay" things really were.

"Right," Oliver said, thumping into the room with two microwaved tikka masalas. He is a big man, is our Oliver. Twenty-three stone and six foot two, we'd once decided after sharing an especially expensive single malt that Oliver had received as a birthday present from his agent that he was ninety-five percent pure muscle. He worked out just about every day, could bench press in excess of six hundred pounds and had the biggest, blackest beard you'd ever wish to meet.

"Okay," he repeated, sitting down in the armchair opposite the badly sprung settee where I sat. "Tell me about this bit you read in the DeLillo novel. *White Noise*, yes?"

I forked with my tikka masala experimentally, and then took another large gulp of my third whisky. "DeLillo's main character is a lecturer in Hitler studies," I said.

"Ah, yes." Oliver tucked into his lunch, the tray balanced rather precariously on his knee – his massive frame making him look as though he were somehow a part of the extra-large, no doubt reinforced armchair rather than merely its occupant. I tried not to look around the musty, manuscript- and book-cluttered room – knowing full well that my eye would light on something guaranteed to put me off my tikka masala. Not that that would take much doing.

Sure enough, I glanced to my left and spotted an old pair of Oliver's voluminous boxers seemingly crawling out from beneath the sideboard.

"He invented the course," I told him, not wanting to dwell on just what Olly's boxers were doing beneath the sideboard in the first place.

"With the help of six million Jews," Oliver said through a mouthful of rice.

"Which is beside the point."

"Not if you're a Jew."

"And are you?"

"Not the last time I looked."

"Then shut the fuck up and let me tell you this, while I'm still sober enough to string a reasonably coherent sentence together."

"Reasonably coherent? You flatter yourself." I could see it was going to be a long day. Oliver was still rather full of himself after the success of his latest charity event (which had involved him pushing a minibus a badly-measured mile) and experience had taught that attempting to resist his mood was futile. Better to just buy into it and hope there was plenty in to drink.

"You're not interested," I said flatly, shrugging and draining my glass. "Your loss, mate."

Oliver chewed thoughtfully for a short while, arching his back every now and then – nursing a strain from the "Big Event". He eyed me suspiciously but I suspected that somewhere beneath that beard he was smiling.

"So this dumb-fuck American college professor runs a course on Hitler Studies and...?" he said, topping up our glasses.

"At the college where he works, there's this other lecturer. I can't remember his name. Not that it matters – the point is, he wants to do for Elvis what this other guy's done for Hitler."

"Let me guess. Elvis Studies?"

"Got it in one." I loaded some rice and tikka masala onto my fork and put it in my mouth before I had chance to reconsider. It actually wasn't too bad – swilled down with a hefty slug of cheap scotch.

"Sounds a fairly preposterous proposal from where I'm sitting," Olly said.

"Couldn't agree more – but the point is, during their discussions, this guy mentions that Elvis read the Bardo Thodol."

"Ah." Oliver nodded as a sliver of understanding peeped over the horizon. "The Tibetan Book of the Dead. Death and rebirth. I see where you're going."

That was one of the things I liked best about Oliver; his capacity as a fellow writer to understand the subtlety of the connections I made as I built myself up for a new project. He never failed to "tune in" and take pleasure in bouncing the ideas back and forth – and for that I was eternally grateful.

"I know the whole Elvis thing has been done to a death, if you'll pardon the pun," I said, "but my story won't actually be about Elvis – it'll be about the boy who convinces himself that the mysterious old man who's just moved into his village is Elvis. A story of adolescent obsession and –"

"Unavoidably homoerotic."

"What?" This hadn't occurred to me and I could have almost been annoyed with him, had it not been for the gift of possibilities his comment provided.

"No matter how hard you try," Oliver said, "you just aren't going to be able to get away from the older man, younger boy thing. Christ, they even said it about King's *Salem's Lot*."

"You always have to lower the tone, don't you?"

"You think homoeroticism is lowering the tone?"

"I was referring to your mentioning King."

Oliver twitched an eyebrow and I saw a flash of white teeth as he loaded more food into his mouth. I'd barely touched my "meal" so decided I'd better at least make an effort – managing to eat a good half of it before the over processed mush got the better of me and I found myself setting it aside on the floor and helping myself to another scotch. Oliver reached over and took my tray of half eaten food, scraping the remnants onto his and tucking in. For someone who was usually pretty careful and regimented about his food, Oliver had a hell of an appetite for junk.

When he was done, he looked at me and said, "How did yesterday go? Sorry I couldn't make it but... well, I was still too knackered after the bus push. Really twatted my back up, too."

"That's okay. You would have hated it, anyway."

"Too many screaming kids?"

"Too many screaming adults," I said. "Well, almost. You know."

"I do?"

"Probably not." I really didn't feel like telling him about it, seeing the act as something of a betrayal and misrepresentative. Nevertheless, I found myself sharing the full story with Oliver – finishing with some of what Ashley and I had said to each other before I had left that morning.

He stared at the arm of the settee when I had finished, and I saw the emotional exhaustion pass through him – something very physical and somehow removed, an alien presence that had little to do with the story I had told him. He took another drink, eyes still stubbornly refusing to meet mine, and I knew that he was thinking of Donnelly McCrane.

Oliver and Donnelly had met at the Frankfurt Book Fair a couple of years before – Oliver there to sit on a panel or three, Don, it seemed, simply because he had little better to do and his Daddy was "a much respected literary agent". The two, Olly-lore had it, had hit it off immediately. There had been nothing overtly sexual about it initially, neither of them wearing their "fagginess", as Oliver liked to put it, on their sleeves, but as the days had rolled on it had become obvious to the two of them that they were falling very heavily in love. The change in Oliver had been extremely noticeable. All of his friends had commented on it at one time or another and Ashley had been fond of saying, "I never realised just how lonely Olly was before he met

Don. He seems so complete, now." And this had been true. Oliver had entered rooms and claimed them – not because of his bulk, but simply because he was loved – and it had been a wonderful thing to see. Together, they were considerate and perpetually affectionate – even in company – but something happened, as it too often does, and that wonderfully precious thing that had existed between them became something else, something quite different.

It was a subject Oliver had never discussed in any depth – not even with me – and I admired that. Whatever had brought their relationship to an end was between the two of them, and no matter how many times Ashley quizzed him about the details I was still naïve enough to believe that Oliver would never tell.

"You were wrong, you know," he now solemnly said, staring into his whisky glass. "But your reasons for being wrong were right. What you have... it's not a fiction. Not something that can be rewritten. Once certain things are said and done there's no taking them back." Now he met my eyes and it occurred to me that this was perhaps as close as he would ever come to telling me just what had happened between him and Don. "Happiness writes white, mate. Keep the pages of the life you share with Ashley and Nadine clean and clear."

I thought about this whilst Oliver went through to the poky kitchen to fetch dessert. The living room was like an oven, and as I got up to open another window I wondered just how wise it would be to take advice from a man like Oliver Montgomery. It was true that he had a degree of experience that I would never have, and that he could often think his way to the centre of the most complex of philosophies and concepts – but he was a man alone, a man who, whatever the success of his written work, still didn't have the things he wanted most from life. I felt for him, admired him, but his quoting Montherlant (or the ever-reliable Anonymous, if some were to be believed) made me wonder; could listening to him ever make a difference?

The scotch was making me woozy and I hoped Oliver had something sweet and substantial for dessert. I was in the mood for something with rich, thick chocolate and lots of fresh cream, but what I got was warm apple pie with a house-brick sized slab of vanilla ice cream.

"Just like mother used to make," Oliver said, sitting back down in his armchair and putting his feet up on the cluttered coffee table. "One thing's been bothering me," he continued. "You and Maggie. Where the fuck where you? Ashley thought you were out there, but you weren't. So where?"

Oliver was about the only person other than Maggie and me that knew about the cottage in Wales and what had happened there, and he had never been shy of making his disapproval known. He liked Maggie, and he liked me – but he also thought the world of Ashley and he had told me many times that what I'd done had been despicable. The "premeditated" aspect of it all had especially repulsed him, and even though he seemed to accept that it was something that had never happened again and, I assured him, never would, he still got suspicious every once in a while.

On this occasion, I chose to ignore the implication and merely answered his question.

"Stalker spotting," I said. "Maggie's got a stalker. She reckons he phones her up and tells her everything she's done and everywhere she's been. She even reckons he knows when she masturbates, if you can believe that."

Oliver raised an eyebrow but said nothing.

"So I figured..."

"Stalk the stalker?"

"Something like that. Came to nothing, though."

"Didn't spot any likely candidates?"

"Unfortunately, no."

Oliver grew introspective and since the apple pie and ice cream was actually rather good, I didn't push it. His booted feet twitched on the coffee table and he slurped melted ice cream between his teeth, staring into middle space and humming to himself.

"Do you believe her?" he suddenly asked.

I didn't hesitate. "Yes. Absolutely."

"She's a recently bereaved ex-lover," he said, as if I needed reminding. "Do you still believe her?"

A couple more drinks and it could have got nasty. As it was, I sat back, sighed and repeated my original answer, adding, "She mentioned it to Ashley before mentioning it to me – and before you

24

say that that doesn't mean a bloody thing, it does to me, okay? And that apart, you weren't there. She was sincere and clearly worried about Wee Mark."

Oliver nodded and held up a massive hand by way of an apology, satisfied. "She tried the police?" he asked.

"Naturally."

"And?"

"What do you think?"

"As much use as a crepe paper condom."

"You do crepe paper condoms an injustice but, yes, that's about the long and short of it. I had a chat with her and Ashley about it, once Mad Molly had left, and I agreed to spend a little time following her myself over the next week or so – see if I can't spot who the hell it is that's doing this."

Oliver took his feet from the coffee table, knocking a stack of books on existentialism and Consequentialism onto the floor. Sitting forward, he placed his bowl in the space left by the books and rested his Popeye forearms on his knees, his bearded face suddenly more animated.

Pointing a large, callused finger at me, he said, "Now *that's* what I like to see. The proactive approach. Brilliant. Give the bastards a dose of their own medicine. When do we start?"

"We?"

"Maggie's my friend as well. Plus I owe it to Jim."

Jim and Oliver had never really got on – Jim possessing a barely concealed homophobic streak that had actually had the beautifully ironic effect of placing him in a minority of one in our little group of friends. I didn't mention this, however, instead pointing out that it was going to be difficult to be inconspicuous with a twenty-three stone bus-pusher in tow.

But Oliver was difficult to dissuade in his post-bus-push omnipotent euphoria. He sat there before me, happily making plans with very little by way of input from me other than the occasional grunt and all too reluctant nod. Apparently, inconspicuous was nothing more than a frame of mind. It was merely a question of pushing all thoughts of being noticed out of your head. Once that was done, Oliver assured me, you were home and dry.

25

"It's very Cartesian," he insisted. "If we exist because we think, the trick of inexistence is really very simple; stop thinking."

He seemed deeply satisfied with this uncharacteristically inaccurate interpretation and I knew that any effort I now made to talk him out of "helping" me would be futile.

And so we agreed (or Oliver agreed – I simply didn't disagree) that we would start our surveillance the following week, since Maggie was reluctantly spending time with her mother over the weekend. Also, I wanted to spend time with Ashley and Oliver had a short story called *The Cup and the Cusp* that he really needed to get finished before Boots, his agent, really lost her patience, so Oliver decided we would start Monday morning – taking it in two hour shifts and keeping in touch by mobile phone.

As I was leaving later that evening, rather the worse for wear, Oliver said, "You know something? Life isn't so bad after all." It was a strange thing to say, but I attributed it to an excess of alcohol. We said goodbye and I tried not to think about the following Monday.

The silence and stale, overpoweringly thick air hit me full on in the face as I entered the living room and I knew right away that Ashley wasn't home. I stood by the settee for a moment, listening and trying to imagine what it would be like if it were always this way. The emptiness sighed sadly against the back of my neck, brittle and icy even as it made me sweat, its weight bringing with it realisation and disharmony – and I remembered afresh the time before Ashley, the time before Nadine Verity. It could never be like that. That man had never known these two wonderful creatures – he had wandered, solitary and under the illusion that he had happiness of a kind right there in the simplicity and calm. He had been a fool, I decided – calling out Ashley's name, just in case, and receiving no response. Whatever complications it brought with it, I needed people in my life – I needed Ashley and Nadine. I heard natural movement, the house shifting somewhere as timbers warmed or cooled, and I knew I could never live with that alone.

I decided to use the time alone productively, however, and headed upstairs to my office – the booze inspiring or misleading me, it was difficult to say which.

My PC was always on, even when no one was home, as was my broadband connection. I checked my email (more spam trying to sell me the usual selection of Viagra and debt consolidation), and then read through my notes again. My story felt closer than it ever had, so I tentatively opened a new Word document, set it for double spacing, and started typing...

He was a boy who liked to look through other people's windows, I wrote. *The lives of complete strangers held him, took him away from himself in a way that nothing else could, and often he would wonder just what it must be like to be that unknown women – to eat as her, breath as her, to dream her dreams in the dead of the night. Sometimes he would imagine himself as the women, naked before her mirror – depressingly alone as she slipped her fingers deep into her cunt, the pleasure and the pain, the comfort of her own body – and he would masturbate franticly, the come ripping from him violently as he imagined what she would smell like, sound like, taste like as she slipped her sopping fingers from inside her and sucked on them, eyes shut tight against the loneliness.*

More often than not, however, it was the watching that held him, rather than the sexual possibilities. He liked to think that he owned a part of these people – that, unobserved, he could somehow reach deep inside them and touch something essential that even they themselves had been unaware of. Possession, he had once heard his drunken, thieving father say, was nine tenths of the law. Well, if that were the case, Richard was most assuredly a good, lawful citizen.

He was three days away from his fifteenth birthday when everything changed. He was sore from another drunken beating and Mrs. Sutherland was wearing the thinnest, clingiest summer dress he'd ever seen. The breeze pressed it against her and he knew today was a good day – a day of distractions and protracted wrist exercises. Her routine was by now so predictable that he had learned he could actually pass by her at times and arrive at her eventual destination before her – thus making his surveillance even less conspicuous – and, so, when she followed him into the mini market, it was no surprise that she immediately headed for the newspapers over in the far corner, beneath the smeared convex mirror. He remained in his place by the freezers, their chill welcome on such a stubbornly humid day, and watched as she bent to pick up her copy of The Sunday Times. Her buttocks – still firm and pleasingly confined for a woman in her late thirties, he thought – stretched the dress's material and he played with the idea of just walking up behind her, brushing against her, allowing her to know he was there as he spilled into his shorts. How would she react if she knew? Richard wondered. Would she be horrified or amused? Or would some primitive part of her welcome and encourage his peculiar attentions?

She was standing now, the folded paper in her hand as she studied the headline. Her face was difficult to make out in the bulging mirror, but for just a moment he thought she glanced up and met his gaze. A fleeting recognition. An invitation, he was sure. I know, *that look said.* I know, and I like it.

Richard left the shop before her and walked south along the High Street before turning left onto Briarburn Lane and walking the few yards to his favourite bench. Mrs. Sutherland, a widow for more than a year and a half, now, lived at the end of Briarburn Lane and he knew that in a matter of minutes she would pass him and say good morning as if she didn't have a care in the world.

Sure enough, she came breezing along a couple of minutes later. As she entered the quiet lane, he prepared himself – pushing the Armani sunglasses that his father had stolen for him further up his nose and flicking his long, lank hair out of his face. The newspaper was tucked under her arm and he imagined her sweat soaking into it – the print bleaching from the paper and staining her skin. "One right classy fuck," his dad would have called her, and however much it would have irked him to do so, Richard would have had to agree. Mrs. Sutherland was the kind of woman who knew how to hold herself. She was elegant, but not snooty – clearly intelligent, but with a blood-rich sensuality that bubbled just beneath the surface.

Richard braced himself for the exchange of good mornings but, much to his surprise, the expected greeting didn't come. Mrs. Sutherland sat down on the bench beside him, slapping the folded newspaper on the remaining seat space, tucking her hands between her legs in licentious prayer and smiling straight at him. He felt his cheeks flush and his cock twitch – suddenly certain that the game was over.

Her sweet, cocoa-butter summer scent drifted to him and she said, "Our bedrooms look over at one another."

She didn't need to say anymore. There could be no mistake. She did indeed know. A deep sigh whilst she waited for him to say something. A physical readjustment, her hip against his.

"Yes," he said. Feigning ignorance was pointless. How could he have not noticed, given that she so often stood at her bedroom window – staring out across the field that stood between them and hugging herself?

"Why?" she said.

The question confused him. "Why what?"

"Why do you follow me all the time?"

All the time was a bit of an exaggeration, but he didn't think she'd quite see it that way. "Summat to do." He shrugged and let his hair fall over his face.

That sigh again. She slouched down and let her hands rest in her lap. Richard wondered if she realised just how fucking provocative that really was.

"Village life." She smiled at him sadly and he noticed that her two front teeth were rather crooked. "No cinema or nightclubs for miles," she went on, "a crappy selection of DVDs at the local shop... is it any wonder we're all a little fucked up?"

He relaxed a little. Maybe this was going to be okay after all. Hearing her voice so close, so conspiratorial was good enough – but for her to be comfortable enough to swear in front of him...

"You need the Internet," he said, knowing something was required of him and grasping hold of the only area of expertise that he possessed. "That helps. You don't feel so... you know."

"Isolated?"

"Aye."

"It's something I've thought about," she admitted. "Jim – my late husband – he left a laptop but we never got hooked up or whatever the correct term is. I expect it would be too difficult and expensive for me anyway."'

"Nah, it's a piece of piss, and you could start off with a basic package to keep cost down."

"Really?"

"Yes, really."

The morning had certainly taken and unexpected detour, and as Richard found himself volunteering a little too enthusiastically to help the strange but wonderful Mrs. Sutherland set up an ISP, he wondered if any of this was wise. The lonely woman befriends the lonely boy. It was an act of charity, nothing more, he was sure.

As they said their goodbyes, after having arranged a time for Richard to call and help arrange her Net connection, Mrs. Sutherland lightly touched his arm and said, "I don't mind, you know."

I read through what I'd written, sitting back in my chair, legs stretched out beneath my desk. It occurred to me, as it so often did, that the story was already deviating from the course I had envisaged. I saw any number of possible ways of getting it back on track – but knew enough to understand that that would probably be fatal. Far better to just let the story be what it wanted to be.

I closed the document and briefly looked at my notes, highlighting the material I believed I needed to focus on next time and feeling the post-work, post-alcohol hangover start to kick in. Nauseated and a little shaky, I was about to close my notes and head downstairs for a glass of water when I noticed a highlighted comment at the bottom of the page. The highlighting was in red so I knew right away that this was none of my doing (I always used blue or lime green).

Fill in the hole, it said. *That I might happily return.* Shaking my head, I smiled at the screen. Ashley. The quintessence of persistent womanhood. I pictured her standing over the hole, me looking up at her, and I finally understood that I was fighting a losing battle. As attached as I had grown to my hole – and the work it involved – I had to concede that she was right. It was a pointless task, one that would probably never achieve the desired result, and my refusing to fill it in would merely serve to show how pig-headed and obsessive I could be.

Downstairs, the house seemed even emptier than it had earlier. I thought of calling Ash on her mobile but I knew she'd only resent it – thinking I was checking up on her. Maybe Oliver, then? Anything to break the imperious silence. But no. Oliver would be asleep or working, I was sure, cocooned in his own little world of dialectics and dirt.

I put the receiver back in its cradle without dialling and instead did what I knew I had to do. I headed out into the back garden to fill in my hole.

My father once told me that a garden was a place in which a man could safely lose himself. It was a realm of possibility only confined by the limits of one's imagination, a playground for the soul and a heavenly, spiritual release. As a boy, I would watch him late at night from what was now my office window – standing in the middle of the lawn, looking up at the sky with his hands in his pockets. A man comfortable in his skin. A man comfortable in his location.

At times like these, I missed him and Mam more than ever. Warm, almost intolerably quiet summer evenings – the sun dipping beneath our neighbouring houses, cool, long shadows reaching for the back door like unreadable portents, heat beneath one's feet as the air, still thick with midges, began to cool. These were times we, by rights, should have spent together. Mam, Dad, me, Ashley and Nadine. Family as it once was, family as it should be forevermore.

Looking down at the hole, spade in hand, I felt as though I was about to do something far more meaningful than it at first appeared. This was for the good of my marriage, the safety of my child – and as such, it was the right thing to do. Nevertheless, it felt somehow sacrilegious – a sin against something I wasn't entirely sure I believed in.

"Just fill it in," Dad would have said. "You know damn well it isn't going to solve the drainage problem, so why fight it?"

I drove my spade into the mountainous pile of excavated soil, listening as Dad talked me through the process – Mam and Ashley laughing together in the kitchen – and stopped immediately, my spade hitting something unexpectedly metallic.

I looked around questioningly, but Dad wasn't there to provide any answers. I stooped – pulling out the spade and tossing it aside as I worked to uncover the mystery object. It was close to the surface, the soil loose and yielding, so it took no time at all to pull it out and brush it clean.

The rectangular tin looked like it might have once held biscuits or sweets – the faded picture on the lid showing a poor Turneresque scene, the lettering scraped away and rusted. It had weight and as I turned it over in my hands, I felt movement. Whatever was inside was solid and... *soft*. It didn't clunk or clatter, just shifted dully. A quiet thud.

"What you got there?" I jumped and almost dropped the tin into the hole – getting quickly to my feet and juggling it before trapping it against my chest.

"Ashley. Don't do that, for Christ's sake."

"Don't do what?"

"Creep up on me like that. I nearly had a bloody heart attack."

She had a playful look about her eyes and I knew that she too had been drinking. Rocking back and forth on the doorstep, her hands clasped before her, she giggled rather stupidly and said, "Who's creeping? I've been banging and clattering about in here for the last five minutes. You've been spending too much time in that there hole of yours. You've got soil in your ears."

"You've been drinking."

"So have you."

"Bet you're drunker than I am."

"Bet you I'm not."

"Prove it, then." Gotcha, I thought smugly.

She hopped down from the step, eyes squinting suspiciously. "How?"

"Fill in my hole for me."

But Ashley was more interested in the tin I held. She stepped forward and chewed her lip thoughtfully – her eyes a little glassy and distant. More colourful than usual, her skin looked ruddy and reassuringly healthy. A beautiful woman, I told myself proudly. One to cherish and accept – in spite of her faults. A lock of hair flopped over her eye and she blew it away, her attention still focused on the tin.

"So what is it, then?" she asked.

I shrugged and turned it over in my hands again, smelling the coolness of the soil and the sharp, metallic odour. "I don't know," I said. "Well, I do. It's a tin – but I don't know what's inside it."

"You think there's something inside it?"

"It feels like it."

I handed it to her so that she could feel for herself and she shook it experimentally – grinning with strange satisfaction. I'd forgotten she could be like this, youthful and easy to please, and I have to say, I think it brought out the best in me. I could have dismissed it, moved the conversation on until the tin was forgotten – as I might have at another time – but instead of so doing, I took the tin from her and said, "Let's see what's inside it, shall we?"

We squatted down and I placed the tin on the floor between us. The light was starting to fail and birdcall marked the beginning of night. I felt the evening waiting at my shoulder as Ashley and I held our breath – and in my heart I felt a sudden, inexplicable sense of loss.

"Go on, then," she said. "What are you waiting for?"

I'd expected the lid to be rusted in place – immovable, bringing our excitement to an anticlimax. A good whack with a hammer and screwdriver would soon loosen it, of course – but, Ashley being Ashley, she would tire of the idea before I'd had chance to fetch my tools and it would simply be left on the patio for me to open the following day.

As it was, of course, the lid came off the tin very easily and Ashley and I found ourselves staring down at the surprisingly well-preserved leather-bound journal of a woman who (although we didn't know it at the time) would change our lives forever. It looked old, the dark blue leather worn and cracked – but it didn't seem to have suffered unduly from its time buried beneath my father's garden. I wondered briefly if it was something Dad had put there – a time capsule to annoy people who hadn't even been born when he'd thought of the idea – but that had never really been his style. It was too forced for Dad, too deliberate, and if Mam had been the power behind this, well, she would certainly have seen to it that it had been packed with greater care.

"Whose is it, do you think?" Ashley said in a reverential whisper.

"I don't know," I answered. Neither of us had so far plucked up the courage to touch it – as if we imagined it might crumble apart in our hands. I thought of Richard in my story and said, "Ours, I suppose. Possession being nine tenths of the law."

She nodded and looked at me expectantly – her mouth twitching impatiently. "Well?" she said. "Are you going to, then, or what?"

"I thought that you might like the honour."

"Scared?" She grinned and I shook my head, sticking out my tongue at her. The truth was, though, the journal did frighten me a little. I understood the power of words – especially those never intended to be read by anyone else – and whatever this was, I felt certain that it was overflowing with personal mystery and grief. I ran my fingers over the leather binding, trying to summon up a sense of its history and any implicit warning – but all I was truly aware of was the leather's grainy texture and the thumping of the hangover at my temples.

I carefully removed it from the tin and opened it. "It is certain to me that I should not be in this place," I read.

Chapter Three

That weekend was the hottest of the year – the hottest for at least five years, it seemed to me. Nadine staying, as planned, with Ashley's mum and dad, Ashley and I found ourselves able to luxuriate in the heat, give in to its little whims and insistences. We sunbathed in the most irresponsible of ways – grabbing the midday rays like our lives depended on it and even nodding off on occasion (something Mam had always warned me against). The minutes ticked by steadily and we embraced this new, albeit temporary regime, drinking vodka from the freezer and eating when it occurred to us. At one-thirty on Saturday afternoon, I even reached over and slipped my hand into the delightfully sweaty interior of Ashley's bikini bottoms – my fingers working away at her for a good few minutes before she awoke with a start and a patio-shaking shudder. She told me off (apparently the neighbours could have been watching from their bedroom windows) but smiled to herself when she thought I wasn't looking, her hand unconsciously straying to her crotch as if surprised by its assorted possibilities.

I didn't sense the change until the Sunday afternoon. It was gradual, creeping in like a new season – a noticeable (and quite possibly imagined) chill the only harbinger.

Working had been out of the question. This was our time together and even I could never have been so insensitive as to expect to work even briefly during such a rare and pleasant period of respite – however much I looked forward to returning to Richard and his adolescent adventures. I therefore gave in and enjoyed, thinking only of myself and Ashley, but by the time Sunday arrived I found thoughts of the journal we'd discovered tugging at the fabric of my imagination, reshaping it with suggestive contours and colours, and I could no longer resist; I brought it out onto the patio to read whilst we soaked up the sun.

"I don't see the fascination," Ashley said. She was flat on her stomach on the sun-lounger beside me – head on her crossed arms as she stared at me evenly. "It's the diary of a nobody – what could be so interesting about that?"

I'd only given it the most cursory of glances since we'd read the first paragraph together – Ashley growing bored before I'd even got to the second sentence. It was almost impenetrable in places – the spastic handwriting as dense as the use of language – and I had to admit, my initial thoughts had been as dismissive as Ashley's. Upon further reading, however, I was finding it both disturbing and wonderful – not to mention frighteningly synchronistic.

"She was a patient in the asylum," I told Ashley. "A nobody, yes – but an absorbing nobody."

"Asylum?"

"The Sorrow Street Asylum? That was on this site before these houses were built?"

"Oh, right."

I'd told her about this many times over recent months and it was vaguely annoying that she'd needed her memory jogging. I wouldn't say that my work didn't interest her, as such. She was as enthusiastic about the finished project as the most ardent Sonuel Moore fan. It was more that the whole creative process bored her.

"Maggie phoned earlier," she said – the subject of the journal and the Sorrow Street Asylum summarily dispatched. "She wanted to know if you're still going to be helping her out this coming week. Keeping an eye on her and all that."

Since discussing this with Oliver, I was beginning to have misgivings. The thought of possibly becoming embroiled in something I wasn't cut out for didn't really appeal. Nevertheless, I had made a commitment, and however distasteful it might be, I always found it nigh on impossible to go back on my word.

"Of course I am," I said. "I wouldn't say I was going to do something like that and then not."

"I know," she said, watching me carefully, eyes slitted against the harsh light – face misshapen and pouty from resting on her arms.

"She's just anxious, that's all. This is really getting to her, Sonny. She's got it into her head that whoever's doing this to her wants to take Wee Mark away from her. Kidnap him."

"Has a specific threat been made?" I asked – closing the journal and resting it on my lap, suddenly quite concerned.

"Not that I know of." She shrugged. "But you know what she's like. Especially since Jim died. She gets spooked. Her mind works overtime. I wouldn't be surprised if..." She let the sentence trail off and I looked down at her. Her eyes tightly shut, I wondered what she was thinking.

"If what?" I asked.

"I don't know. Forget I said it."

"Easier said than done. If what, Ash?"

Again that shrug. "I just... I wouldn't be surprised if she was making it up. To have you running around after her."

"That's the most ridiculous thing I've ever heard in my life."

"Is it?"

"You know it is. Why on earth would she want to do a thing like that? It's bloody preposterous."

"I don't think it is," she said, quietly, her eyes still closed – speech a little slurred. "Unlikely, possibly – but given that she has no man in her life right now other than Wee Mark I'd say it was anything but preposterous. She's still grieving, love. A grieving, lonely woman is a peculiar creature. A woman is a peculiar creature full stop."

I saw an opportunity and unashamedly took it. "You won't get an argument from me on that," I told her.

"We disappoint you?" Finally she opened her eyes again, watching me carefully – measuring every twitch and tremor like an emotional seismologist.

"I didn't say that."

"You implied it."

"It was a joke, Ash. Lighten up."

I watched her buttocks clench as she did her pelvic floor exercises – a thoughtful and deliberate tensing that reminded me of a thug cracking his knuckles. A pool of sweat had formed in the small of her back and a lone hover fly set down beside it, supping heartily. Ashley reached behind her and slapped it away.

37

"It's not easy, you know," she said.

"What isn't?" I wondered if she meant slapping flies away or clenching one's buttocks.

"Being me. It's not easy being me." Her voice held a treacly, retarded quality that I'd heard before and didn't particularly like. Introspective and suddenly quite gloomy. I tried to figure out where this had come from – and how I'd failed to spot its imminent arrival. "It's all well and good you taking a cheap pop at womankind in general, but... it's just not easy. Being me. Being a woman in the twenty-first century. *Being*."

I knew better than to argue with her. It wasn't what she needed and it most certainly wasn't what *I* needed. As she spoke, I imagined her shrinking on the sun-lounger – Alice-like and vulnerable. Her voice became weaker and weaker, until it was little more than a whisper, and I listened without interrupting, hoping she might purge herself.

"I used to think it would all amount to something," she said. "Something I'd be able to see and touch. Something tangible. I'd spend a few years in preparation, doing the emotional groundwork, and then, one day, everything would just fall into place and I'd be... you know, fulfilled. But it's not like that at all. Every day it just gets harder and harder, even though I know how lucky I am, and sometimes... I just... I should be happy, so why is it so hard? I just... I'm not *giving* anything."

None of this was new to me, of course. For a good few years, since well before Nadine had been born, I'd heard it or something very similar at least every couple of months. It all came down, as I saw it, to a lack of fulfilment and self-worth brought on by one very simple underlying problem; Ashley was too bloody idle to do anything about it. She wanted to feel of value. I tried to point out that Nadine and I needed her, that our lives would be lousy without her, but that didn't help. Ashley was a clever woman. Cleverer than me in many ways, she could have walked into any number of rewarding positions if she'd put her mind to it. But that would have required discipline and commitment – the willingness to march to the beat of someone else's drum.

I waited a moment, just to be sure she had finished, and then said, "I don't know what to say that I haven't already said a hundred times.

If you're that unhappy, we can change things but to be frank, every time I suggest a solution, you don't want to know."

"That's because all your suggestions add up to the same thing," she said in a sulky whisper. "Get a job."

"Is that really such a bad idea?"

"Yes."

"Why?"

"Because it's not addressing the underlying problem."

"Which is?"

"I don't know."

It was difficult to know where to go with this. The more we talked, the more pointless the task seemed to become. I looked at the garden – the hole finally filled in, the lawn looking fairly healthy now that the summer storms had stopped and given it time to dry out, the green stained fencing so reminiscent of childhood – and tried to understand how we had reached this place. I didn't understand the problem and I was damn certain Ashley didn't, either. So how on earth were we to ever find a solution?

I was about to say this to her when I heard the familiar sound of footfalls coming along the path at the side of the house. Someone whistled the Dambusters March through his teeth and Ashley rolled her eyes at me – sitting up and putting on a long, thin blouse that covered up the important stuff. I usually locked the side gate when Ashley was sunbathing, but today I'd forgotten and, sure enough, it opened and Old Man Ned came strolling round onto the patio – hands clasped behind his back, stooping as though he was about to speak to a very short child.

Ashley hated Ned. He lived a few doors along and ever since she'd seen him with a pair of binoculars once she'd insisted he was a Peeping Tom – a dirty old man, she told me, "whose eyes undress me, find me not up to scratch and help me back into my clothes". I, on the other hand, liked Ned. He was one of those old-fashioned storytellers; ninety-nine percent bullshit and always on the lookout for an audience, but generous with his wit and hospitality. Where Ashley saw a pervy old git, I saw a lonely old man with a rich store of local lore and old style common sense.

"Hello, Ned," I said, getting to my feet and offering him my seat beside Ashley – much to her chagrin. He waved a hand and declined, without so much as a glance at Ash. "What can we do for you this fine day?"

"Is it a bad time, lad?" I was dressed only in shorts – my bare chest a little too red for comfort. "I wouldn't want to intrude if you and your good lady were enjoying the sun."

"We were just going to have a cup of tea. Care to join us?"

"Actually, no. Thank you. I can't stop. I was just wondering if you might have a few minutes to spare to give me a hand with summat."

Ashley hadn't even said hello – unless a weak and fleeting smile counted as a greeting. She sat on the lounger with her legs pulled up, hugging the blouse to her, and, I have to admit, I wanted to give her a good shake.

Before she could speak up with some excuse to keep me from helping Ned (I swear, I could hear the idea forming in her head), I jumped in and said, "Sure, mate. Now quick enough for you?"

"I reckon now would be just the job," he said, showing his crooked, stained teeth. "If that's all right with Ashley. You don't mind me stealing him away from you for a few minutes, do you, love?"

There was nothing even remotely convincing about her smile. She shrugged her shoulders and started making herself more comfortable. "Be my guest," she said. "The conversation was getting a little tedious and repetitive, anyway."

Old Man Ned's living room faced east, like ours, so at this time of day it was pleasantly cool – especially with the windows open as wide as they were. I stood amidst all the clutter – horse brasses, aspidistras, more books on the Battle of the Somme than I think I've ever seen in one place at the same time in my life, four Tiffany lamps in various states of disrepair, two circa 1973 tiled coffee tables, two televisions (one LCD, the other a fourteen inch black and white portable), cable decoder, DVD player with somewhere in the region of three hundred DVDs, video recorder, stacks of magazines and newspapers, one threadbare armchair and a settee that looked hardly used – as I stood amidst all this, I felt a deep moment of peace, of tranquillity, almost.

Old Man Ned stood in the doorway watching me with a vaguely amused air as I took in my surroundings. During our short walk from my house to his, he had told me of his new pet project – a book, "not like what you write, or owt, just a little thing about the stuff that's happened round these parts" – and I now understood his problem. If he was to do it properly, he'd explained, he reckoned he needed a computer – something easy to use with "one of those Internet things". The thing was, he had little room for a desktop, especially if the other rooms were as cluttered as this.

"I thought of getting rid of the bookcase," he said. "Putting it there. But that'd mean getting shot of a load of me books, and I can't say I find that all that attractive."

I thought of Richard and the delightful Mrs. Sutherland. He would know exactly what was required under such circumstances.

"There won't be any need for that," I told him, turning to the doorway where he stood and smiling. "All you'll have to do is buy a laptop instead of a desktop, then you can use it wherever you like and put it away when you're finished."

Ned raised an inquisitive eyebrow and shuffled further into the room – almost cracking his shin on one of the coffee tables. He seemed less stooped in his own home, more at ease and less inclined to see himself as the old man the world insisted he was. He perched on the arm of the settee and said, "One of those things that look like a briefcase?"

"A laptop, yes," I said.

"But... they're not... they're not *real* computers, are they?"

I wasn't really sure what he meant, so I didn't respond – chewing my mouth thoughtfully and praying that he'd say something to clarify his point.

He sighed and dried the palms of his hands on the knees of his jeans. Shaking his head, he said, "I know. I'm showing my ignorance. It's just that it doesn't make a whole lot of sense from where I'm sitting. They're *tiny*, so how can they be as good as real computers?"

Now I understood. Ned was of a mindset that insisted that big was better. Whether it was a generational thing, I didn't know, but Ned wanted to *see* something for his money. When he bought a computer, he wanted a fifty-foot bastard.

For the next five minutes I did my best to convince him that laptops, and miniaturisation in general, were good things. He resisted

41

with the occasional derisive sniff, but ultimately he accepted my arguments – reluctantly agreeing that a laptop was the only workable option if he didn't want to get rid of anything.

"I reckon you're just feeding me a line cos you don't much fancy helping me hump all those books out of here," he said with a wry grin as he showed me to the door. "Want to keep yourself fit for that woman of yours." He winked and although I would never have admitted it to Ashley, it was one of the few times I felt uncomfortable around Old Man Ned. I didn't want him talking about Ashley, in any way, shape or form – and so I smiled politely, gave him a pat on the shoulder and left.

It was true I'd enjoyed his company. It was also true that it was good to be back out in the steadily freshening air.

That evening, I sat alone in my office – trying not to dwell on the silent afternoon with Ashley that had followed my visit with Old Man Ned. My head ached from too much sun and vodka, and I felt an overwhelming sense of loss. A full, busy life suddenly meant nothing. It was an act of misdirection, nothing more, and understanding that was of no help whatsoever. Ashley had a point, I thought. Being happy was hard. Being *truly* happy was hard. Other people seemed to manage it, but I couldn't help asking myself just how real all that was.

Before going to bed, blanketed in depression and wilting perceptibly, Ashley had stopped by my study for a moment – leaning against the jamb and staring in at me. I'd stared back at her, admiring her still slim figure in the shorts and T-shirt she wore, unable to resist her sad, gem-like eyes. In that instant, I was wholly convinced that she thought I hated her. I didn't know where the thought came from, but it made perfect sense. She saw herself as the problem – forever upsetting the apple cart – and in her mind, that was more than enough of a reason for me to hate her.

"It's still hot," she'd said. "The weather. I wish it would cool down a bit. It's unbearable."

Before I could respond, she'd left – her gaze falling to the floor as she turned away, movements fluid but curiously ungraceful. It was all so premature. A space where there should have been occupation and vitality, a void that time could as yet see no way of filling. Something to be mourned, if not understood.

I thought about writing. It was true I felt like shit and should really have joined Ash in bed – but I just wasn't sleepy and the thought of laying awake beside her, listening to her breathe as she listened to me breathe, filled me with a deep and oppressive brand of despair. But I wasn't up to writing. The headache and my mood would compromise the fiction, I was sure, and I'd only end up discarding it, and so I picked up the journal and turned to the page I'd marked earlier.

I do not know or particularly care what day it is, I read. *I should not be writing, and yet they let me, possibly grateful of the stillness it inspires in me. I am purged thrice daily, and only once into these threateningly blank pages. Weak and empty. It is their preference. It makes for compliance, the soul silenced and stilled, a dispirited and broken creature less likely to rail against their stoical and otherwise intolerable conventions. She is the worst. The Warty Nurse. I call her this because she isn't worthy of a true identity and the wart on her nose seems to grow bigger shift by shift. She delights. That is what I sense more than anything. She delights in seeing me empty and husk like, standing in the doorway to the water closet and watching as the watery, foul-smelling stool erupts from me. Her pleasure as I wipe myself unsteadily, full knowing I will never be as clean as I wish to be, is nigh on intolerable – and had I the strength I would surely claw out her hateful, twistedly gleeful eyes.*

The Warty Nurse knows the worst of me. She knows that all the enforced vomiting they can inflict on me won't stop me pleasuring myself beneath the sheets once the lights are turned down. She knows that however they might restrain me, I will always find enough movement to take me away from this hellish place. Sometimes a thought is enough – and this knowledge offends her so greatly that she can think of nothing more than how best to steal from me, how best to hollow me out that I might be filled with piety and rectitude.

This morning she inflicted a further indignity on me – or that was how she no doubt viewed it. I have suffered far worse and with a certain readjustment of thought it was not quite so bad as it otherwise might have been. I might say I even derived a degree of physical pleasure from it, being of such a Nature.

"Kneel on the bed, please," The Warty Nurse said, cheeks flushed,

fingers laced on her tightly starched belly. "Quickly now. We haven't got all day."

She cannot reach me. That is what this woman will never realise. Probe and invade as she might, her fingers like the tentacles of some extraordinary sea monster within me, she can but scratch the surface of who I am – and surely will never understand the things I have done... the things I am convinced I will do again.

When she sang to me under her breath, whispery words and broken melody – with urgency and not a little fear – I thought I felt something loosen between us. It was difficult for me to see it clearly at the time, but now I understand it in that way that can only come in the dead of night, when the angry halls are dark and broodingly silenced. A little of her power over me has been exiled, I now see. With that act, she gifted me something I'm sure she never intended. She took pleasure from the thing she did to me, of that I am convinced, and I better than any know that pleasure always has its price. I have learned and still learn. The lesson has become the pleasure, in some unfathomable way, but this is something The Warty Nurse would never be capable of grasping. She still believes that this place grants her certain freedoms – that my imprisonment in this place I do not belong disempowers me and negates any opportunity there might be for me to impose my Will and correct the balance. But she is wrong. So very wrong. My understanding of her True Nature lends me a degree of liberty that she will never acknowledge until it is far too late.

A boy once held me. When I was a girl – a maiden and his equal in strength and intellect. A Sunday afternoon graveyard, solemn and sensual. I knew little in those times, little of the things my looks and scent would demand of me, but I knew enough to see that this boy was enamoured of me. He pushed and brushed against me at every opportunity, blushing and bulging as he panted an apology. I liked the game, but that afternoon behind the church he went farther than any had a right. I will not say I did not enjoy the act. I find pleasure wherever I can. It is my way. Rather it was his presumptuousness to which I finally objected. He believed he had some God-given right to enter me, to tear the very thing that was, then, so precious to me. He pushed me to the ground, and I did not try to stop him – as easy as that would have been. Hard and fast, it was, some might say, a cruel introduction into the ways of men, but it was one for which I was nevertheless grateful.

Three days later, the boy was found disembowelled down by the docks. I do not know if this was my doing. I do not recall. I like to think it was.

Her voice was distant and soft – at the far end of a long, extending tunnel. Close, yet light years away – delicate and, yet, somehow jarring and brash. She spoke again, and I saw a naked woman kneeling on a bed, buttocks large and relaxed as she waited and waited and...

"Sonny?" Ashley shook me gently by the shoulder and I sat up quickly – my neck and back immediately issuing formal, written complaint (in triplicate). "You're getting too old for shit like this."

I'd fallen asleep face down across my desk. My right cheek was both sore and numb, and I had pins and needles in my fingers. Add to this the stiff neck and back and I think it's fair to say I wasn't in the best of shape.

Ashley appeared somewhat amused by my dishevelled and disjointed appearance – and after the afternoon and evening we'd had the day before, I could only find that promising. Wearing only a faded matching sky-blue bra and thong, her hair falling about her face as if in an effort to conceal a scar or defect, it struck me that the worst was over, for the time being, and maybe we could be happy after all.

"I owe you an apology," she said, brushing my hair back from my brow.

"Do you?" My mouth was dry, my tongue sticking to the roof of my mouth.

"You know I do. I was an arse."

"It happens to the best of us," I said graciously. "Don't worry about it, love."

"You forgive me?"

"There's nothing to forgive." I sighed and pulled her onto my knee, holding her around the waist as she put her arms around my neck. "It's just... it's life, love. It does that to us all every once in a while. It doesn't have to make sense, it just *is*. Oliver would no doubt call it existential."

Ash nodded thoughtfully, grinning as she said, "Sartre was a fucking pain in the arse, too, then?"

"Naturally."

We held each other for a while longer – examining each other's sunburnt bits and checking for melanomas like grooming gorillas. Ashley smelt of sleep and crisply baked flesh, just the faintest lingering whiff of her feminine hygiene spray and last night's deodorant. Beneath that was something more personal, something particular and yet ephemeral. Her essential smell that existed just beyond the more describable frequencies.

"I do love you, you know," she whispered into my ear, head resting on my shoulder. "I know I have a bloody funny way of showing it sometimes, but I do."

"I've never doubted it," I lied.

Ashley took me to bed. We had at least a couple of hours before Pippa, Ashley's mum, brought Nadine back and Ash seemed determined to finish our weekend alone on a high note. As out of sorts as I was, I did not resist – falling into our tried and tested method of lovemaking and actually finding that, yes, the intimacy and release helped. I held her like my life depended on it as I penetrated her and she cried quietly as we worked together, fighting for her curiously elusive climax. Downstairs, the telephone rang – and we ignored it, caught up in our sudden desperation and something I would later think of as akin to panic.

Ashley finally satisfied, after much hard work on both our parts, we settled back in each other's arms and listened to the sounds of the street outside. Children playing, cars and the occasional motorbike passing by – the susurrations of the newly resurrected breeze in the trees. It took me back to my childhood, my teens. Growing up in this place with so many dreams and unfulfilled ambitions. I'd wanted so much, but above all I had yearned for simple contentment – a wife, a child, a facsimile of the wonderful (and quite possibly unattainable) example set by my parents. Where others might lie in their beds dreaming of rock stardom and excess, I would dream of times such as this – love and leisure, simple understanding. I had believed that all obstacles in a relationship were surmountable, that any broken part could be easily fixed with patience and application. Naïve? Perhaps.

Ashley moved so that she could get a better look at my face, plumping the pillow and making herself more comfortable. "Happy?" she said, lips soft and a little pouty.

"Happy," I said, not wholly convinced but determined not to show it. I would fight my way to happiness if that was what was required, and in the meantime I would just bloody well fake it.

"So yesterday is all forgotten?"

"I'm sure I haven't got a clue what you're talking about."

"It's that easy, eh?"

"If we want it to be."

Those soft lips pursed and I thought she was going to disagree – insist that nothing was that easy. But she merely smiled and said, "You really believe that, don't you? You really believe that we can make things the way we want them to be."

After a little consideration, I said, "I believe it's possible, but not necessarily probable."

Sitting up and turning to face me, hugging her knees – naked and uncharacteristically vulnerable – she sighed and shook her head. "It's early and I've just come my brains out. You're going to have to explain that."

"I think every individual has the capacity to create the life of which they dream," I told her, "but one thing invariably gets in the way."

"That one thing being?"

"Life itself."

"Life gets in the way of life?"

"Life gets in the way of *a* life. Or, rather, chance, rogue elements do." Not bad for a Monday morning. Olly would have been proud of me.

"Define 'chance, rogue elements'," Ashley said, eyes crinkling with smug self-satisfaction.

"Random events and encounters," I told her, knowing full well I was getting in way over my head. "Unpredictability. Sensitive dependence on initial conditions. That kind of thing."

"A moody, irrational partner?" Blessedly, she was grinning. Her eyes lit up and she chuckled to herself, shaking her head and adding,

47

"Sorry. No, really, I am. That isn't a fair question."

"Sounds fair enough to me," I said with mock-solemnity. "And it's a very interesting point, actually. I suppose what you're really asking is do I think you've held me back? Does that sound about right?"

"Well I wouldn't quite –"

"It's unavoidable, really," I continued, laying it on thick and hoping the humour was evident (my life probably depending on it). "Man is the driving force behind the whole, incredible patriarchal system, naturally – whilst Womankind is... how shall I put it? Womankind lacks vision and insight. It continually strives to stem the flow of progress, ever fearful that it will be left behind and –"

Grabbing my sleepy penis beneath the sheet, Ashley said, "Much more talk like that and I *will* stem the fucking flow. *Permanently*."

I surrendered gracefully, giving in to yet another chance, rogue element.

I'd just come off the phone to Oliver – returning his call and agreeing that we would carry out our first surveillance of Maggie together, until we got into the swing of it – when Pippa, as prompt as ever, turned up with a frighteningly serene Nadine. The two looked a perfect fit, grandmother and granddaughter, the latter riding the former's hip as if it were the most natural thing in the world. Even in her mid-fifties, Pippa was a stunner. Slight and energetic, auburn hair tied back and a light dusting of make-up highlighting her fine features, she was the archetype I'd once imagined Ashley growing into. Authoritative, but only occasionally imposing – comfortable in her own skin and with her place in the world. But daughters rarely become their mothers in my experience, whatever the clichés state to the contrary, and Ash certainly wasn't the exception that proved the rule.

She came through to the living room without needing to be asked, putting Nadine down and sitting in the armchair beneath the window with a perceptible sigh – stretching her legs and wiggling her toes. Ashley was still in the shower, no doubt begrudgingly washing away the remnants of our second sweaty sex session of the morning, so I offered Pippa a coffee and she declined with a smile.

"I'm cutting back," she told me. "All those toxins, just not good, you know – especially for a woman my age."

I perched on the edge of the settee and playfully patted Nadine's Pampered bottom as she waddled past. "Ah, I see," I said. "And just how old are you, now? Thirty? Thirty-five?"

"Fifty-five, as well you know."

"A lot to be said for toxins, then, from where I'm sitting."

"Then I'd say you need to sit somewhere else."

I laughed and shook my head, steadying Nadine when she nearly tripped over my foot. "How was she?" I asked Pippa, indicating Nadine with a nod. "Behave herself?"

"As good as gold. We spoilt her rotten, of course, so she'll probably give you hell all week. Makes for an interesting life, though, right?"

"We don't know how to thank you."

"A progress report would be good." When it became clear that I didn't have a clue what she meant, she added, "Ashley. She seemed a little distracted and in the doldrums the other day."

I didn't like talking about Ashley to her mother. I didn't like talking about Ashley to anyone. It always struck me as just about the worst thing anyone in a relationship could do, because it implied a weakness within the unit, a lack of loyalty and honesty. It had been difficult enough talking to Olly, but with Pippa I often felt that, as nice as she was, she was inclined to judge her daughter harshly. Ashley was not Pippa, and for Pippa this was a disappointment and an affront. Nevertheless, she was concerned and I supposed I had no real choice other than to tell her how Ash was doing now – even if it meant being less than generous with the truth.

"She's fine," I said. "She was just in need of a bit of a break. We both were, if I'm honest."

Nadine, her dark blue eyes large and perpetually astonished, climbed onto the settee beside me and snuggled in, whispering a Kylie song under her breath. I rearranged myself, putting my arm around her whilst Pippa studied me sceptically.

"There seemed more to it than that," she insisted. "It looked to me like she was having one of her bad times again."

It was easy to forget that others had seen Ashley at her worst, too. I was so used to protecting her and bearing the brunt of her moods and depressions that it could almost have come as a surprise to see that

Pippa had been there before me – had had to guide her through the difficult years before we'd met. Ashley rarely spoke of her childhood and early teens, but I'd always got the impression that, in spite of the inevitable conflicts, theirs had been a fairly harmonious household. Now I looked at that again and wondered if, perhaps, it had been more difficult than I had realised. Ashley as a teenager. Not exactly an alien concept to me, since we'd met when she had been just sixteen. But maybe I had seen the best of her. Where Pippa had had a troublesome, moody and depressive daughter to contend with, I had had the mischievous and fun-loving girl who nearly always made me smile.

Pippa was not easily misled, and I knew better than to try. "She had a bit of a blip," I admitted, "but she seems to have got over it just fine. She's back to her old self this morning."

"You're sure?"

"Positive. She gets like that when she's tired, that's all."

"Oh, I think it's a little more complicated than that, Sonuel, as well you know." She glanced at the hall doorway, ensuring the coast was still clear, and then added, "Maybe there's nothing clinically wrong with her. I don't know. I'm not qualified to say. But she has it rough at times, and that can be hard on those around her.... I want you to know, Sonny, that we are here for Ashley, too. For Ashley and you. You don't ever have to feel alone."

It was an unexpected and moving speech – one I was in no way prepared for. I started to mumble an ineffectual reply, but Nadine beat me to it.

Shuffling her bottom to the edge of the settee, she hiccuped and then, with raised chin and dimpled cheeks, said very precisely, "Splendid."

An exaggeration, but welcome nevertheless.

Chapter Four

Ashley sat on the edge of the bed in jeans and T-shirt, bare feet rubbing thoughtfully against the carpet. I watched her from the doorway, listening to Nadine playing in her room across the landing, then entered and sat on the bed beside her.

Pippa had left a good fifteen minutes ago, and by rights I should have been meeting Oliver for our possibly quite ridiculous surveillance of Maggie – but something had changed with Ashley since her mother had left, and I wasn't too comfortable leaving her alone.

She smiled rather unimpressively, her eyes not in the least convincing, and then turned her attention back to the carpet and her feet. When she sighed, I felt Sunday afternoon returning and tried desperately to think of some way to get the Ashley of earlier that morning back.

"You shouldn't be here," she told me quietly.

"I know but..."

"But what?"

I considered possible answers. Make something up, or stick with the truth? I reached over and took her hand. It felt cool, a little clammy. Maybe she was sickening for something. I sincerely hoped so.

"What's up?" I asked. "Did Pippa say something?"

"Not to my face," she said. And I immediately understood. "Why did she do that, love? Why couldn't she just ask me how I was instead of treating me like... I don't know, someone you have to tiptoe around? I'm not that bad, surely."

I had to tread very carefully – without letting it show. Ashley was watching me intently and I knew that if I leant too far in either

51

direction I'd be in big trouble. "I just think that she didn't want to risk bringing you back down if you'd picked yourself up again," I said. "I can't say I was too comfortable with it, but I think I understand it. A little."

She nodded and got a better grip of my hand. "I know," she said. "I just don't like it. It's too reminiscent."

"Of what?"

"Of childhood," she told me.

I will never forget the day Ashley and I first met. I was twenty-four and generally rather full of myself. University was behind me and I was now finally fluffing my feathers and preparing to be the one thing I'd always dreamed of becoming; a successful writer... any kind of writer, for that matter. I idealistically saw opportunity everywhere, optimism dripping from me like perspiration, and it didn't matter to me in the least that I hadn't yet published anything, or that I was doing any menial job I could find just to make ends meet. The fact was, I was writing – and when I told people I was a writer, rather than a bartender or window cleaner, it no longer felt like a lie.

It was a good time for me. A new decade, a new outlook. I partied with friends, forever bemoaning the decline in the innovative delights of the music we played, wrote a thousand words a morning come hell or high water and worked at whatever temporary work I could find, delightfully seeking inspiration in my surroundings and sifting through the minutiae for "true meaning". A good time... or perhaps not. I fooled myself, I suppose, like many of us do. Nothing was fixed or pinned down. I drifted and the world about me drifted. Transient and quite possibly highly unforgiving, I wrote about damaged, lost souls – and ignored the flashes of recognition.

I'd never really liked Estby Bay. It was a seedy seaside town that seemed perpetually out of season – bleak and broken, the arcades shiny but flaky, the beach a minefield of dog shit and broken bottles. So why did I end up there on that fateful weekend? Quite simple, really; Oliver. Had it not been for his insisting that I should hook up with him and a few "scene" gays he was having a lot of fun with at the time, I would have stayed at home, written a few thousand words, had a quiet wank and never met the beautiful (and young) Ashley Levine.

"We've got a caravan," Olly had told me. "It won't cost you a fucking penny, mate. And those fuckers'll love you so much you won't have to buy a drink all weekend." I remember I'd expressed some concerns about his friends possibly expecting "something in return", but Olly had been quick to put my mind at ease. "With me there, you won't have a thing to worry about," he'd told me. "And apart from that, you'll pull a cute girly the first night there."

It had struck me as a whole load of nightmares rolled into one, but Oliver hadn't been about to take no for an answer. And so we had arrived late Friday afternoon in three cars, the rain bouncing and the temperature more reminiscent of January than July, and my fate was sealed. Oliver and his friends (Rich, Christian and a few others I can only remember by their dreads and piercings) fussed about unpacking, Oliver frequently telling the others not to be such a "bunch of fucking obsessive pansies" and squeezing in and out the inadequate door on his way to and from the cars. I knew right off I was out of my depth – especially when Rich flung his arms around my neck and started crying, telling me that he would never forgive that "horridific, beastly man" (Olly) for what he had said ("you've got a pimple on your nose, mate") – and so, within half an hour or thereabouts, I decided a walk alone in the rain was my best option.

The Esplanade was relatively deserted, the families that had braved the beach for the day long gone – either returning to their caravans or B&Bs, or feeding coins into the clattering and buzzing machines in the arcades – and as I walked, my shirt and jeans already soaked through, I tried unsuccessfully to think of somewhere I'd less rather be. Cars and lorries passed on my right, burning exhaust fumes mixing with the curiously filthy and unappetising smell of fish and chips, and the sea rolled in shades of grey on my left – and the only promise of shelter or respite I saw was the roofed-in brick and wood seating areas that looked out to sea. It was either that or cross the road for the shops and arcades I found so unappealing.

I jogged the remaining few yards as the rain started to come down more heavily, cursing Oliver for talking me into coming with him, and finally plonking down on the bench, mumbling to myself obscenely. Only when I'd finished talking to myself did I glance around and notice the young woman sitting at the far end of the bench – feet up as

53

she huddled into the corner made by the bench and the shelter reading Joseph Heller's *Good As Gold*.

I remember she wore heavy-duty, black leather work boots, torn and tattered jeans and a red and black plaid shirt – her shoulder-length hair shaggy about her face, complexion tanned and a little ruddy. She eyed me suspiciously over her book and then, unable to help herself, grinned and said the first words I ever heard her speak:

"If it helps," she said, "you've cheered me up no end."

Ashley had never really been inclined to talk about her childhood. As she told it, it had been fairly typical and uneventful – something to be forgotten simply because there was little to remember – but that had always seemed somehow suspicious to me. So to be finally sitting on the end of our bed together discussing this was both a relief and a worry. I imagined every childhood horror under the sun, torturing myself with ominous and wholly uncharacteristic images of her father, but felt myself relaxing as she spoke.

"That's what I remember more than anything," she told me. "People talking about me. Behind my back. Even from my bedroom, I'd hear Mam and Dad going on about me, worried about this, worried about that. It was bloody ridiculous."

"They're parents," I insisted. "That's what they do... we'll be the same with Nadine."

She looked at me sharply, pulling her hand away from mine. "No, we won't," she said, an edge of anger communicating just how serious this was. "We'll be anything but the same, Sonny. I don't want Nadine being brought up feeling that... that she doesn't have a say in her own life. If we discuss anything about her, we do it with her around."

"That isn't possible," I said softly, taking her hand again and hoping I was doing this right. "Sometimes we'll have to discuss her privately, just between the two of us – it's vital."

She nodded and I felt something start to uncoil just beneath my diaphragm. "But only when it's absolutely necessary and only when we are quite sure she can't hear us, right?"

"That sounds about right to me," I told her.

I still didn't really understand what was going on here. I knew as well as anyone the various resentments that could develop and fester over the years between parents and a child, but it still seemed virtually unthinkable that Pippa and Len could have done anything to warrant this kind of reaction. I thought of my own parents – my own childhood – and felt a flash of anger at Ashley's ingratitude; she still had her parents, could still fix the things that were broken, if she so wished. Whereas I... I had nothing in need of fixing. My parents and I had reached a place of balance and unspoken acceptance. We had been who we had been, and whatever our faults, we had admitted a quiet admiration for one another. But that still didn't mean that there were not things I wanted to discuss with them – both trivial and of great importance – or that I missed them any less.

"They've always thought of me as a problem," Ashley continued. "That's what it comes down to."

"I don't think that's strictly true, love." Pippa and Len had always seemed reasonable, loving people to me (although Len had been something of an obstacle in the early days) and this just didn't fit with my image of them at all. I was doing my best to be patient, but this just seemed to be getting more ludicrous with each passing minute.

"Take my word for it, first and foremost, I'm a problem to them. A whole fucking *series* of problems.... Don't look like that, Sonny. You don't know. You've only seen what they want you to see. The truth is, whether I'm right or wrong, that's how it seemed all the way through my childhood. That's how they made me *feel* – sitting in the living room, talking about my 'moods', about whether I was doing drugs or fucking boys, wondering if they should get me 'professional help'. I was a *normal* kid, for fuck's sake. A *normal* teenager, but to them I was... I was going to say I was some kind of freak, but that's too excessive. Even *I* can see that. They were wrong, but they weren't quite *that* bad."

That was something, at least. I started to tell her that I understood what she was saying, where she was coming from, but before I'd said more than a couple of words, she was speaking again.

"Did I ever tell you about the time they caught me reading de Sade?" she asked.

We spent the rest of the afternoon and early evening talking in the shelter – looking out to sea at the ships waiting to be piloted into port and resisting the temptation to shuffle closer to one another. Heller sat on the bench between us like a wordy old chaperone and I tried not to dwell on the fact that it had been he who had introduced me to the word "oxymoron". Ashley laughed easily, but almost always attempted to deny it with a quickly following frown – and this made me work all the harder, delighting in this insight into her nature. When she moved to make herself more comfortable, I thought she was about to leave, and my sense of relief when she stayed was both fascinating and revealing.

I knew she was younger than me, of course. She looked eighteen or nineteen, but spoke to me like an emotional and intellectual equal – so it wasn't something I was unduly concerned about. If she was old enough to appreciate Heller, I couldn't see that there was a problem.

"So what brings you to the wonderful Estby Bay?" she asked me.

"My friend, Oliver," I told her. "I'm spending two whole nights in a caravan full of queers."

"Looking forward to it?" She smirked and set Heller on her lap. I wondered if this was an invitation to move closer.

"I'll be sleeping on my back with one eye open," I said.

"I'm sure they'll be gentle with you."

The evening grew late. We drank coffee and ate cakes in a café just off the High Street, and then Ashley announced that she had to be getting off. Her parents would be wondering where she'd got to. I offered to walk her back to her B&B, but she assured me she would be fine – and anyway, it was just around the corner and, as she told me, I had a caravan of queers to take care of.

Before parting outside the café, we made plans to meet the following morning and Ashley leant in and kissed me. It was a rather chaste, tentative little closed-mouth kiss on the lips – but still I found it both touching and arousing. She blushed and smiled at me and, impulsively, I reached out and caressed the side of her face.

"Nine thirty," she said. "At our shelter."

"I'll be there at nine."

"Playing hard to get, eh?"

"I get the feeling it'd be a waste of time," I said.

"I think you could be right."

We were standing in the doorway to Nadine's bedroom, watching her play with her Action Man figures. Her favourites were a couple I'd preserved from my own childhood – far superior to the modern equivalent, with spiky hair and hands that still gripped. She picked up the one I'd always called Jack (Blue polo neck, jeans and a beard) and sat him on the edge of the bed, maternally patting him on the head and chattering away to him in Baby-Speak. Ashley held my hand as we watched and I waited for her to continue telling me about the de Sade incident.

"I don't remember ever being like that," she told me. "Carefree. Maybe I was and just don't remember it, I don't know..." She trailed off, smiling as Nadine pushed Jack from the bed with one hand and caught him with the other. "I tried, but I just... I wanted to understand everything, I suppose, and I guess that might have made me seem moody and introspective to Mam and Dad. I don't know. Either way, I think they should have known better."

"You were telling me about de Sade," I reminded her.

She stared at me blankly, then nodded and leant against the jamb, hugging herself. "De Sade," she muttered. "What a thing to get so uptight about. A tosspot pornographer-philosopher. You know what he's like. Literary tedium at its best. Once the novelty wears off, it just gets predictable and anything but arousing. I'd read a couple of hundred pages of Juliette, played with myself a few times, but I'd just about had enough of it. It was too twisted for me, but, well, that in itself was interesting. I was fifteen and I was already beginning to understand that everything, no matter how perverse, can be rationalised and justified, if one was willing to work hard enough at it. Granted, it might not be a rationale or justification you or I would recognise or accept, but I already understood that morality is highly subjective. For all his faults, de Sade taught me that.

"Of course, Mam and Dad didn't 'get' any of that. All they saw was their fifteen-year-old daughter with her hand down the front of her jeans reading a mucky book. It didn't matter that I was just scratching the top of my leg, or that I was reading it in the living room and not trying to hide anything from them. I considered myself old enough to read whatever the hell I liked – Mam used to lend me her Jackie Collins when I was just fourteen, for God's sake! – but

57

apparently I was mistaken. De Sade was the spawn of Satan. They never said as much, but they might as well have. I tried to talk to them about the book. Explain that I had learnt some important stuff from reading him, primarily that he was a twisted old tosser who tried to intellectualise his filth – but they just wouldn't listen. That was what was really awful – the way they both just kept right on talking as if I hadn't said a word. They just didn't hear me, Sonny. No matter how calm I was, no matter how loudly I shouted – they just didn't hear me. They didn't want explanations, they didn't want the truth, they just wanted me out of the way so they could talk about me and revel in the drama of it all….

"They sent me to bed without any supper, can you believe that?" she said. "Just like a kid who's broken a window with a football, they sent me to bed without any supper and stayed up until three in the morning discussing what was to be done with me. I sat at the top of the stairs and listened, of course. They might not have let me have a say, but I wasn't about to let them talk about me without my at least having some idea what they were saying. They're C of E – you know that, right?"

I nodded, almost too overwhelmed to speak.

"Well can you believe that at one point they actually mooted the idea of taking me to a Catholic priest?"

"Let me guess," I said, trying to lighten things a little. "They wanted to have you exorcised?"

"Something like that, yes," she answered flatly, my attempt at humour going straight over her head. "Maybe exorcism is exaggerating it a bit, but they wanted to scare me into seeing that some of the choices I was making were bad – and for all of fifteen minutes they were convinced a Catholic priest was the perfect solution."

It seemed preposterous that Pippa could consider something so bizarre and, well, plain stupid – but I was now utterly convinced that Ashley was making none of this up. All these years, she'd kept this to herself and, yes, that had initially made me doubt her, if I'm truthful. I was her husband, for Heaven's sake – and I was supposed to know everything there was to know about her. But now it was out, and I thought that maybe I understood her a little better. It was an added insight I'd never figured on.

Ashley looked at me and smiled a heartbreaking smile. "It's not as bad as it sounds, I suppose," she told me. "I had friends who had it a hell of a lot worse. It's just that when I hear her talking like that it brings it all back, makes me feel powerless and insignificant."

"Maybe you need to talk to her," I suggested. "To both of them."

"Maybe I do." It was the closet we had been in a long time, and we both seemed to acknowledge this. I thought that perhaps this was what had been needed all along – Ashley opening up, letting me in – but I also knew that that was probably too much to hope for.

When I finally left to go meet Oliver, she seemed rather more settled – still introspective, but settled nevertheless. She carried Nadine downstairs with her and stood at the living room window, watching me go, the two of them waving. Proud, I walked with purpose and the utterly misguided sense that everything was going to be all right. A corner had been turned, I believed, and we were once again heading in the right direction.

We met at our shelter the following morning, as arranged, and the first thing I noticed and took as an encouraging sign was that Ashley had made something of an effort. Gone was the work-wear, only to be replaced by a short, pale yellow skirt and a tight, white sleeveless top. Her hair tied back loosely and her face lightly made up, she looked beautiful and, as Oliver would say when he met her later that evening, far too good for me.

It was much brighter and drier than the day before, the sun already starting to burn through the clouds and warm the pavement beneath our feet. It suddenly seemed a mammoth task to fill the day ahead of us and I felt a pang of doubt, finding it momentarily impossible to believe that the magic of the evening before could be maintained. The conversation would be stilted and hackneyed, and whatever the warmth of the day, the air between us would be dead and cold – in spite of my best efforts.

But I needn't have worried. Ashley all but skipped over to me and immediately linked my arm – talking ten to the dozen and leading me down the concrete ramp used by the fishing boats and the lifeboat to the sorrowful, shifting sands. She was well rested and in good spirits, open (I thought) and enthusiastic. She was really looking forward to our day together, she told me. She wanted to know everything there was to know about Sonuel Moore – about my writing and my life, the things that made me "tick". I smelt her freshness on the breeze and relished my closeness to her, already aroused, already a little in love.

"Have you read *God Knows*?" she asked me. We'd found a fairly safe patch of beach, free of broken glass and dog shit, and sat ourselves down – side-by-side, staring out to sea and watching the fishing boats. The breeze was a little cooler down here and I wished we'd had a windbreak. Colourful stripes and as much nostalgia as you could handle.

"For my sins, yes," I said. I didn't want to talk about Heller. He was a one-book wonder, with little to recommend him other than the occasional belly laugh. Better than some, but still vastly overrated.

"You don't like it?"

"I've read better," I said, with little real enthusiasm – remembering something Oliver had said to me the night before. I'd been telling him about Ashley. His E-inspired friends had apparently decided that arguing about the sleeping arrangements was a "silly" thing to do and had decided to draw lots. Oliver had looked jaded and seemed to be regretting the whole weekend – which was satisfyingly ironic, given that I was now enjoying almost every minute of it. Sitting down on the opposite side of the table to me with a can of beer and a packet of KP salted peanuts, barely managing to squeeze in, he'd sighed and rolled his eyes at me, shaking his head at the squealing.

"What is it they say?" he asked. "Be careful what you wish for?"

Now I thought about that as Ashley considered what I'd just said about the Heller novel. I'd always wanted someone like her – beautiful, young, intelligent and well read. Someone I could have a conversation with *and* have fun with between the sheets. But maybe, I now thought, *just maybe* that was too much to ask of myself. I had the distinct feeling that Ashley was about to prove that she understood Heller far better than I ever would.

But she was smarter than that. I assumed she wanted something more from our budding friendship for instead of launching into a discourse on Heller's merits, she merely shrugged and said, "I know what you mean. I enjoyed it but he can be so irritating in places."

"That applies to most writers," I said. "Even me."

"I'm sure it doesn't."

"I'm sure it does."

We argued playfully for a while longer and then, much to my surprise, Ashley took hold of my hand and stood, pulling me to my feet. "There's something I want to show you," she said, leading the way north along the beach.

It took us a good fifteen minutes to get there, walking on the sand making it feel more like half an hour, and when we arrived my first reaction was to wonder if it had really been worth it.

The sand dunes were deserted. It was a harsh and barren place – even with its razor-like blades of lyme grass – and I understood why few people chose to make the walk this far north along the beach. From the top of the highest dune, a view of a nearby chemical plant was the biggest treat – heavy industry further to the north – and as I slid back down to be with Ashley it was all I could do not to comment ironically on the wonderful sights.

"I never said it was picturesque," she told me – grinning wryly and reading my thoughts. "But that's not why I brought you here."

"It's not?"

"I thought you'd have worked that one out for yourself. Clever man like you."

"I've led a very sheltered life."

"Brought up by nuns?"

I nodded. "And every one a novice."

"Bless. I can see I'm going to have to teach you a thing or two."

"I'm a fast learner."

As private as this place seemed to be, I didn't really expect Ashley to be so uninhibited. I was expecting sex with our clothes on – hurried fumblings whilst we anxiously looked over our shoulders – but what I in fact got was a completely naked Ashley who didn't really seem to care whether we were observed or not. It was awkward but sensitive, and we giggled uncontrollably afterwards, but there was now no doubt in my mind; as quickly as this had come about, it was not just about sex. I had fallen for her as surely as the tides washed the shore – and as we lay together afterwards, my hand resting against the warmth of her sex, I braved all the possible outcomes and told her so.

"You telling me you love me?" she asked.

"Yes," I said. "I love you. I'm *in* love with you."

"That's good, then."

"It is?"

"Naturally. I don't do that for just anyone, you know."

"I'm pleased to hear it."

She snuggled in closer to me – pulling her skirt and blouse over her, but not yet ready to get dressed. "Sonny?" she said quietly.

"Yes?"

"Is this where we should be? This moment. Is it what was intended or did we make it happen?"

Post coitus, I preferred conversation that was a little less challenging – who would be number one next Sunday, that kind of thing – so this caught me a little unprepared. I shuffled about a bit and made thoughtful noises, and then rolled on my side to get a better look at her.

"I don't think there's a distinction," I said. "What we make happen is what was intended. Free Will and all that shit. Where we are is where we should be, because we made the necessary choices to get there."

"But what if we make the wrong choices?" She was on her side, too, now, her clothes pressed to her and her eyes large and wet with emotion. "What if... what if we don't know all the facts and, because of that, make choices we wouldn't normally make?"

"You having regrets?" I asked quietly, feeling an icy, nauseating dread bleed through me.

She shook her head. "No," she said. "But I think you might. I'm only sixteen."

Back at the caravan, Oliver chased Rich, Christian and the others the hell out of it and sat me down in the living area with a large scotch and what I thought was a sympathetic look (it was hard to tell with the beard). He sat down on the adjacent couch-bench thing and gave my knee a pat.

"Right," he said, "now we are alone, do you want to run that one by me again?"

"I've fallen for a sixteen year old," I told him. "Ashley. The girl I was telling you about. We made love in the sand dunes, and then she told me. She's only sixteen."

Even then, Oliver had seemed somehow imbued with wisdom. He possessed such self-confidence that the natural effect of this was to make him look as if he had all the answers, had done it all before and had every imaginable experience already tucked firmly under his belt. Whether this was the case or not didn't really matter; I saw a man not much older than myself, someone I trusted and believed in, and I instinctively knew that that was enough.

"And the problem in that is?" Oliver asked.

"She's *sixteen*," I repeated.

"Not jailbait, then." Oliver sighed and tried to make himself more comfortable on the too-small couch. "I repeat, and the problem in that is?"

"Not everything that is legal is right," I told him.

"So you think your relationship with this girl –"

"Ashley."

"You think your relationship with Ashley is wrong?"

Straight to the crux of the matter. Oliver's beard twitched and I got the impression that on some level he was finding all of this rather amusing. His disproportionately small nose crinkled and he quickly put a large, roughened hand to his face and sneezed.

"Look," he continued, before I had chance to reply. "I probably know you better than anyone, right?"

"Probably." I didn't bother checking him against a list; Oliver was too perceptive for it not to be true.

"And I know from years of association that you don't fall in love easily. Correct?"

This was true. I was good at keeping a part of myself back. For a long time it had seemed a prerequisite to survival. I nodded.

"So when you tell me you've fallen for this Ashley, I know it's no joke. You love her and you're in love with her, and I'd bet you've already told her as much."

"After we made love in the sand dunes," I confirmed. "It seemed the right thing to do."

"And she's in love with you?"

"It certainly seems that way, yes. Apparently she doesn't do that with just anyone."

Oliver was starting to look a little smug. He finally seemed to have managed to get comfortable and the conversation was on track. All was well with the world.

"Right. So we've established that the feeling between the two of you is mutual and as real as any of us can assume. Now we come to the age thing. She's over the legal age of consent, but you still don't think of the relationship as 'right' –"

"I didn't say that."

"But you –"

"What I said was that everything that's legal isn't *necessarily* right. I didn't say I actually believed that."

Oliver's brows were knitting and the little I could see of his lips suggested he was, at the very least, growing impatient with me. I'd seen the same expression earlier that morning and five minutes later Rich had been crying again.

"Then what *do* you believe?" he practically hissed.

I shrugged. "I dunno. It... she seems older than sixteen. She's well-read, intelligent and funny, and I'm comfortable with her – but some people are going to have a problem with it, aren't they?"

"'Some people' will always have a problem with something," Oliver told me. He reminded me of someone trying to potty-train a toddler. "That doesn't mean it is or should be a problem."

"Other people's attitudes will create yet another obstacle, though," I said. "There's no getting away from that."

"Do you want to be with her, for fuck's sake?" he said angrily.

"Yes," I stammered.

"And she wants to be with you?"

A quick little nod.

"Then stop being such an arse. We're having a party tonight. Bring her along."

Chapter Five

After calling him on his mobile a couple of times, I finally caught up
with Oliver at the library. Dressed in a black T-shirt and black jeans,
sunglasses tucked into the neck of his shirt, he looked hot and tetchy.
The temperature had dropped a degree or two, but it was still
oppressively warm and humid – even for someone who wasn't Olly's
size – and as he told me how he had followed Maggie to her mother's,
where she had dropped off Wee Mark, and then on to where we now
were, I noticed that, as well as seeming tetchy, Oliver looked
generally out of sorts. There were soot-like smudges beneath his eyes
and the colour of his skin made me think of cheap power-cut candles.
I asked him if he was okay, but he just ignored the question – fairly
typically, I guess.

"She takes some keeping up with," he told me. We were in the
fiction section. Oliver and I were near the Bs, Maggie the Ds. "The
word 'nimble' doesn't even begin to cover it. I'm not built for
endurance events. Short, sharp bursts of extreme power, that's me."

"The mind boggles." I turned and surreptitiously looked around
the library – from the reception to the first floor minstrel's gallery that
was the poky and insubstantial reference section – and quickly said,
"Anyway, any sign of anything suspicious?"

Oliver pulled a William Boyd novel – *The New Confessions* –
from the shelf and absently thumbed through it. "Not a sausage," he
said. "A guy followed her down her mother's road for a short while,
but I quickly eliminated him from our investigation."

I frowned at him quizzically.

"Postman," he explained. "A man with a big sack. He could have
been very distracting, were I not so conscientious."

Maggie had moved on, a couple of books tucked under her arm, and was now standing by one of the computers – as if trying to make up her mind what to do next. I glanced around the library again – even looking out the floor-to-ceiling windows to ensure that there wasn't anyone watching from outside – but everything seemed as it should be.

"She looks lost," I said.

"The natural state of the contemporary individual," Oliver informed me. "No escaping it, I'm afraid."

"You paint such an uplifting picture."

"I'm glad you think so," he said.

Oliver and I had known each other for as long as I could remember and through all the years I'd never quite escaped the feeling that some part of him existed on an entirely different plane. This seemed especially so since the split with Don – the break-up somehow exaggerating his need for introspection and solitude. It wasn't too difficult for me to imagine Oliver wandering around his hovel, talking to himself in much the same way as he was now talking to me, and as we followed Maggie out of the library I found myself wishing that both Maggie and Oliver were not so alone. I understood loneliness, and I saw its not so subtle effects in my two friends. It followed them like a shadow, stalked them like a jilted lover...

I stopped quite suddenly. Oliver walked on a couple of paces before realising I was no longer at his side. He turned and looked at me enquiringly, the muscles at his jaw twitching impatiently through his beard.

"We're going to lose her, if you don't get a bloody move on," he said.

"She's lonely," I told him.

"Well, yes – I would think that goes without saying. So what's your point?"

I continued walking. "I'm not sure. It's not a new idea. Ashley was saying something quite similar the other day but I dismissed it because... what with what happened in Wales and everything it was a bit... you know."

"Too close for comfort?"

"Yes. The thing is, I never realised until now just how lonely Maggie really is. Everything about her just yells loneliness. When I said she looked lost in there, I got it wrong. She knew exactly where she was and where she needed to be next. It wasn't that at all – it was more that –"

"There should have been someone at her side," Oliver said sadly – sliding his sunglasses from his T-shirt and putting them on.

I studied him with a sideways glance, for the moment forgetting why we were following Maggie. For the second time this week I got the distinct impression that Olly was saying more about himself than anyone else. He took up a lot of space, did our Oliver, but he was still a man with much space to share. Too much space, I suspected.

"Yes," I said quietly, wishing I hadn't brought up the subject.

We continued following Maggie, dropping back a bit further at Oliver's suggestion – trying to pay a little more attention to the ever-changing people around us. From the library, she headed to Asda for a few groceries, also buying a water pistol that looked capable of quelling the most unruly of rioters. I assumed this was for Wee Mark, and shuddered at the thought of him running around like a mini-Stallone squirting everything in sight. I never understood why parents did that (and I'd been as guilty of it as the next dad). The water pistol had "trouble" stamped all the way through it and it seemed obvious to me that it would be confiscated and placed somewhere out of reach within minutes of Wee Mark receiving it.

"Common sense goes out of the window where kids are concerned," I said, and Oliver nodded.

"Individual perception," he muttered. "Can't be trusted, mate. There is a definite need for external interpretation in these and all matters."

Maggie was at the checkout. Oliver continued to waffle on about the necessity for objectivity, "image degradation" and how untrustworthy the senses were. Maggie caught my eye and I looked away, encouraging Oliver to hang back by the tinned peaches. The supermarket was actually a far easier place to watch her and take in her possible stalkers and as Oliver told me how it was vital for the sanity of the individual that a certain distance was placed between himself and that which he observes, I scanned the lines at the checkouts, the milling crowds in the aisles, for likely candidates.

"Have you any idea just how untrustworthy your senses really are?" Oliver was saying. "Or, rather, how untrustworthy our ability for interpreting what our senses tells us is. Every minute, we're colouring and shaping the world the way we want to see it. And for all we know it may bear no resemblance to the *actual* world. This tin of pears, for example," he said, taking a tin of peaches from the shelf, "might, for all we know, be a tin of peaches."

"It is a tin of peaches," I told him, paying particular attention to a suspicious looking man in an England football shirt.

"Eh? Oh, yes. Well for all we know, this tin of peaches could well be a tin of pears."

"Isn't the label a bit of a give-away?" I asked distractedly.

"Only if you assume we all read labels the same way." He turned the tin round and shoved the barcode under my nose. "What do you see?" he asked.

Oliver, as I had suspected earlier, certainly wasn't himself today. I decided to humour him – keeping one eye on Maggie and England Shirt.

"Black lines and numbers," I said.

"Exactly. But, I ask you, what does a barcode reader see? Product type, I.D., price – probably a whole load of stuff that hasn't occurred to us. So which interpretation is right?"

"Depends on individual requirement, I'd say." England Shirt paid for his celery and tomatoes and left without so much as a glance in Maggie's direction.

"What?"

I shrugged. "We read it how we are programmed to read it."

Oliver thought about this, and then nodded. "So neither interpretation is wrong."

"And, strictly speaking," I said, just to complicate matters further, "neither is right."

Oliver put the tin back on the shelf, sniffing indignantly. "I've never liked peaches anyway," he told me.

On her way back to her mother's, Maggie seemed rather more tense – glancing over her shoulder every few minutes, endlessly switching the carrier bag that held her shopping from one hand to the other – and this rubbed off on Oliver and me. We hung back as far as was reasonably possible and spoke in whispers, walking the relatively quiet streets with little hope of spotting her stalker. At the corner of Sutherland Street and Richard Road – the former being where her mother lived – Maggie stopped and sat on a low garden wall, placing the carrier between her feet and putting her face in her hands. Neither Oliver nor I knew quite what to do.

"Maybe she's just composing herself before seeing her mum," Oliver said. "You know what a pain the old tart can be."

We'd both had our run-ins with Maggie's mum, Francesca, over the years – the silly, chain-smoking harridan never quite managing to understand that not all of Maggie's friends were intent on ruining her life – and even in my parentless state, I genuinely did not envy Maggie. If Ashley had had it bad with Pippa and Len, I was sure that even she would acknowledge that Maggie had been to hell and back five times over with Francesca.

"If she were doing that," I said, "she'd be in the Brown Jug knocking back a few vodkas. That's more Maggie's style."

"So what do you think's wrong?"

"I don't know... it's hot – maybe she's feeling a bit under the weather."

"You think we should...?"

As we watched, Maggie started to slump forward – her body going limp and insubstantial. Oliver and I glanced at each other and then we were running, not in the least concerned that we might be blowing our cover to any unseen observer.

I got to her before Oliver, kneeling down in front of her and doing my best to support her as the last of her strength departed. Her face was ashen and her flesh sticky and cool, and as Oliver helped me carefully lay her down on the pavement I was suddenly quite convinced that she was dead. First Jim, and now her – poor Wee Mark left to whatever fate awaits an orphan in the twenty-first century.

"Put her feet up on the wall," Oliver said. "She's just fainted."

"Should I loosen her clothing?" It was a stupid question, given that she was wearing baggy shorts and T-shirt.

"This isn't Wales," Oliver told me – and had I not been so concerned about Maggie I think I would have swung for him, as big as he was.

"I'm quite aware of that," I said, glowering at him as Maggie started to come round. He held up a hand by way of apology and I turned my attention back to Maggie – who I helped back onto the wall, once she felt well enough.

A few people had come out of their houses to make sure everything was all right, some genuinely concerned, others merely wanting something to talk about over their pints later that evening – and whilst Oliver did his best to assure them that everything was just fine and dandy, "just a little too much heat", Maggie looked at me with the saddest look of longing and asked, "Did you see him?"

I shook my head, wishing I had something more positive to tell her – even considering, albeit very briefly, making something up.

"You must think I'm going barmy," she said.

"Someone's bothering you. Why on earth would I think that?"

"Because you and Oliver don't see him at all, and I see him everywhere."

"Your stalker?" I got a peculiar feeling we were now talking about something else entirely. Her eyes darted from one side of the street to the other, taking in the willow on the patch of common opposite, the rubberneckers and Samaritans, and I wondered if she had been drinking. But I was sure this was too early even for her.

She looked about to tell me something vitally important, leaning in to me conspiratorially and taking hold of my hand. "Yes, my stalker," she said.

"You see him?" I asked, taking her too literally. "Everywhere?"

Shaking her head, the colour coming back to her lips and cheeks, she smiled sadly and said, "No. It just seems that way. When you don't know who it is, you realise it could be anyone. When you realise it could be anyone you... it might as well be everyone. Every stranger is as much of a threat as any other."

When she forced a too optimistic smile, I was finally convinced there was something she wasn't telling me. I knew I couldn't force the issue, however. Maggie would tell me (or possibly someone else) in her own good time.

"If it helps any," I said, "we didn't see anyone who looked in the least bit suspicious. No one followed you from the library to Asda, and there wasn't anyone in either place who paid you any undue attention."

"Just because you and Oliver couldn't see him it doesn't mean he wasn't there," she said – and I thought about what Oliver had said about the tinned peaches. Maybe it was true. Maybe we just weren't equipped to read the information the way it needed to be read. Maybe we were too subjective – too locked into our own interpretation. Maggie was a bright, down-to-earth woman – not someone I would normally consider prone to paranoia – but now I found myself wondering, conversely, how much of this was about *her* lack of ability. I remembered that stifling little cottage in Wales, and it seemed nigh on impossible that this was the same woman before me I had so intimately known there. Something essential had changed and, yet, once again I was at a loss to say just what it was. I wasn't equipped to read the information in the way in which it needed to be read – and the frustrating force of this finally hit home, the futility of my attempt to understand and quantify weighing down on me like the unrelenting summer heat.

When Maggie had recovered some more, with the help of a cool glass of "fizzy water" brought out by the old lady on whose wall Maggie was sitting, Oliver and I walked the short distance to her mother's with her. Oliver pointed out, rather unnecessarily, that if the mystery man was indeed watching her (I'd kept as alert as possible, and I honestly couldn't see how) we had almost certainly blown any chance we had of catching him. Maggie didn't seem all that bothered. She merely pulled at the sweaty patch of T-shirt just below her cleavage and shrugged apathetically.

"I don't want to sound ungrateful," she said, "but I'm not sure it was such a good idea, anyway. He... he knows me too well." She laughed and I thought I heard the depressingly dull chime of resignation therein. "It's almost as if he knows what I'm going to do before I do it."

As I walked home alone, Oliver deciding to risk the unjust disapproval of Francesca and stay with Maggie until her and Wee Mark were safely home, I thought about this and found the inevitable comparison between Maggie's problem and my story about Richard and Mrs. Sutherland. Richard "stalked" from the front, so to speak, knowing Mrs. Sutherland's routine so well that he could arrive before her and, he wrongly believed, avoid any kind of suspicion. Would a real-life stalker operate like that?

I made a mental note to mention it to Oliver when next we spoke.

It was a pleasure to return home.

I felt the morning fall delightfully away as I stepped over the threshold – all the confusing thoughts and my concern for Maggie stripped off like a damp and dirty coat – and paused for a moment at the bottom of the stairs to acknowledge this moment of ease and stillness. I heard activity upstairs, Ashley singing along with the CD player in our bedroom – an old Exile Inside track *Katrin*, if I wasn't mistaken – and smelt something I couldn't at first identify, it was so distant and unexpected. I waited. I breathed. I closed my eyes and silently sang along.

A certain kind of order.

The smell of fresh paint.

Upstairs, I found Ash and Nadine in our bedroom. It was a hectic, disordered sight that I could never have predicted after the past twenty-four hours – but it was nevertheless uplifting and amusing.

Ashley had stripped down to her pants and bra. I was sure there was a logic to this but it wasn't immediately apparent. In something of a reversal of this, Nadine looked flushed but elated in one of my old shirts – which Ashley had apparently cut down to prevent Nadine tripping on it. Both held paintbrushes in their hands, and both looked positively demonic in their enthusiasm.

As Nadine ineptly daubed undercoat on the radiator, "singing" along with Exile Inside, Ashley walked over to me, being careful not to trip on the dustcovers, a stupid but wholly endearing grin on her face.

"It seemed like a good idea at the time," she said, glancing over her shoulder at Nadine – who now had a brush in each hand and a look of lip-sucking concentration on her face.

"There are laws against child labour," I told her, reaching out and giving the elastic at the waist of her pants a twang. "Think we can get her to mow the lawn when she's finished?"

"I'm sure she'd be more than willing to give it a go," Ashley said, watching Nadine proudly. "What she lacks in skill, she makes up for in enthusiasm." Looking back at me, hair falling in her face and reminding me of that first day in Estby Bay, she said, "You don't mind, do you?"

"Why should I mind? It's needed some paint splashing around for a while now and, well, I was hoping if I left it long enough –"

"I'd get off my fat arse and do it myself?"

"I wouldn't put it quite like that."

"Yes you would."

I nodded with mock solemnity. "Yes, you're probably right, I would."

Ashley smiled and bent in to kiss me – the move quite sudden and forceful. She caught me hard on the corner of my mouth, and had it not been otherwise quite so pleasant I might have flinched at the pain it caused as my lips were mashed against my teeth.

"What was that for?" I asked.

"By way of an apology."

"You have something to apologise for?"

"This morning?"

"What about it?"

She sighed. Paint dripped from the tip of her brush onto the dustsheet on the floor. "I don't know," she said. "It's just that sometimes I forget how hard it must be for you. I whinge about my parents and –"

"I have no parents to whinge about?"

She looked away. "Yes."

"You can't think like that, love," I told her, my hand at her waist. "This morning was good. You needed to get it out and I'm glad you did. I'm just a little surprised you didn't tell me sooner."

Ashley brushed the hair from her face with the back of her hand, looking out of the window at the roofs of the houses over the road. Leaving a smear of paint on her cheek, she looked vulnerable and somehow heroic. My wife, the Noble Figure.

"I know," she said. "I'm not sure I can explain it. I suppose it was... I suppose it was something I just didn't want to think about. I locked it away, I think, and this morning Mam just managed to press all the right buttons – or the wrong buttons, if you prefer."

"You gonna talk to her?"

Shaking her head, she said, "I did consider it for a while, but I can't really see what good it would do. Her and Dad aren't going to change now, so it's perfectly possible that I could just be stirring up trouble for no good reason."

"Some would say getting it out in the open was a good enough reason in itself," I pointed out.

"And maybe they'd be right. I don't know. I just don't think I want to take that chance."

"It's your decision." I wasn't entirely sure I wanted the status quo disrupting myself, if the truth were known. Pippa and Len were decent enough people from where I was standing, and – in spite of the problems Len had had with me in the early days of my relationship with his daughter – I believed I could depend on them to be there for me as well as Ashley, in the unlikely event that I should ever need their help. I wouldn't exactly say they were replacements for the parents I'd lost. Far from it. Pippa and Len didn't even come close. But it was nevertheless good to know they were there – if only to baby-sit.

I offered to help with the painting, but Ashley was having none of it – she and Nadine had everything under control, thank you very much. I therefore decided I'd try to get a little work done on the *Ma Boy, Ma Boy* story – feeling that I'd left it long enough and that if I didn't get back into it soon Richard and Mrs. Sutherland would slip away from me, if they hadn't already. Ashley hadn't finished speaking, however, and before I could excuse myself, she laid a hand on my arm, leant in close and whispered something in my ear that I heard, but nevertheless had to get her to repeat.

"I think we should try for another baby," she said.

I opened my mouth to say something, then closed it – realising I didn't have anything like an appropriate response. I wasn't even sure I knew what would qualify *as* an appropriate response! Nadine was enough. We were just getting by as it was, for heaven's sake. But another baby would be nice. Impractical but nice. Company for Nadine. Yes, that was a plus. Not too much of an age difference. A little sister. Or brother. Yes, a brother. She'd like that and –

Ashley took her hand from my arm – trying to read my confused and no doubt confusing features. Her excitement was already on the wane, that much I could see, but I wasn't sure there was anything I could do about that. An only child like Ashley, I'd always wanted a large family. When we'd married, quietly confident that all we had to do to realise our dreams was work hard and persist, I'd held tight to the ideal, trying with all my might to deny the reality. But circumstance is a great antidote to idealism, and however much I shared and desired the dream, I just didn't think that now was the right time.

"You don't think it's a good idea," Ashley said, taking a step back and examining the slowly stiffening bristles of her brush.

"I'm not sure," I said. "It was just a little unexpected and... well, I just think the timing's a little off."

"We're comfortable financially," she pointed out. "And... I know we've been a bit iffy, lately, love, but I'm working on that and, well, it's not like it's anything serious, is it?"

She really wanted this. Her eyes shone eagerly and her mouth twitched nervously. She blinked. A slightly desperate smile. And I very nearly gave in there and then.

"That's true," I said. "But it still isn't something we can afford to rush into."

"I agree." And now a step towards me. The hand on my arm again. "We need to discuss it thoroughly before we make a decision." She massaged my wrist, slowly running her hand back and forth as she stared mesmerisingly into my eyes. "Over dinner," she added. "Tonight. After we've put Nadine to bed."

Agreeing, albeit reluctantly, I left the two of them for the relative safety of my office – doubting that I would be able to work, but now even more in need of some time alone.

I closed the door behind me and sat down in front of my PC, looking at my notes. My head was full of babies and stalkers and "individual perception", but I nevertheless found myself reading through a paragraph highlighted in red, and which I only distantly remembered writing.

Mrs. Sutherland is no innocent, I read. *It is a myth that her kind are – and for her to be anything other than a predator would be unrealistic and unconvincing. Her foremost wish is to consume and be consumed.*

My first thought was that this in no way fit with the existing image I had of Mrs. Sutherland. I saw her as vulnerable and needy, a little desperate and intrigued by Richard's fascination with her. But a predator? It was an interesting idea – one that I knew had its correlation in reality – but it would inevitably throw up its problems, not least, where would the "Elvis" character fit in?

I opened the story file and sat with my fingers resting on the keys – suddenly feeling the need to write, but quite unable to do so. I'd had worse days. All in all it hadn't been too bad, in spite of Maggie's problems and Ashley's wish for another baby. But still I felt it all suddenly weighing down on me – an interminable sense that something was out of place or missing, that I'd forgotten something or had failed to see a vital clue, a banality that would nevertheless help me see more clearly where I fit in, what this was all about. I sat back in my chair and looked at the door, contemplating going back to Ashley – telling her that we would try for another baby... telling her that we wouldn't try for another baby. It was open a fraction, as if silently inviting me, and I wondered how that had happened. I distinctly remembered closing it, wanting to block out the moderately depressing strains of Exile Inside (Nadine had been singing the lyrics "fuck the whole world" when I excused myself). I'd come in, closed the door behind me and briefly leant against it – relishing the peace and order.

I got to my feet and opened the door a little more, looking out onto the landing to make sure Nadine wasn't toddling about – up to her mischief – and then closing it again, realising the latch mustn't have caught properly the first time. It was an old house and nothing lined up quite as it should. Dad had always complained about it and now I supposed it was my turn.

Without giving it any more thought, determined to find a way in, I hit the keys the minute I sat down – opening a different door entirely and finding Richard waiting for me.

He didn't like the way in which the sun sat in the sky like a threat, I wrote. *It made him think of vultures in old cowboy films, patiently waiting for their chance to swoop down on the carrion and eat their fill – ripping out long, elastic strands of intestine, popping out eyeballs with their paradoxically precise beaks. He stood on the doorstep and squinted up at it – wishing it away behind a cloud or, better still, on the other side of the planet entirely, his reality cloaked in blessed cool and dark night. Yes, just him and Mrs. Sutherland, and the night. Maybe then she would tell him her secrets, take him into her confidence in ways he could now only imagine and let him understand why she was being so kind to him – why she had not simply had a word with his dad about how Richard was stalking her.*

It was a mystery, even he had to acknowledge that. At first he had put it down to loneliness. Her husband had popped his clogs and she didn't know many people in the village – or few she actually found herself liking. But there seemed more to it than that.

As he walked the short distance across the field to her house, slipping his sunglasses on against the mocking glare of the sun, he struggled to make sense of it.

Mrs. Sutherland – or Maggie, as she insisted he call her – was an intelligent woman. She had picked up the stuff he had taught her about the Internet and the laptop in general in next to no time. In fact, now that he thought about it, she had been suspiciously quick to get the hang of it. Which begged the question, if having him install an ISP for her and having him teach her all about "that stuff" had just been a ploy to get closer to him, why?

Maggie spotted him from the bedroom window and came down to let him in. Today was going to be newsgroups day. What Richard still thought of as the Wild West of Cyberspace. If you were going to get in trouble or flamed to pieces, that's where it would happen. He'd thought of inadvertently clicking – accidentally on purpose, as his gran would say – on one of the porn groups, just to see how she would react, but when he saw her waiting for him at the door he knew he'd probably bottle it and end up playing it safe, not wanting to fuck up whatever it was they had together.

Wearing only a pair of obscenely tight pale blue shorts (the seam highlighting the crack of her cunt, much to Richard's delight) and a tatty old Sex Pistols T-shirt, she looked pretty and very unlike the woman he had taken to following.

"I thought you'd decided not to come," she said as he took his sunglasses off and tried not to stare at her crotch. His eyes felt like ball bearings – her beguiling delve the strongest of magnets.

"Dad went off on one about my hair," he said. "He reckons I'm a bender."

Maggie gave him a sympathetic look – rolling her eyes as she stepped back to let him over the threshold. The kitchen smelt spicy and fresh, but over all of that Richard was aware of her smell, innocent as baby powder, heady and exotic as incense. In the shade and relative cool of the kitchen, he felt her closeness – wanted to move towards it. She understood him, that was what he felt more than anything. Not that much younger than his father, she nevertheless had a far more worldly and unfettered view. Richard didn't need to explain to her that the length of his hair was no reflection of his sexuality or that the music he listened to wasn't just unintelligible noise. She knew these things already – had probably lived them herself and remembered their affect admirably. When she smiled at him and said "Some people will just never get it, will they?" there was nothing fake or insincere about it. The world of dilemmas and contradictions he inhabited was more than familiar to her.

"He doesn't want to get it," he told her. "He just wants to sit on his arse in front of the telly getting boozed up."

Richard had never spoken to anyone about his father like this. Under normal circumstances, his instinct was to conceal and protect – because the bottom line was, everything reflected on him. His father was a drunk and a thief, and if he admitted that to anyone he would be tarred with the same brush. Maggie wasn't like that, though. She didn't give a shit what his father was like. It was him she was interested in.

"He does that a lot, does he?" she asked as he followed her through to the pristine, sunny living room.

"Enough. More since Mam buggered off."

"You must miss her."

He considered dressing it up a little for her. Then he remembered this was Maggie he was talking to, not some well-meaning and utterly facile teacher, and said, "No, not at all. She wasn't much better. Glad to see the back of her. Just wish she'd taken him with her."

They sat on the settee – Maggie perched on the edge beside him whilst he sank into the soft, luxurious cushions. "You mean that, don't you?" she asked.

Richard nodded and felt his cheeks flushing. It wasn't that the admission embarrassed him – but rather the familiar, slightly seductive tone of her voice. He didn't know whether it was imagined or for real, but there was an intensity to this exchange that was making him hard – and he was sure she could see that.

"I'd be better off all on my own," he told her.

"Without anyone?"

"Without them."

Maggie seemed to have forgotten his reason for being here – and he wasn't about to remind her. The truth was, he was actually quite enjoying this. There was something promising and loaded about it – something he had sensed in a less obvious form the first time Maggie had sat down on that bench beside him and started talking. He couldn't understand it, and wasn't sure he wanted to, but it had been enough to make him stop his other stalking activities, feeling that he was – however ridiculous it might have sounded – somehow being unfaithful. He'd continued for a short while, but none had lived up to what Maggie had grown to mean to him. She lived in the back of his mind and overshadowed everyone and everything.

And he liked it.

"So you're not going to turn into some recluse living in a tin shack on the wild and windy moors, then?" she asked, grinning – her knee rubbing against his as she twisted to get a better look at him.

"Nah. I'd go nuts. I like people too much."

"All people?"

"Some more than others." Richard was rather pleased with that. It was an obvious attempt at flirting but it was his most classy and natural to date. She studied him and for a moment he thought he might have blown it. Her frown was slight but perceptible, the tightening around her mouth a little worrying. And then her shoulders relaxed and she grinned.

"Anyone in particular?" she asked, giving his knee a playful nudge with hers and winking.

Richard was unsure how best to play this. He didn't fully understand the game – didn't really know that it was *a game – and was afraid that he might inadvertently break some unspoken rule. He thought of what his dad would do, and then chose the opposite course of action.*

*"Just some old, computer illiterate bird I've been seeing a lot of,"
he said, grinning – thinking, however hard he tried not to, of her too-
tight shorts, of that sweet delve, of what it would be like to –*

*She slapped him hard on the leg – laughing as she told him, more
than a little ironically, that he was such a charmer. Her hand lingered
on his thigh, and he laughed with her – wanting to keep its warmth
there for as long as possible.*

*"You don't really think of me as old, surely," she said, when her
laughter had abated somewhat.*

Richard shrugged. "Not really," he said. "But..."

"Uh oh. But?"

*"But, I dunno. You're just not like the girls I know from school, I
guess."*

*"I should hope not," she said softly. "You don't like them much,
eh?"*

"Depends."

"On?"

*This was getting more personal than he liked, but he knew that if
Maggie was to continue to trust him, it was important that he held
nothing back from her.*

*"On what you mean by 'like'," he said. "For the most part they're
just fucking clueless but, well, I still..."*

"You still can't help wanting to bonk their brains out?"

*Maggie smiled wickedly, and as unsure of himself as he was, he
couldn't help grinning back at her – his cheeks growing hotter by the
minute, his need more urgent and focused. She held his gaze, a little
ruthlessly, and he wished he'd left his sunglasses on. It was wrong
that she could read him so easily and successfully. When she squeezed
his thigh a little more firmly, he shuddered and, desperate for her,
considered getting up and running from the room. Feeling exposed
and susceptible, his heart beating out warnings he couldn't even begin
to interpret, he tried to answer her – but all that came out was a
nervous, faltering little laugh.*

*"I know," Maggie said, giving his thigh a final pat and taking her
hand away as she turned and looked out the window. "None of it is
easy. Even for me," she added, looking at him over her shoulder.*

"You should bear that in mind."

"But..." It was the best he could do under the circumstances.

"There are no buts, love. Certain aspects of life just... well, they don't get any easier, let's put it that way. Since Jim died... village life isn't all that healthy for a relatively young widow. I could dry up and turn to dust in this place, and few people would be any the wiser."

"I would be," Richard said. He blurted it out, it was true, but Maggie seemed to understand and appreciate this show of fellow feeling and solidarity. She smiled a smile as sweet as buttermilk, eyes downcast and unreadable, and nodded as he said, "I'm your friend. And I'd miss you."

His erection was subsiding, his arousal replaced by a sincere compassion that surprised even him. Suddenly he found he would be happy just to hold her – for now, at least – and he took courage from this, reaching out and touching her arm.

"I know," she said, taking his hand in hers. "Come on, let's go upstairs."

He wasn't stupid enough to read too much into the invitation. It was fairly common for them to spend time in her bedroom and, sure enough, once there they settled down to the task of trawling through various newsgroups for interesting facts on everything from Satanism to Elvis Presley – Maggie reluctantly admitting that she was a closet Elvis fan. Richard couldn't help being disappointed, though, however realistically he'd viewed the invitation.

"The one thing you really have to protect with newsgroups," Richard told her, "is your identity. Use a fake name and a second online email address if you decide to post. That's enough to keep you anonymous from most people, but always remember that, you know, you're never completely anonymous, so don't break any laws."

"Do I look like the criminal type?" she asked bumping her shoulder against his.

"Well I dunno, but those shorts should certainly be outlawed." It was out before he had chance to think about it and, much to Maggie's amusement, he stammered an apology immediately – hoping she would move the conversation along and save him further embarrassment even as he wished for an in-depth analysis of his

statement.

"I thought you'd like them," she said, her voice little more than a whisper – sing-songy and mellifluous. "I put them on especially."

"I... I do... I do like them but..."

"You're scared to let me see just how much you like them, is that it?"

Unable to speak – suddenly flustered and close to tears – Richard nodded quickly, feeling juvenile as he swallowed hard on the emotion.

"I didn't do it to embarrass or tease you," she told him. "I just wanted to make you happy. You've helped me and I just thought you could do with some cheering up. I can easily change into something else, if it'll make you feel better."

"No!" Richard said, and she laughed – they both did, the tension easing and the strangeness of the topic gradually becoming less significant as Richard finally grasped just how unshockable Maggie was. "I mean, you can if you want to – but you don't have to on my account."

Silence. But not quite. The window was open and, Maggie continuing to stare at him thoughtfully, he heard birdcall and, somewhere far off, horses whinnying. It was a moment of temperate and curiously soporific expectation and he thought of making himself more comfortable – plumping the pillows on which Maggie dreamed nightly and resting his weary head – convinced that the deliberations with which Maggie was occupied would take an age to reach their conclusion. Dulled by the stress and excitement, he yearned for a moment's respite – but when Maggie finally stood up and started removing first her T-shirt and then the crotch-cutting shorts, he felt his energy and excitement return.

"I'm taking a big risk," she told him. "I'm trusting you to be discreet. If you don't think you can keep this to yourself, tell me now, Richard. Our secret?"

It was too good to be true. Like something out of the wettest of dreams, Maggie stood before him, the crotch of her thong damp with sweat or passion, and all he could think of to say was, "Who have I got to tell?"

"That isn't the answer I need," she insisted. "I need you to promise me. Even if there were someone you were convinced you

could trust, you wouldn't tell them. Right?"

He would have said anything right then – anything to stop this from ending – but when he gave her his word, he meant it. He would never betray her. It would be their secret. He would never tell a soul.

"I promise."

We sat across the table from one another in relative peace and silence. Ashley had prepared a meal of roast beef and Yorkshire pudding, my favourite, but now that it was dished out neither of us seemed in the mood for eating – picking at our food in a desultory manner and willing a breeze to blow through the optimistically open kitchen door. The heat was the obvious culprit – stealing away our appetites like a thief in the night – but for me there was more to it than that. I was worried about where tonight's conversation might lead, but as well as that I was also concerned about *Ma Boy, Ma Boy*. The story wasn't heading where I'd expected, and whilst this in itself wasn't a problem, I was worried about the nature of the story. There was at least one precedent for it in reality that I knew of, but I wondered if it didn't perhaps smack of an adolescent wet dream. I for one would have loved to be seduced at fifteen by a sexy older woman but, however desperate she might have been, it just didn't strike me as all that likely. Where was the attraction in a spotty kid who was going to come at the first sniff of sexual intimacy?

Ashley reached across the table and held my hand. "Penny for them," she said.

"Could you ever imagine yourself seducing a fifteen year old boy?"

"Could you ever imagine yourself seducing a sixteen year old girl?" She smirked and rubbed her foot against my leg. "It's a silly question, but, yes, I suppose under certain circumstances it's something that might conceivably happen. Story?"

"Yes," I said, thankful of the allusion. "I have a lonely widow about my age who, for whatever reason, has ensnared this fucked up kid in... you know – her web of frustrated sexuality. And I just don't know how believable it is."

"Do you believe it?"

"When I'm writing it, yes."

"And when you read it?" Ashley wasn't usually so inclined to talk about my work and I appreciated the effort she was making. Her fingers interwove with mine and she pushed her plate aside, resting her other arm on the table and patiently waiting for me to speak.

"That's more difficult to judge," I told her. "I don't read my work the way a reader does. I read it critically. So I always have a degree of difficulty suspending disbelief."

"Is it worse with this one?"

"Not really, no. I'm just worried that people will read it and think, 'Yeah, right – and *that's* going to happen'."

"It happens in real life all the time," she pointed out.

"But that doesn't mean it makes good fiction."

Ashley didn't understand. Her brow creased and her thumb rubbed rhythmically against my fingers. "Sorry," she said. "You'll have to explain that.'

"Sometimes you have to tone down 'reality'," I told her. "Otherwise the fiction just becomes ridiculous. Coincidence is the obvious one. We all know we live in a world of coincidence. Events line up in a seemingly meaningful way and some yell synchronicity while others, quite rightly, dismiss it as coincidence. It's the norm, a natural and common part of life – but the minute you stick it in a work of fiction belief starts to crumble, unless you are very good at what you do."

"And this applies to things like relationships between fifteen year old boys and older women?"

"It's a hard subject to get right," I said, nodding. "A real-life situation like the one in my story could exist – I might even go so far as to put money on it – but that doesn't necessarily make the fiction viable. It's like... it's like they are parallel universes, with slightly differing physical laws."

"If you start rabbiting on about String Theory, I'm out of here," she said, mouth twitching into a thoroughly bewitching grin.

"A cack-handed analogy?"

"Some would say."

"Some being?"

"Anyone who considered it a cack-handed analogy, I guess."

Feeling suddenly unaccountably at ease, I looked down at the barely touched plate of food before me and followed Ashley's lead – pushing it to one side as, beneath the table, I kicked off my trainers so that I could better play footsie with her. The dreaded subject hadn't been mentioned yet and even though I realised it was as inevitable as governmental sleaze and corruption, I really didn't care. Everything would fall into place eventually, fact and fiction. *As it was,* I thought, feeling a little intoxicated, *so shall it be.*

Sure enough, a few minutes later – just when we were half-heartedly considering getting up to wash the dishes – Ashley said, "So, have you given it any more thought then?"

"The baby?" I said, deciding it best to face the subject head on.

"The baby." She sat back and let her hands fall loosely into her lap, a woman seemingly a world apart from the Ashley of the day before. Hair mussed up and dark with sweat where it touched her neck and forehead, she once again took me back to Estby Bay – to the implicit promise of those first days together, the promise which had only been partially fulfilled.

"I've thought of nothing else since finishing work," I told her.

"And?"

"And I still don't know. I want us to try for another. There's nothing I'd like more than a house full of kids – *our* kids – you know that."

"But?"

"But it's a big decision and I think we need to consider it carefully before rushing into anything."

She slumped a little, studying her knees – making a barely perceptible whistling noise as she breathed slowly through her nose.

"You don't think I'm up to looking after two kids," she said.

"Did I say that, love?"

"I'm not looking for an argument, Sonny." Sitting up and folding her arms on the table, she rocked forward and added, "The truth is, I'm not sure you'd be wrong if you did think that. I know I'm not perfect and I know I get things wrong, but... I really don't want Nadine being an only child. I don't want her to be our obsession, love."

I was about to tell her that I understood absolutely where she was coming from when the back gate squeaked and clattered and we heard heavy footsteps coming round the corner into the back garden. I rolled my eyes and Ashley shrugged back at me.

"We'll discuss it later," she whispered hopefully as Oliver entered like a dyspeptic old bear and sat down at the table – the chair groaning alarmingly.

Something was bothering him, that much was obvious. Ashley greeted him in the usual way – "Now then, fuckface" – to which the standard response of "hey, you old slapper" was not forthcoming, and I asked him how the delightful Francesca had been – with much the same result. His face looked puffy and flushed in carnation-like patches, and I thought that it might be something physical. His heart, maybe – finally letting it be known that too much was being demanded of it. But when I asked him if he was ill, he just shook his head and stared into middle space – preoccupied with whatever problem he no doubt saw it as his duty to solve.

"It doesn't make sense," he finally said.

"What doesn't?" I asked – Ashley pulling a wide-eyed face and getting up to make a start on the pans.

"Maggie. There's something I can't put my finger on. Something you told me..."

"About Maggie."

"And her stalker." His fingers tapped urgently on the tabletop and then he stiffened, grinning as he said, "Masturbate!"

"I'd rather finish the dishes first," Ashley mumbled.

Oliver ignored her, turning to me and continuing. "You told me," he said, "that Maggie told you that this guy even knows when she masturbates. Correct?"

Ashley glanced over her shoulder at me. "She said that?"

"Yes."

I wasn't too keen on her suspicious tone. Thankfully, Oliver wasn't in the mood for conversational diversions.

"And she was speaking literally?" he asked. "It wasn't hyperbole, right?"

"It seemed pretty literal to me."

Oliver sucked his teeth thoughtfully and sat back. "Well there you go," he said. "That's what I don't get. Unless Mags sits at the window when she takes care of herself, which doesn't strike me as her thing, how the hell does this bloke know something so intimate?"

Drying her hands on a tea towel, the pans now forgotten, Ashley faced us and said, "Maybe it's someone who's known her intimately in the past."

I didn't for one minute seriously believe that Ashley knew Mags and I had history. If this had been the case I was sure she would have just come right out and confronted me. Nevertheless, I felt the full weight of the irrational dread sitting in my stomach like a stodgy, half-digested Yorkshire pudding. I didn't want to be the one to answer her, fearing something in my voice would betray me, so sat sweating whilst Oliver formulated a reply.

"So why doesn't she recognise his voice on the phone?" He sniffed and shook his head, scratching at his beard. "Nah, I don't think we're dealing with an ex – and even if we were, that still wouldn't really explain how he knows when she masturbates."

"In just about every other respect, Maggie's a creature of habit," I pointed out. "Who's to say she isn't as regimented in that aspect of her life, too."

Oliver gave this rather more consideration than it probably deserved. He looked from me to Ashley and then back again, shaking his head as he said, "She's a passionate woman with an exhausting toddler to contend with. She'll do it when mood and circumstance allow – and I for one wouldn't fancy trying to predict such episodes. No, something isn't right here. This guy has too much information."

"According to Maggie," I said.

Ashley looked ill at ease. A little discombobulated, as my dad would have said. She pulled out her chair and sat back down with a sigh – mouth heavy and ruminative. "I'm not sure I'm comfortable talking about Mags like this," she said sullenly. "I think if you've got anything more to say on the subject, you should say it to her."

Not usually so reluctant to talk about our friends behind their backs – especially when we were trying to "help" them – I was a little suspicious. She caught my eye and, as Oliver noticed the uneaten food and reached across to help himself to Ashley's plate, flicked a surreptitious glance at the door. It took me a moment longer than it should have to realise that she wanted rid of Olly.

"Easier said than done," he said, picking up Ashley's knife and fork and tucking in, even though the food was by now stone cold.

"What do you mean?" I asked.

"She's fed up with talking about it. She's now working on the principle that if she ignores him he'll just go away. You know," he continued, chewing on a rubbery piece of Yorkshire pudding, "I went back to her place with her and Wee Mark once she'd finished arguing with that cunt Francesca about something the little fella had or hadn't done. Don't think it helped that I was there. She actually accused Mags of 'showing off' in front of me – can you believe that?"

"Yes," Ashley and I said in unison.

"Anyway, like I say, I went back with her to her place and we had a beer in the back garden whilst Wee Mark soaked everything in sight with that stupid fucking water canon thing she got him. I like Maggie. She's a sweetheart and I'd do anything for her, especially now that Jim's no longer around to frown his way through my 'life-style choices'."

"He wasn't that bad," Ashley said.

"He was bad enough. But, anyway, that's beside the point. Like I say, I love Maggie right down to the soles of her boots – but she can be a right frustrating cow, at times."

"She's a woman," I said, and Ashley kicked me under the table – playfully enough, I guess.

Oliver scraped away at the plate – his frown deep, a fleck of mashed potato in his beard. "We were talking about quite general things," he told us, "but I couldn't escape the feeling that there was something she wasn't telling me. It was like there was a subtext to everything she said, and all I had to do to get to the truth was deconstruct what she was telling me. Except it wasn't that simple."

"It seldom is," Ashley said, growing perceptibly bored.

Whilst I had shared very similar insights to those of Oliver when Maggie had spoken to me after her funny turn, I didn't think now was a good time to mention it – given that Ashley was obviously determined to continue our baby discussion and didn't particularly like the fact that we were talking about Maggie behind her back. I therefore did my best to move the conversation along, allowing Oliver to finish Ashley's dinner before saying, as delicately as possible, "I think it's about time you buggered off, mate. Ashley and I have things to do."

Ashley – flushed and with a fine, glossy patina of sweat on her upper lip – clearly wasn't too keen on my choice of words. Her mouth crinkled and tightened and she gave an indignant, spastic little twitch of her head.

Oliver regarded me with earnest, narrowed eyes. He looked better than he had all day, but still there was a paleness to his usually ruddy features that wasn't exactly helped by the blackness of his beard. With a slow nod of resignation, he got to his feet and started for the door, stopping at the threshold and looking back at us.

"I've been intrusive, I know," he said. "But this is serious. I don't know what, but *something* is going on here – and sooner or later we'll all have to discuss it."

Chapter Six

Old Man Ned looked rather too pleased with himself. He held the open laptop out towards me as if it were a briefcase full of money and grinned the grin of the just and proud, telling me of his little adventure to PC World and how he had succeeded in getting "one bugger of a deal". His eyes gleamed with delight and his hair had been slicked back especially for the occasion. All in all, he was like the proverbial dog with two tails – insisting that the salesmen had thought they'd seen him coming, but oh how wrong they had been.

"They reckoned I was just some gullible old fool who didn't know his arse from his elbow," he said. "But I proved the buggers wrong. Didn't let them just sell me any old tat."

I groaned inwardly, my smile fixed and as genuine as I could make it under the circumstances. Ashley had gone round to Maggie's to see if she could get to the bottom of whatever was going on and I therefore had Nadine with me. She stood beside me in Ned's living room, hands clasped behind her back as she had seen Ned do, and glanced at the books and DVDs and other various bits of junk and clutter. Mouth open, she looked astonished that so much could fit into such a relatively small space.

Ned stared at me expectantly. "Only paid a grand for it," he said. "Got a five year cover plan, too. Not bad for an old fool, eh?"

I didn't have to heart to tell him he'd been ripped off. A few hundred quid would have easily got him all he needed and more, but it was too late now and I therefore merely said, "Quite a machine you've got there, mate. A good, well future-proofed piece of kit."

"Which means?"

"You won't need to upgrade for a long time."

Moderately satisfied by this, he sat down on the settee, Nadine between Ned and me, and watched as I inserted the mobile broadband dongle he'd also bought into the USB port. I figured it would take ten minutes at the most to get him up and surfing, then I could show him the basics and leave him to it for a while – hopefully before Nadine got restless.

As it turned out, it took a little longer than expected, but, all in all, it was relatively painless

"There," I said. "You're now officially online, old chap."

"It's done?"

"Yup."

Quite typical of most of the "silver surfers" I'd encountered over the years, Old Man Ned picked things up a lot more quickly than he had originally envisaged. Leaning into the laptop with Nadine and me, he was soon pointing and clicking as though it was what he'd been put on this earth to do. As his confidence grew, the heavy-handedness that had at first been apparent slowly disappeared and his fingers grew more nimble – moving the cursor about without having to give it a second thought. I introduced him to Google and, sure enough, the first word he typed in was "porn". I stopped him before he could click on the search button, however, reminding him that Nadine was present and giving him a friendly warning about the dangers of Net porn.

"It's the first thing most folk search for when they go online," I told him. "And I for one have nothing against it. But there are dangers."

"Police, you mean?"

I shook my head. "They're only concerned with kiddie porn, quite rightly. What you have to watch out for are scams, viruses and hackers – that kind of thing."

"Safer to buy a magazine?" He grinned ruefully and I chuckled. I didn't feel entirely comfortable discussing Internet porn with an old man. It didn't exactly conjure the most appealing of images. I therefore agreed and quickly moved the subject along.

"Think of something you need to know for this book of yours," I told him. "Type that in."

Ned thought for a while, Nadine studying him fixedly. His fingers hovered over the keys – trying to decide, I imagined, on just the right keyword combination. I'd taught him about the importance of keeping his search as tight as possible, only broadening it by deleting the more specific keywords if absolutely necessary, and I was flattered to see that he now appeared to be taking my advice. His lips tightly pursed, shoulders hunched, his arthritic index fingers tapped in the chosen combination and he sat back – rather dramatically awaiting his search results.

Sorrow. Street. Mathewson.

The UK results were limited to just thirteen clearly irrelevant sites and Ned looked disappointed. This was a big day for him. He'd invested in an expensive computer, seeing it as the fount of all human knowledge, and it appeared it hadn't yielded the desired information. What was he to deduce from that, other than that he'd wasted his money? His sigh seemed to say that he should have known better than to even try. He was not of the Technological Age – and he was most assuredly not of the Information Age!

"Not what you were looking for?" I asked him, as sensitively as possible.

"Doesn't look that way." He squinted harder at the screen and then shook his head positively. "Nope," he said. "Nowt there that rings any bells. Guess it was a bit of a long shot."

"It is a little... *specific*," I told him. "You were looking for someone who used to live here, right?"

"My great aunt. She was a bit of a one. Had a right reputation locally." He smiled to himself, warmed and protected from the disappointment by the memory. "Local historians always seemed to include at least one story about her in their books and pamphlets and for a while, before things got really bad for her... well, happen you could say she was a bit of a local celebrity like. Until they locked her up and threw away the key."

"Locked her up?" I asked.

"Up?" Nadine repeated gravely.

"The asylum," Old Man Ned told me, and the hairs on my arms stood on end.

"The Sorrow Street Asylum?"

"Aye, that's the fella. She used to have these monumental mood swings. One day she'd be depressed and introspective, the next so full of energy the words used to fair spill out of her. She wrote prolifically during her 'up' periods, and sang endlessly – but she also had a habit of making a bit of a nuisance of herself around town... well, I suppose it was more of a village, then, which probably didn't help matters all that much. Folk like her get lost in the crowd, these days – but then it was different. It didn't do to draw too much attention to yourself."

"Which is exactly what she did." Ned seemed about to stall or lose his way, and I didn't want that to happen. Nadine seemed to find his voice curiously soothing, so I didn't have to worry about her growing bored and restless – and I desperately wanted to hear more about his great aunt and the asylum. "Sounds like she might have been bi-polar, to me."

Ned shrugged. "Possibly," he said. "Hard to say. All I know is the family stories my gran used to tell me when I was a bairn. The auld bugger used to scare me witless, but I loved every minute of it. Remember it vividly, even now. Sitting up in bed, the blankets heavy and coarse, not nearly warm enough as I watched the snow falling through the window. Gran sat on the edge of the bed, dressed all in black because Granddad, may he rot, hadn't been dead long – her thick, greying braided hair falling down her back and making me think of the weird loaves of bread Greek Jimmy's mam used to make, before Ernst Parkinson's horse trampled her to death. And she always started the same way. No 'once upon a times', no gentle wandering into that night's story or owt. Always the same flat claim to fact. 'And this is how it happened'.

"She was a big, solid woman, was Gran – and... well, I wasn't inclined to doubt her or that statement. That was how it happened, because she said so – and that was all the proof I needed."

He was starting to drift and I tried to get him back on course. Tapping the laptop, I said, "So this great aunt was sectioned?"

"Committed, they called it in them days."

"Committed. Yes. Of course."

"It was a lot easier, too. This was after the Lunacy Act was introduced, but even then it wasn't that difficult to get someone put away for good – especially with the right contacts. People didn't even have to be loopy. Not by modern standards. Anything that was deemed too eccentric could easily be labelled 'dissolute and immoral' and Bob's your uncle. I tell you, most of the young uns of today?

Wouldn't stand a chance in Hell.

"The way my Gran used to tell it, it was the gentlemen and lady friends what did it for my great aunt. She chose her words carefully, did Gran, cos I was only a bairn, but looking back and reading between the lines it's fairly obvious Great Aunt wasn't fussy who she had her fun with. Apparently, it was the last straw. This on top of the eccentric behaviour, arguing with strangers in the street, barking like a dog in chapel, urinating on the village green to name but a few incidents... well, after all that, summat just had to be done."

"And this is all going to be in this book of yours?" I asked. I'd considered telling him about the journal but, rather selfishly, I decided to keep it to myself. The professional aspect had to be considered. Ned was just a hobbyist writer, whereas I had a living to make. If there was anything of use in the mystery woman's journal, I had first dibs. It was a moral given.

"Some, maybe," Ned said. "Depends on what feels right. She was family, after all – and if I can't do her justice I reckon I don't have the right."

We talked about this a while longer, until Nadine finally started to get whiney and tired. I made my excuses, told Ned that he knew where I was if he needed any help with the laptop and left – Nadine in my arms, holding on to me tightly, her damp little face pressed into my neck as she hid from Ned's farewell attentions. Once again I experienced a sense of relief; Ned was a nice old guy, but there seemed to be an intensity to my encounters with him that I couldn't quite understand. His house had a faintly musty, feverish smell to it – the far-off smell of illness and dependence – but that wasn't it; I expected worse smells when I entered an old man's home, and, frankly, it didn't bother me all that much. Now that I was out, it seemed that the intensity was connected to something else entirely – something essentially Ned, something recessed and hereditary.

Back home, I put Nadine down for her afternoon nap and texted Ashley to see how long she was going to be. I wanted to do some work but didn't much feel like starting only to be interrupted.

My text was answered a few minutes later when Ashley walked into the kitchen looking hot and dejected. She pulled out a chair and sat down with a thud, throwing her phone and keys onto the table and kicking off her shoes. She had shiny, sweaty patches beneath her eyes and a light sheen across her forehead – her fringe damp and clumpy with sweat.

I'd just made myself a coffee and offered her one, but apparently she needed something more immediately satisfying – taking water from the fridge and drinking straight from the bottle (something she insisted was a filthy habit... whenever *I* did it).

"Tough afternoon?" I asked.

She rolled her eyes and took another swig from the bottle. "You could say that," she said. "Olly was right – there's something more than just this supposed stalker going on with her. I've never seen her like that."

"Like what?"

"Impatient with Wee Mark, for starters," she told me. "She actually slapped his legs at one point, over practically nothing. I've never seen her do anything like that before, Sonny. It wasn't pleasant."

Leaning against the sink unit and sipping my coffee, I asked, "You try to talk to her about it?"

"Naturally. That *was* why I went round there, after all."

"And?"

A gulp of water and a shrug. Head back and a weary sigh. "It's like Oliver said," she told me. "She was evasive and dismissive. It was as if she regretted ever telling us about it."

"Do you think this stalker's caught on to the fact that we know and he's told her to... you know, get us out of the picture or else?"

"He's a stalker, love, not a Mafia don."

"Even so, he seems to know the more intimate aspects of her life – which suggests to me that he's not just some dumb kid getting his rocks off by spooking the neighbourhood Pretty Young Widow."

Ashley frowned and dangled the bottle of water between her legs. "You think he has... what?" she said. "A degree of expertise in these matters?"

"I'm not sure. I'm just thinking out loud, really. But now that you mention it, he doesn't even need to be all that much of an expert."

"I don't follow."

"Listening and spying devices. You can get them all over the place on the Net. He doesn't even need to be able to see her while she's in her house – just hear her. And he can do that from outside. But if it's someone who's had access to the place, a workman or whatever... well, there's no telling what he might have rigged up."

Ashley mulled this over whilst continuing to re-hydrate herself. "I don't know," she said. "It all sounds rather too Machiavellian for my liking. Why would someone be so obsessed with Mags? Some celebrity I could understand, but *Maggie*. No, it just doesn't make sense."

"So what do you think's going on, then?"

She shrugged and fingered her hair back from her sweaty brow. "I really don't know," she said despondently. "All I know is that Maggie now pretty much insists that it's nothing – that he'll get bored and stop soon enough – and that her mood is down to Jim."

"Missing him, you mean?"

"I assume so. I asked her why she was being so hard on Wee Mark and she just apologised and said, 'It's just Jim'…. Maybe that is the root of all this, after all."

"You think she's fabricating it?"

"I dunno. What do you think?"

"When you said something similar the other day, it seemed unlikely. Now... now I'm not sure I know either."

"Well one thing's for certain," Ashley said.

"What's that?"

"We can only help her if she'll let us – and right now I'm not at all sure that's what she wants."

"Then why on earth did she mention it in the first place?"

"Her fear isn't a closed system," she told me. "You have to remember that, Sonny. Things go in, things go out – and whether she's making all this up or not, it's real to her. Something's happened to make her reconsider involving us."

Once again I retreated to my study, determined to get some work done but ultimately too tempted by the journal I'd left resting on the corner of my desk – in a space usually reserved for correspondence. Ever since Ned had told me about his loopy great aunt I'd felt the familiar itching at the back of my mind. Like the inexplicable need to phone an old friend I hadn't heard from in years, it had persisted all through my conversation with Ashley and I realised as soon as I (very firmly) closed the study door behind me that work was once again out of the question. I forgot about Maggie. I forgot about Richard and the beguiling Mrs. Sutherland. I forgot about Ned and his great aunt. I even forgot about the conversation I had had with Ash last night – sitting up into the wee small hours and finally, albeit reluctantly, agreeing that we would indeed try for another child. Everything fractured and fell away as I sat down and opened the journal to the page I had marked.

That morning I had snatched a few minutes to read a couple of paragraphs whilst I had drunk my morning coffee. It had been an uneventful, difficult to read passage – the handwriting cramped and seemingly rushed – that had largely dealt with the day-to-day routine of the asylum. I'd read of the bland cod she'd endured for supper, the walk she had taken with the Warty Nurse, out among the other "lunatic paupers" – and saw between the lines the mystery of who this woman had been only partially illuminated. An educated woman who hadn't been committed to a "Single House" asylum, a woman clearly so estranged from any family she had that the authorities of the day saw no other option than to place her in a county asylum – either that, I suspected, or a prison. As I again started to read, I once more flashed on the image of the horrific asylum in Stoker's Dracula – allegedly based on an actual, relatively progressive asylum near Whitby. Was that really what it had been like? Storms whipping the inmates into a collective frenzy? Patients eating spiders and flies as they muttered and chuckled to themselves? It seemed somehow appalling that a woman who was apparently so literate and intelligent should be subjected to such base, dehumanising conditions – whatever her crimes or predilections.

It is preferable to stare out of the window at such times, I read. *The sky, however many clouds, whatever the quality and arrangement of the stars, is a blank canvas onto which memory and fantasy can be liberally daubed. Each night is a soulful* tabula rasa *and even though I know I can follow my whims wherever I wish I find myself returning time and again to those first days with Chadwick. It is yet another form of masochism, I naturally realise, but I can no more resist such*

97

delightful pain now than I could then – and so I wallow and wait, blessing him for the things he taught me, the sensations to which he introduced me, even as I curse him for his betrayal.

He was a rogue and charlatan – a confidence man and a cad – but that day he walked into my life, he appeared every inch the gentleman. I was not the naïve child he imagined, however. No gent would ever have approached me in broad daylight as I then was – and I didn't flatter or deceive myself; this attractive, graceful fraud saw nothing more in me than a business opportunity. Addressing me so openly was merely an act of speculation and I was more than content to go along with it – accepting his offer of drinks and supper, happy to let him do most of the talking.

A sharp, crescent moon on the wane. Grimy, rain-stained windows – such a cruel barrier, so crude and unforgivably real. Thinking of Chadwick, I move and feel myself stir. A wicked, personal pleasure under the circumstances. And I smile, falling into such irreproachable night as that first evening comes back to me – the rich food and heady wine, the intimacy of his fire-lit, dancing-shadowed parlour, the damp-fur smell of his dogs and the feeling against my thighs of the rough fabric covering his fainting couch as I slid forward and opened myself for him. Even then I had been under no illusions. To this man I was no more than a means to an end. To forget that would be fatal, but to always remember it, to always carry it close to my heart like a ganglion of love and loathing – to do this latter was to arm and armour myself, and I well understood the possible strength of my position.

He was older than I, this chimerical man I knew only as Chadwick. I a mere nineteen years, he could have been my father – a man of two score years at the very least, though this was something we never discussed. He limped badly when the weather was damp, most of the time, as I remember it, and had an infantile aversion to soap and water that made it almost intolerable to be confined with him for long periods – but whatever else might be said of him, Chadwick was enterprising and, for the most, amusing to be around. I liked him as much as sense and caution would allow, and gladly took whatever was offered.

I watch a gossamer cloud obscure the waning moon, and shudder at those other, more immediate memories.

Do they read my jottings, I wonder before going any further. Does the repulsive Warty Nurse sit on my bed and finger these very pages whilst I am away being purged and provoked? It doesn't concern me. She has already revealed something of her True Nature and if I am of such perverse interest to her, then so be it. I do not care. I cannot care. That I incriminate myself and others, confirm their assumptions, is not my concern. I am beyond that, now.

The confidence tricks we worked together were many and varied, simple but effective. Fraudulent and fake charities, the sale of items that were not ours to sell (a friend of Chadwick's replicating the requisite forms and deeds) – we practiced many routines and did rather well out of it. I wanted for nothing and my relationship with Chadwick developed those traits that would at another time have made me wary. We settled into a kind of domesticity, taking rooms together and living as husband and wife – my sense of myself as someone somehow apart from the rest of Humankind growing as we built cautious walls around us, trusting only in ourselves, and even then with certain qualifications. I enjoyed Chadwick as he enjoyed me, allowing him to take our intercourse to whatever extremes he so desired – but now I see the relationship for what it truthfully was; a way station, a temporary respite for us both... a pause whilst the Fates nodded.

He taught me to dally with death, my climax all the richer as the rope tightened around my neck. I became more accustomed to associating pleasure with pain – inseparable twins that I nurtured at my bosom and cried with in the night, my comfort, their placation – and all the while both he and I grew in stature until we had the respect of even the wealthiest of our peers. They did not and could never know us. We both accepted that whatever our appearances, we could never risk becoming a part of "society". It was too dangerous and so we projected an air of aloofness, speaking to nobody, never accepting invitations and most assuredly never making them. We came more and more to rely upon ourselves for our entertainment but that, naturally, became a burden in time and we found ourselves laughing less at our shameless and highly profitable exploits and instead retreating to familiar haunts. We gambled and drank in places where our true identities and occupation were known and applauded, and for the briefest of times it was idyllic – a blessed relief for both Chadwick and me to let the pretence and fakery fall away, to break through the shell of proprietary we had created and be born again.

Everything seems inevitable, now. It could not have persisted. Such perfection is only ever fleeting, as my present circumstances testify. The world turned and we danced and drank our way through the monotony of success. And I felt my grip on it all gradually loosen, the ambition and pleasure going first, the sense of complicity following quickly at its heels. Change. Unexpected silences. My suspicion growing day by day, moment by moment. The clock in the parlour ticked, the sound of long forgotten childhood Sundays, and suspicion became intractable certitude.

We were too close of a match – too alike in our appetites and habits. The very thing that had made us such a success, each being able to predict so perfectly whatever the other was going to say or do, was, it seemed, to be our downfall. Naturally, I had a choice. If I so wished I could indeed choose to ignore what common sense and instinct was telling me. I could accept and silently condone, allow the obvious infidelity and betrayal to go unchallenged and unpunished. But that required more than I was willing to give. That *spoke of indignity and compromise – a significant shift in my position that was wholly unacceptable. And I wasn't about to let that happen. I couldn't let that happen.*

This is what I remember:

The gas low, the shadow deep and alive. A rich and crumpled burgundy fabric on the bed – something oriental and corrupt. The unmistakable stink of hashish turning my stomach with its promise of apathy. The scratching of rats in the walls. Far off, voices in the street, the steady rumble and creak of a barrow.

And on the bed – fish-belly white contrasting so starkly with the deep burgundy – Chadwick and his whore. My *Chadwick and his whore, for whatever lies I may have told myself to the contrary, that was how I had come to think of him. A possession, a part of me. And all my grand claims to common sense and wariness, to understanding that what we had together was about nothing more than profit, simply couldn't conceal that one, insistent fact; I had, in some distorted way, fallen in love with him.*

If only he hadn't deceived me everything would have been all right. His whore was a rare beauty – unblemished skin, hair black as an Egyptian's, eyes like polished Whitby jet highlighted, appropriately, with kohl. I could smell her sweat and juices over the hashish as she reclined beside a still asleep Chadwick, watching me lazily, fingers lightly brushing the surprisingly coppery hairs at her pudendum – and I saw in that moment just how uncomplicated it might have been. Chadwick could have had his Egyptian whore. I could have had his Egyptian whore. If only he hadn't lied to me, the games we could have played together!

I later discovered her name was Mary. Mary the Beauty, her fellow whores and protectors called her.

After I had killed them both with the hammer I had carried through the streets in my purse, I took some moments to enjoy the two of them – saying farewell one final time to my Chadwick and caressing Mary by way of an introduction. Even in death, the Egyptian whore with the name of The Virgin tasted sweet and salty, the sweat in the foods of her cunt still drying.

Her tongue was of no use to me now, so I helped myself to her fingers.

The door was open again. I'd taken great pains in closing it and it seemed pretty unlikely that Ash had looked in without my noticing. I stood and examined the handle and catch, closing and opening it a number of times, utterly unable to see how it could click open unaided. On the landing, I closed the door from the outside and stood looking at it for a few minutes – sure an explanation would come with time. Nothing happened without good reason, I told myself as I examined the jamb and hinges for irregularities. Something had happened to cause the door to open and it was merely a matter of thinking outside the box – of trying to think back to my childhood, to the time when my parents had stood on this very landing and perhaps pondered the same puzzle. Had they had problems with this door, too? I imagined Dad standing beside me, hands on his hips as he earnestly regarded the challenge. "The top hinge is pulling it out of alignment," I imagined him saying. "Fix that and you fix your problem." It seemed a simple enough solution but when I looked at the hinge again I saw exactly what I had only moments before; there was absolutely nothing wrong with it.

I found Ashley in the living room – watching a Time Team repeat and texting Molly. Slumping on the sofa beside her, sighing as the delightful Carenza explored her trench, I said, "Did you by any chance look in on me while I was working?"

"Yes," she said. "But you weren't working, you were engrossed in that journal. Why?"

"It was just that my door was open and I remembered closing it." It was something of a relief to have an explanation but it was nevertheless rather disconcerting to once again discover that I could lose myself so completely.

"I closed it after me," Ashley insisted, too preoccupied with her phone to notice my unsettled look. "I know you don't like noise when you're busy so I always make a point of closing it properly."

"So why was it open, then?"

She shrugged. "You tell me. Maybe it was the wind. Did you have your window open?"

"Naturally. It's stifling up there."

"Well there you go, then. Air pressure, darling – happens all the time."

"Air pressure opens doors?"

She frowned and stared at the chimney. "I can't say for certain, but I'm fairly sure it does. It can close them with one hell of a slam, so why not?"

I was still far from convinced but let the matter drop – happy (for the time being) to tell myself that in spite of what she had said to the contrary, Ashley had simply forgotten to close the door properly. Believing that was far easier than believing her air pressure explanation.

"Who are you texting?" I asked, knowing full well that she and Mad Molly nearly always exchanged vaguely adversarial texts at this time of the day.

"Who do you think?" Her thumb continued working away as she glanced up at me.

"Mad Molly?"

"Natch. And getting madder by the minute."

"In what sense?"

"In the I'm a Christian and I'm okay sense," she said, singing it to the tune of Monty Python's Lumberjack Song. "She's convinced that all Maggie's problems stem from the fact that she hasn't had Wee Mark christened. Can you believe that?"

I nodded and moved closer, so I could read her reply. "Coming from Molly, I'd believe just about anything," I said. "Maggie hears her talking like that and she'll break her teeth for her."

"If she said that about Nadine, I'd fucking kill her," she told me.

"Indirectly, she already has," I said. It had been something Ashley and I had been in complete agreement about. Both of us essentially atheists, from Church of England backgrounds, we saw no reason to pander to family tradition and have Nadine baptised into God's care or whatever the hell it was they did. Hypocritical and meaningless, it was not something either of us could sanction – even for the sake of appearance – and the more Pippa pushed, the more convinced we became that it was the right decision; Pippa only attended church for christenings, weddings, funerals and occasionally at Christmas, so her spiritual advice didn't exactly come with the best of credentials.

"I never thought of it like that," Ashley was saying. "The cow. How dare she?"

"Careful," I said as she angrily texted a reply. "Don't forget she has God on her side."

"Aye, well he can go fuck himself, as well," she said – her cheeks flushing as her thumb worked its secular SMS magic. "The arrogant bastards. Who do they think they are?"

I liked it when Ashley was like this. It reminded me of the girl I had fallen in love with – full of ideas and opinions, forever prepared to challenge and disagree. I watched her as the texted with a new-found energy, the muscles in her neck twitching as she delivered her pronouncement on the Arrogance of Gods, and I thought back to the party on the evening of the day we had first made love – all the little gay boys falling in love with her as she sat like a queen (in the usual, non-faggy sense of the word) in the corner, chattering on about her favourite authors and, as the evening rolled on, swapping beauty tips with "da boys". Oliver and I had watched her from a distance, both with a sense of relief, though for very different reasons. Oliver was grateful that someone had managed to distract his "baby homos" whilst I was merely relieved; seen in this light, the beautiful, energetic young woman I had fallen in love with hadn't seemed so young or verboten after all. She beamed a confident maturity, gesturing madly as she explained the finer points of exfoliation, and when Oliver had turned to me and said "Now do you see that her age can never be the problem you imagined?" I nodded. "And it's only going to get easier," he went on. "You'll grow into each other and by the time she's in her twenties, you'll wonder why you even gave the thought head room. You'll see."

That Ashley had evolved into the woman beside me, and for all the apparent differences, it was good to be reminded of this. We'd thought of ourselves as soul mates, sitting up into the wee small hours, discussing everything from Chomsky to the ridiculous amount of miming on television music shows – and it was true that much of that "connection" had been lost, or was now, at least, taken for granted, but at heart we were still the same two people, held together by more than circumstance and duty.

"Do you know what really gets me?" Ashley was saying – her message sent.

"No – what really gets you?" I asked, smiling and taking hold of her free hand.

"'Witnessing'," she said. "The way all religions think they have the right to ram their bloody stupid fairytales down other people's throats. It wouldn't be so bad if they waited to be asked, but people like Molly don't. It's against their religion." She laughed at her own little joke and then continued. "Did I ever tell you about that time I was in Boots down town?" She had, many times, but I shook my head anyway – knowing that this story was merely a bridge to take her to others. "It was pitiful. There was this young bloke in a wheelchair. A paraplegic by the look of him, and probably an ex-biker. Long, shaggy black hair, death's head hawk moth tattooed on his bicep, facial piercings – you get the picture. The cheeky sod winked at me when I went by, so he was clearly a man of taste and intellect."

"Goes without saying." This was what I always said. Life was a pantomime, and all the more bearable for it.

"That's what I thought," Ashley said, glancing at her phone impatiently. "Anyway, this bloke was waiting to be served with the rest of us and out of the blue this woman with bad psoriasis comes over to him, going down on her haunches like she was Princess Fucking Di or something.... I hate speaking ill of the dead, but she had that squatting down thing all wrong, in my opinion. Coming down to people's eye-level. Isn't that like a physical dumbing down? Sitting on a chair, yes – that I can understand – but squatting near someone in a wheelchair? No, I think not. Patronising if you ask me."

"You were telling me about the guy in Boots," I reminded her – only just managing to avoid tagging *again* on the end.

"Eh?"

"The bloke in the wheelchair?"

"Oh, yes – I hadn't forgotten." She elbowed me playfully. "I like to tell a story my own way, thank you very much."

"Well excuse me."

"How would you like it if your editor constantly told you to cut the suspense building stuff?"

"She does."

"And your response?"

"I try to slip in more when she isn't looking."

Ashley smiled and glanced at her phone again before continuing. "She was a lot like Molly, this woman," she said. "You could see it before she even opened her mouth. 'Zealous' and 'uncompromising' are the two words that most immediately spring to mind. She saw this bloke, thought he was an easy target and, so, squatted down beside him and started in with the patter.

"It was fine to begin with. The bloke took it in his stride – answering 'rock and roll' when she asked him what he believed in, that kind of thing – but when she told him, with a reassuring pat on the arm, that everyone walks in Heaven, things started to go wrong for her."

"He didn't believe her?" I asked, ironically.

"He clearly thought it was the biggest load of tosh he'd ever heard in his life," she said. "'Take it somewhere else, love,' he told her. 'Throw in a digital alarm clock or a Parker pen and I still aren't buying.'"

"Nice. And how did she take that rather impressive little knock-back?"

"With typical Christian grace," Ashley said. "Beatific smile, the lot. Think Molly when she's at her most irritatingly patient and you're half way there.

"Anyway," she continued. "That was when she really fucked it up. She said something about how it was understandable for him to be bitter and cynical, but that he had to understand that God saw beyond all that. He was omniscient and He could see into people's hearts and understood that all the bluff and bluster in the world didn't alter that we were all His children. She waffled on some more but the guy in the wheelchair hadn't got past 'bitter and cynical'. He waved a hand in front of her face, as if to see whether or not she was in a trance, and then repeated the phrase – asking just what gave her the right to be so fucking presumptuous. She started to say more about God, but he cut her short, telling her he'd worked very hard to reach the level of contentment he had and he sure as hell didn't need some God-hugging imbecile selling him eternal salvation in the form of a working pair of legs. 'Life isn't that simple, love,' he told her. 'So save it for Sunday school and spare me your falsehoods and fictions.'"

"And all this happened in Boots?" I said.

"You bet. You really haven't lived until you've spent a busy Saturday afternoon people-watching in Boots."

"I'll put it on my bucket-list," I said. "So how did the woman react to that?"

Ashley started to reply, telling me about the "stunned silence" and "air of anticipation", but the beep-beeping of her phone interrupted her. She held it out before us and snuggled in closer to me – suddenly anxious and unexpectedly reluctant to read Molly's response. She breathed rapidly against my arm and finally thumbed the button and opened Molly's message.

"Maybe I'm wrong about everything I believe in," the message read. "But what if I'm not?"

Chapter Seven

I'm normally a very heavy and reliable sleeper, getting my eight hours and waking grumpy but refreshed, but on the rare occasion when insomnia strikes, I know better than to try to fight it.

And so the early hours of the following morning found me at my study window – looking out at the night sky and thinking about what Molly had said. Was that what it all in the end came down to? I wondered. Religion nothing more than a conglomerate of hedge-betters? In the grip of sleeplessness, it was all too easy to see her point – to see that Ashley and I were, indeed, the ones taking all the risks, whilst the most she had to lose was a little face. But was that enough to justify a life lived in the clutches of a bunch of people who, when all was said and done, was primarily concerned with perpetuating a myth in order that their own tenuous positions might be maintained? It seemed a ludicrous proposition, to me, and not one I ever saw myself subscribing to – however desperate the circumstances.

Before slipping away from me into sated sleep, Ashley had said something that had left me feeling a little unnerved, however. Yawning, she had rolled contentedly away from me and said, "Maybe we all get what we believe in." It had been nothing more than a stray thought voiced as sleep started to claim her, but it had nevertheless caught my attention and imagination – so much so that, however uncomfortable it made me feel, I now found myself playing with the idea, staring down at the back garden and wondering what my father would have said about the afterlife.

Both Mam and Dad were practical people. They had come from that post-war, working class generation that had had no real time for anything other than the day to day task of "getting by". They had both known hardship – Dad often holding down two jobs, Mam supplementing this further with a few hours at the corner shop, money nevertheless tight – but in time their hard work and sheer, unwavering resilience had paid off and they had found themselves in a relatively comfortable position. Money, they knew, didn't just magically appear in their pockets, and their frugality could sometimes be annoying, but experience had imbued them with a brand of common sense and lack of pretence that served them well in all aspects of their lives together. Dad, especially, could be spectacularly unimpressed, on occasion. His right eyebrow would raise in acknowledgement of something quite remarkable or noteworthy (the first shuttle disaster, for example) and that would be it. He might ponder the causes with the rest of us over a pint down the pub, but the event didn't touch him because... well, the event didn't touch him. His practical side, dominant as ever, looked for threats to or benefits for his family, saw none and therefore concluded it was of no real concern to him. And this was the philosophy that he, and to a lesser degree, Mam, lived their lives by – at first through necessity, and then habit.

Dad would have undoubtedly found Ashley's "what if" fascinating, of that there could be no mistake. He was not a man wholly cut off from metaphysical musings. But at the same time he would not have placed any undue importance in such matters. It was pleasantly diverting nonsense to discuss around the fire when there was "nowt on telly", nothing more – and all the tea in China would not have prompted him to take it any more seriously than that. "It's an interesting idea," I imagined him saying. "But I can't see it catching on."

One time, I remembered, he had taken me to a strange little circus that had come to town. It was a rather pitiful set-up that claimed to "emanate from the fine and utmostly noble Indian circus tradition", and Dad went to great lengths to ensure that I was under no illusions as to the origins of these fine, exotic people. "Southampton or somewhere like that," he said. "Take my word for it, mate. They wouldn't know Indian circus tradition if it bit them on their very white bums." In shattering the illusion so thoroughly, Dad could have so easily ruined the outing for me. But he was smarter than that, and he knew there was nothing his son liked more than being "in" on a secret. A significant part of the enjoyment I experienced that evening came not from the clowns (all of whom seemed made-up caricatures of our family doctor) or the tentative and utterly unconvincing lion tamer, but rather from the sense that Dad, Mam and I knew something that no one else did. Eating a hot-dog with onions, the onions an attempt at masking the overriding scent of shit and piss, I sat on the hard, wooden bench and surveyed my fellow audience members, gauging their reactions and judging them, on the whole, poor, gullible fools. I felt like a secret agent on the verge of uncovering the greatest international conspiracy in recorded history – and only when a magician came on to perform The (Authentic) Indian Rope Trick did I turn my attention back to the circus's single ring.

The magician looked like a cross between Mahatma Ghandi and Wilfrid Brambell – scrawny and smeared, I was convinced, in gravy browning. He waddled splay-footed into the centre of the ring and introduced himself as Gupta Singh – the last in a long line of "oh so very fine Indian fakirs". Dad chuckled and bent down to whisper in my ear. "Looks a bit of a silly fakir to me," he said, and I laughed out loud – the questionable "Indian" magician fixing me with a stare before continuing with his historical preamble. "For centuries," the silly fakir continued, "the secrets of true Indian magic have been handed down, generation to generation, through mine, the most supremely noblest family in all of India and the sub-continent! Never once, oh no, were these most precious of secrets written down. To do so would be an insult to the gods, and to those who have gone before. Words are spoken at the chosen time, and the memories are locked away, the secret guarded most precisely."

I was growing bored with this clearly fabricated monologue, as, it seemed, was just about everyone else in the audience. People coughed and bums and feet shuffled. A kid a few rows back inflated his empty crisp packet and then popped it between his hands, earning an even longer stare than I – and further back, hidden in the shadows where the poor lighting failed to reach, someone shouted "get on with it!"

Things were not getting off to a good start for poor old Gupta Singh, and as I looked out of my window at the night sky, I remembered that, as a child, I had actually felt sorry for the silly fakir. He had worked so hard at creating a feeling of suspense – put so much effort into imbuing his ancient and utterly commonplace trick with an air of authenticity – and no one watching him that day had even come close to appreciating or understanding this (except maybe me). Gupta Singh heard that cry of "get on with it" and took a dignified bow. "As you wish," I remembered him saying. "Sanjeet!"

A skinny brown boy, hair the shade of blue-black that looked as if it had come out of a bottle, came through the curtains at the back of the ring – carrying a rope, a basket and a scimitar.

I recall the fakir barking instructions to the boy in what I assumed was Hindi, but could have been nothing more than a clichéd parody. The boy didn't respond quickly enough, and this earned him a swift slap across the back of the head. Rubbing the spot where the silly fakir's hand had connected, the boy handed the fakir the rope – an undramatic act that seemed the leave the audience and the fakir rather unimpressed. Another slap followed and then Gupta Singh turned his attention back to us, his oh so very patient and most noblest of audiences.

"In the back streets of Bombay, my esteemed and upright father taught me the illusion I am going to share with you today," he pronounced. "It is filled with grave danger and so I must with respect ask you to remain utterly and most completely silent. Thank you so very much."

And with that, the fakir threw one end of the rope into the air and, in spite of his instructions, we gasped. The rope ascended gracefully, uncoiling like the lithest of dancers – the thrown end disappearing into the darkest, impenetrable heights of the not so big big top. Mam grabbed Dad's hand and I was a little shocked that she and the rest of us could be so easily impressed. Indian snake-charming music was, in the greatest act of predictability I'd ever witnessed, being played into the tent and the rope seemed to shimmy in time to it, only stopping when it reached its limit – its "earthly" end dangling a few inches above the ground, the other concealed within darkness at the highest point of the tent.

The fakir surveyed his audience with a smug look on his face, and for a moment I thought the trick was over. I looked around to see if anyone was going to applaud, but the rest of the audience was captivated – wanting and expecting more.

Apparently not one to disappoint, the fakir bent down and

dramatically picked up the scimitar that the skinny boy had laid on the floor beside the large basket. With a flourish, he showed it to the audience – swinging it in impressive, light-catching arcs before shaking it threateningly in the skinny boy's face. The boy flinched and pulled away from him, throwing his arms up in front of his face like Fay Wray when Kong came a-calling. It was a decent enough attempt, but he overstated it somewhat and Gupta, not wanting to lose his audience, cut the scene short, telling the skinny boy to get up the rope before he was in "abso-bloody-lutely big trouble".

Dutifully, and with monkey-like grace, the boy ascended the rope and disappeared into the darkness.

The fakir took a bow and we all applauded. I remember feeling a little disappointed. This time I was sure the trick was over, and, yet, I felt that there should be more. Magicians rarely disappeared people without bringing them back. David Nixon had always brought them back, as did Paul Daniels – so I saw no justifiable reason why Gupta Singh should leave poor, skinny Sanjeet up there in the darkness. It was wrong and, more to the point, it was incomplete.

Before I'd even had time to think about what I was doing, I stood up on my seat, much to Dad's amusement, and shouted, "Bring back Sanjeet!" My call was taken up by others, and before long the whole tent was chanting "we want Sanjeet, we want Sanjeet!"

I smiled to myself as I remembered my mother's flushed face – the embarrassment that had quickly become pride in her son the leader of men, her son the champion of skinny little Sanjeets the world over. Dad had winked at me approvingly as I had sat back down, patting me on the knee and saying, "We'll make a union representative of you yet." At the time, I hadn't caught his irony – and certainly wouldn't have understood it if I had – but now I saw as well as he that, like him, I would never make a union rep, even if my politics had allowed; I was not and would never be a leader of men, I was an observer, a chronicler of events and traits, even then.

Gupta Singh took my peasant revolt in his stride, however. He smiled kindly on me and the rest of his shabby audience and bowed his acceptance, looking up at the rope, one hand cupped at the side of his mouth as he yelled, "Sanjeet, you can be of the coming down now!" We all waited, holding our breaths, saucer eyes searching out movement in the darkness at the top of the rope. The silence hung about us like a fog. Not a sound. Not a movement.

Gupta started to look worried and then, sensing our growing impatience, annoyed. He called Sanjeet again, to no discernable effect, and shook his fist angrily at the heavens before tucking the scimitar into his dhoti and ascending the rope himself – telling us he would not be long, "please to be bearing with me."

"So that's what they meant by 'authentic'," Dad said.

"What do you mean?" Mam asked.

"If I'm right, the next bit's pretty gory." He put a large, reassuring hand on my head. "It's just an illusion, but we can leave now if you want."

I naturally chose to stay – already looking forward to telling my friends about whatever it was that Dad thought was going to happen. Dad whispered his warning to those seated around us however, telling them that now might be a good time to get young children the hell out of there. The warning rippled through the audience, and by the time we heard Gupta and Sanjeet arguing in the darkness at the top of the tent, a good third of those watching had left.

Somewhere in the darkness there was a great commotion. The shouting got worse – Sanjeet's squeals of protest accompanied by curses in a tongue it was difficult to imagine anyone understanding – and when we heard the great swooshing sound of the scimitar cutting through the air, Dad was already nodding to himself. I heard a scream – we all did – and watched as something fell from the darkness and landed with a wet thud at the bottom of the rope.

It took me a moment to work out just what it was, but when I did I finally understood why Dad had issued his whispered warning. This was not something your average kid should see and even I – had I not been warned in advance that it was gory but, after all, nothing more than an illusion – with my love of horror movies and all things vampiric could have conceivably found it difficult to stomach. The arm twitched a few times, blood leaking apathetically from one end, fingers reaching out desperately at the other – and I knew as soon as I identified it as an arm that such a skinny, gravy-stained limb could only belong to poor, victimised Sanjeet.

Or that, at least, was what Gupta wanted us to believe. As the limbs rained down, followed by the prime cut of torso and, finally, the googly-eyed head, my mother covered her mouth with her handkerchief and muttered something about how revolting and obscene this was. I, however, was transfixed. I'd moved beyond the false reality of the illusion and was already contemplating the problems it posed. How did the rope stay up? What was in the darkness at its zenith? Where could you get amputated limbs and blood that looked so *real*? These were just some of the questions I asked myself as Gupta Singh descended the rope and, shaking his head indignantly, collected the various body parts and placed them in the basket.

"Ghastly sight," he said, staring into the basket – arms akimbo. He reminded me of Yul Brynner in *The King and I,* full of disdain and self-destructive pride. "So very sorry you had to witness it." He looked around, at a loss for something he apparently needed, and then approached a gentleman in the audience. The man had a raincoat folded in his lap like my father and Gupta pointed at it. "Might I borrow that?" he said. "In order that I might preserve the poor boy's dignity. I assure you, if it is in any way damaged, you will be suitably recompensed."

The man looked at his wife and then shook his head. "Forget it," he told Gupta Singh. "You cut the poor fucker up – use your own bloody raincoat."

Gupta started to protest, explaining that he would, indeed, use his own raincoat if, indeed, he had one – which, indeed, he didn't – when Dad got to his feet, apparently bored with the illusion and wanting it out of the way so that The Tumbling Tornadoes could take their turn at trying to entertain us. "Here," Dad said, tossing Gupta his own raincoat. "Take mine."

Gupta caught the raincoat and bowed gratefully – shuffling hurriedly over to the basket of bits and draping Dad's raincoat over it.

"That isn't your best raincoat, I hope," Mam whispered. Dad patted her knee and told her not to worry. It was his old coat, but even if it hadn't been, it wouldn't have mattered because *it was just an illusion.* "Illusions leave stains, too, dear," Mam said, and Dad chuckled knowingly.

I remember Dad nudging me. I never loved him and Mam more

than when they were conspiring with me – sharing secrets or preparing me for what lay ahead, commissioning my help in a joke or a prank. I realised as I looked down at what I supposed would, in reality, always be Dad's back garden that I had a tendency to romanticise my childhood and the relationship I shared with them – but I now saw their wisdom for the uncomplicated thing it had been. "Watch this bit very closely," he said. "See if you can see how it's done."

Gupta faked grief and sorrow, telling the audience a sorry tale of woe. He insisted that Sanjeet – the son of his dead brother – had not been a bad boy. It was merely that "the demons" occasionally got "under his skin". "The death of his father hit him very hard, you know," Gupta Singh said. "Sent him fair round the bend, if the truth be told. But I did my best for him. Me a poor man of the cloth, as you people are wont to say, and some time circus performer. A man alone with an unruly, disrespectful teenager! It was doomed to end this way from the very day he set foot on my doorstep!"

The audience was growing bored and restless again. Even the least intelligent among us had by now worked out that this was all part of the act – and we just wanted it over as quickly as possible. My need to know the secrets behind this bloody trick was on the wane (my bum numb and the dust making my eyes itch) and Mam was looking through her bag for something she probably didn't need, as was her way during times of extreme boredom. Dad kept his eyes on his raincoat; old or not, he wasn't about to lose it.

"It is a very sincere tragedy," Gupta Singh said. "Make no mistake." (Years later, I would hear George W. Bush use this same three word phrase after the very real tragedy of 9/11 and think of Gupta Singh. Two silly fakirs together.) "Every day this will live with me and torture me. I will sleep not a wink and –" He stopped, hearing a noise behind him and turning to look at the basket.

Dad sat up straighter – nodding to himself and smiling a little smugly. "This is the bit, mate," he said to me. "Keep your eye on that basket. Don't let anything Gupta or anyone else does distract you."

Ever the obedient son, I strained against the urge to blink – my eyes misting counterproductively, tears quickly spilling as Gupta walked tentatively back to the basket. I wiped away the teary blur and concentrated, not allowing any stray thought or flicker on the periphery of my vision to take my mind off the matter at hand. Gupta glanced over his shoulder at his audience, feigning trepidation and shuddering perceptibly, but this barely registered at all, so intent was I on keeping my wits about me and not letting any trick or misdirection win me over.

"It is his ghost, I am sure," Gupta said in a stage whisper. "Come back to haunt a poor, old man. What will on this earth become of me?"

Dad wasn't at all impressed by this melodrama. The eyebrow rose, and that was it.

It wasn't the greatest of reappearances, it had to be said. The music, which had continued to play in the background, faded away – and in the silence, the lights began to flicker. Dot, dash, dot, dot, dash, dot, dash. A code with the sole purpose of distracting. But I was no fool. I concentrated hard – so hard my fists clenched and my held breath made my temples throb. Flicker, dot, dash. The silence of the audience as it mulled over the possibilities of what would happen next and whether or not now was a good time for them to leave, too. Mam buried in the darkest depths of her handbag. These things threatened to take my mind off that blasted basket – but I refused to succumb, redoubling my efforts and squinting my eyes against the unreliable light, determined to absorb and understand every detail so that when it came time to tell this tale to my friends, I could do so with authority.

The lights flashed and the basket trembled. Dad's raincoat, covering the basket in a bizarre attempt at preserving Sanjeet's "dignity", fluttered around the edges and then, ever so slowly, began to reshape itself.

As Sanjeet rose in one piece from the basket, wearing my father's raincoat, it's fair to say that I didn't see anything that might suggest how the illusion had been accomplished. I had my theories of course – involving pits beneath the ground and twin Sanjeets – but, disappointingly, I saw nothing that might categorically give the game away.

On the journey home there had been much discussion, but what I now remembered most as I pressed my forehead against the cool glass and looked down at where my hole had been was the dream I had had that night so long ago in my childhood.

It had been simple and harrowing – unconcerned by illusion and obsessed with its own twisted reality. In my dream, a dead boy ascended the rope, heading for an eternal void he could only begin to imagine. In my dream, the boy struggled to keep his grip – wanting to fall but knowing instinctively that that would be even worse than whatever awaited him at the top of the rope. In my dream, the boy was me.

I wanted to go back to Ashley and sleep. Remembered dreams were unimportant. They had no place, I told myself, in the life I now found myself living. But try as I might, I could not stop myself from thinking about boys and ropes – the void waiting – and, inevitably, I suppose, after a number of replayings the boy became Jim. Poor, cancer-worn Jim with his bigotry and his love for his wife and son. With atrophied arms and legs, he hoisted himself into the darkest depths of oblivion, and down below, Maggie – who had once, in that cottage in Wales, stimulated my prostate with the index finger of her right hand – reached out to him, vainly calling him back to her. Goodbye. Don't go. Return to me. Let me go with you. The torture of a lover's death.

When Maggie started to climb the rope after him, I blinked hard against the image and tapped my forehead on the cool glass three times in an attempt at reinforcing my reality. Save the symbolism for Richard and Mr. Sutherland, I told myself. There's no place for it here. It doesn't help. It only confuses the picture.

Movement distracted me. I was only distantly aware of it. It came from *somewhere,* but where, exactly, I couldn't immediately say. I glanced over my shoulder, expecting to see Ashley sleepily watching me from the doorway, but saw only my darkened, dormant study – the door (thankfully!) still firmly closed. And then it came again. Low down and to my right.

Outside.

In Dad's garden.

Where my hole had been.

I stepped back quickly, suddenly afraid to be seen and, perhaps more to the point, afraid *to see.* Someone was in Dad's garden – in *our* garden – and I wasn't sure I wanted to be witness to such bare-faced, intrusiveness, even as I realised I had no real choice and that this was something that had to be dealt with, and dealt with quickly.

Moving to one side so that I was partially concealed by the curtain, I once again looked out – spotting immediately the shadowy figure standing over my backfilled hole. The security lights hadn't come on, but in spite of the heavy, impassive darkness, I knew right away that the figure I was seeing was that of a woman.

Leaning in closer to the window, I started as she looked up at me – meeting my eyes and, I was convinced, smiling.

Leaving my study, I headed downstairs.

The night was surprisingly refreshing – the chill air immediately bringing me out in a rash of goose-pimples. I stepped out purposefully onto the patio, the paving cool and rough against my bare feet, and closed the door behind me – not wanting to make even the most obscure of invitations. It occurred to me briefly that I should have brought something with which to defend myself, but it was too late now and, if I'm truthful, I no longer thought that this was a threatening situation. There was a stranger (I assumed) prowling around in my garden, I was unarmed and very nearly naked, and, yet it didn't seem to me that I was in any kind of danger. In retrospect, I was naïve at best, bordering most assuredly on the foolhardy – but hindsight can only measure and quantify so much, and at the time there were influences of which I was only dimly aware at work.

Surprisingly, the security lights still hadn't come on. I stood stock still for a moment, listening intently and letting my eyes adjust, knowing that the woman I had seen from my study window was watching me, just waiting for me to make my move, I was sure. I stared in the general direction of where my hole had been – but the night still held tight to its secret, and no amount of squinting and straining could alter that. For a moment, I was aware of just how vulnerable I really was, taking an involuntary step back before my sense of security flooded back with a vengeance. I was not in danger. My world was as it had always been; safe, predictable – far removed from the trials and threats so common to others. I saw no reason why any of that should change – or, if it were to change, I saw no reason why now should be the time.

She was beautiful. That was what struck me first. Flesh the colour of concentrated moonlight, she stood silently before me – her hands hanging limply at her sides, naked and more vulnerable than I could ever be. Young – possibly in her mid-twenties – she nevertheless carried her large breasts lower than I would have expected, and her body showed scars and infirmities I would not have expected to see in a woman her age. Her ankles seemed puffy and swollen, and, among the too numerous healed non-medical scars, a partially healed laceration ran from the top of her right thigh to her knee. Eyes hooded, unkempt hair falling about her face, she seemed to look through me rather than at me – and, yet, I was quite certain that she was aware of me. She made no sign that this was the case (to begin with, at least), but I knew, just as I had known that I was in no real, immediate danger from this "stranger".

"Are you all right," I said quietly – not wanting to alarm her. She was standing where my hole had been, a few feet away from me, and now she looked up and, for the first time, met my gaze. Her eyes were quite unremarkable, but the look... that look was something else entirely. Hearts don't break. Souls don't crack open and seep spirit into the night. Time doesn't stand still – and the minds of strangers rarely connect in any meaningful way. And, yet, that was what seemed to happen to me that night. The woman stared into my eyes and reached out to me over a distance that was more than just the space between us. Her mouth opened and I thought for a moment that she was actually going to answer my question – but instead she merely smiled, the fingers of her right hand moving to the coppery, dense hairs at her vulva. I thought of Mrs. Sutherland – that fictional Maggie, Richard's walking, talking wet dream – and very briefly entertained the notion that I might have invented this encounter. A sleepless night of memories and dreams, sleepwalking, hypnagogic hallucinations, the spillage and seepage of fiction and mysterious memoir.

Her fingers slipped inside herself and she shuddered, still smiling that smile, her eyes still locked on to mine. She tilted her head back, tossing her unruly hair and staring down her nose at me. A wet little hiccup of a sigh escaped her and, still playing with herself, she started to walk towards me.

118

I didn't want to turn and run. I didn't want to avoid any part of this strange encounter. Whilst I wasn't actually aroused by this clearly damaged woman, I was attracted to her – attracted to the questions she represented, to the reason behind this shameless display. I wanted to understand her, help her even, and perhaps more pointedly, I wanted her to thank me.

She approached and I prepared myself for whatever was about to happen. This wasn't a sexual encounter, I kept telling myself. If Ashley were to witness this, she would understand immediately that the woman was clearly ill – disturbed and delusional. There would be no accusations, no teary threats and tantrums – and, yet, I hoped against hope that Ashley would remain in bed. I didn't want her or anyone else seeing this. Not because I was in anyway embarrassed by the encounter but, rather, because she was mine, nobody else's. Whatever life had subjected her to so that she should arrive here at this time of the morning, I was suddenly completely convinced that it was no one's concern but the woman's and my own. She had come here to see me, to ask my help – and as ridiculous a thought as it might have been, I acknowledged it as a kind of truth.

"It's okay," I said as she approached. "Everything's going to be all right." As far as reassurances go, it was admittedly pretty lame, but very briefly it seemed to reach her. She faltered and stopped, her eyes clearing as she took in my features. She pulled her hand away from her sex as if it had bitten her and gasped, truly registering my presence for the first time. She started to say something, and then shook her head – the befuddled thought quickly lost. And then the veil once more descended. Her expression fell away like a dying moth and she started walking towards me again, drawing her feet level with each other before taking another step, like a bride walking down the aisle.

Three steps apart, then two – and, finally, the woman was only a single step away from me. I expected her to stop there, but she didn't. She continued until our skin touched, until she moved into me and through me. I felt nothing – no shock or sense of dislocation, no fear or euphoria. The cooling night air raised a fresh rash of goose pimples, but that was it. The woman entered me, and left. She took nothing, but neither did she give anything.

I turned and watched her walk away, and then sat down on the lawn.

Someone was tugging at my sleeve. Someone or something. A dog, perhaps, or a persistent child. I pulled away, turning, determined not to succumb. I just wanted to be left alone in peace, alone so that I might finish my walk in the garden – passing through the archway into the bright, colour-rich day with all of its promise and reward. Briefly, I felt the grip on my sleeve –

what sleeve?

– loosen, and I spun away, the colours and flowers blurred and indistinct, but beautiful nevertheless. This was freedom. Those who fought for liberty knew nothing. It was attainable without brotherhood or bloodshed. A walk in the garden was all it took. Away from it all, adrift in a world of symbols and smells...

But then it was tugging at me again, speaking this time, shaking me as I pulled away. "Sonny! For fuck's sake, Sonny, what on *earth* do you think..."

Holding tight to a rhododendron, I pushed the voice away, determined not to recognise it or give in to its heavy-handed seduction, singing to myself, blocking it out.

This time more softly. Concerned. Afraid. "Sonny. Sweetheart? Come on, now, wake up, love."

I wanted to tell her that I was awake – didn't she fucking understand that? – but it was too late. The rhododendron turned to dust as reality rushed in at me, the early morning breeze too loud, the climbing sun a vile accusation. A pain ripped down my neck to my right shoulder when I moved and I felt suddenly wet and cold, my body sore and numb at the same time.

"Love?" Ashley was leaning over me, kneeling on the backfilled soil and holding my arm. I was in my hole again – or if not in it, on it – and I didn't have a clue how I had got here. I remembered the woman, and I remembered sitting down on the grass. But that was it. "What're you doing, sweetheart?" Strangely, she was close to tears, her throat working hard as she put her warm, dry palm to my forehead, eyes blinking rapidly. I tried to reassure her with a smile, a reply as yet beyond me, but this had entirely the opposite effect, her face crumbling as the full force of the sobs claimed her. "I thought you were dead," she spluttered, a little anger creeping in now. "Jesus, Sonny, you scared the fucking life out of me! What the hell are you doing out here? You'll catch your bloody death."

I sat up and she helped me brush the soil from my shoulder and the side of my face, waiting for me to answer but apparently happy to give me the time I needed. "I don't know," I finally said. "I couldn't sleep so... I remember coming out here to cool off and... I guess I must have sat down."

"You guess, or you did?"

"I did." I considered telling her about the naked woman, but given the state I was in I concluded that that would only alarm her further, and so decided against it. I needed to make sense of it myself first.

"So you weren't sleepwalking or anything?" she asked.

"No, absolutely not."

"So this... it's... you're not worried or anything?"

"What have I got to be worried about?" I answered lightly, wanting to put her mind at ease, but now that the safety of my dream garden had been taken away, I felt afraid and confused. Sitting shivering under an early morning sun, the events of the night before made no sense whatsoever. Dreamlike as they had been, I was nevertheless convinced they had happened.

"Oh, you know," Ashley said. "Us. The new baby and everything."

"I'm not worried, Ash," I said, still not fully recognising this for the lie that it was. "I came out here because I was restless and hot. I fell asleep. That's all there is to it."

"Honestly?"

"Would I lie to you?"

"Yes."

"Well I'm not. I've no reason to lie. Not to you."

"I'm pleased to hear it."

"I'm pleased you're pleased," I joked. I felt no guilt, only relief. Whatever had happened, I needed time to think about it – to put everything in its place and see the whole picture for what it really was. And I couldn't do that with Ashley looking over my shoulder, however much I might have wished otherwise.

"Let's get you inside and sorted before Nadine wakes up," she said – grabbing my forearm and pulling me to my feet. Every bone and fibre ached and I winced, steadying myself against the fence post when my knee popped a little alarmingly. "You're getting too old for this shit," Ashley told me as I hobbled up the garden path, my body slowly returning to me. "You need to start taking better care of yourself. Sleeping in the garden isn't good for anyone, but a man your age? No, not good, pet."

"What do you mean, a man my age?"

"Well," she said, shrugging. "You have to admit, you are knocking on a bit."

She was smiling, hoping I'd take the playful conversation further – but the truth was I was feeling every one of my thirty-eight years, and I didn't much feel like joking about it. I didn't want her to stop smiling, though. It was such a refreshing, uplifting sight. And so I stopped halfway to the back door – turning her to face me.

I didn't joke. I didn't trivialise her smile. Leaning in close, smelling baby powder and the slightly sweaty, familiar warmth of our bed, I kissed her softly. A sparrow chattered tunelessly and the sun warmed my painful right shoulder – and I felt something loosen in Ashley. Her weight shifted as the last of the fear and anxiety drained away, arms limp at her sides like a schoolgirl being kissed for the very first time. She closed her eyes, the experience focused in her lips – sight unnecessary, a mere distraction – and when we parted, the smile was broader than ever.

"What was that for?" she asked.

"Just because."

"I call you an old man and I get a kiss in return. I'll have to remember that."

"You didn't call me an old man," I pointed out. "You said a man my age."

"There's a difference?"

"Yes. I like being the age I am."

"Old, you mean?"

"As old as the woman you feel – isn't that what they say?"

"You're going to feel me?" The fear had gone entirely, now. She was just Ashley again. My wife – beautiful and unfulfilled, loving and lovely and sometimes a little lost. I remembered the woman, hurt and distant before me –

strolling down the front / with a finger up her cunt / ship ahoy / ship ahoy

lost and mysterious, and pushed the image away – not wanting anything or anyone to spoil this moment.

"Once my old bones have recovered, who can say?" My neck spasming painfully, I nevertheless held and kissed her again. "Sorry if I scared you," I said. "It won't happen again."

"Good." She pecked me on the cheek and brushed soil out of my hair, avoiding my eyes. "I really thought you were dead, you know. I saw you there and... I don't know, it was like there was no other explanation. And all I could think of was Maggie. How bad it must be for her without Jim. How does she cope, Sonny?"

"I don't know, love." I pushed her hair from her face; the ley lines of pillow creases still criss-crossed her cheek. "I suppose she just has to – for Wee Mark's sake."

Ashley considered this. It was the obvious answer and, yet, I got the feeling that she didn't find it all that plausible. "Do you think she resents him?" she asked.

"Jim?" I wanted to get in, have a couple of ibuprofen and take a shower – but I felt I owed Ashley a little consideration after the scare I had given her.

"No, Wee Mark."

I was confused, the woman of the night before still taking her peculiarly bride-like steps at the back of my mind. "Why would she resent Wee Mark?"

She shrugged and shook her head, dismissing the thought if not my question. "I don't know," she said, walking slowly back to the house with me. "I'm being silly but... it's just that... I don't know – if she feels how I felt when I saw you just now, it just seems to me she'd resent anyone who stood between her and Jim."

"And you'd resent Nadine?" It was the best answer I could think of.

Ashley smiled and shook her head. "No, I don't suppose I would," she said.

"Well there you go, then."

"How did you get to be so wise?"

Already feeling somewhat better, I followed her into the kitchen.

"Sleeping out under the stars?" I ventured.

Chapter Eight

As I watched him pick up his knife and stare at his reflection in the blade, I felt the by now familiar ache at the back of my neck. The ibuprofen had helped somewhat, but this dull, burning sensation had persisted – pushing my head unconsciously forward and weighing me down, so much so that had it not been for Ashley and my wish to keep up appearances, I would have cancelled my lunch with Oliver and spent the afternoon sleeping.

Oliver had spoken little more than a handful of words since I'd arrived at our favourite pub cum restaurant – five minutes late and dripping perspiration (which was only in part caused by the heat). He'd greeted me sullenly, his beard twitching in acknowledgement.

"I never thought vanity was your thing," I said – sipping my beer with a cursory glance at the menu.

"It's not," he answered, silently daring me to contradict him. "I'm just checking the cutlery for water stains. That's all right with you, I assume?"

Oliver could be as naggy and belligerent as the next man, especially when his work wasn't going well, but there was an undertone to the way he spoke today that suggested this was something more serious. He put his knife down beside his fork and stared out the window at the car park, giving me the opportunity to study his face more carefully. He still didn't look well. His eyes, distant and curiously sad, were ringed with sfumato bruises and, in spite of the glorious weather we'd been having, his skin was pale and puffy. It didn't take a genius to work out that he hadn't been sleeping.

Since that morning, I'd done my best not to think of the events of the night before – filing them away until I had time to examine them more closely, with the luxury of not being interrupted or watched. It had been far easier than I had expected and I had managed to sail through the couple of hours I'd spent with Ashley and Nadine without either of them figuring out that something wasn't quite right with me.

"Something strange happened to me last night," I told Oliver. To this day, I still don't truly know why I did it. I convinced myself at the time that it was merely a way of drawing Olly out, of getting him talking, but in retrospect, I'm not so sure. I felt alone, I think – alone and compelled, scared, even. Maybe I just wanted him to see that he wasn't the only one with shit going on in his life... or maybe I wanted to get him talking so that *I* might see that I wasn't the only one with shit going on in my life. Either way, it got his attention. He turned his face from the enthralling sight of the pub car park and regarded me, a quizzical, raised eyebrow making me think of Dad again, as I added, "You won't believe a word of it but, I swear, to the best of my knowledge, it happened."

"*To the best of your knowledge?*" It was good to see the wry smile distorting his in-need-of-trimming beard. "This is going to be interesting."

"It's no joke, mate," I warned.

"Even better."

"How'd you work that one out?"

"I'm not in the mood for jokes," he said. "Right now, I need a joke the way the Pope needs a vasectomy."

"And that's no joke," I joked.

"Amen." He folded his arms on the table after shooing Polly, the waitress, away with the menu (she knew us well and was more than familiar with Olly's various idiosyncrasies; unless I was mistaken, Polly actually seemed to find them endearing). "So this isn't going to end up being a disappointing alien abduction story, right? You aren't going to do a Whitley on me, I hope?"

"God forbid."

"He can't, you're an atheist."

"And God doesn't forbid atheists, too?"

Olly chuckled and sat back. "You've been taking lessons off that wife of yours," he said. "Sometimes I feel sorry for Molly."

"You do?"

"Not really, no. I'll tell you who I do feel sorry for, though."

"Who?"

"That kid of hers."

"Veronique."

"Veronique, yes. It's about time we stopped fucking pussy-footing around, in my opinion, and started acknowledging religion for what it really is."

"That being?"

"A form of child abuse."

He wasn't about to get an argument from me on that one – as extreme as some might consider the statement. Now that I'd started, I didn't want deviate.

I smiled and shook my head. "Anyway, no," I said. "It's not an alien abduction story."

"And your next door neighbour hasn't turned out to be a Bardo Thodol-reading Elvis Presley?"

Polly was standing a few feet away, pretending to wipe a table down as she eavesdropped. A bright girl who clearly found her job rather tedious, this was something she regularly did, with us, at least, and Oliver and I had silently agreed long ago just to let her get on with it. We talked about our fiction in the same way in which we talked about our lives, and if she could distinguish between the two she was a better man than I was.

"Do you want me to tell you about this..." I glanced at Polly. "Do you want me to tell you about this story or what?"

Oliver held up his hands in submission. "Sorry," he said. "Go ahead. Don't let me stop you."

And so I told him of the evening before – or, rather, earlier that day. I started with my restlessness, telling him how the heat and paint fumes had got to me. Ashley had gone out like a light, I explained, leaving me to listen to her breathing – steady and increasingly annoying. Faced with the choice of tossing and turning with the very deliberate intention of waking her up or getting up myself, I had opted for the more honourable course of action – going through to my study, not really knowing what I was going to do once I got there. I told Oliver a little of the texted conversation Ashley had had with Molly, and how this had coloured my thoughts, leading him to the reminiscences about my parents and the silly fakir with his Indian Rope Trip. By this point he appeared to be growing bored – glancing out of the window at the car park again – and so I moved quickly on to the woman I had spotted from my window, standing where my hole had been. I built on this, filling in the details as accurately as I could, but still Oliver continued to stare out of the window – the only indication that he was hearing me the occasional grunt and sniff. Finishing with my heading back into the house with Ashley, telling him that I hadn't wanted to worry her anymore than I already had, I sat back and awaited his no doubt incisive comments.

I was therefore disappointed, to say the least, when he waved a hand dismissively and said, "Hypnagogic hallucination."

"It wasn't a hypnagogic hallucination," I told him, doing my best to keep my voice down. Polly was a couple of tables away, but I could tell that she was still picking up enough on her radar to know that this was one of our more interesting conversations.

"How do you know?" His voice was laconic, way too soothing. He made me think of analysts; disinterested, unsurprised – perpetually impartial and locked into his own discipline. I wanted to grab him by the hair and bang his fucking head on the table.

"Because I've studied my Oxford Companion to the Mind, too," I told him impatiently. "It doesn't fit any of the bloody criteria."

"Those being?"

"I hadn't just woken up," I said, counting the points off on my fingers. "In fact, I hadn't been asleep *at all*. I wasn't on the verge of falling asleep – "

"To the best of your knowledge."

"*I wasn't on the verge of falling asleep,*" I reiterated. "The colours weren't vivid, the way you'd expect them to be with a hypnagogic hallucination and – "

"That's all well and good," he said with a hollow sigh. "But what do you suggest as an alternative explanation? Do you seriously believe that that woman actually *walked through you*?"

"Don't be so bloody ridiculous."

"What, then?" He leant in close over the table and added in an ominous whisper: "You think she was a *ghost*?"

Oliver could be a pain at the best of times. His peccadilloes were trademarked and accepted as par for the course. How many times had I said or heard other people say over the years of our friendship "oh ignore him – it's just Olly being Olly"? Too many to count, certainly –

but it had never been an issue, not really. His bluntness, his occasional lack of tack, was just that. It was Oliver and there was nothing behind it – no hidden agendas, no real animosity, even. This, however, was different. Oliver was setting out to attack me, it seemed, but still I got the distinct impression that there was more than that going on here. This wasn't about me.

"What the hell's wrong with you, Oliver?" I asked him.

He glanced out of the window again; childish denial and avoidance tactics were the order of the day. "I don't know what you're talking about," he insisted.

"Yes you do." I wasn't about to let this go. "You look like shit and you're being a bigger twat than usual. What's up, man?"

I felt something give. The tension that had been building between us eased and he turned his bloodshot eyes to mine and slouched down in his chair, stretching his arms out on the table. His lips so tightly pinched that they disappeared completely within his beard, I experienced an overwhelming sense of relief – both because Oliver was finally going to share something of himself with me, and because the attention had been taken from me. I no longer had to talk about myself.

When he spoke, he said only two words. *Donnelly McCrane.*

I was under no illusions. I knew Oliver well enough to know that he didn't give anything away without a fight – and therefore saw immediately that whatever it was that had caused his anxiety and preoccupation, it in truth had nothing to do with Don. That he was willing to share something of their relationship with me – after so jealously guarding the details for so long – merely served to underscore the seriousness of the situation.

"What about him?" I asked. "You seeing him again?"

Oliver shook his head. "Haven't seen him in a long time," he told me. "I hear from him occasionally – Christmas and so on – but that's about it."

"So what's the problem?"

"Oh, you know – it's one of those times."

"I'm not sure I follow."

"Last week was the anniversary of the two of us moving in together." He looked over his shoulder at Polly, decided to leave her to it, and then added, "I thought I was over it. The love and the lies but... it's as fresh as it ever was."

I didn't know what to say. Oliver had made himself more vulnerable than he ever before had and my mind was working overtime. That there had been love in their relationship didn't surprise me – but lies? This seemed unthinkable, and I have to admit that what I finally said was more out of curiosity than sympathy.

"What do you mean, lies?" I asked.

Oliver had once told me that people placed too much value in the "truth". He had been drunk at the time, the two of us tucked away in the corner of the grotty nightclub where Maggie and Jim had been holding their engagement party, but his twisted logic had made a kind of sense since I had also been well into my cups. His argument had been relatively simple; we die. We die and, yet, we none of us truly accept it until we are forced to. "Existence," he'd said, "is underpinned by that one right motherfucker of a lie and all other lies are, in comparison, poor imitations. And why do we do this? In an attempt to attain happiness for ourselves and others. Take you and Ash, right?" he'd continued. "You slipped it to Maggie that time down in Welsh Wales, yes?" As drunk as I'd been, I'd still known what rhetorical meant. "You gave her a right good fettling – practically fucked her in half, I wouldn't mind betting – and then what did you do, mate? I'll tell you – you both came home and lied. Lied and, through omission, continued lying. And why? Happiness. You enjoyed Wales. Maggie enjoyed Wales. And Ashley? Ashley loves you. She loves you and she's happy with your relationship because she knows nothing of your little indiscretion. Lies did that. Without lies, we probably wouldn't be here 'celebrating' today. Imagine what Jim would do if he found out." It had been a fairly typical Oliver observation, and not something I'd really paid all that much attention to – but now I found myself wondering if one of his cock-eyed philosophies had finally come home to roost.

"Just that," he now said. "Everything we'd had together had been founded on lies. Oh, yes, he loved me all right. There was absolutely no doubt about that. He loved me so much, in fact, he left his wife and three kids for me."

I gasped and sat up a little straighter – the effect a little melodramatic, but genuinely reflective, nevertheless. "He did *what*?"

"Left his wife and three kids, without my ever knowing about them." Oliver looked deflated – kicked and worn down. His breathing sounded slightly asthmatic. "I never even so much as suspected," he told me. "We moved in together and it was all so... well, it was just right. I worked, we lived in each other's pockets – we did that whole domestic thing. And we didn't have to work at it. It just all came so naturally. Then one day the duplicitous little toe-rag just blurted it out. Told me that it didn't change anything, not really, but there was something he had to tell me."

"A wife and three kids."

"A wife and three kids. He insisted he loved me. Leaving them was the best thing he'd ever done, he said – which, frankly, just made me fucking cringe. It hadn't been good between them for a long time but he'd never realised why until he met me. He went on and bloody on for hours, but I think he saw right away just how much of a mistake he'd made. In the end he was all but begging. I still hadn't said anything and he just kept at it. It was like... it was as if he thought saving what we had together was just a matter of keeping talking. Force me to remain silent. Wear me out and down. Don't let anything or anyone else in. You know what the worst part of it all was, though?"

"What?" I could hazard a guess.

"Lost potential," he said with a bitter little laugh. "It could have been so good, Sonny. Don and me... I trusted him. Trusted him enough to open myself up to him in a way I've never done with anyone else. I was prepared to think of myself as half of a couple – and I don't need to tell you what a big step that was for me. We weren't two people, we were *a couple*, and the future was looking brighter than it had in a long, long time. And then he dropped his bombshell and all that promise went out of the window."

"Why?" I understood what Oliver was saying. He felt somehow betrayed. His relationship with Don had been deeper than he had ever realised. Don had withheld some pretty important stuff – but surely it hadn't been something two grown men couldn't work out.

"Isn't that obvious?" he asked.

"I can't say it is, no," I answered. "I mean, yes – what Don did in

131

not telling you was wrong. There's no disputing that. He didn't involve you in the decision-making process, apart from anything else. He had a whole heap of baggage that you knew nothing about. But... wasn't that something that could be fixed? Isn't that what relationships are all about – learning the dos and don'ts together?"

Oliver smiled patiently. I was clearly being naïve. "I wish it were that simple," he said. "It might work for some, but I can't live like that. I need to live a life that I know to be as dependably true as a life can be, and I was no longer sure I could find that with Don."

I thought of quoting some of his historic, drunken rant on "truth" back at him, but decided against it.

"And now you're regretting splitting with him?" I asked – greedily wanting to keep the conversation moving, to delve deeper into his mysteries and thereby ignore my own.

"I suppose I am," Oliver said. "Or maybe I'm not – I don't know. It was the right decision. That much I do know. The right decision for me... probably for us both. But that doesn't stop me missing him. Especially at times like this."

"Have you talked to him since?"

Nodding, Oliver said, "We've talked, but we haven't really *talked* – if you see what I mean. And even that was a good while ago, now."

"Then maybe now might be a good time to get back in touch with him," I suggested. "See if you can't find a way of moving on from this – if not together, then apart."

"I don't want to get back with him." He said it too quickly – afraid that his most secret wish might gain a foothold.

"Don't you?"

"I don't know," he answered, rather more honestly, I thought. "I'm just not sure I could get what we had together back. Up until that point, I'd never even had to think about trust. It had just been there. If I got back with him now, that would be the predominant theme. We'd have to rebuild and I'd have to gamble and I'm just not sure I could do that."

"He's not worth it?"

"Probably. But that isn't the issue."

"So what is?" I was reminded of that fateful day at the caravan site when Oliver had helped me see that I couldn't turn away from my love for Ash just because she had been only sixteen. It seemed only fitting that I could now return the favour.

"Whether I can go back." This seemed to confuse even as it clarified. He frowned deeply and looked about to say more, but at that precise moment my mobile rang.

I glanced at the caller I.D. and held it up for Oliver to see. "Ashley. You mind?"

"Be my guest. Tell her she gets a slap next time she dares to interrupt me, mind."

"You wouldn't stand a fucking chance."

I knew something was wrong the minute I thumbed the answer button. I heard the faintly conch-shell whooshing sound of space, echoing, distant voices and urgent activity. My immediate thought was that something had happened to Nadine, but as Ashley spoke, purposefully but with a barely contained anxiety... hysteria, I might even have said – as she spoke, I realised with relief that my wife and daughter were safe. Something terrible had happened but thankfully not to them.

"I thought she was dead," Ashley said – the second time that had happened to her today. "Wee Mark was playing with the little boy next door – if beating shit out of him can be considered playing – and I just walked right into the kitchen, the way I always do, carrying Nadine because she wasn't in the mood for playing with Mark. And I thought she was dead.

"She tried to kill herself, Sonny. Maggie tried to gas herself."

"She wasn't going to call in," I told Oliver as I drove. "Her and Nadine were just going for a walk to the park and then straight home. But Ash had forgotten to have a wee before coming out and she didn't much fancy using the bogs in the park so..."

"That was a bit of luck." Oliver hadn't said much since getting in the car and I couldn't fathom how he was feeling about all this. It had been fairly clear when I first told him what had happened that he had been upset and concerned, wanting to get to the hospital as quickly as I, but as we drove he became more introspective and monosyllabic.

"Let's just hope a bit of luck is enough," I said, and Oliver nodded – shifting his bulky frame and trying to get comfortable in the confined space.

That was when it really hit me, I think. That realisation that someone with whom I shared the secret of my infidelity might already be dead. Alive in our hearts and minds until we were told otherwise, but quite possibly dead to those at the hospital with her. It seemed absurd that we didn't know – that we continued to drive on in ignorance – and so I gave Oliver my phone and asked him to phone Ashley, even though we were now only five minutes from the hospital.

"Voicemail," he said.

"Keep trying."

We found Ashley in the waiting room with Maggie's mother – Nadine and Wee Mark playing rather too noisily in the children's area in the corner of the room. She got to her feet immediately and walked over to meet us, allowing me to take her in my arms as the resolve that had apparently kept her going through all of this finally left her. Oliver stepped to one side and waited patiently whilst Francesca scowled at him suspiciously – no doubt counting the ways in which we had conspired to bring Maggie to this dark, alien place. I could almost hear her thinking "no one in my family has ever done anything like this before... what am I going to tell people?"

Ashley, with an effort, succeeded in getting herself under control. She stepped back and dabbed at her nose with a sodden clump of tissues and took a deep, fluttering breath. Tugging at her blouse, she fought for composure – shaking out the kinks and creases.

"They haven't told us anything," she said. "I've asked a dozen times but they just keep us waiting – fobbing us off like we don't matter."

"I'm sure they'll tell us something as soon as they can," I said. "Their number one concern right now is going to be taking care of Maggie. You wouldn't want them to compromise that now, would you?"

She shook her head. "No, it's just that I feel..." She faltered, the tears threatening again. "Until the paramedics got there it was just me, Sonny," she said. "Just me and Mags, you know? And I thought... I was the only one who could help her, and now there are all these other people she doesn't know and..."

Oliver stepped forward, touching Ashley's arm with a gentleness that his size belied. "I'll have a word," he told her. "See what I can find out."

She nodded gratefully and Oliver left, lumbering over to the reception desk. I knew from long experience that Oliver would not throw his weight around. He didn't have to; when people saw him coming, and then heard his usually well reasoned arguments, it was enough. Like everyone else he set out to "charm", the receptionist would bend over backwards to please him.

"She isn't helping," Ashley said, nodding in Francesca's direction. "If I have to listen to her telling me that she knew something like this was going to happen for much longer, I swear I'll put her through a bloody window. She hasn't got an ounce of feeling, that woman – for her daughter or anyone."

"She never did strike me as the motherly type," I said, watching Oliver lean over the reception counter, speaking softly to the young woman. She was already hooked, I thought. She would do whatever it took to make him happy – even the one thing he would never want.

"That's understating it," Ashley told me, glancing over her shoulder as the woman in question got to her feet and joined us – a stern, suspicious look robbing her face of the little beauty it might have possessed. "Uh oh," Ashley added in a hurried whisper. "Speak of the devil."

I greeted her politely enough but all I got in return was a terse nod and sniff. "What's he doing?" she said, looking over at Oliver. "Is he asking about my daughter?"

"He's just seeing if they have any more news," I said, sensing her unfathomable displeasure and not at all in the mood for her particular brand of stupidity.

"It's not his place." She glowered at me and on another occasion I might have been intimidated. She was a friend's mother – a one-time figure of authority who had demanded feigned respect in the very least. Even now, after all these years, my instinct was to bow down, give in to her imagined position and let her rule me the way she still tried to rule her daughter. But today I wasn't having any of that.

"Tough," I said.

"What did you say?" She was flabbergasted. Ashley's mouth hung open and I considered reaching over to close it for her – the way I'd once had to do for our baby daughter, lost in a forgotten yawn. I could be impressive when I put my mind to it, both my mother and Ashley had said that at one time or another. It was just that I didn't often make that choice (which probably made it even more impressive when I did).

"I said, 'Tough'," I said. "We're here to do whatever we can to help," I continued. "To help Maggie and Wee Mark – not because we have to, but because she's our friend and we love her. Now, if that interferes at all with your cock-eyed idea of how things should be, I feel for you, I honestly do. But, like I say, it's tough – because right now you aren't our priority. Understand me?"

She was not a woman to bow out gracefully. Hers was a very fixed idea of how the world should work, and anything or anyone that challenged that had to be dealt with in no uncertain terms. She took a measured step towards me, eyes righteously ablaze, and pointed her finely sculpted chin up at me.

"How dare you?" she hissed. "Who are you to think you can talk to me like that?"

"Your daughter's friend," I said.

"And that gives you the right to treat me like something you've trodden in?"

"No," I said, spotting the misplaced flicker of victory in her bitter smile. "What does, however," I quickly added, "is the fact that that's *exactly* how you've treated us over the years, and how you seem intent on treating us today. Oliver's trying to help, but all you see is a challenge. Why is that, Francesca?"

I wondered if perhaps I had gone too far. She was a woman in her sixties, a widow, and really I knew nothing of the life she had been forced to live.

Turning from us, she returned to her seat.

"That was a bit harsh," Ashley said.

I thought she was joking, but Ashley seemed serious enough. She watched Francesca sit back down and the pity Ashley felt was obvious in her soft features and the dejected sag of her shoulders. I'd only been doing what I thought best, I explained, a little annoyed that Ashley had sided with Francesca. "I just didn't like her attitude towards

Oliver – especially when he's just doing his best to be helpful. It simply wasn't fair."

"That's all well and good," she whispered, "but her daughter's fighting for her life in there. However she behaves, she deserves our compassion."

"This from the woman who was ready to put her through a window?"

Ashley wasn't up to this, and I think I realised it just in time. I backtracked quickly as the tears started to bubble up, telling her that, in all seriousness, I understood what she meant. We had to think about Mags and Wee Mark. That was what was important right now.

Nodding, Ashley let me take her in my arms as Oliver approached. She felt warm, slightly feverish, and I suddenly understood that, in spite of what I had just said, she and Nadine were my main priority in all of this. If tiptoeing around Francesca was what it took to get Ashley through this day, then so be it. If necessary, I would happily kow-tow endlessly to the old tart.

"The doc'll be out to see us in about five minutes," Oliver told us.

It was actually closer to fifteen, but under the circumstances nobody seemed inclined to point out his lack of punctuality. He looked about twelve, his white coat oversized and stained brown at the cuffs and collar, and I couldn't help feeling I knew him from somewhere. I was sure I was mistaken, but that was most certainly the impression the gentle smile gave me.

"You must be Maggie's mother," he said to Francesca. A natural.

"Yes." She looked up at him and for the first time today – perhaps the first time ever – I saw honest emotion on her face. Anger, hatred and fear commingled as she asked, "Is her little boy going to be motherless as well as fatherless?"

The doctor, who had introduced himself as Chris Compton, took this in his stride – smiling beatifically and shaking his head as he said, with a maturity that his appearance belied, "No, I'm glad to say there's absolutely no chance of that. Maggie is going to be just fine. We'll be keeping her in, just to keep an eye on her and so that we can assess her, but there's really nothing for you to worry about, I assure you."

"That's easy for you to say," Francesca told him – and, the plastic chair beneath his bulk echoing his sentiment, Oliver groaned.

Chris Compton had seen it all before, I was sure. The professional smile remained fixed and dilated as he clasped his hands before him and said, rocking on his heels a little, "I'm not sure I follow."

"It really isn't that difficult," Francesca told him. "You said there's nothing for me to worry about, and I said that that's easy for you to say. Is that really so complicated?"

Now that we knew that Mags was out of danger it appeared that the rules had once again changed. Ashley, until this time holding my hand tightly – her palm clammy – stiffened and tightened her grip, the muscles at her jaw clenching. "Do you have to be so fucking rude?" she asked Francesca – leaning in so close that her breath lifted Francesca's greying fringe. "The gentleman's trying to help – just like Oliver was," she added, a graceful recognition of the fact that I'd probably been right after all. "And all you can do is throw attitude back at him. Aren't you familiar with the phrase 'thank you'?"

Doctor Chris Compton looked for a way out, glancing over his shoulder before apparently realising that his work here wasn't quite finished. He blushed and started to tell us that Maggie was resting and that it would probably be best if we came back the following day to see her, but Francesca, bless her, was already in full flow.

"You think someone deserves my thanks, do you?" she said. "That it? Well let me tell you something, my girl, I have no one to thank. *No one.* Why? Because no bugger has ever done me any favours – especially that bloody jumped up daughter of mine."

"How can you say that?" Ashley was indignant – her voice choked and rich with something akin to grief.

"Because it's true," Francesca told her. "She's just like the rest of you – puts herself first, never considers the consequences of her actions." She pointed at Wee Mark, playing quite nicely with Nadine. "Look at him. A lovely little boy. A bit of a bugger, but what boy his age isn't? And what would have become of him if she'd died? No mam or dad, his remaining grandparents knocking on a bit. Where would he have ended up?"

"And that doesn't tell you anything?" Ashley asked, the tears falling freely now. "She was prepared to leave the little boy she loves behind and that doesn't tell you anything?"

"It tells me she's as selfish now as she's ever been."

Chris Compton had heard enough. With real authority, he went down on his haunches in front of Francesca and said, "There's something you have to bear in mind, here. Maggie is ill. She's done nothing wrong and she certainly doesn't need guilt and recriminations."

"I'm her mother," Francesca told him. "I'll be the one to decide what she does or doesn't need."

"And I'm her doctor," he answered. "If I think you're going to interfere with her recovery I *will* recommend that you aren't allowed to see her."

"You can't do that."

"I think you'll find he can," Oliver said. "And if it were up to me, I'd have him make that recommendation now."

Francesca regarded him with total and unyielding hatred. Her hands clenched in her lap and her neck stiffened with indignation and in preparation for what was about to come next. Around us, the waiting area became busier. A couple of paramedics rushed a guy on a stretcher through the double doors at the north end of the room – the guy looking in a bad way. I heard clattering and chattering, concerned whispers and the inevitable tears, but nothing really sank in other than what Francesca was saying and the self-righteous sneer that bitterly distorted her features.

"So you think, what?" Francesca said. "That I'm not fit to be around my own daughter, is that it? That I'm bad for her?"

Unwaveringly, Oliver answered. "Yes," he said. "Actually, now that you mention it, I do."

"And you're qualified to say? Someone who'll never know what it's like to be a parent?"

"You're all upset," Doctor Chris Compton tried vainly to interject. "Maybe you should all just – "

For all his weight and muscle, Oliver was really a quite gentle chap. Yes, he could lose his temper as easily as the next man – and, yes, there had been occasions when he had been more than happy to use his fists – but at heart, he was a pussycat... an admittedly very large pussycat, but a pussycat nonetheless. Faced with such a personal slight, however, hitting him in a place all but guaranteed to be tender,

I wasn't sure how he might react – and therefore braced myself. In his shoes, I would have found it difficult not to pin her to the wall and rip her bloody vindictive head off.

But Oliver was better than me. I'd always suspected it and now I had my confirmation. He took a breath that seemed to go on forever, and then, with grave consideration, said what he had to say.

"I've had to watch you undermine Maggie's confidence time and again over the years," he said. "So, to answer your question, yes, I do think I'm qualified. In my opinion, speaking as someone who actually may one day be a parent, I think Maggie would be far better off without you."

And there it was said – the one thing we'd all thought at one time or another, I suspected. First my attack, then Ashley's (in spite of her not being too keen on what I'd said to Francesca) and now this. It really wasn't her day.

Vitriol and cruelty wouldn't have been surprising. A further assault on Oliver and his sexuality wouldn't have caught any of us of guard – except for our poor, unsuspecting doctor friend. But what Oliver got by way of a reply was nothing like that at all.

"Maybe you're right," she said, in a tone that suggested she thought nothing of the sort. "I've tried my best to keep her away from negative influences, but maybe that's where I went wrong. Maybe I should have just let her get on with it.... So we'll see, shall we?"

Francesca stood suddenly, almost knocking the crouching doctor over. She straightened her jacket and looked at the three of us. "Yes, we'll see," she repeated, and left saying, "You take care of her. I wash my hands of the whole sorry mess."

Midnight – that hour for witches and ghouls, when coaches turn back into pumpkins and horses into mice – found Oliver and I sitting on the low garden wall, drinking beer with whisky chasers and staring drunkenly at the place where my hole had been whilst we made half-hearted attempts at working out what to do about the problem of Mags and her mother. We had returned late that afternoon, bringing Wee Mark with us, and after much discussion and a little food, Ashley had put the kids to bed and retired herself – our agreement that the three of us would do whatever we had to to get Maggie through this hanging in the air with faux sincerity. It was more responsibility than any of us wanted, but now that Francesca (or Oliver?) had so supremely dropped us in it we had no real choice but to do the best we could.

"That's where the hole was, right?" Oliver asked – pointing with his Stella bottle. I answered in the affirmative for about the tenth time, and he nodded to himself. "Interesting. And you're sure you didn't, you know, unearth any bones or anything?"

This was a new line of questioning. It required another shot of scotch.

"Bones?"

"The physical remains of the dead," he elucidated keenly. "You know. The shin bone's connected to the knee bone. The knee bone's connected to the shoulder bone – "

"Thigh bone."

"Whatever. You get the gist, though, right? Bones."

"Bones?"

"That's what I said. Bones. Dig any up?"

I thought about the day before – watching Time Team with Ashley whilst she'd fired theological texts back and forth with Molly. Two bodies in a grave. Phil brushing away at the skull with loving attention.

"Disarticulated," I said.

"I beg your pudding?" Oliver was pouring himself another whisky. He seemed in a better frame of mind than he had earlier – but then he was knocking it back as though prohibition was about to be introduced.

"Disarticulated," I repeated.

"I heard ya, but I don't get ya. Explain, please."

I wasn't sure exactly what I meant, and, yet, it somehow made perfect sense. Nothing was where it should be was about the best explanation I could come up with, but Oliver seemed to find this satisfying enough. Intoxicated, the world made more sense; expressing that sense, however, was something of a chore.

"So no bones, then?" Oliver said – sounding rather too disappointed for my liking.

"No bones," I assured him. "Only the journal."

"Only the journal." He emptied his whisky glass and poured us both another before asking, "Only the journal?"

It was the one aspect of my life I'd intended to keep to myself – at least for the time being – but now it seemed my secret was at least partially out. I considered back-peddling, making something up to put Oliver of the scent, but of all my friends and acquaintances, he was by far the shrewdest and least likely to be diverted. And so I followed the only workable course available to me and told him the full story.

Oliver didn't reply immediately. He walked over to the spot where the hole had been and squatted down – drinking and fingering the soil ruminatively. He hummed to himself as he sometimes did when attempting to mull over an imponderable, then stood and faced me – quite suddenly, his features difficult to read in the poor light.

"It's not disarticulated," he said. "You haven't got it at all, have you?"

I didn't have a clue what he was talking about and said as much.

Sitting back on the wall beside me – the wall where I now couldn't help feeling that all of this had started with Maggie telling me about her stalker – Oliver put his glass down by his feet and leant in close. "It's connected," he said. "The woman in the journal and the woman you saw last night – they're connected. Surely you must have spotted that. They're one and the same, mate – they have to be."

The proposition was ludicrous. Real life just didn't work like that, I told myself – it was untidy and beyond sense or explanation... lived in denial, as Oliver might have said, whilst form and order was relegated to works of fiction and the failing crutch of religion. My life, like every other, was like Phil's Time Team skeleton; the thigh bone was not connected to the knee bone, so fuck the word of the Lord.

And, yet, I could certainly see what Oliver was saying.

"So you think she was, what? A ghost?" I said. "My unearthing the journal disturbed her?"

Oliver shrugged. "Dunno, mate," he said. "Maybe the journal just got into your head and, you know, you hallucinated her."

"I didn't suffer an hallucination," I told him, a little pissed off that we were back to this. "Hypnagogic or otherwise."

"You have to admit it as a possibility, at least."

"I don't have to do anything of the sort." In a vain attempt to make the whole thing more real to him, I got to my feet and stood where I had been the night before. "I was here, right?" I said – as if this in itself were a proof. "And she was over there." I pointed, my hand not quite as steady as I would ideally have liked. "I say something to her. Ask her if she's all right, something like that, and then she starts walking towards me with... well, you know."

"A finger up her cunt. Yes, you told me." He sighed and arched his back, the injury from his last bus push still bothering him. "Listen," he said, "just answer me one thing, Sonny. You say you spoke to her, yes?"

"Yes."

"So what did you say to her?"

I briefly wondered what it would feel like to hit him over the head with a beer bottle.

"I asked her if she was all right."

"Your exact words were, 'Are you all right?'"

"Yes," I said – really meaning "maybe".

"Are you sure about that, Sonny?"

I couldn't stick him when he acted the smug little shit. He nodded to himself with leering satisfaction when I didn't reply and said, "There. That's what I mean. If we can't remember what we said, *exactly*, how on earth can we rely on what we remember of a particular incident?"

"Because it's all we have, you fucking prick." I hadn't meant to say that last bit out loud, but now that I had I had to admit it felt rather good.

"Fucking prick?"

"That's what I said, didn't I?"

"And you're sure about that?" He was grinning now. I wasn't convinced this was a good thing.

Oliver patted the wall beside him. "Sit down," he said. "There's something I think I should tell you."

What Oliver said next would change the way I would view the world and the events happening around us incalculably. It was true that some part of me still insisted on rationalising, on finding writerly explanations in the most ridiculous of places, but, essentially, I accepted what he told me as fact – and in so doing was forced to

143

accept a whole new realm of possibility. As he sat beside me on that wall, talking to the whisky glass held between his knees, I heard his weariness and confusion surface but, for my part, only found in this a kind of confirmation. It didn't matter that I didn't actually understand what was happening to Oliver, not then – only that it allowed me to see that I wasn't going insane, that in some obscure way I was not alone.

"It must have been... I don't know," he said, "a few days after the bus pull. The night after you came round for a bite to eat, I think. I'd been working all day on that bloody story for Boots. She wants it for this anthology shit. Thinks it'll up my profile because there's something by Paul Auster and William Boyd in it, too, and I was fed up to the back teeth of it. She knows I hate writing to a fucking brief, thick bitch." He shook his head at the futility of it all and sipped his scotch – holding it in his mouth before continuing. "So I thought I deserved a break…. That what I told you earlier? About Don? It was all true. He's been on my mind a hell of a lot and... coupled with the exhaustion of working until close on midnight I wasn't exactly in a very good frame of mind. I watched a shitty DVD – something with De Niro in it – drank, and read some Camus. Not a good combination. Within an hour I was drunk enough to appreciate the irony of my existence but still sober enough to step back from it a little and realise that it could be a hell of a lot worse and that there was nothing in my life that couldn't be fixed. It would have been a very entertaining scenario if it had been happening to someone else, but I couldn't really find it in my heart to appreciate it. I... I wanted to lose myself, Sonny. You know how that feels, right?"

I nodded slowly. "Show me a man or woman who doesn't and I'll show you someone who's already lost."

"Exactly." We clinked glasses and he continued. "So that was where I was in my head. Exhausted from the work and endlessly wondering how Don was doing, if I'd made the right decision – thinking that maybe I wasn't destined for greatness after all and that perhaps I'd finally reached the point where I, like billions of other people, was going to end up alone in a fucking old folk's home, unloved and with shit running down my leg."

"Just your average day in Oliverville, then."

"Don't be flippant," he said sternly. "This is serious."

"Sorry."

"I should think so, too."

Interrupting his narrative was not a good idea. Like any writer, Oliver had a way of telling a story that was very much his own – his thought process easier for me to understand than it was for others more because we were friends than anything to do with the fact of our both being writers. Everything had a point, for Oliver. Everything was seamlessly connected – one thought leading him to the next – and to break the chain was to risk bringing the story to a premature end.

I waited, hoping that the damage was not irreparable, and after a long and studied silence, he finally continued – haltingly to begin with, and then with more grace.

"I was... it was tempting to just, you know," he said. "Just give in and mope. Indulge myself in the unhealthiest of ways. But thankfully I caught myself just in time. I tossed Camus in the basket with the other fucking waste paper, poured the rest of the booze down the sink, told De Niro to fuck off and went out for a walk.

"It was after midnight by this point. It was overcast and there was a storm in the air. Sticky, but it still felt bloody good to be out there. Everything was so frigging *silent*. So calm. Just what I needed, I thought.

"You know the cemetery on Park Lane?" he asked me. "The old one?"

I knew it well enough. My parents were buried there – one of the last two, in plots Dad had bought years before, before the council had opened the new, flat, wind-plane of a cemetery over by the municipal golf course. It was everything a cemetery should be, the one on Park Lane. A Victorian antidote to the stark uniformity of its modern equivalent – and as a child, I like many others had enjoyed playing there among the crooked headstones and the family tombs, collecting conkers when the season was right and wondering if the dead really did "walk" at midnight, as my cousin had insisted.

Very quietly, I said "yes" – not wanting to interrupt Oliver's story further with memories of my own.

"That's where I ended up," he told me. "The gates hadn't been locked, unusually, so I just walked in without thinking. After Camus,

145

it seemed curiously life-affirming and my mind cleared almost immediately. I walked along the narrow, broken Tarmac paths, through the topiary archways and between all those *graves* and I just felt this completely un-fucking-expected calm descend. Don't get me wrong. I was still thinking about Don. Everything that had been going around in my head for the last hour or so was still there, but I could deal with it better. Whether all those graves acted as a *memento mori* and helped me gain some perspective, I don't know, but I definitely felt better... initially, at least."

The night air had cooled considerably whilst we had been talking. I wore only jeans and an old tee shirt, my feet bare, and when Oliver mentioned the graves and, more especially, the topiary archways, the hairs on my arms stood on end. I recalled yet again something from my childhood. A childhood only with great effort finally overcome, those archways had at one time haunted my dreams. There had been nothing all that original to the imagery in those dreams, just the simple, age-old motif. Through those evergreen portals, something *other* had existed – a world separate from the one with which I was familiar, something alien and, yet, subtly connected to the very thing that made me who I was. I hadn't understood it as a child, and as I thought about it now I still wasn't sure I fully grasped its finer points. All I really knew was that I was chilled and suddenly quite sure that the place to which Oliver was very pointedly leading me was one from which it would not be easy to return.

He seemed to sense my trepidation, pausing for a moment as if to let my thoughts catch up before pouring himself yet another drink and continuing.

"There's an old oak in the north-east corner," he told me. "I used to play there when I was a kid. With a girl called Glenda." He laughed at the memory. "She was a right sort. Always seemed to have nits and a snotty upper lip, but she was uninhibited and a bit of a tomboy, so we got on like a house on fire. Even lost my virginity to her, later on."

"I didn't think a man of your standards could stoop so low," I said with mock-disgust. "I mean, *a heterosexual act!* What next? Two point four kids and a mortgage?"

He smiled but in essence ignored me. "She was actually a nice lass," he told me. "We did it a few times and it wasn't bad. I think we

146

both suspected something wasn't quite right but... well she was kind and surprisingly understanding – so that oak tree has a lot of good memories for me. I learned stuff about myself there that otherwise might have taken years for me to understand. So that's where I headed. The oak tree."

This seemed to be taking forever and my instinct was to hurry him – prod and guide him. I resisted, however, setting the lager aside now and concentrating on the scotch, in need of warmth and a softer focus.

"I sat under that oak and I could almost hear Glenda laughing in the branches above me. I stopped thinking about Don. I stopped thinking about my work. I even stopped thinking of the old folk's home and the shit running down my leg. Suddenly a nine-year-old Glenda was there beside me – lifting her skirt to examine a pimple on her fanny, just as she had during our first summer together – and the ease and innocence of such a strong memory was... well, I suppose for the briefest time I actually achieved what I'd set out to; I lost myself. Nothing mattered except the memory and as I explored it more and more, remembering Glenda's earthy, chip-fat smell, I found myself growing calmer and calmer.

"But I didn't sleep or doze," he added quickly. "I'm going to stress that now because I don't... well, you'll know what I mean soon enough."

Someone was watching us. The back of my neck prickled and I suddenly found myself looking up. I thought I saw Ashley at my study window – staring down at us – but it was only the night's shadow, smoky against the pane.

"I wanted to remember everything," Oliver said. "About Glenda and the games we played, I mean. So I got to my feet and started walking in circles around the oak – singing the old songs and remembering the game of solitaire I'd made for her by digging holes in the ground with a stick and collecting the right number of pebbles.

"And then something made me stop. It wasn't a noise, as such but... I was aware of a movement. For one ridiculous moment I imagined it was Glenda, squatting for a piss on the other side of the tree as she so often would, but whatever I heard or felt was too heavy for that."

This was what he had been building up to. He got to his feet and

147

stood with his back to me, whisky glass in one hand, the other hanging limply at his side.

"We never liked each other," he told me. "And if I could have chosen who to see that night, his name would have been way down on the fucking list, I can tell you. But I guess life doesn't work like that."

I felt eyes on me again, but I tried to ignore the sensation – knowing that if I thought about it too deeply I would find myself returning to the night before, to my own mystery with her measured, bride-like steps and her wandering fingers.

"Of all the people," Oliver said, sipping his whisky, elbow high as a salute, and shaking his head. "Of all the people it could have been..."

"Who was it?" I asked, unable to help myself.

Oliver looked over his shoulder and appraised me. Only when he was apparently satisfied did he answer.

"Jim," he said, and turned away.

Chapter Nine

Watching her dress was an affirmation. She wasn't perfect – this much he knew from the steady hours he had spent surveying the limitless contours of her body – but she had taken pretty good care of herself, and it was certainly true that he would be proud to be seen out with her... were they to ever actually go out together.

"I'm sorry," she said quite suddenly. Richard was confused. As far as he was concerned, she had no reason to apologise. "It was a little over the top," she added, but he was still none the wiser.

Standing by the curtained window, wearing only what they now referred to as "the criminal shorts", Maggie's face was obscured by shadow. A hand moved to her face and he thought for a second that she was dabbing at her eyes.

"Over the... What was?" he asked, propping himself up on an elbow.

"Me," she told him. "I just... it helps, that's all."

And then he understood.

At first it had surprised him. Even now, after a month of "being with" Maggie, he could not really think of himself as "experienced" – but he suspected that no matter how many women he had been with he would still have found her actions a little surprising, to say the least.

It had been like all the other times they had spent together – heady and wholly involved, so intense he doubted his luck as well as his ability to control himself. Maggie had understood, however, as she always did, whispering sweetly in his ear, soothing him as she guided his hands, telling him that they had all the time in the world – that they had forever and nothing or no one would ever come between them. And everything was going to be all right. Her kisses had left blemishes of warmth on his neck, a flush to his cheeks, and as the two of them had worked towards their climax, it had happened.

Very deliberately, Maggie had bitten her lower lip – drawing blood and taking herself over the edge.

Maggie now dabbed at the bite with the tissue and stepped out of the shadows. He saw she was crying and felt lost and confused. He should say something, tell her as she had told him that everything was going to be all right, that it would be okay – nothing and no one would ever come between them. But he couldn't. Nothing he said would ever make a difference because she was a women and he was just a boy with a stiffy. And at the end of the day –

"It's just something I've always done, occasionally," she said. "Jim used to hate it so I stopped doing it with him. Tonight, with you, though... I just didn't think you'd mind."

"I didn't," Richard said quickly. "It didn't bother me at all. Whatever it takes, right?"

She was studying him carefully and he really didn't know what to make of all of this. What was he supposed to say? Nothing seemed appropriate, nothing seemed convincing to his fifteen-year-old ears.

"Do you have to go home tonight?" she asked him.

"No," he said – relieved that the strange moment seemed to have passed. "I told Dad I was staying at a mate's. Like he gives a shit."

"Good," she said. "There's something I want to show you."

Richard knew what disappointment was. He'd lived with it all his life, his parents a constant reminder of its ineffable reality. Every Christmas and birthday had highlighted it in all its ignominy, and only by lowering his expectations had he found a way of making it a little more bearable. He saw the world as merely the possibility of more disappointment, however miraculous his present – and, so, when Maggie told him that she had something to show him, he merely smiled and waited as she walked over to the DVD player and put a disc in.

"I know you think it's all so, so old fashioned and tacky," she said, "but I like him and I really want you to give it a try."

Surely enough, it was as disappointing as he had anticipated. He'd never actually disliked Elvis, would even go so far as to say that he sort of admired the guy, but the '68 Comeback Special wasn't exactly new to him – and, truth be known, he actually thought some of it was the worst television he'd ever seen. The black leather "in the round" jam session was pretty cool, as was the "If I Can Dream" finale, but the choreographed sequences were just bloody appalling. Nevertheless, he dutifully lounged beside Maggie on the rumpled bed and absorbed as best he could every minute of it.

"It might sound ridiculous," she told him during a silly dance-fight scene, "but he's just always been there. He's been a constant in my life and... I don't know, that just seems pretty special. You know what I mean?"

Nodding, he said, "With you it's Elvis, with me it's Marmite. Got me through so pretty bad times has Marmite. Don't know where I'd be without it. If it wasn't for Marm – "

"Yes, all right, I get the message." This was better, he thought. Back to how it was before that lip-biting nonsense. She slid down the bed a little and put her head on his chest, slapping his knees out of the way so that she could see the telly more easily. "I still don't know how you can have the audacity to compare Elvis to Marmite, though," she said – tongue firmly in cheek. "A girl like me could find that quite offensive."

"You're trying to tell me that there hasn't been a time when you wouldn't have fancied your Mr. Pelvis between a couple of slices of bread?"

Richard still wasn't completely sure what Maggie thought of him. It was clearly true that she found him physically attractive, but when she considered him before answering what was, when all was said and done, a perfectly innocuous question he felt somehow wary. She knew things he probably never would, he realised. Her experience went beyond this village and the people in it – and whether he should have or not, he found that threatening.

He dead husband was a prime example. She had told Richard hardly anything about him at all, held back, it seemed, that part of herself so completely that it was almost as if she'd wished him dead – either that or she just didn't want to share that part of her life with Richard. And yet Richard felt that Jim was somehow always present. He resided in the soft furnishings and the choice of wallpaper, and persisted in Maggie's choice of perfume. Whenever Richard went to the toilet – about the only time he was ever alone in the house – it wasn't Maggie he imagined sitting on the loo prior to him. He didn't think of her hissing trickle as he once would have, or the way she'd sometimes hum a tune to herself distractedly as she finished draining off – but instead imagined Jim thrutching, reading the Telegraph, perhaps, or gripping his knees with his hands in preparation for the final push. And the more he tried to ignore the image, the more stubbornly insistent it became.

"I'm a little more realistic than that," she finally told him. "He wouldn't have fit."

It was a poor attempt at a joke and they both knew that something wasn't quite as it should have been. They were both trying too hard – Richard with his predominant thoughts of Maggie's dead husband, she with he didn't know what. She rolled away from him and stared at the ceiling, taking hold of his hand and lacing her fingers between his. There was a tension he didn't understand, a quiet consideration that made him want to leave – find someone his own age and get off his fucking head – even as he in turn wanted to roll over and embrace her. It was the lip thing again, he thought. She was still worried for some bloody ridiculous reason that it had upset him – that he would be like Jim, that old fart of a frigging ghost, and tell her not to do it again. But when she spoke, squeezing his hand more tightly, he saw that it wasn't that at all.

"People never really get it," she told him, "but it was bad – it was bad and without Elvis and his music I might never have made it. And, yes, I do know how sad and pathetic that sounds, but it's true and I sure as fuck aren't going to deny it just because of what people think."

This last was stated almost angrily and Richard now turned to face her – placing a hand on her bare arm and gently running it up and down. "It doesn't sound pathetic," he told her. "It sounds... well, reasonable, you know?"

"You think so?"

"Aye, I do. If your childhood was owt like mine..." He shrugged and looked away, not wanting to even think of going there.

"It was pretty horrendous," she said. "Jim could never understand how it still affected me so much and... well, I just used to tell him he didn't have a clue what isolation was like until he'd lived the kind of childhood I had. It changes you in unimaginable ways – and changing back just isn't that easy or simple."

Richard wasn't quite sure what she was saying. "Isolation?" he asked.

"My parents were divorced," she told him. "It was a nasty business and Dad... he just dropped out of my life."

"Wish mine would."

"Yes, I know, love – but my dad was nice. Apparently not nice enough to fight for his daughter, but nice enough that I missed him more than I ever thought I would. He left and it was just me and Mam. A bad situation made worse by the fact that she moved me to the back of beyond – a poky little cottage miles away from the nearest village. It was bloody awful. She made out she was doing it for my own good, that keeping me away from negative influences was what every parent was meant to do. Which is true to a point, I suppose, only she... she took it to the extreme."

"You went to school, though, yeah?"

"To start with – but the cottage was damp as hell and I was ill a lot of the time. I started going less and less until... well, I guess I must have slipped through the net. Mam taught me, after her own idiosyncratic fashion, but most of it I just picked up myself from books and magazines and the telly. Mam liked the way things were working out, you see, so she indulged me. Any books or records I wanted and they were there. Most of the time I didn't even have to ask. They just appeared. As if by magic. Anything to keep me there with her, away from all the shit going on in the world... away from all the fun.

"What's the longest you've gone without speaking to anyone?" she suddenly asked him.

He shrugged. "Dunno. A day or two when Mam left, maybe. Something like that."

"I once went six whole months without saying so much as one word to another living soul."

"You're joking."

"I wish I was. I didn't need to speak to Mam, you see, and anyone else... well, I was alone, Richard. Utterly and completely alone in this strange little world of books, television and Elvis. It got so's I didn't need to speak and then, before too long, I just didn't want *to. Speaking made me feel even more isolated, so I stopped doing it all together."*

It wasn't too difficult for Richard to imagine what this must have been like. Hadn't he been in a similar place before that strangely mythical day when she had sat down beside him on that bench and started talking? He didn't like to look back at those times, now – however recent – but the similarity between himself and Maggie was striking, and he wondered if perhaps she hadn't understood that better than he during that first encounter. Two people locked in their own insular version of reality, looking for a way out without ever realising it.

"When did it all end?" he asked. "You're isolation, I mean."

"August, nineteen-eighty-three. I was sixteen and it was the sixth anniversary of Elvis' death. It had been a fairly average summer but I'd still managed to spend a lot of time in the garden. I'd developed quite a taste for sunbathing and when Mam wasn't home I'd strip off naked and soak up whatever sunshine there was whilst listening to Elvis on my Walkman. It was, looking back, a lot better than it could have been, that summer. I wouldn't say I was exactly happy, but I'd somehow constructed an existence that helped me deal with the peculiar circumstances. I didn't need to leave. I didn't need to get away. By this time the very idea of the outside world frightened me. Whatever else Mam had done to me, she'd provided me with a sense of security that I just couldn't imagine being replicated any other way. Elvis sang "In the Ghetto" and the sun warmed me and all was not well with the world, but it was bearable and at least I was safe."

"But something changed?"

Maggie shuffled closer to him, their shoulders touching. He suddenly wished he had known her then – that they had been the same age and had been locked together in shared isolation, brother and sister, perhaps, thrown into an incestuous but completely real relationship like those characters in the book he remembered his Mam reading. Not so much Flowers in the Attic, *more* Dandelions in the Cellar.

"Something changed," she whispered. "At first I couldn't put my finger on it. My times in the garden were different. I usually undressed in my room and would come out in a robe that I'd take off once I was comfortable, but now I started undressing out there – slowly, enjoying the act itself. It was confusing for me. I knew about sex, and masturbated a lot – sometimes three or four times a day if there was

154

nothing interesting on the telly – but this was different. I didn't feel alone. I felt as if there was someone in my garden with me. Watching me. Wanting me. I couldn't see anyone but... well, initially, I didn't look very hard. It confused me, but I liked it. I'd been alone for just about as long as I could remember and now I felt someone was there with me and I realised it was a good feeling. If I was being watched, I didn't care. It was a kind of interaction and that was better than nothing, so if someone was spying on me, so be it. I wanted to be watched and whether I was imagining it or not I was determined to put on a show."

"That's why you didn't mind me watching you," Richard said – the whole thing finally making sense. "You saw me as..."

"My way out," she told him. "A way to escape my isolation. My salvation." She laughed softly and rolled on her side so that she could look at him. "After Jim died, you see," she said, "it was almost like being back at home with Mam. I felt cut off, too safe and secure, too reliant on myself. And then you started watching me and it was like being back in my garden again, feeling his eyes on me and knowing there was an opportunity there if I was just willing to take it."

Three days before, Richard had come very close to breaking their cardinal rule. Talking to the brash, sickeningly successful Alan Altman outside the chippy he had listened with uncharacteristic patience as the prick had told him of his latest conquest – a girl called Kara Jackson. Kara was a stuck-up bitch with more airs and graces than a royal banquet, but she had the blackest hair imaginable and legs that Richard, before Maggie, had imagined himself working his way up on numerous occasions. She had all the personality of a sheet of A4 paper, but Alan, like most of Richard's year (many of the girls included), had nevertheless wanted a piece of her. The difference was, he had apparently succeeded where all the others had failed – and he had taken great pleasure in sharing the details with Richard. After five minutes of hearing how wet and tight her cunt had been, how she had pissed herself when she had come and let him fuck her up the arse – Richard had grown bored and said, "What does she smell like?" It had been a stray thought voiced, one inspired by the memory of the very smell he was smelling now – that warm oceanic smell of sleep and sex, the Maggie smell – and Alan had thought it hilarious. "Shit an' spunk after I've finished with her," he'd said, laughing at the ridiculousness of the question – and right then Richard had been so close. It would have been the easiest thing in the world just open his mouth and tell Alan about all the things he and Maggie had done together, how great the sex was and how he loved the simple closeness that came with conversation and history. But he'd held his tongue and now, smelling her smell – smelling their *smell – he was glad he had.*

"It was four weeks before I saw him," she said. "But by then I'd already made up my mind what I was going to do."

Richard listened as she told him her story.

"By the time he revealed himself to me, I'd had time to prepare. I had clothes and toiletries in an old sports bag of Mam's, food in case the journey was long and a couple of my favourite books. It didn't matter who he was. I knew he wasn't dangerous, because he'd had plenty of opportunities to harm or take advantage of me and hadn't taken them, and that was all I really cared about. But that's not to say I didn't have an idea who he was. It was all too obvious to me then. All those years of isolation, I'd actually had a companion, even if I'd never realised it, and it seemed only natural and just that he should be the one who would now rescue me.

"It was one of the cooler days of the summer but that afternoon, I still followed my usual routine while Mam was out at work. The only part that differed was that this time I took my packed bag out into the back garden with me and locked the door – knowing in my heart of hearts that this was a place I'd never return to."

She paused, seemingly judging the weight of what she had just said. Pressing even closer, Richard put his arms around her after first pulling the sheet up over them. The evening, like that long ago day in August, was cooling.

She laughed to herself and something about this made Richard want to hold on more tightly. Maggie was going to drift away from him, he suddenly realised. Nothing he could do or say was ever going to prevent that. As she had once decided to walk away from that cottage and her mother, so she would one day choose to leave him – to pack a few things in a poxy sports bag and head off into the sunset.

"When I look back and think of all the things that could have

happened, it's bloody remarkable that I survived," she told him. "But I was lucky. I had my guardian with me, my shadowy, rock and roll ghost, and that... well, it helped. People just knew. They steered clear. All he had to do was place a hand on my shoulder and that was it. They just knew that I was under his protection and if they messed with me, they messed with him."'

"Rock and roll ghost?" Richard asked – deciding that it was time for a little clarification.

"Elvis," she said, quite matter-of-factly. "Oh, don't worry, I know exactly how it sounds, but that doesn't matter. Whether he was in my head, my heart or my reality – when I went out into the garden that afternoon and started stripping off, I knew he was going to rescue me. Maybe he already had in some way, I don't know, but this time when I felt his eyes on me I didn't ignore them. I turned and stood before the thick privet – trying desperately to keep my hands away from my pudendum, wanting him to see everything, wanting him to know that I trusted him.

"Have you ever heard the birds stop singing?" she suddenly asked.

"No," he said. "I don't think so."

"It's eerie and exciting," she told him. "And that's exactly what happened when I stood in front of the hedge. Everything went quiet. Everything. The birds stopped singing, the breeze stopped altogether, even the beating of my heart in my ears stopped. I couldn't hear anything and I couldn't think. I didn't need to think. I was just waiting. Testing. Convincing and proving. If anyone had seen me, anyone other than the man – anyone other than Elvis – they would have thought I'd lost the plot completely. But who else was going to see me? Mam was at work and as far as the rest of the world was concerned I was all but dead. Dead, certainly, as the man who rescued me that day. So I didn't fight it. I stood and waited, and when the privet parted and he stepped out looking older but somehow more healthy and natural – I knew that I was doing the right thing.

"The birds started singing again, the breeze picked up and he said in that unmistakable drawl, 'Honey, you're gonna catch your death.'"

That last line hand been delivered with such humour and accuracy that Richard had been unable to help himself. Desperate not to offend her, he had nevertheless found it impossible to restrain his laughter – sitting up and hugging his knees whilst Maggie smiled on patiently.

"Okay," he said. "Okay, you got me. That was good. For a minute there you really had me going."

"That's what he said," Maggie told him calmly, still smiling. "As God's my witness."

"Elvis stepped out of the privet and said, 'Baby, you're gonna catch your death'?"

"'Honey'."

"Oh, sorry, my mistake."

Maggie merely continued to smile at him. She reminded him of a teacher – someone prepared to wait as long as it took for the penny to drop. The seconds and then the minutes ticked by and finally she said, "Like I've already said, I know how it sounds, but it's not as simple as that. Whatever they say, whatever evidence there is to the contrary and however ridiculous it might seem, Elvis was there for me that day. Maybe I imagined him – I really don't know – but he was certainly as real as anyone else in my life... more so, in many ways."

"But you don't actually think that Elvis is still alive, surely?" He said this cautiously, his voice low, all suggestion of amusement banished. He didn't want to upset her and after all, who was he to judge or claim to understand the life she had lived?

"Maybe." She paused, staring up at the ceiling again. "Yes, if I'm truthful, I think I do. There, I've said it. It's taken me years to acknowledge it, but, yes, whether I imagined him or not, I think he's still alive." She looked at him out of the corner of her eye. "Now," she said, a mischievous twist to her mouth. "What do you make of that?"

"In my humble opinion," Richard told her, knowing there was really only one way to deal with such an admission, "I think you're nuttier than squirrel shit."

Laughing, Maggie sat up quickly and knelt beside him, slapping his chest and telling him that he was a beastly boy and he should treat his woman with a little more respect. Richard welcomed the reaction, pleased to see that he was more adept at handling these situations than he had originally believed, and when she kissed him he realised just how little any of this actually mattered. Thousands of people believed Elvis was still alive – people with far less compelling reasons than Maggie – so why should this make a difference to anything?

"So where do you reckon he's living now, then?" he asked her after they had made love again.

Wiping the sweat from beneath her breasts with the sheet, she grinned and shrugged – still flushed from the fucking (which this time hadn't involved any lip biting). "Somewhere local," she told him. He couldn't say just how serious she was. And didn't even bother trying.

"Why do you think that?" he asked.

"Just stands to reason."

"It does?"

"I think so, yes." Her breasts dry, she moved on to her cunt – cleaning herself absently. A temporary measure, one that would prompt her to change the sheets before they decided it was time to sleep, but an already familiar one.

"Why?"

"Because he wouldn't want to be too far away from me."

"Ah, right, of course."

"I'm serious," she said. "Whatever other people think, he and I had a very special relationship. We both knew what it was like to be cut off from the rest of the world and neither of us wanted to go back to that. When it came down to a choice between living your life in a kind of isolation or cutting yourself off from your family, we both chose the latter. He found me, and in a way, I found him. It just makes sense that we'd never be too far apart."

"So how local is local?" Richard had an idea. Something that Maggie might enjoy. Something that they both might enjoy.

"Dunno."

"In the village or farther a field?"

"Oh, in the village. Definitely in the village."

Maggie seemed to understand that Richard was on the verge of suggesting something interesting. She sat cross-legged on the bed beside him, eyes wide, shaved cunt looking bruised and beautiful, and said, "What?"

Richard grinned victoriously. "Let's see if we can find him," he said.

I'd written all the morning and most of the afternoon away – skipping lunch altogether and losing myself in the strange order of my increasingly peculiar and (though loathe to admit it) increasingly poor fiction, not at all concerned that I might be avoiding having to address the issues that Oliver's admission of the night before had brought to the surface. I was well aware that the events in and around my life could no longer be ignored – that each was somehow linked to the other, however tenuously, and that one could not be contemplated without the other – but upon waking, Wee Mark and Nadine Verity wreaking havoc at the breakfast table, I'd found myself unable to look directly at the questions that most assuredly had to be addressed.

Stepping out of my study, pleased to see that the door hadn't opened by itself again, I found Ashley standing on the landing staring in at our bedroom with a dejected, forlorn look. Her arms hung limply at her side and her shoulders rolled forward. A strand of oily hair had escaped the hasty ponytail and fallen across her cheek, curling at her jaw line. Perfect, I thought a little uncharitably – recognising her attitude at once and wondering if I could slip back into my study without her noticing.

She needed me. I needed her.

I stepped back and she turned.

Her smile suggested too much effort and I softened immediately – remembering the girl she had been, the woman she was. I thought about how hard I'd had to work to make her come the last time we'd made love, and how lovingly grateful for my patience she had been. This was the same person who had waited for me in that shelter all those years ago, who had made love to me in the sand dunes and been there for me when my parents had so suddenly and cruelly died.

"I should have finished it while I had chance," she said – meaning the half-decorated bedroom.

"I think that's the least of our concerns right now." I walked over and put my arm around her – the two of us staring in at the partially painted walls. "As long as we have a fully functional bed, what does it matter?"

"I want it right," she said. "I want it how it should be."

"Then let me help. Even with Wee Mark around, we'll soon have it out of the way with two of us at it."

"You don't think I can manage it on my own."

This was exactly what I'd been hoping to avoid. Ashley's shoulders stiffened and I reluctantly let my arm drop – taking the initiative before she decided to shrug me off.

"I *know* you can manage on your own," I said, keeping it light. "I just thought we'd get it done more quickly if we both got stuck in."

I felt guilty and confused. Ashley stared at the floor in the bedroom and it felt like the harshest of accusations. She turned, shaking her head, and started walking down the stairs. I followed, still wanting to retreat to my room but knowing that this was far from over.

In the living room, Ash turned to face me – and I saw something completely unexpected in her face. I'd imagined the standard look of uselessness and confusion, but what I actually saw was anger – pure, unadulterated anger. Her eyes were watery and intense, her teeth clenched so tightly that I thought they might shatter, and when she took a step towards me, I impulsively backed away.

"*That* was unnecessary," she told me, pointing at the ceiling. "You didn't need to do that to me. If you wanted to do the decorating, you should have got off your fat fucking arse and done it a long time ago – before I had to try to do your job for you. But now that I've made a start at it – *now* that I've made a start at *your* job – don't think you can just waltz in and take over, because that just isn't bloody on."

I didn't know how to react. This was so out of the ordinary, even for Ashley, that my first thought was that she was hysterical, and maybe I should slap her. For her to be angry over something that was, when all was said and done, quite ridiculous was beyond my capacity to understand – but still I managed to control myself, still I managed to walk calmly past her into the kitchen, where I poured myself a glass of water and gave her a moment to calm down.

She followed me and stood in the doorway waiting for a response. I didn't want to speak, afraid of what might come out – utterly convinced that whatever I said, no matter how hard I tried to moderate my reply, it would somehow mark the beginning of the end for the two of us.

"You're just going to stand there drinking water?" she said.

"For now," I answered, staring out of the kitchen window and trying to fix on something – a solidly rooted shrub, a fence post, something that would keep me grounded, stop me drifting off into the ether.

"Typical."

"What's that supposed to mean?" I turned to face her, thudding the glass down on the worktop so hard it almost broke.

"Meet action with inaction," she said. "Your standard response. Do nothing."

This was bloody preposterous, and my wife would have known that.

"What do you think I should be doing?" I asked, somehow managing to keep my anger in check.

"Anything," she said. "Just stop being so fucking calm and calculated. Shout if you want, slap me, tell me what a lousy, lazy twat of a wife I am – just don't stand there looking at me as if I'm a plot development you can't get a sodding handle on."

"You're not a lousy, lazy twat of a wife," I told her, determined to stop this before this got out of hand. "Ash." I walked over and put my hands on her shoulders. Surprisingly, she let me. "Listen, love, we've had a pretty weird twenty-four hours and we're both upset and exhausted. Maggie nearly died and you were the one who found her. That's a right bugger of a shock, but we've got to stay strong for Mags and Wee Mark. We are all they've got and we can't afford to let this tear us apart. Really, we can't. They need us. Nadine needs us. And *I* need us, love."

"I'm not a lousy, lazy twat of a wife?" There was no humour in this, just a gentleness that contrasted sharply with her mood of just moments before. She still wasn't the wife I knew and loved, still caught in the maw of her black dog, but she at least seemed rather more manageable.

"Absolutely not. You didn't really think that that was what I was implying, did you?"

"I don't know," she said. And now the tears started. "I just get so much wrong – and don't say I don't, because I know I do. I try but it never seems enough."

"For me?"

"No, for me."

This seemed to me to be the crux of Ashley's problem; a deep-set disillusionment with her own abilities. I wondered briefly if Pippa and Len had been to blame for this – with their ridiculous attitude to her when she had been a girl, an attitude that had, to one degree or another, persisted into adulthood – then dismissed it, seeing the cause as unimportant now. I held her close, stroking the back of her head and whispering to her reassuringly.

"You aren't that girl anymore," I said. "You're not answerable to anyone and you really don't need to measure yourself quite so harshly."

"But I fall short," she said. "Always."

"Says who?"

"Me."

She was right, of course, but I wasn't about to say as much. Her inability to finish a job, to stick at something until it reached its inevitable conclusion, could be frustrating, to say the least – but that, I suddenly realised, didn't mean that she deserved to torture herself like this. She was my wife, and whatever her faults, however hard she made it at times, I loved her – loved her and, especially at peculiar times such as these, needed her more than ever. At times, it was certainly true, I could have happily walked away from her – left her and Nadine and moved in with Olly as Don had (or *not quite* as Don had) – but those were moments of extreme frustration and anger and the reality was that right at that moment I could never have imagined myself walking away from my wife and child.

"Don't you think you're being a little hard on yourself?" I asked her.

"I don't know. Do you?"

"Absolutely. Just look at the last twenty-four hours or so – the way you've saved Maggie's life and looked after Wee Mark on top of all the things you normally have to do. Not many women would be willing to do that.... I mean, can you imagine Molly volunteering to look after Mark?"

"She's looking after him and Nadine this afternoon, while we go visit Mags."

"Oh," I said, momentarily at a loss. "Yes, but... but that's only for a couple of hours. It's not something she'd gladly do for the full duration of Maggie's stay in hospital, now, is it?"

163

"Probably not," she conceded.

"Well there you go, then," I said, rather too pleased with myself. "Stop beating yourself up so much. You don't deserve it."

"I can't help the way I feel," she told me.

"To a degree, you can." I stood back and fingered the greasy strand of hair behind her ear. I was amazed by my own composure and wondered, perhaps, if it had anything to do with the fact that Oliver and I had each taken the other into his confidence – that I now had a collaborator to help me unravel the various threads and conundrums. "One step at a time," I told her. "Look at the things you've achieved, not all the negative shit. You haven't left the bedroom half unfinished, it's half completed. Change the little things and the rest will follow."

She was smiling. That was something, at least. "You've been watching too much daytime telly," she told me.

"That's where I get my best story ideas."

"Teenage Mum Fucks Brother For Drugs' Money and Kills Mother in Drunken Rage When Caught In Flagrente with the Family Pooch?"

"You've been looking at my manuscripts again, haven't you?"

"I like to know you aren't libelling me," she said – and I felt a pang of guilt when I thought of Maggie Sutherland and her dead husband, Jim. Granted, it was hardly biographical but it would be clear to any of our friends just where certain elements of the story came from, even if I changed the names. With time, Maggie might find it flattering (in fact, there was no might about it – she would love it) but that still didn't stop me having an uneasy feeling. When I allowed my reality to creep into my fiction – or, more especially, someone else's reality to creep into my fiction – the responsibility became all the greater. I had a choice. Make it the best story I'd ever written, or delete it.

Another pressure I didn't particularly need.

Ash pulled out a chair and sat down, stretching one arm out on the table beside her like a gymnast awaiting treatment. Head back against the wall, she sighed, closing her eyes. "I don't know how you put up with me," she said.

"I love you," I said – the simplest, most accurate answer I could think of.

"And that makes it easier?"

"Not always, no."

"So why? Why do you put up with me?"

"Ash?"

"What?"

"Shut the fuck up."

She opened one eye and looked at me, smiling. "You don't get out of it that easily," she told me. "Why do you put up with me? Seriously. No smart-arse writer replies."

I thought about my answer very carefully. She'd opened both eyes now so I saw just how important this was. She tilted her head questioningly, clearly growing impatient, and I struggled for that one validation – the one thing that would explain everything about my relationship with Ashley.

"Because I can't imagine my life without you," I finally said.

Oliver came with us to see Maggie. He said nothing to me about the night before and what he had told me, as I would have expected with Ashley around, but during the journey there he did mention Don again – telling us that he had spoken to him on the phone that morning and he was doing okay. Olly had told him about Maggie and Don had asked if it would be all right if he visited her. Not wanting to do anything that might make Maggie uncomfortable (he said), Oliver had told him that he would have a word – see if Maggie was up to it. I got the distinct impression that Oliver had no such intention. I also felt, however, that Oliver had been the one to phone Don, not vice versa, and wondered if he knew any better than I just what it was he actually wanted.

Mags was sitting up in bed when we arrived – looking exhausted and more than a little embarrassed. Oliver had brought her dressing gown and things in that morning, but it was so warm in the six-bed room that she sat on top of the sheets in only a short nightie. Faded hearts on a white-grey background. Something Jim might have bought her a long time ago.

She sat up straighter as we approached the bed, trying a smile on for size and then letting it fall as Ash hugged her and the two of them crumbled into each other. Oliver and I stood back – me at the foot of the bed where I had an unfortunate but nevertheless intriguing view up Maggie's too-short nightie, Oliver on the same side as Ashley.

Maggie had almost died and I was looking at her cotton knickers, remembering what it had been like with her – how she had liked to go on top, how she could be so tender and, yet, so exuberant and unrelenting. If I tried very hard, I could still recall the delves at the backs of her knees, the curve of the small of her back – the way in which she'd clawed at the rug in front of the open fire as she had reached her climax. She had tasted of forgotten summers and winter streams, and what we had done together had been so wrong and, yet, exactly what we had both needed at that time.

Ashley continued to hug her and I continued to look at her knickers, lost in a reverie the force of which surprised even me. Oliver caught my eye. I found chairs for us all.

"I feel like such a bloody idiot," Mags said as the three of us sat down. "Such a bloody, *selfish* idiot."

"Don't be silly," I said, letting her take my hand. Ashley smiled encouragingly, proud of her considerate and caring husband. "What you did... it's not easy, Mags. No one makes a decision like that lightly and..."

"What he's trying to say," Ashley kindly interjected, "is that we understand and we certainly don't think badly of you."

Mags was filling up again, her smile appreciative and twitchy. Her hand was sweaty in mine, but I didn't want to pull away; it wasn't in the least bit unpleasant. It was personal and primitive, cave-dwelling and vital.

"Now I can see how wrong I was," she said, sobbing a little, "but I just felt that there was no other choice. It seems ridiculous, now, but everything closed in on me and... there was this dark cloud. Not outside and, you know, not in my head, either. It was in the kitchen, up near the boiler, and I just felt like I was bleeding into it. I know it wasn't real, and I think I knew then, but... it was horrible."

Ashley took hold of Maggie's other hand in both of hers, squeezing as she tried to keep strong, pushing back her true emotions and blinking rapidly. "You don't need to think about that now," she said. "You've got all the help you need and everything's going to be just fine. Isn't it?" she asked Oliver and me.

We both nodded with rather too much confidence and I said, "Molly's looking after Wee Mark, so you've got Jesus on your side, too, now. Won't go far wrong with Jesus to watch out for you."

Maggie laughed true and hard, surprising the three of us. "It must be bad if it's come to that," she said. "As long as He doesn't want me for a sunbeam."

Oliver sat forward, forearms on knees. The chair, like most chairs, was too small for him and his discomfort was very obvious. "You'll have to watch her when you get out of here," he said, grinning. "You're just what she's looking for. A mission. A charity case. That's what they do, these Christians, catch folk when they're at their weakest and then twat them up completely with the Word of God."

"I'm not exactly in the best of places right now," Maggie admitted. "But the day I'm that far gone you have my permission to take me out and shoot me."

We all smiled politely. I found the image a little disturbing. However different it was to the events of the day before, it still smacked of self-destruction. Oliver and I looked at one another and he sat back in his chair. I knew he was regretting telling me about seeing Jim's ghost, or whatever the hell it had been, just as I wished I'd never told him about the naked woman in my back garden – but I somehow thought it was all for the best. Looking at Mags, I knew it was.

"I tried to tell you," Maggie was saying. "But it just wouldn't come out right. All that stalker business... rubbish."

I remembered the day that Oliver and I had followed her. It seemed a silly episode now, one that I couldn't readily understand or explain, and I couldn't help feeling that I had somehow been made a fool of. I didn't appreciate having my time wasted, being sent off on a wild goose chase, but this was Maggie – and what she had asked of us had been the only possible solution she could find to a problem she didn't fully (or even partially) understand.

She squeezed my hand more tightly, holding on for dear life, and I heard her stomach rumble; complaint, hardship, need and confusion. These were the cornerstones of Maggie's condition, possibly of all our conditions, and I couldn't imagine her finding a conclusion in this place with its insufficient antiseptic veneer and its marauding superbugs.

"You see, I knew," she told us. "I knew from day one, but I just couldn't make sense of it. It was all so... it was what I wanted. I'd been given the one thing that I wanted, but now that I had it I just couldn't make sense of it and I found that I didn't want it, after all. What is it they say, 'be careful what you wish for'? I should have known better. It was like – you know that Stephen King book?"

"Carrie?" Ashley said.

"The Shining?" I ventured.

"Pet Semetary," Oliver said knowingly, and Maggie nodded.

"That's the one," she told us. "He brings his dead kid – "

"Gage," Oliver kindly assisted.

"Is that his name?"

"As far as I recall."

Maggie shook her head at the folly of giving a child such a dumb name and then said, "Anyway. He brings his son, this Gage, back to life but he's different. It's not his son anymore. Well, that's what it was like for me. I got my Jim back but he wasn't the same. It wasn't like it was before. Or, rather, it was."

"You got Jim back?" Ashley asked quietly.

Oliver was starting to look uneasy and it wasn't difficult to see why. I tried to catch his eye but he merely continued staring at Mags.

"Yes, in a way," Maggie said. "He was my stalker. I saw him everywhere. I saw him or I saw *signs* of him. It wasn't like he walked into the living room, sat down and started watching *Dave*. He was... oh, I don't know, it's hard to explain. The phone calls started and it was... I couldn't believe it was him, to start with. I thought it was someone playing a cruel joke. But I think I knew. Really."

"And that's why...?" Ashley said, and Maggie nodded. "It wasn't like it was before so you wanted to go to him so that it could be?"

Maggie squeezed my hand again – this time so hard my knuckle cracked.

"No," she said adamantly. "Absolutely not. No, Ash... no, I didn't want to go to him. Maybe before I would have. But now... no. Now I just want to get away from him. I was trying to escape him, Ash. If he can do that to me, torment me like that, I want nothing at all to do with him."

We were all at a loss for something appropriate to say. Oliver finally looked at me and I thought for one dreadful moment that he was going to tell Maggie that he had seen Jim, too. His teeth flashed in the midst of that increasingly unruly beard and he drew breath, preparing himself. My eyes widened in warning and he looked confused, brow creased, button nose twitching as if with an itch.

And then Ashley was speaking again, and any opportunity he'd had went blessedly out of the window.

"You don't want to be with him?" She sounded rather too incredulous for my liking. On the journey to the hospital, Ash had made a point of telling Oliver and me that we should present a united front, allied alongside Maggie in a show of force against whatever troubles were besieging her. It had all been very martial and quaintly Churchillian, but we'd got the point and had seen no reason to oppose her. And now here she was expressing, albeit implicitly, a quite possibly inappropriate degree of disbelief.

"I don't want to be with him," Maggie said, with more resolve than I'd ever seen her display. Her shoulders stiffened and she released my hand, lacing her fingers together in her lap and frowning deeply as she tried to explain herself more clearly. "When Jim was dying... I knew. We both knew, you know? From the very beginning. We won a few battles together, but, ultimately, we knew the cancer would win the war, whatever the doctors said to the contrary. And there was... well, I know it might sound odd, but there was a kind of comfort in that. We talked about him dying and... we didn't accept it, but we tolerated the inevitability of it, I suppose. And that made the time we had together better, you know? It was still hard, but the added pressure of having to tiptoe around the issue was gone. Before the cancer we'd had problems. He wouldn't talk, not in any real way, and we were starting to drift. The cancer... we had to talk. A lot of the time there was nothing else to do. And even now, feeling the way I do and after everything that's happened, I still miss that Jim."

"But?" Ashley said.

"But the Jim that's been stalking me... haunting me, I suppose... that Jim's a different Jim. He's more like the old Jim and... I want nothing to do with him, Ash. Nothing whatsoever."

Chapter Ten

It was the time I needed – time to think, time to lose myself in the physical nature of the job at hand. Nadine and Wee Mark had been watching me for the past twenty minutes, sitting silently and intently on the floor in the doorway like two drowsy little buddhas. I envied them their intense focus and that ability to pull back from the world around them, to sleep at the most improbable of times. Getting lost in physical activity, in comparison, was the best I could do – and as I put the finishing touches to the radiator, I remembered something I had read in the journal the day before. Pregnant with Chadwick's child, overjoyed that the father was dead and that she had got away with his murder and the murder of his lover, the mystery woman had communicated this part of her story in her usual philosophical, slightly manic style – colouring her world with expressions of dissension and welcome solitude. The pregnancy changed her, unquestionably, but at heart she was essentially the same determined, self-serving, morally destitute woman she had always been, though most of her efforts were now directed towards securing some kind of security for her as yet unborn child. I'd read of how she had left the town where she had lived with Chadwick, leaving everything behind for fear that profiting so obviously from his death would attract suspicion, and how she had eventually found herself in a small coastal village – living rough there for three nights (sleeping behind a building that she later discovered was a makeshift morgue used primarily for bodies that were washed up on the beach whenever there was a shipwreck) until she found temporary employment and accommodation. To one such as myself, a stranger to her world and, yet, one who was becoming increasingly familiar with it, it seemed that she had at last found a kind of peace. She considered her unborn child and worked, only occasionally subsidising her pay with illicit acts of one kind or another, and neither she nor I felt any real loss for Chadwick.

170

Gary William Murning

Now, Nadine and Wee Mark watching me avidly as I started cleaning my brush, I remembered one line in particular. *Children, the prospect or reality, bring with them the wealth of generations forgotten.* It struck me as such a simple and, yet, profound statement – suggesting portals and keys to greater knowledge, the negation of the Ego and the possibility of so much more. I wanted that, I realised, returning my daughter's beautifully uncluttered stare. I wanted what she gave and in spite of all the weird shit that was going on in our lives, I found I wanted the child Ashley and I had mooted the possibility of – the child that incident had put on hold, the two of us too exhausted at the end of the long day to do anything other than kiss each other good night and turn out the light.

"Everything finds its own time." It was something both my mother and father had been fond of saying, and it had never seemed quite so appropriate as it did now. I looked from Nadine to Wee Mark. They'd both been as good as gold and I felt as though the three of us existed in the eye of the storm. Such calm didn't so much find its own time as make it, I thought, and it was our duty to embrace and appreciate.

I knelt down in front of Nadine and Wee Mark. Their chins rested in their hands, legs crossed, they regarded me evenly – smiling slightly and going a little cross-eyed as I leant in close.

"Boo," I said quietly, and Nadine giggled. "What you up to, guys?"

Wee Mark shrugged. "It wasn't me," he said.

"What wasn't you, mate?" We, Ashley and I, were already more than a little familiar with Mark's habitual denials. Nothing was ever him – even when there were no breakages or misdemeanours to pin on him.

He shrugged again. "Dunno," he said sulkily, "but it wasn't me."

"Not me, too," Nadine chirped up, sticking her head between Wee Mark and me and tilting it from left to right gleefully, grinning all the while. They'd been stuffing themselves with sweets; I could smell that artificial, sugary smell on their breaths, but sweets were not forbidden at this time of the day so I ruled that out.

"It wasn't, eh?" I said, giving her a playful little tickle under the right arm. Wee Mark lifted his left arm by way of an invitation, so I tickled him, too. "Who was it, then?" I asked.

171

A synchronised shrug. "Vanessa?" Wee Mark ventured, apparently intent on helping.

"Ah, right. Vanessa." I still hadn't figured out if there was something genuinely in need of denying, here, or if Wee Mark was merely sticking to type. I imagined him fifteen years from now. *I know my rights. I'm not saying owt until I've seen my brief. This is police harassment.* And this for nothing more than a caution over a faulty indicator light.

"So what did Vanessa do?" I asked in a conspiratorial whisper. All pals together.

The language of the toddler; shrugs, sulks and tantrums.

Shrug.

Shrug.

"Oh, well," I said. "Vanessa's good, really – just like you two. I'm sure she'll tell us what she's done wrong eventually cos that's what good boys and girls do, right?"

They looked at each other and then nodded uncertainly. What did I know? Who was really fooling whom? I got the distinct impression that I was out-of-my depth.

Children, the prospect or reality, bring with them the wealth of generations forgotten.

Ashley was standing in the doorway behind Nadine and Wee Mark. In the week since Wee Mark had been staying with us, she had battled her depression admirably – pulling herself up by her bootstraps, as Mam would have said, and dealing with only those things she felt absolutely necessary. Standards had slipped a little, it was true, dust dulling every surface, pots taking longer to be washed – but she wasn't being quite so hard on herself and she was at least letting me help out where I could, now. She looked well enough, but it was obvious that she was tired and far less concerned with her appearance and her personal hygiene than she normally would be. Dressed in shabby jeans and a white blouse that had a Bolognese sauce stain on the left breast, no shoes or slippers on her feet, she seemed rather more slumped and sallow than I would have ideally liked, but strong nevertheless. When she smiled, I saw something I hadn't seen in what seemed like a very long time; power, sexuality – the kind of command I now largely associated with her religious

172

arguments with Molly.

"You look like you could do with a beer," she said. "These two little tykes been behaving themselves?"

"It wasn't me," Wee Mark said, craning his neck and looking up at her.

"What wasn't him?" Ashley asked me.

Now it was my turn to shrug. "This is something we have yet to ascertain," I told her, "although I have a feeling it's more reflexive than anything else, this time. They haven't moved for the past twenty-five minutes."

"What did you do – Velcro them to the carpet?"

"A few well-placed nails did the trick." Ashley laughed hollowly, Nadine joining in whilst Wee Mark glowered at her as if this were the greatest betrayal imaginable. "You look tired," I said, revising my earlier thoughts on how strong she looked.

"I am – a little. Nothing forty winks won't fix."

"Still, not long now, anyway, eh?"

A pause. A scratch of her armpit. A rub of her neck.

"Actually," she said, "I was wanting to talk to you about that."

"Do I want to hear this?" I asked, getting to my feet.

"Probably not."

"But I have to hear it, anyway?"

Nodding her regret, she said, "I'm not comfortable with the idea of her going back there, Sonny. Not yet. Not on her own."

"They've said she's okay to go home, love," I said – feeling my heartbeat start to race. I didn't want Maggie staying with us. As much as I liked her, it would just be too much living in the same house as her – sharing a bathroom, sharing a history.

"They say a lot of things," she pointed out. "I just don't happen to agree with them, this time."

"Love, we haven't got room."

"Of course we have... and if we haven't, we'll make room – simple as that."

"I'm just not sure it's a good idea."

"Why?"

Because Maggie and me fucked each other's brains out in a cottage in Wales one time. I fell asleep with my head on her thigh and

173

my fingers tangled in her pubic hair – and I don't think it's something that could ever happen again, but I just don't want to take that chance.

"I don't know. I just think it'll be a better idea if she gets back into her old routine as quickly as possible."

"The same old routine that..." She glanced down at the kids. "The same old routine that made her do what she did?"

I couldn't see a way of opposing her without seeming petty and heartless. To avoid my own discomfort I had been momentarily prepared to abandon Maggie to her fate – to trust in the word of an underfunded, triaged-to-death system and curl up in my secure little nest with my family without so much as a thought for moral or ethical responsibility. Many things I could dismiss. Many things I could rationalise away. Many, *many* things I could do without feeling so much as an ounce of remorse. But this would not be one of them.

"No," I said, "that's not what I meant. That's not what I meant at all. We'd be there for her and help her establish a more healthy way of living." She started to say something but I held up a hand to stop her. "You're right, though. It smacks of throwing her in at the deep end and... you're right. We have to have her stay, for a short while, at least."

Nadine and Wee Mark continued to watch the monkeys in the zoo.

Ashley stepped carefully between them, hugging me with her chin on my shoulder. "You know something?" she said. "You're the best husband and friend anyone could ever wish for."

It resisted. I tried every way I could think of to get in, but nothing came – no natural progression from the earlier scenes with Richard and Maggie in bed together, no halting, divergent threads, nothing. I sat in front of my PC, checking email and reading the *London Review of Books* online whilst I waited for inspiration to strike, the journal safely locked in the bottom drawer of my desk in an attempt to avoid it further distracting me. But still nothing came. I read a jokey email from Oliver, and then a more serious one about the week before and what we had told each other – and I realised immediately that whatever slim chance there might have been that I would get some work done today, it was now gone.

The email read:

From: Oliver Montgomery [mailto: Oliver@local4net.co.uk]
Sent: 10 August 2005 09:15
To: Sonny
Subject: Deus ex machina

Sonny,

I want to dismiss it, mate – rationalise everything I/we thought I/we saw. But can't. To do that would be like turning away from a physical proof of a natural law. That probably doesn't make a whole lot of sense, but I'm guessing you'll know what I mean. Is this something we can understand without rationalising it away? I don't know. It's certainly a challenge. We can't just ignore it, though – that much I do know. Maggie sees Jim, I see Jim and you see this dead woman who's possibly the same woman who wrote the journal you found. Is this coincidental, or is there something bigger we aren't yet seeing?
   We need to talk. And soon. Call me. Oliver.

Standing at the window, I looked down on the back garden – where all of this seemed to have started for me. I thought about my hole and thought about the hot and humid day when Maggie had sat beside me on the very wall I was now looking at and told me about her stalker. Did Oliver have a point? Was there something bigger we were failing to see or were we simply getting caught up in each other's delusions?

Nadine and Wee Mark were in the back garden. I watched them come out of the garage together carrying my spade between them and chattering away animatedly. Wee Mark held the business end of the spade, Nadine the handle, and both looked ready for action as they headed for the patch of garden where my hole had been. Doc and Sleepy, off to mine them some gold, Snow White waving them off from the doorway to their cottage. Idyllic. Peaceful. Self-sustaining.

But where is Snow White, boys and girls? Surely she hasn't let her two favourite dwarfs wander off into the forest all by themselves, has she?

I took the stairs rather more quickly than I should have – almost losing my balance at the halfway mark and only recovering fully when I reached the bottom and shouldered myself off the opposing wall and into the living room. I felt a familiar soreness ignite in my lower back, bile rising into my throat as I remembered just how sharp the blade of that spade actually was. Little toes in soft shoes. Infantile enthusiasm and inability. What the *fuck* was she thinking of?

Ashley was asleep on the settee. I gave her a hard shake as I passed quickly by – dashing through the kitchen and out the back door, shouting to her to get herself out the back, *now*. I'd forgotten our conversation of earlier that day. I'd forgotten that I was the best husband and friend anyone could wish for. I'd forgotten all the good, supportive, encouraging things I'd said to her the day after Maggie's suicide attempt. I saw a sharp spade and two precious toddlers left unattended. I saw Ashley asleep on the settee. I saw looming tragedy and a capacity for anger in myself that seemed limitless and frightening.

I had once determined to always be reasonable with those I loved. But now I was older and wiser.

Nadine and Wee Mark were struggling to work out the best way to use the spade together. They didn't seem to be in any immediate danger so I stood close by, ready to leap in, should it be required, and waited for Ashley to join me.

My heart was still beating ten to the dozen and my shoulder hurt where I'd bounced off the wall. I thought again of all the things that could have happened – all the other stuff they had access to in the garage (which I knew for certain I had locked earlier that morning) – and turned to Ashley as she shuffled up beside me looking sheepish and sleepy.

"What the fuck were you thinking of?" I said.

"I just sat down for a few minutes," she said.

"What about the garage?"

"What about it?"

"I locked it when I'd finished cleaning my brushes. How did it get unlocked?"

"Search me," she said. "I haven't been in there today."

"You must have been."

"Oh. Because there's absolutely no way that someone so perfect as you could forget to lock it, right?"

I thought about how rushed I'd been after finishing the decorating – how I had wanted to get to my room as quickly as possible and get some writing done before the day was over. I'd had an idea, one that, as it happened, I hadn't been able to develop in any particularly usable way – but that wouldn't have prompted such carelessness in me, I was certain.

"I sure as fuck aren't perfect," I told her, "but I know I locked that door."

"And I know I haven't been in there today. Why on earth would I need to, Sonny?"

"How should I know?" I almost added something scathing and highly offensive, something that even now I am ashamed to write, but stopped myself in the nick of time – saying instead, "All I know is I look from my window up there and I see these two coming out of the garage carrying a spade and you nowhere to be seen. There are all sorts of things in there that they could have got into. You know that as well as I."

"I didn't unlock the door," she insisted.

"Maybe you didn't," I conceded, "but neither did you keep an eye on what they were doing. Christ, love, they're *kids*. They have no sense of danger."

"You think I don't know that?" She was getting angry, now. Angry and emotional. The tears started to well and her hands clenched at her side; when either one or both were released, there would be bother. "You think I'm fucking *thick*, is that it? You – what? – think I'm some kind of bloody imbecile who likes to just sit back and watch her helpless, beautiful little daughter toddle into all kinds of danger? Is that it?" The hands unclenched and the tears started to fall. "How dare you, Sonny? How bloody dare you? I'm exhausted. Don't you understand that? I'm exhausted and I sat down for two minutes while they played on the rug in front of the telly and the next thing I bloody know you're shaking me awake and talking to me like I'm a useless piece of shit you've just trod in! Who the *fuck* do you think you are?"

I started to speak, and then realised there was nothing for me to say. I would never be right. However serious and genuine my concerns, the Universe would always find a way of tilting ever so slightly and changing my truth and its interpretation.

"I try," she was saying. "You *know* how I try. But it's... I get tired and lost. The vertical shifts and I just feel like if I don't sit down, I'll fall down. Everything is still important. I still love and care, I still have an overwhelming need to protect. But I'm drained. Wrung out. I'm drained and wrung out and I have to sit down."

"You should have given me a shout," I said, more softly now. Wee Mark was getting a little rough and dangerous with the spade; I gently took it from him. He accepted this with unexpected grace, him and Nadine chasing each other back and forth across the patio, squealing excitedly.

"I know," Ashley said, watching the kids a little dreamily. "I know, really I do – but I never meant to fall asleep. I don't even remember closing my eyes. It was time for me to just grab a few minutes, you know? My head was a bit all over the place thinking of Maggie and what she did – how bad she must have been feeling to do a thing like that – and... it is preferable to stare out of the window at such times. I needed to lose myself, I needed to..."

She continued talking but I wasn't actually listening. Something about what she had said was familiar – familiar for, it seemed, all the wrong reasons. I'd heard much of it before, of course. This was different, however. This familiarity took me somewhere else entirely and I couldn't immediately see where that was. I worked back through all she had said, trying to listen with one ear to what she was now saying so that I could at least nod in the right places, and when I finally pinpointed it, I felt a sudden, almost uncontrollable need to sit down.

It is preferable to stare out of the window at such times, she had said – and I knew without having to refer to the original material that it was a direct quote from the mystery woman's journal. The journal that Ashley had never shown the slightest interest in and which I now, for reasons I hadn't studied too closely, habitually locked away in a desk drawer whenever I wasn't around.

"I don't know what else I can say," Ashley continued. "I know I get things wrong but I try, Sonny. What more can I do?"

I thought about the unaccountably unlocked garage door. I thought about my study door, unexpectedly open with no real explanation. I didn't have the slightest idea just what was going on here, but of two things I was certain: none of this was Ashley's fault, and Oliver had been right in his latest email; we did need to talk – and soon.

"You can forgive me, for starters," I said.

"Forgive *you*?"

"I've just remembered something," I lied. "I did forget to lock the garage door."

I spent a good half an hour getting things sorted out with Ashley. Maggie was due to be discharged from hospital later that day and so we aired the spare bedroom and changed the sheets – even though they didn't actually need changing. Once this was done, we got the kids looking spick and span and, before going to meet Oliver at the pub, I obediently dropped them around Molly's.

Ashley had been quick to forgive me for wrongfully accusing her, but all through the afternoon – with its forced and false cheer – I had been unable to escape the feeling that something had changed between us. It wasn't that we had lost each other's trust, it couldn't be anything as grand or as simple as that, but, rather, it was a feeling that we were no longer the centre of our relationship. I thought of the line she had spoken – the line from the journal – and I felt us spinning further apart, drifting off into a confusing maelstrom of unborn babies, dead husbands and ghostly Elvises. I held her, hoping she was going to shower before going to pick Maggie up, and it was easy to fool myself into believing that all was right with the world. We were strong and it would take much more than a little weirdness to tear us apart. But it just wasn't that clear cut. I loved my wife and daughter and, as I had thought many, many times, I could never even think of leaving them – and, yet, I found myself wishing for escape, searching for respite, hoping against hope that Oliver might have somehow worked all this out so that we could put it all behind us and reclaim our usual, utterly boring and predictable lives. I would never run, but I wanted to. I would never be so fucking cowardly, but cowardice nevertheless had its attractions.

It was difficult getting away from Molly. Veronique hugged her mother's legs and stared up at me from the doorstep whilst Nadine and Wee Mark raced enthusiastically into the house – and Molly regarded me solemnly.

"A nice little mess we have here, eh?" she said. "I still can't quite believe that Maggie would do such a thing."

"She's been under a lot of pressure," I told her – rather too defensively.

"I'm not judging her, Sonuel." I wished she'd just call me Sonny; Sonuel always sounded peculiarly biblical when she said it.

"I'm pleased to hear it."

"You don't think much of me, do you?" When Molly wasn't looking all stern and evangelical, she was actually quite attractive. She had a vulnerability around the eyes and mouth that made me think of bruised peaches and little girls on the verge of tears. Petite and doll-like in her apparent fragility (something Veronique had inherited from her), the overwhelming feeling I had for her was pity. Maybe that was arrogant of me, but the truth was a significant part of me considered Molly foolish – naïve and frighteningly misguided for one so intelligent.

"I don't think much of your beliefs or your attempts to impose them on others," I admitted, "but as far as not thinking much of you... I like you, Molly. I like and trust you."

"I'm glad," she said. "I only ever do what I think is right, Sonny. You do understand that, don't you?"

"I do – but now isn't really – "

"It's just that I genuinely believe that Maggie... she's lost, Sonny. We all are, to a degree, but it's especially true with Maggie. You've got to see that."

The funny thing was, I knew exactly what she meant. I saw it with Mags and in the wake of recent events, I thought I also saw it with Oliver, Ashley and myself. Adrift. Looking for meaning and order amid the chaos. As I had observed many times before, that was what my fiction had always been about. And hadn't that need for understanding and apparent direction now spilled over into my reality?

"I do see that," I told her. "It's just that we don't all choose the same way of dealing with these things."

"And Maggie's way of dealing is better than mine?" It was a fair point. I just wished Ash had been there to shoot her down in flames.

"Your way wouldn't work for Maggie, Molly," I said, as patiently as possible. "If I thought it would, I'd be out buying her a Bible right now, believe me, I would."

"Really?"

"If I thought it would help her and stop her doing anything like that again, yes – of course I would."

"Then you'll help me?"

I looked at my watch. I was already late. Oliver would be well into his third drink by now.

"Help you?"

"I just need the chance to be alone with her for half an hour, Sonny, that's all," she said. "I won't push things. I just want to sit and talk to her without Ash sticking her oar in. Maggie needs to see that we do have choices, Sonny, that's all. If I can make her see that... well, then the rest's up to her. I won't force anything on her."

"If the chance presents itself naturally," I said, "what you choose to do is your own business. But I won't help you, Moll."

"Even though it might help her?"

"Maggie has fully-formed ideas on how the world works. All you'd succeed in doing would be to call her judgment into question and place her under even more stress. I'm sorry, but I won't help you do that."

"And you don't believe you owe Maggie the chance to be well again?" she said, her lips thin and tight. "After what you did to her in Wales?"

I'd clearly underestimated her.

It had always seemed entirely natural to me that what had happened between Maggie and me should remain secret. As far as I had known, Oliver had been the only other person who was aware of it – and I'd never had reason to believe that he would tell anyone about it. Now, however, I was faced, yet again, with another reality entirely. Somehow, Molly knew about that cottage in Wales – knew about it or had spotted Divine Clues and drawn Frighteningly Accurate Conclusions. How she had come by the knowledge wasn't my prime concern right now, however. Standing beneath the tatty canopy on her doorstep, taking in her composed and vaguely didactic features – brow creased and intense, eyes unblinking as her lips all but disappeared – I toyed with the idea of just denying everything. It was the simplest and most obvious solution. Oliver would never have told her anything of what had happened between Maggie and me, and I couldn't even begin to imagine a scenario where Maggie would share anything with Molly, let along something so clandestine and intimate – so the natural conclusion to draw seemed to be that Molly had somehow put the pieces together herself and simply got lucky. By nature and doctrine, I imagined her to be a deeply suspicious woman, so it didn't take a great leap to figure out that her apparent knowledge could well be founded on nothing more than supposition and, perhaps jealousy.

"I don't know what you're talking about," I finally said.

She smiled as if this had been just what she had been expecting me to say. "Yes you do," she told me. "Not long before your marriage to Ashley, you and Maggie spent some time together in a little cottage in Wales. What went on there, Sonny, is your business. I'm not threatening you. This isn't about me telling Ashley. That isn't going to happen. What you did is between you and your god – "

"I haven't got a god."

"You and your conscience, then," she said impatiently. "What you did is none of my business, that's all I'm saying – and I have no intention of making it my business. All I want you to think about is what you did to her and whether or not you owe it to her to let me at least try to help her. Is that too much to ask?"

"How do you know?" I asked, avoiding her question for the time being. "About Mags and me. How did you find out?"

"God opened my eyes," she told me, smirking. "Is that what you want to hear, Sonny?"

"I want to hear the truth."

She nodded thoughtfully and looked down at Vanessa – who seemed to have fallen asleep against her leg. "The truth," she said. "Of course.... I'll answer your question once you've answered mine. Will you help me?"

"I can't do that."

"Because?"

"Because I don't believe it's fair on Maggie. It's not something she'd want and... why didn't you just go and see her at the hospital?" I asked, suddenly realising that Molly had apparently missed a very obvious opportunity.

"What?" She blinked.

"The hospital... did you even go, Moll?"

"You know I didn't."

She was right, of course. I did know this and up until now it hadn't seemed in the slightest bit strange. Molly had been quick to volunteer to take care of the kids whilst we visited and it was a routine we, with all our various preoccupations, simply hadn't questioned. We all had our role to play, and Molly had without argument accepted what *it seemed* she had been given without so much as a single grumble.

"But now you want me to help you have some time alone with her," I mused. "Why didn't you just drop by one afternoon when you knew we wouldn't be there, Moll?"

She carefully prised Vanessa from her leg and gently shooed her into the living room to play with Wee Mark and Nadine. Once this was done, she sighed – as deep as a well and brittle round the edges – and leant against the jamb.

"I'm not perfect," she told me. This seemed quite an admission coming from her. From me, it would have been a fairly standard disclaimer (my equivalent to Wee Mark's "it wasn't me") – but with Molly it carried a certain gravitas. "People think that I'm full of myself and they think that *I* think I'm perfect. But I'm not and I don't." She swallowed and I saw just how difficult this was for her. "I wanted to go and see Mags," she continued. "And not just for the reason we discussed. I wanted to be there for her but..." She shook herself and shrugged, smiling weakly and grappling for composure. "It's just that place," she said. "Let's just say it doesn't have very good associations for me."

"The hospital?"

"The hospital." Pushing herself off the jamb, she folded her arms and said, "So you're not going to help me?"

"Let me talk to Maggie," I said, suddenly feeling sorry for her – but not really intending on doing any such thing.

"Thank you, Sonny."

Only when I was walking into the pub car park did I realise that she still hadn't told me how she had known about Maggie and me.

I found Oliver in a booth in the eastern corner of the room – over by the entrance to the restaurant. He was slumped with his head in a book. I noticed as I sat down opposite him that, rather ominously, it was a book on neuroscience.

"You're late," he told me, without looking up. "I've been sat here like a jilted lover for close on an hour – even Polly's been looking worried. You better have a convincing explanation."

There was a large whisky on my side of the table. "This mine?" I asked.

"Naturally."

I took a decent gulp of it, feeling it kick me all the way down to me toes, and squinted through its heat as I said, "I dropped the kids off at Molly's. You haven't by any chance mentioned anything about Maggie and me to her, have you?"

"Why would I want to do a stupid thing like that?" He sipped his beer and regarded me evenly. Oliver was an honourable man. For me to even think of asking such a question was preposterous.

"I don't know," I said. "I'm just at a loss to think of another explanation."

"She's suspicious?"

I shook my head. "It's gone beyond that. She knows everything."

"Welsh Wales?"

"Everything."

"Shit." He turned his beer bottle on the table and gave a little "oh well"-shrug. "Too late to worry about it now, though. You'll just have to roll with the punches. I assume she's going to tell Ash."

"You assume wrong."

He looked surprised. "I do?"

"You do. Apparently that's between me and my god."

"You don't have a god."

"That's what I told her."

"And?"

"She made an amendment." Oliver seemed confused, chewing on his beard and continuing to turn his bottle on the table, so I elucidated.

184

"It's between me and my conscience."

"Ah, I see," he said. "That's very generous of her."

"Still doesn't answer the question of how she knows, though, does it?"

This was really beginning to niggle. Oliver hadn't told her and I could never believe that Maggie – wonderful, tragic, discrete Maggie – would ever let anything slip. That, as far as I could see, left only two other possibilities; either Molly had somehow worked it out for herself, as I had thought earlier, or someone else knew about this – someone who had carelessly or very deliberately shared the information with Molly.

"Is it that important?" Oliver said. He glanced at the book, which he had placed face down on the table beside his beer – clearly considering whether he should pick it up and start reading again. "It's not like she's going to tell Ashley, so what's the big worry?"

"If she knows about it, other people can, too," I said. "Jesus, Olly, for a bright bloke you can be pretty fucking dense at times."

"Bless you," he said, raising his bottle in a salute. "So, what, you think the whole town knows about you and Maggie, now, is that it?"

"I didn't say that."

"No, you didn't."

There had been a time when we had all been comfortable with who we were and our place in the world – and I remembered that time, now, sitting across from Oliver, watching him sip his beer as he struggled uncharacteristically to find something to say.

A long ago summer. Before Nadine. Before Donnelly McCrane. Just Ashley, Oliver and me. We'd toyed with the idea of going abroad, but the general consensus was that this would be foolish; there were delights enough in our own country that we still hadn't sampled, so why waste a fortnight trudging around Spanish souvenir shops eating authentic British fish and chips? We had packed everything into the car, intending to travel the country looking at historic sights, henges, the remains of Roman villas and generally soaking up the heritage we so rarely acknowledged. We'd planned in great detail beforehand – working out the best route on the Net and sitting up late most of the week before our departure arguing about whether we could make Stonehenge in time for the Summer Solstice, and if this was a good time to enjoy the place, anyway, given the inevitable hordes of New Age Travellers. As it turned out, though, all our planning and arguments had been academic. We never made it to Stonehenge and, in fact, we only just made it out of the county.

Peace and contentment are rare. I knew that that day, sitting across the table from Oliver in the pub – and, remarkably, I think I knew it that day when, only a little over half an hour into our journey, we pulled into a small campsite just outside Helmsley, intending to stop only long enough to have a bite to eat.

I remembered the simplicity of the place. Little in the way of amenities, a handful of tents and a couple of tourer caravans nestled into the side of a craggy-peaked hill – and I'd known immediately that this was where we were going to spend the two weeks of our holiday.

Oliver picked the book up and marked his place by folding the corner of the page. Setting it down again, he said, "A penny for them."

"I was just thinking of that summer we spent just outside of Helmsley," I said.

"Ah." He smiled fondly. "The Grand Tour. It was nice – in that way that only the unexpected can ever be."

"Simpler times," I said.

"Perhaps. Or simpler people. Maybe we just got lucky."

It was a time and place I hadn't thought of in a very long time – and its effect on me was strangely calming. I recalled the long, lazy days spent staring at the simple but nevertheless quite beautiful landscape, eating and drinking and talking about whatever came into my head to two of the people most dear to me, and I felt somehow cleansed. The events of recent weeks were still important – they still had something to tell us, some code we had yet to decipher – but I felt suddenly less tainted by them, more like the old, more familiar me.

"Is it as simple as that?" I asked. "Luck?"

I was looking for profound insight – something we could build on – but Oliver merely sipped his beer, wiggled his eyebrows at me and then burped. "Fucked if I know," he said. "The more I think about such things in light of recent events, the more nonsensical it all becomes. I take it you, like me, haven't had any more visitations?"

"Not exactly," I said.

"That's not what I want to hear, mate."

186

"I'm well aware of that but there's *not exactly* all that much I can do about it."

"I suppose all we can really do," he finally said, after a thoughtful pause, "is put all our cards on the table, look at what we've got and take it from there. What happened, Sonny?"

I told him about the argument I had had with Ashley – how certain we had been that neither of us had been responsible for the unlocked garage door and the sentence she had used from the mystery woman's journal. He listened without interrupting, letting me waffle on about my study door, how it had a habit of opening by itself, and enduring a five minute monologue on the possibility that, however tenuous, everything that had ever happened in my life had a connection. He didn't even flinch when I used a crass spider-web analogy, merely nodded patiently and blinked slowly.

"Even Helmsley," I continued. "Even that has its place in the bigger picture."

"How?" Oliver asked, intrigued.

"The story I'm working on," I told him. "It has elements of Maggie's story in it, heavily fictionalised, but I've only just realised it also uses the landscape we experienced that summer. There's a remote cottage, a garden – and even though I don't actually put it down on paper, the scenery I see in my head is the scenery we saw during that holiday and when Maggie escapes from that garden, that's the world she initially runs to... those hills and valleys, the boldness and texture."

Oliver leant forward, arms folded on the table. "Maggie?" he said.

"Maggie Sutherland," I told him. "The character from my story."

"And this Maggie Sutherland," he said, after a moment's consideration. "She has a dead husband called Jim, right?"

"I know," I said. "It wasn't intentional. It just sort of bled into it. You know how it is. You don't see what you've done until you step back from it, and by then you're too committed to the story to be able to do anything about it."

"You plan on changing the names later?"

"Yes – of course."

"But in the meantime, it's Maggie and Jim."

"Not really."

"Yes, really." He sighed and sat back, shaking his head slowly. "Any other time, I would have said run with it. As long as the fiction has integrity, do what you've gotta do. But the way things are now? It's unhealthy, Sonny."

Abandoning Richard and Maggie to their fates was not something I was prepared to even think about. The respite they had at times recently afforded me had been a godsend and I wasn't about to give that up without a fight.

"In what way?" I asked, doing my best to set my jaw the way the square-shouldered hero always did in the old black and white movies.

A little too patiently, he said, "Look, I'd never presume to tell you what or what not to write. I'm a writer, too. I know how these things work. But this... this reality is hard enough for us to grasp without you complicating matters further by fictionalising elements of it. I just think it'd be wiser if you set it aside for a while. Just until we get all this sorted."

"And you think that's possible?"

"That you can set it aside?"

"That we can get this sorted."

"I really don't know." He prodded the book on neuroscience with a callused index finger. "I was hoping this might provide some insights but..."

"Nothing?"

"So far, no."

"You're still looking for the logical, scientific explanation?"

"Is there any other way?" he asked.

"I don't know," I admitted – and then added, on a whim, "We could try looking for a creative explanation, I suppose."

Oliver looked tired of the subject. He sat back and let his arms drop into his lap but, in spite of himself, he said, "I'm not sure I know what you mean."

"We're both writers," I said, improvising. "We make our livings creating problems and then solving them. We build theme around apparently unrelated incident in order to find a deeper meaning, something that makes sense of existence. So why don't we just apply the same technique to the problems we're facing in our lives?"

Now that I'd spoken the words aloud, they seemed ridiculous and hollow. Desperation rang at their heart, and as I watched Polly cleaning glasses behind the bar, I wondered if it was any easier for her. Was hers a world of inexplicable happenings, too, or was it just the usual round of hand to mouth banality? I tried not to imagine what she was like away from her work – what her *life* was like away from her work – but it was difficult. I wanted the comfort of another's detail, the subtle escape of her problems and delights. It was the only way. Forget a creative explanation, just run. While I still had chance.

Before I had left to take the kids to Molly's, Ashley had said to me, "Do you ever wish you could just sit back and watch yourself – see where you're going wrong?" I'd dismissed the question, told her that she needed to stop thinking quite so negatively. We all did things wrong. It wasn't unusual. As far as I was concerned, in spite of the events of earlier that day, she had far less to worry about than most in that department. It was a moment of loving generosity, but now I once again found myself thinking about what she had said. I didn't want to watch myself – I wanted to watch other people, explore their possibilities – and, yet, this was just what I had in part suggested to Oliver.

"Do you think that's a good idea?" he asked me. "It's like I was saying about you putting Maggie and Jim in your story, mate – the way things are now, it just sounds unhealthy."

I could certainly see his point, and, yet, in spite of my misgivings, it seemed perfectly clear to me that it was a far better approach than Oliver's. To me, seeing him with his tatty little book on neuroscience, it seemed he was even more inclined to run from our shared truth than I. He wanted to explain it away; I wanted to understand what it said about us and the world we inhabited.

Or that was what I at least told myself.

"I don't agree," I told him. "Writing our way through this might be just what we need. A collaborative project. A factual novel. It makes perfect sense to me."

"It's not a prospect I find all that inspiring," Oliver said sulkily.

"What else can we do?"

He poked the book with a finger. "Keep looking for plausible explanations?"

"Second hand, discipline-biased explanations, you mean?"

"That's rich," he said.

"What is?"

"You talking about discipline bias. This from the man who believes the novel can answer all our questions."

"And you don't believe that?"

Oliver considered this, beard curling into his mouth like a sea anemone – and then he pushed himself to his feet, saying, "I need a piss. I won't be a minute."

Left alone, I went to the bar and got myself another scotch – a beer for Oliver. I didn't much feel like returning to the booth, the book on neuroscience not the best of company, and so remained there watching Polly finish cleaning her glasses.

She was a pretty little thing with a penchant for short skirts that I couldn't help but admire. Quick to smile, hands energetic and slender, she reminded me of a young horse my father had once taken me to see. Excitable. Powerful without the arrogance to realise it. Naturally healthy and curious. If I'd had a sugar lump, I'd have gladly given her it.

I tried to glance away when she caught me staring at her, but it was too late. She smiled and I smiled back, and she walked over to me – putting the final glass and towel on the bar between us.

"Your friend abandoned you?" she asked.

"Toilet," I said. "Temporary respite."

"I take it you've had a bit of a disagreement," she said – and I suddenly felt I had to go carefully, here. Polly seemed sweet, but I didn't know anything about her other than that she wore short skirts and enjoyed listening in on other people's conversations.

"Not really," I answered. "We just differ in our approach, sometimes."

"To your work?"

"Amongst other things, yes."

Polly nodded knowingly, and then said, "I loved *Of When*, by the way."

Of When had been my last novel, and it was fair to say that I was surprised Polly had read it. It wasn't that it had sold badly (in fact, it had done rather well and had attracted reviews that even Oliver had found quite impressive), but rather that I couldn't *see* Polly reading it.

190

She had the look of the closet fantasy fan, maybe occasionally dipping into the occasional space opera. *Of When*, in comparison, had been a broad literary novel that had examined the various effects experienced by a community when the child is abducted from its midst. The "crime" element had all but been ignored. I didn't want to see the natty or scruffy D.I. complaining about the compromised integrity of his crime scene or bagging evidence. What I'd wanted was to walk around with the parents of the abducted child – trudge through their nightmares and watch as they fell apart with accusations and frightening insights. I wanted the underbelly, the if-onlys, the precise methodology of secrets and grief. A hard novel to write, I remembered – whilst Polly talked of the novel's intensity and my incredible ability to get to the "grimy heart of the matter" – how it had seemed to spill over occasionally into my family life. It hadn't affected my relationship with Ashley in any obvious way, but nevertheless there had been times when we had sat together on the settee, silently watching the telly, and the mood had become that of my novel. At such times, I imagined that we both knew *exactly* what it would be like to have a child abducted. I didn't have to play with imagery and metaphor, I didn't have to think myself into the character. It was there. Around us. Within us. A primeval fear, something essential and marrow-like. I smelt it on the air like an impending storm and tasted it like blood on the back of my tongue.

"It really was very moving," Polly was saying. "Moving and unnerving. It made me see things about myself that were... well, you know."

"I do?"

"Not what I otherwise would have expected," she said, with a shy smile.

When Oliver finally returned from the toilet (I rather unkindly wondered if he'd "met" someone in there), Polly quickly handed me a crumpled piece of paper that she'd been writing on as we rounded off our conversation. "I really need to speak to you," she whispered urgently – casting a nervous glance in Oliver's direction. "Call me, okay?"

"I..." But before I could say more, she had returned to the other end of the bar where she served a twentysomething a fashionable drink in a bottle and purposefully avoided looking at me.

Back in our booth, Oliver said, "I was thinking about what you were saying while I took a dump."

"I thought you only wanted a piss." I looked at Polly's mobile number under the table and then shoved the piece of paper in my trouser pocket.

"I changed my mind," he said, "so fucking shoot me."

I pointed an index finger at him and let my cocked thumb drop. The recoil was decidedly unimpressive.

Blowing smoke from the barrel, I said, "You were saying?"

"I was thinking about what *you* were saying – about fiction answering all the questions," he said. "It can, but only on a personal level. And never for the reader, only for the writer."

"The act of writing?"

"Exactly. It's not passive. The writer takes a reality and refuses to accept it for what it *appears* to be. He works with it, finds the pertinent questions and sets about answering them – if only for himself. It's different with the reader. Yes, the reader participates, but he's only a passenger filling in the gaps. It may inspire him to take journeys of his own, but he'll never take the same journey the writer has – and he'll never have all his questions answered."

"I won't argue with that," I said. "But what are you saying? My creative explanation idea wasn't so bad, after all?"

"I'm not sure," he told me. "It might work, but not as a collaboration in the sense you seem to be suggesting. These experiences are personal, however connected they might be. We can only answer our own questions, not each other's."

The afternoon continued with more talk of my creative explanation until we finally returned to the subject of Maggie. Oliver wondered about Jim, whether he was "haunting" Maggie and him in the traditional sense, and if so, why? There didn't seem to be any obvious logic behind it and we both agreed that this, together with its possible connection to my experiences, was something we should both examine individually in our "creative explanations". It seemed too coincidental for it not to mean something, I thought – but kept this to myself, not wanting to colour Oliver's interpretation.

"So what do we do about Maggie?" Oliver asked. We were both

well into our cups by this point, Polly once again hovering as she cleaned tables and pretend that she hadn't given me her phone number and we'd never met and were actually complete strangers and probably wouldn't like each other anyway. Oliver had carefully torn a page from his book on neuroscience and was vainly trying to fold it into, I assumed, an origami duck. As a duck, it made a great Cthulu.

"Meaning?" I asked, wishing I'd been on beer rather than scotch.

"Meaning, what do we do about Maggie?" he said, growing impatient with me and his duck. "Do we tell her that I've seen Jim, too, or don't we?"

"It might make her feel better," I ventured. "But... she's a hell of a lot more... you know – more like her old self, but it still might... I don't know."

"Could go either way, right?"

"Right. It becomes something else once we tell Mags."

"A whole nother can of worms."

"Exactly."

Oliver held up the origami monstrosity, balancing it gently in the palm of his hand. "What do you think?" he asked.

"What's it meant to be?"

He shrugged. "Not sure," he said. "But if I had to hazard a guess, I'd say... a hypnagogic hallucination?"

Chapter Eleven

The room was stifling – and as cluttered and chaotic as ever. I listened and I felt, trying not to let my mind drift, not wanting to appear rude but also not wishing to miss anything that might shed light on any aspect of the situation in which I found myself. Old Man Ned, seated in the armchair, feet up on one of the coffee tables, wandered aimlessly through what little knowledge he could dredge up, and I patiently jotted the occasional note on my smartphone, feeling no closer to understanding.

It had been close on three weeks since that afternoon in the pub when Oliver and I had decided that we would attempt a creative explanation of our predicament – and it was fair to say that we were still no nearer understanding any of this. The exact details of Oliver's progress were unknown to me. We had agreed that we wouldn't discuss any aspect of our individual efforts for at least a month, but it was nevertheless plain to see that it was presenting him with as many problems as it was me. Oliver had been sullen the last time I'd seen him, and it was true I was suffering a similar mood. I looked and wrote and invented, but even with all that effort, nothing worthwhile revealed itself. I poured through all the accepted explanations – hauntings, psychological or neurological conditions, sociological phenomena – but the fictions I built were stale and unforgiving, and so, leaving Maggie and Ashley playing with the kids in the back garden, I had decided on this approach. Old Man Ned. A walking, talking creative explanation.

I told myself that it didn't matter that I suspected much of what he said to be bullshit, at best. What mattered was that the ideas came freely and unexpectedly. The associations had to be unhampered – random and removed from the kind of logic that only served to corner reason and interpretation. Ned prattled on, and as irritating as this might be, I felt lifted, occasionally hopeful as I went with it – happy to be lulled, even as I fought to stay attentive.

"I'm not good at the names and stuff," Ned was saying. "And dates. Not at all good at dates unless I've got a book to look 'em up in. But I am good at remembering the story stuff, if you know what I mean. That's what history's all about, for me. Got nowt to do with dates and kings and that kind of thing. It's all about what happened to Jack and Jim the day they tried to get a look inside the loony bin. That's the stuff that makes me tick."

I heard the familiar name and even though I realised right away that it was purely coincidental, I felt every muscle in my body tense.

"Jack and Jim?" I asked.

"Two lads I knew when I was a bairn," Old Man Ned told me. "Right pair of buggers, they were. They must have been about ten, at the time, and they was into everything. Wasn't a week went by when the bobby wasn't having a word with them."

"Rough uns, eh?"

"Nah," Ned sad, rotating his ankles on the coffee table. His right slipper had a hole the size of an old penny in the sole and through it his Paisley sock looked grubby. "Truth be known, they were as soft as second-hand shite. They never got into any fights, nothing like that – that I recall, anyway. It was more like they were just naturally curious. They took their neighbour's motorcycle to pieces one day, right there in his back yard while he was getting some kip after working nightshift, just to see how it worked and fitted together.... They were naturally curious, aye, but they weren't smart enough to understand that there were consequences. Soft as second-hand shite, like I said."

Ned's laptop was on the other end of the coffee table. The screen showed a web page that I'd briefly glanced at when Ned had brought me into the room. Now, thinking about Jack and Jim and just how relevant a name can be, I glanced at it more closely. It appeared to be a local history site. Not unusual for Ned. I saw a man's photo – sepia and stiff, and another of a pretty young girl with eyes that looked as though they could lift you off your feet and dance you quixotically through unimaginable streets. They looked Victorian. Possibly Edwardian. I saw the words "tragic murders" and wondered if that wasn't a little tautological.

"Their auld fella used to give them some right bloody beatings,"

Ned said, smiling dreamily. "But it didn't do no good. When something occurred to them, they just had to do it. They never saw beyond the event."

"And they got into the asylum?"

"Near enough," Ned said. He nodded. "Aye, near enough. They climbed one of the back walls and got into the gardens. From what I heard, the grounds were pretty well tended. Lots of topiary hedge archways and knot gardens. But it was mature and there were a lot of handy hiding places for a couple of tykes like Jack and Jim. They were in there for about four or five hours before anyone spotted them and chucked them out. Dark by that time, too – which only served to make it all the more awe-inspiring to the rest of us kids."

I imagined those two children – short back and sides, snotty noses, clothes little more than rags – hiding among the topiary, peeping out and pointing, sniggering and shuddering at the shadow people they saw taking the air with shuffling feet. Those two boys had not been unique. They had done nothing unusual for ten-year-old boys. At their age, I might have done the same. This didn't help me, however.

Since discussing our problems in the pub with Oliver, I had made no progress with the *Ma Boy, Ma Boy* story – and I now tried to superimpose one story over the other, seeing the Jack and Jim of Ned's story as Richard and Maggie Sutherland, creeping into the asylum with the sole purpose of finding their Elvis. It seemed a ludicrous approach, but I soon saw that this was far from the case. Richard and Maggie wanted more. They wanted to see, to understand and assimilate – just as those two boyhood friends of Ned's had. And wasn't that at the root of this? The eternal quest to have curiosity satisfied, to have appetite sated?

Ned was eyeing me suspiciously. He put his feet down from the coffee table and leant forward, resting his forearms on his bony knees. "So what's this all about?" he said. "And don't tell me that it's for one of them books you write, cos I reckon there's more to it than that."

"It's for one of them books I write," I told him stubbornly, and he nodded knowingly.

"Fine," he said. "You don't want to talk about it. I can understand that. Just answer me one question, though. Does it have anything to do with that lass of yours?"

I didn't know whether he meant Ashley or Nadine. He told me he meant neither.

"Maggie?" I asked. "Maggie isn't my lass."

Watching me very carefully, Old Man Ned inhaled noisily through his nose and said, "I don't even know who Maggie is – but I'd have to guess that that's probably a 'no'. Not Maggie."

"Then who?"

I felt the heat rising from the pit of my stomach – a feverish heat that once again took me back to my childhood, to the sickbed times, the delirium and fear, the confusion and comfort. I was not immortal. I depended on others. And sometimes it was just right to accept that. Sitting back, I imagined my mother kneeling on the floor beside the settee – soothing me with downy words and calm caresses – and the heat rose in my face and I closed my eyes, not wanting to accept the implication of what Ned was saying, not wanting to hear his answer.

"Sheila Mackenzie," he said – and I opened my eyes.

"Who?"

"That's what they call her, son. The woman you are seeing. Sheila Mackenzie."

The whisky was cheap and as harsh as hell, but I couldn't say I cared all that much. It hit the spot and that was what mattered. I helped myself to another and listened as Old Man Ned explained himself.

"There's not a whole lot more I can tell you, really," he said. I got the feeling that this wasn't entirely true, but said nothing. "Not a lot's known about her and I even have my doubts that that's her real name, but she's been haunting Sorrow Street ever since they knocked the asylum down and put up these houses, as far as I can tell."

"She's a ghost?" I asked. It was a ridiculous question but it was all I could think of to say. After everything that had happened it seemed something of an anticlimax. Oliver and I were bigger than all this. We deserved better. A ghost was beneath us. What did Ned think this was, a fucking *Most Haunted Special*?

"If you want," he said. "Always seems a bit too simplistic for my liking, though. The word 'ghost' has a dismissive air about it, these days. As I see it, it's more complicated than that."

On this, we were in agreement. "More complicated in what

197

sense?" I asked.

He shrugged and smiled, pouring himself a whisky and sloshing the urine-coloured liquid around the grimy glass. "Wouldn't be complicated if I knew that, now, would it?" he said. "Like I said, I don't know a right lot about her – and I certainly don't know that much about ghosts, as we insist on calling them... but one thing I do know, all the stories you've read or heard about hauntings won't help you one iota because, as I see it, these things define themselves. Each one is unique and nothing'll change that."

"Meaning?"

Old Man Ned swallowed a mouthful of the vile scotch, his throat clicking with the effort, and shook his head hopelessly. "I'm not sure," he said. "I think I'm just saying that to generalise them is to probably insult them, and that's not something I'd much fancy doing myself."

"Ghosts are individuals, too?" I said – hiding behind irony, since the whisky didn't seem to be helping all that much.

"If you want."

We said nothing for a minute or two, both of us staring into the middle distance – our gazes crossing, but never meeting. I didn't know whether the conversation we'd just had had been a positive development or not. I wasn't alone. Sheila Mackenzie had walked these paths before, apparently been seen by others – and, yet, I could find no real comfort in that. It was too commonplace and, if anything, I found Ned's belief that ghosts were specific creatures more reassuring.

"How did you know?" I asked him. "How did you know that I was seeing – that I had *seen* – this Sheila Mackenzie woman?"

Old Man Ned sucked his top lip thoughtfully before speaking. I felt the by now familiar heat rising in my face again and wished Ned's living room were not quite so cluttered and stuffy. I wanted my mother. Childlike in my fear and lack of straightforward understanding, I wanted her on the floor beside the settee – cooling a flannel in a bowl of icy water and dabbing my brow.

"It was obvious summat was going on," Ned finally said. "You... I couldn't put my finger on it. It was more of a feeling than anything else. And then I saw you from my bedroom window that night. Down in your garden. And it was plain to anyone looking that you were seeing something that no one else could."

"You saw me from your bedroom window?"

Old Man Ned nodded and I realised just how compromising the whole incident could have been. Any one of our closest neighbours could have seen at least some of what had happened – and if they had, just what, exactly, would they have made of it all? Would they merely dismiss it as typically eccentric behaviour coming from a writer or would they see it as something more worrying? Ned, ironically, was one of the few people on Sorrow Street we actually talked to – the other people I had grown up knowing either dying or moving away, their replacements two-dimensional in comparison, worthy of only the occasional nod. Ned clearly understood at least a little of what was going on in my life, and his seeing, whilst not exactly ideal, was bearable enough. But the thought of those unknown people, those ill-informed, possibly bigoted creatures seeing me in such a bizarre situation made me feel sick to my stomach.

"Aye," Ned said, "I saw you in your garden. I couldn't sleep because of the bloody heat, so I was stood at my open window trying to catch a breeze and there you were – large as life and twice as ugly."

"Shit." I glanced at the floor beside the settee; I could no longer imagine my mother kneeling beside me with her cooling bowl of water and flannel. I was on my own in all of this. No parental guidance, no opinions I would reject in a fury only to quietly accept later. Whatever happened now – wherever this went and however I got there – I suddenly realised it was all down to me. No one could make the decisions for me, now. No one could explain the finer points of how this was affecting my family and me. I had the capacity to understand, to draw my own conclusions and act on them – but suddenly I knew *exactly* what loss was. Alone without the support of my parents, sure that all our neighbours thought I was some kind of madman, I felt myself adrift.

"I wouldn't worry about it," Ned said reassuringly. "From what I could tell, no one else saw you – and if they did, so what? They don't figure in all of this, as far as I can see. They're just people, and people don't matter when they aren't *your* people."

"Your people?"

"Those close to you. Your friends and family. They're the only ones that really matter. The rest are just strangers. Here..." he reached across and topped up my glass, "... you look as if you need another."

In truth, it was probably the last thing I needed. My head was spinning as I tried to think. He had seen me. He was impartial, the quite possibly objective observer I needed.

I sipped the whisky and thought, and then said, "What did you think when you saw me? What were your... you know... what were your impressions?"

He considered my questions gravely, sucking his top lip again and sitting back in his chair – staring at the corner of the ceiling above the telly, as if there imagining my garden and me. Before speaking, he put his hands on his knees and stretched.

"My first thought was how I wished I still had a body like yours," Ned said. "Granted, you aren't exactly the best of specimens, but you did look well, that night – well and fit. Like a man who could move mountains, if he had to. I looked at you and I thought, 'There's a man with a job on his mind'. You looked as if you had summat to do, that was it. And then you just stood there and it was as if all the energy suddenly went out of you. You were limp, if that makes sense. You stood there upright enough, but you still looked like a rag doll. Anyone else watching wouldn't have got it. They would have just thought you were sleep walking or summat, but I knew there was more to it than that because, more than anything, you reminded me of your dad – and he was certainly never a one for sleep walking."

The corner of the ceiling lost its attraction and Old Man Ned stared at me pointedly. I couldn't see what my father had to do with this. As I remembered it, he and Ned had never exactly been best buddies. It was true that they had talked on occasion, and Dad had helped Ned out now and then the way I did – but it seemed ridiculous that Ned should claim knowledge of my father intimate enough to know whether or not he walked in his sleep.

"How on earth do you know?" I asked, perhaps a little too sharply.

Ned waited for a count of ten, and then said, "Your dad saw her, too, Sonny. He saw her, too."

I stood by the gate and watched my wife.

Nadine and Wee Mark played on the lawn – clumsily and

clownishly kicking a partially deflated football back and forth – and Ashley read a magazine quietly on the sun lounger, wearing a pink bikini and sunglasses. She hadn't yet spotted me and I took a moment to compose myself, pushing all thoughts of what Ned had said to me out of my head for the time being and instead focusing on Ashley – on how good she looked in the bikini, on what we could be doing if our life together were not crowded with the lives of others, on how we seemed to have forgotten about the new life we had planned on creating together. I felt loss and confusion, it's true, but right then, more than anything, I was aware of our love and fragility.

As I had been leaving, Old Man Ned had very pointedly told me to give Ashley his love. He had insisted, jokingly, that she had a lot to put up with what with me and my "other women" – telling me to tell her that if she felt she ever needed to spend some time with a real man, she should give him a call. He knew nothing of my one-time relationship with Maggie, of course, but it had been a joke that had nevertheless failed to miss its mark – and as I walked quietly across the patio in Ashley's general direction, I flashed on a sickening image of Ned standing over her, hands fiddling in his pockets as he drooled and dreamed.

"Sonny," she said, shielding her eyes and gazing up at me.

"Ashley."

"You do realise you're blocking my sun, of course."

"Of course."

"Oh, well that's all right, then." She pushed herself up on her elbows – sweat dribbling from the delve at her collarbone, her cheeks and the tip of her nose already a little too red. "And you don't fancy sitting down for a minute or two?"

"You want my company?"

"Always," she said coyly. "Plus it would be really nice to have my sun back."

"I never had you tagged as the mercenary type," I said – pulling the white moulded plastic chair over and sitting down beside her.

"There's a lot you don't know about me, lover-boy."

"Is there?" I realised we were both still joking – just letting the conversation take us wherever the hell it wanted – but this was not a comforting thought.

"Actually, no," she told me after a moment's consideration. "There's nothing you don't know about me."

"Are you sure?"

"As sure as I can be."

We silently watched Nadine and Wee Mark do a bizarre little dance across the lawn, and then I asked, "Where's Maggie?"

"Upstairs resting," Ashley told me. "It was a bit too hot for her and she'd been helping me change the kids' beds so I chased her for a lay down."

"It's working out better than I envisaged," I admitted.

"These things usually do, in my experience."

"Except when they don't."

"Naturally."

The "dancing" on the lawn was getting rather rough. It was fast becoming a drunken barn dance (sans barn and fiddler). Wee Mark took a run at Nadine, clearly intending to swing her around by the arm again, but Nadine stepped deftly aside – sticking her foot out and tripping Mark up. He landed with a characteristic Wee Mark thud, his chin bouncing off the lawn. His milk teeth clattered together and his eyes watered, but he didn't cry – merely jumped straight back to his feet, laughing as he chased Nadine in circles on the rectangular lawn. I couldn't help but admire his resilience. The world was not a threat to the Wee Marks of this world – not through ignorance, as some might expect, but simply because such creatures possessed within them the sublime capacity to overcome.

Ashley was staring up at me. She'd raised the back of the sun lounger so that she could more easily watch Nadine and Wee Mark with me – and when I looked at her I noticed that the bra of her bikini had slipped slightly to reveal the dark areolae of her nipples. While the kids were busy rolling about on the lawn, I slipped my right hand inside the left cup – impressed and aroused by her firmness, damp flesh against damp flesh, the friction of attraction and need.

"Not here, Sonny," she said – but she didn't push my hand away, instead rubbing herself experimentally through the damp, sweaty material of her bikini bottoms. "We can't."

I squeezed and brushed my thumb back and forth across her erect nipple – feeling myself grow hard and slick.

"Where then?"

"I don't know. Tonight. In our room."

"But I want you now."

"Sonny." Longing and disappointment in equal measure, the unspecified insistence that I be reasonable – that we both remember our circumstances and show a little restraint. I felt sick. I wanted her to take me away, help me stop thinking, but all I got instead was caution and care, the prevailing of intellect over instinct.

But she was right. Maggie was upstairs sleeping and the kids were playing on the lawn. I could hear our neighbours out in their gardens, radios coming and going on the breeze, and smell a barbeque being fired up. What choice did we have other than, for the time being, abstinence?

"I know," I said. "I just want you."

I withdrew my hand and Ashley took hold of it in hers, kissing my knuckles. "And I want you, too," she said. "More than ever. What can we do, love? We both knew this would be a little restrictive, but it is only for a little while – and it's not as if it isn't for a good cause."

"Do we know how long it's going to be?" I asked, rather uncharitably.

Ashley shook her head. "Not much longer, I'm sure."

I could still smell Ned's on me. Ashley didn't say anything about it when I leant over and kissed her, but I could tell she too caught that oddly indefinable whiff – and didn't find it in the least bit attractive. I therefore decided a shower and a change of clothes was probably a good idea.

"Just try to be quiet, okay?" Ashley said. "Don't wake Maggie up."

I promised to do my best but, as I ascended the stairs, I thought that it was pretty unlikely that Maggie would be able to sleep through someone using the shower or the bathroom in general – given that her room was right next door.

Pausing on the landing, I sniffed under my arms as best I could – wondering if I could forestall the shower until later. Pulling the fabric of my T-shirt to my nose, I inhaled deeply – getting an immediate hit of sweat and stale urine, something overripe and fruity. Not at all pleasant, it at least settled the question and, without giving it another moment's thought, I pushed the bathroom door open and stepped inside.

The wound on her thigh hadn't healed. She squatted over the toilet staring straight at me, and that was all that I could initially register. It hadn't healed and it looked infected and if she didn't get something done with it soon it was very likely going to kill her. I took an involuntary step back, starting to apologise for bursting in on her like that as I took in her breasts, the healed scars, the tangle of coppery hairs at her pudendum – and then this peculiar, wholly unfathomable reality started to hit home. I heard her bowels loose, saw the filthy fluid erupt from her, and I understood that this was again the woman from the journal. Her eyes held mine and I thought that Sheila Mackenzie was such an unlikely name, such an impossible association for such an exotic, repulsively attractive creature. Nameless, she had been more appropriate. Without a label, something to bring her back down to a wholly human, wholly real level, she had been somehow more appealing, not so much of a threat – but seeing her here now, knowing her as Sheila Mackenzie and also knowing that, if what Old Man Ned had told me was true, my father had also seen her... seeing her here now like this made me understand that what she actually was was dangerous.

"Mine," she said. The first words I had ever heard her speak. Her voice was rich and a little too deep, not at all the voice of someone who hadn't spoken in decades – and as she stood, as if to approach me, I watched her mucus-like shit hit the toilet seat and wondered if the dead sang. In their graves did they perhaps exercise their voices by singing Abide With Me? Or did they merely whisper through eternal night, saving themselves for Friday Night Karaoke at the Club Resurrection?

"Mine," she repeated. "Nothing ever belongs except to those that really need. Nothing. Everything is mine. I want. I need. I am. Mine. I take what is mine because I've never been given anything. Not in life, not in death. *Mine.* But can it be? Mine. Never... enough. I purge. I empty myself to make more room, but then more is needed. Too much space. Not enough to fill it. Effort. Struggle. Never enough."

She started to walk towards me, hands out – beseeching. I tried to slap her hands away, feeling her strength and resistance, her *solidity,* and backed quickly away – hitting my shoulder hard against the edge of the door, slamming it shut and blocking my exit.

Today, I sit here and try to find the right words to express just how I felt when faced with that... that what? Horror? Even that seems too inexact and woolly. I need a word, just one, to tell of the scale and complexity of my emotions, of my fear, but repeatedly I fail. I picture myself in that bathroom, Sheila Mackenzie's cold hands stroking my face as I grow hard in spite of my fear and confusion, the smell of her liquid motion thick on the air – gaseous and virulent – and everything I write seems cliché, inaccurate at best, a mere shadow of an ideal, Platonic form.

I felt something alien, something I had once known – a remnant from a previous time. It hurt, my chest and throat tight, and I thought of release, the desperate, vital need to expel. I grew harder as Sheila Mackenzie whispered and pleaded, but that wasn't it.

A scream.

I needed to scream.

I needed to scream and if I didn't give in to it soon that tight, burning pain in my chest, throat and ears would, like a bizarre fulfilment of some childhood urban myth, travel to my brain and I would die of an embolism.

"Sonny." Now she was using my name. I pushed myself back all the harder against the closed door, willing myself to melt through it – ghostlike and insubstantial as I once imagined the woman before me to be. A hand caressing my neck. Fine fingers tracing my jaw line, cupping it as my name was repeated. I closed my eyes against whatever horror would come next, the scream so close – so, *so* close – and tried not to listen, tried not to hear this dead woman speak my name.

"Sonny – what is it? What's the matter? Sonny?"

I'd never enjoyed making a fool of myself. Some people seem to thrive on it, dancing like the wildest of imbeciles at parties, shouting and drawing attention to themselves in the streets, falling in love like dopey, misbegotten puppies time and time again – but not I. I wanted normalcy, the quiet life where no one was unduly concerned about or attracted to me. I wanted nothing that would draw me out of my tight little unit. So when I opened my eyes and saw Maggie standing before me – the hair plastered to one side of her head whilst sticking up on the other, dressed only in washed out pink knickers and bra, face flushed and harsh with wide-eyed concern – I felt, on top of a dizzying sense of dislocation, the kind of embarrassment that just made me wish I'd never been born. The mortification worse than the time my mother had walked in on me whilst I masturbated in my room as a teen, I wanted to turn and run, get away from Maggie. But the door was firmly closed behind me and Maggie – dear, sweet, suicidal Maggie – was before me, leaning in to me with a cool hand on my face.

"Sonny?" Her voice was soft and brittle around the edges. The voice of a mother, rich with emotional need and the instinctual reassurance I was familiar with from my own childhood. "Sonny, it's all right. It's only me. Hey. Come on, now. It's okay." She was smiling at me, even though we both knew this was not the time or place. "What's wrong, love? You seemed to, I don't know – I thought you blacked out for a bit, there."

"I'm okay," I mumbled – mouth dry and all but unresponsive. "I was a little dizzy, that's all."

"That was no dizzy spell," she said. "Credit me with some sense, Son – it was like you were somewhere else."

"I'm fine, Maggie – honestly." I pushed past her and went to the sink, splashing cold water on my face. "I just didn't expect to see you in here. I came in, saw you there and started – and then the reflected sunlight from the window caught me in the eye and I just went. That's all."

"That isn't what happened." There was such certainty to her tone – such implacable need and, if I wasn't mistaken, anger, that I turned to face her.

She stood with her back to the bathroom door, hands by her side, shoulders sagging with the weight of her own burden. Her figure was fuller than Ashley's, especially at the hips, and as I took in her tense and unwavering form, I saw the woman she would become. Frumpy. It had been one of Mam's favourite words. "I saw Mary Oswald the other day and by God is she getting frumpy." As she grew larger, so would her underwear – as comfortable and capacious as she, without hard edges or sharp corners, spoilt only by silent recrimination – but she, unlike many, would nevertheless be a pleasing sight. If she lived long enough, Maggie would grow into the woman Nature had always intended her to be. I wanted to be around to see that. I wanted us *all* to be around to see that.

"That isn't what happened, at all, Sonny, and you know it," she said. "You saw something. You came in here and you saw something that wasn't me. What did you see, Sonny?"

She was a potential alley, a kindred spirit. At that moment I saw it with the utmost clarity. Maggie and I shared secrets and mysteries. We knew things about one another that no one else did, and I suddenly understood just how unifying and beneficial this could be. Where Oliver had all but insisted that he and I approach our problems separately, only coming together with our ideas when some kind of conclusion had been reached, Maggie would push for us to face our demons side by side. She would embrace my reality and see it as an affirmation. If she was mad, I was mad – and where the mathematics would suggest that that was twice as bad, Maggie would only ever see it as half the friendless misery it could have been.

"I didn't see anything," I told her.

In my study, I closed the door behind me and leant back against it – eyes closed, heart seemingly growing larger with each thud-thud until it felt as though that was all I was; one gristly, engorged-to-bursting heart, thud-thudding against the injustice of the world. I tried to steady my breathing, aware that I was close to hyperventilating and righteously pissed off that there were no paper bags in the house. *Just plastic,* I thought. *A medical emergency where only paper will do, and all we have is plastic.* It seemed ludicrous and, yet, wholly fitting – and as my breathing finally started to regulate itself, I sat down before my computer and put all thoughts of paper bags out of my head.

I thought that maybe I should have just told Maggie the truth, after all. But what was the truth? That I had seen a woman who had possibly been dead for seventy years or more and that, if what Old Man Ned had said were true, my father had also seen her? That Oliver had also seen Jim and we were both working on an explanation by writing individual fictions that might, ultimately, have nothing at all to say about the predicaments in which we found ourselves? I just couldn't see how bringing Maggie into all of this, allowing her to see that the psychological explanations the shrink had given her were false and laughable, could actually help. Surely it was better that we keep her out of it – spare her the worry and confusion. That had to be the kindest route to take.

But what if she told Ashley?

I didn't even want to think about that. To have that last, insubstantial shred of control ripped from me just made me want to... what? Hide? Run away? Repeatedly bang my head against the wall until I was dead? I didn't know what it made me want to do. I didn't even know how it made me *feel*. All I knew right then was that I didn't want her telling Ashley, and that I suddenly didn't have the strength to try to prevent it. Whatever was meant to happen would happen – and the best thing for me to do was simply sit back and let it.

I moved the mouse and looked at my notes for the *Ma Boy, Ma Boy* story. I hadn't written any more of it for a good while – taking Olly's advice and instead focusing on the quest for the elusive creative explanation – but now I found myself once again drawn to it. It didn't matter to me that the world around me was getting stranger by the minute, or that I was still no nearer understanding any of it. It didn't even matter that Maggie Sutherland and Richard (not to mention Elvis – mustn't forget Elvis) might only serve to complicate my reality further. What mattered right then was the fiction and the fact that I thought I saw a way back in. Unwilling to even think about what I had seen and heard in the bathroom or what Ned had told me, I just wanted to be back in that unnamed village with Maggie Sutherland and Richard – sharing their dark little adventure whilst somehow negating my own.

Richard breathed in the night and thought that this was the most perfect way of living he could ever have imagined. The darkness concealed them and he had to keep reminding himself that, should they let their guard down and step from the shadows, they could still be seen.

"I'm certain it's him," Maggie was saying. Dressed in black jeans and a black turtleneck sweater, her hair tied back and her face smeared with boot polish, he suspected she was enjoying this a little too much. She spoke in urgent whispers and crouched with him behind

a holly bush – grabbing his hand excitedly whenever the man they were surreptitiously observing passed the uncurtained window. "It has to be – I just know it."

"How did you work that one out?"

"It was none of the others and there's no one else it can be," she told him.

Richard reminded himself that this little game had been his idea – and so far it had been a right fucking wheeze, as his granddad was fond of saying. They'd spied and letched and generally discovered things about their neighbours that they would never otherwise have imagined. The widow who lived over the road from Maggie liked to "read" lesbian porn in her garden shed, for example, listening to The Archers on a tinny old transistor radio, whilst Mr Smithwaite two doors along had a woman visit three nights a week – a pretty, erect young thing whom he took in his arms and taught the foxtrot. Just that, Richard thought. The fucking foxtrot. *All innocuous enough, and certainly not something that either of them had been or were ashamed of. It was their game. Voyeuristic, yes. Intrusive, absolutely. But they were hurting no one, and the sex they shared after each little "outing" was bloody amazing.*

Now, however, he was beginning to wonder if this were such a good idea. The whole Elvis gig – the jokey plan to hunt him down – had been something they had both embraced, each getting something unique and no doubt highly individual out of it, but tonight was different. Maggie was still caught up in the fun of it all, enjoying the "fancy dress", SAS element of it, but something had changed. She seemed especially hyper – her hand sweaty and fidgety in his, constantly looking over her shoulder and whispering commands. Under slightly different circumstances he might have found it amusing, endearing, even – but her insistence, faked or otherwise, that this really was Elvis only served to underscore the peculiar, obsessive quality of her mood.

"He doesn't have to be in the village," Richard pointed out.

"Yes he does."

She was so insistent that, initially, he wasn't inclined to argue with her. What did he really know about anything? He was just a boy and she was a woman with a soft body and years of experience behind her.

The years between a childhood of isolation and the liberation that had ultimately brought her to this place had been tumultuous, he knew. An addict for a while, she had slept rough under bridges – hung out with the kind of no-hopers that made his dad look like the fine upstanding gentleman he wasn't – and at one point a little over fifteen years ago she had been close to suicide, desperate to escape the memories of where she had been and, indeed, where she then was. But none of that altered the fact that this assertion that Elvis was alive and well and living in the village, whilst moderately entertaining, was simply ludicrous – and so he found himself arguing with her, gently enough, it was true, but arguing nevertheless.

"That doesn't make sense, and you know it," he told her. "He could be anyway – whatever you say about him not being too far away from you. Why would Elvis move to a fucking shithole like this?"

"Anonymity," she said, "and, like I've already said, to be near me. You weren't there, love."

"I know I wasn't, but it still doesn't make sense."

"Who says anything has to make sense?" He supposed she had a point. Just. "That's where we all go wrong, if you ask me. We want everything to be neat and tidy. We want perfect, acceptable explanations – and the reality is totally removed from that. Not everything has meaning, not everything has significance. It just is."

Richard was about to tell her that he understood that – that he didn't need every problem to have a pretty little solution and he sure as fuck didn't expect to have every question answered – when he noticed a movement at the dining room window of the house they were watching. The man was looking out, a glass of whisky in one hand, a book in the other, and for a moment Richard was convinced he was staring directly at them. He grabbed Maggie by the upper arm and pulled her roughly into deeper cover – feeling the sweat prickling his armpits as Maggie's foot snagged on something unseen and she fell on top of him.

"He saw us," Richard hissed.

Maggie laughed, pushing herself up on one elbow and kissing him hard on the lips – flesh mashing painfully against a cruelty of teeth. "Silly boy," she said, "didn't you see his mouth moving? He was looking at his reflection – he was looking at his reflection but he was seeing and talking to Jesse. It's what he does, love."

"Jesse?" Richard was breathless, convinced they were going to be caught – imagining the beatings he'd get from his old man. He loved being with Maggie and delighted in the sense of unity this little game brought with it, but he was suddenly quite scared – unable to see where this was leading and just how deeply involved he was. It was true that Maggie was the one taking all of the risks. If they were caught and their relationship was discovered, she would be the one who would be punished most severely. He would no doubt achieve victim status and get away with nothing harsher than a little woolly jumper counselling. But he didn't find that in the least bit reassuring. That she was prepared to take such risks – for a game, for a phantom... for a delusion *– was all the more disturbing. "Who the fuck's Jesse?"*

"His dead twin brother, love," Maggie said, whispering in his ear – one hand resting at his neck. "He always talks to Jesse. Always has and I guess he always will. They probably need each other more than ever, now."

"But it's not really Elvis," Richard insisted. "This is just a fucking game, Maggie. It's not Elvis and he's not talking to his dead twin brother. Stuff like that just doesn't happen."

She wasn't listening to him. Looking out through a gap in the bushes she was watching the man at the window. "I always thought that was the most evocative aspect of his life," she said. "His mother dying was bad enough, but Jesse... El's life started with death. It was with him, always, in his reflection and his shadow – in the way he walked and possibly even in the way he sang. Jesse, greedy and hungry Jesse – living through his vibrant twin brother. Vernon and Gladys should never have told him about Jesse. It marked him from day one."

Maggie sat back against the fence with a sigh – pulling Richard into a sitting position beside her. "I know what you're thinking," she said. "You still think I'm nutty as squirrel shit and you're scared."

"I'm not scared," he insisted – succeeding only in sounding even more afraid.

"But you do think I'm nutty?"

"I didn't say that. I just don't understand what's going on here."

211

"And therein lies the problem," she said, putting her head back and looking up at the stars. "That stupid fucking need to understand – to make sense of everything."

"I can't help the way I am," Richard protested.

"Actually, on the whole, you can," she said. "But I wasn't really talking about you. I was talking in general. About everyone, me included."

"So we're all stupid to try to understand?" It beat double maths, but as far as lessons went, it wasn't exactly the most stimulating or comforting of premises.

"When it gets in the way of living the life, yes," she said. "Sometimes the only true way is to take it for what it is, without questioning every little thing. Somehow I know that that man at that window is Elvis. If I think about it too much, I'll talk myself out of the truth of it because, on a logical level, it just don't fucking compute."

"So how do you know?" Richard asked.

"Because I had his twin sons," she said.

I desperately wanted to write more but Ashley was shouting up to me from the bottom of the stairs and, however badly I might have wanted to ignore her and dive back into the turbid, rippling illusion of my story, I couldn't really ignore her.

I stood in the open doorway of my study for a second or two, composing myself and preparing my story – just in case Maggie had done the dirty deed and told Ashley what had happened in the bathroom – and then walked to the top of the stairs and looked down at her.

"What is it?" I asked, trying not to sound too impatient and, yet, making it clear from my tone that I was busy.

"You've got company," she said. "Can you come down?"

Outside in the garden, the day bleeding into the brick and mortar as the temperature once again began to rise, I found Old Man Ned sitting on the wall beside Maggie – the stalker wall, as I'd now started to think of it. He'd dressed for the occasion in cream slacks and a pastel, powdery blue short-sleeved shirt, hair combed back and deck shoes suitably crisp. I wondered if he'd merely dropped in on his way to somewhere else or if this really was for our benefit.

"Ned," I said, noticing that Maggie had got him a beer (it couldn't have been Ashley; she would never have been so encouraging).

"Now then, stranger." He tipped his bottle at me and winked. Maggie was watching me carefully and I felt prickly heat rising between my shoulder blades. "Long time no see," Ned said ironically.

I smiled and pulled up a plastic chair as Ashley ushered Nadine and Wee Mark indoors for their naps. "What can I do for you, mate?" I asked – exhausted and confused, my head heavy with the cheap whisky he'd given me earlier.

"More what I can do for you," he said.

"He's been telling me about the asylum that used be here before they built the estate," Maggie said. "I didn't know that."

"Not many people do."

"I thought this might be of interest." Old Man Ned handed me an old, yellowing pamphlet, many of its pages loose or ripped. "I thought I had it somewhere, but I wasn't sure. Had a hell of a job finding it."

I took it from him, wishing he didn't know as much about my situation as he did and knowing that Maggie was already putting two and two together and coming up with God alone knew what. Leafing through it as casually as possible, I noted tables of figures and statistics, crude line drawings and page after page of cramped, antiquated typesetting. A smoky, damp smell like singed fur rose from it and I quickly thanked Ned, setting it on the floor by my chair.

It would be of no use to me. I knew this, and so did Ned.

"It's pretty fuzzy," Ned was saying, "but it's probably worth a look. It's amazing what you can sometimes uncover if you look in among all the dross hard enough." He was smiling at me and I quite suddenly didn't want him here. It wasn't just that I was concerned that he might let something slip and unintentionally give Maggie even more to work with. It was more that I felt as if Ned had taken a step too far. He seemed to want to help, but his concern was intrusive – *invasive*, even – and I now found myself wondering about his motives.

Just watch your step, I imagined Dad saying – unable to decide if this were a genuine recollection or not. *Folk have a bloody habit of only doing what they want to do. They usually have an agenda all of their own, in my experience.*

"I'm sure it'll prove really useful," I told Ned. I sounded cold and distant, not at all the kind of response Ned had grown accustomed to. His brow twitched into a passing shadow of a frown and his eyes narrowed suspiciously.

"Even if it's only to stick under the leg of a wonky table, right?" He wasn't giving me the benefit of the doubt, merely playing the game – carefully assessing this rule change.

"Well, now that you mention it..." I returned his smile and Maggie watched this exchange with obvious puzzlement. She looked about to say something, and then thought better of it.

"I see you got that hole of yours filled in, then," Ned finally said. "Solve the problem?"

"We haven't had much in the way of rain," I pointed out. "It's hard to tell."

"Thing with something like that is, you get one thing fixed and something else crops up. But you're a smart bloke. You knew that already, right?"

I knew he was talking about more than just drainage problems – but Maggie thankfully seemed to have missed any implication, and I was therefore prepared to let the matter drop. I didn't want to prolong this. Rightly or wrongly, I now saw Ned as part of my troubles and getting rid of him quickly became a priority. I said little, allowing him and Maggie to rabbit on ceaselessly about local issues. I listened patiently, nodding in all the right places and glancing imploringly at Ashley when she came back out from putting the kids down for their nap. There was no escape there, however; I'd made my bed.

"That Internet thing that Sonny here helped me put in has been a godsend as far as news and other information is concerned," Ned was saying. "Don't rightly know what I'd do without it, now."

"It's not something I'm all that familiar with," Maggie said. "When my husband died, well, he left a laptop but we'd never got round to putting the Internet on it. He wasn't a much of a one for anything like that, really. Just used the laptop to do his spreadsheets and that was about it."

"You should get Sonny to set it up for you." Ned said this innocently enough, but I couldn't help feeling that he knew more than he should. "Then we could send each other emails," Ned continued. "I like my emails. I have this friend, Sheila, and she lives... well, let's just say a long, long way away – and we email constantly. Four or five times a day. You wouldn't believe the things we talk about."

"I can imagine," Mags said – far too taken with him for my liking.

"Oh," he said, smiling at me, lips wet and obscenely fleshy. "I don't think you can. I really don't think you can."

I'd had enough. I didn't know what he was playing at but I wasn't prepared to listen to another word. However uncomfortable he had at times made me feel, the overwhelming sense I had had of him was of a man I could trust. Now I felt differently. Ned was bad. Ned had his own agenda. Ned wanted to wheedle his way into our lives and...

... and what? I didn't know. Maggie Sutherland and Richard whispered together behind the holly bush at the back of my mind and I again saw Sheila Mackenzie squatting over the toilet in our bathroom and voiding herself in the most foul and violent way imaginable, and Ned waited, peeling the label off the sweating lager bottle with those knobbly, arthritic fingers of his. I looked at Maggie, feeling her eyes on me. "What did you see?" she had asked me earlier, and I now found myself wondering just what it was s*he* saw – what it was she saw when she looked at the world around her, what it was she saw when she looked at me. Where was the centre? *Who* was the centre? How was I to make sense of this when the sun beat down, my head hurt like buggery and *Maggie kept staring at me like that?*

Ashley smoothed sunscreen on her arms, oblivious, and a mean-looking wasp landed on Maggie's knee. She slapped it away and then whispered to me, "Are you all right, Sonny?"

Only a matter of weeks ago, she had tried to gas herself and, yet, here she was asking me if I was all right. I knew I should have found it humbling – should have been shamed into getting a grip and coming clean to those closest to me. But I didn't. Her question was yet another intrusion, and my reply was terse enough to make Ashley look over at me.

"I'm fine, Mags, love," I quickly repeated, this time more moderately – even managing a fairly convincing smile. "Just got a wee bit of a headache and my eyes are fucked. Too much time spent staring at a computer screen."

"I know that feeling," Ned chuckled. "I forget to blink, at times.

215

Next thing I know, my eyes are tearing and everything's gone all foggy. Not good." He put his empty bottle down beside the wall and got to his feet. "Well," he said. "I better be going. Leave you young people to get on with whatever it is young people do these days."

"Young?" Maggie said. "I wish."

"Everything's relative, pet," he said, and I walked with him to the front gate, where he paused and regarded me earnestly. "What did I do to upset you?" he asked.

"You shouldn't have come to my home." Even I had to admit that that sounded pretty pathetic.

"I thought I was doing you a favour," he said. "I had t'get up in the bloody loft to find that pamphlet. I don't know why I bothered, now."

"That's the problem, Ned." He squinted, pigeon chest rising and falling monotonously. "Neither do I."

"You think I'm up to something?"

"Are you?"

"Oh, look – I'm going. You've obviously seen your arse, lad, and I really don't need this."

"Why did you bring Sheila into the conversation?" I asked. "That wasn't funny, Ned."

"Neither was your attitude." The sun was dipping behind me; Ned's eyes watered with the callous glare and for a second or two I felt sorry for him. "Where do you get off being so cold with folk what're trying to help you?"

His self-righteous indignation was wasted on me. I didn't want any part of his little game. All this time, he had been doing his best to find a way into my life – making suggestive comments about my wife and generally pretending to be the harmless, lip-sucking old man that he (to me, at least) quite clearly wasn't. Watching him walk away, not saying anything more that might stop him, I thought that maybe I should have taken more notice of Ashley from the beginning.

Back on the patio, where Ashley and Mags were sunning themselves and nattering about something that, thankfully, seemed to have nothing to do with me, I sat on one of the arse-sweating plastic chairs and picked up the pamphlet. I saw very clearly that this was the last thing I needed. The day had been difficult enough already without my piling even more uncertainty and enigma on top of it all.

According to Ned, my father had seen Sheila, too. This strange woman had haunted both our lives, father and son, and, yet, I had seen nothing of this in Dad. I had no memory of him that even remotely suggested he had been struggling to understand something on the scale of my own ordeal. So had that just been Ned's way of getting to me? Did he see that by involving my father he somehow completed the circuit? And if so, why? Why would it be so important to him that I be so unnerved?

Maggie got up to fetch herself and Ashley a drink, pausing beside me to see if there was anything I wanted. Her shorts were as tight as Maggie Sutherland's, I noticed, and I tried to keep my eyes from dwelling on her "camel's toe" – looking up at her face and squinting against the sun. She smelt of cocoa butter and sweat, and placed where I was I suddenly found myself imagining leaning in to her, pressing my face against her groin, breathing her in as I had all those years ago in her mother's cottage in Wales. I didn't want her. If it meant hurting Ashley or risking all that we had built together, I didn't want to love Maggie in that way ever again. But if there had been guarantees... if I could have known for certain that Ashley would never find out and that it would leave no discernable impression on our lives, then I would have seized whatever Maggie-related opportunity might present itself.

"Name your poison," she said, peering down at me – still clearly trying to figure out just what was going on with me.

"A scotch would be nice," I said, wanting a little blurring around the edges. "Plenty of ice."

"You think that's a good idea?" she said, quietly – so that Ashley couldn't hear.

"I do."

"After what happened in the bathroom?"

"I can always get it myself."

Her thighs tensed, and I thought that maybe she was feeling it, too. An energy, a need – that hunger that could never be truly satisfied. *Are you wet, Mags?* I wondered. *Do you need escape?* I imagined her running her fingers over her thighs, rubbing her crotch hard before holding out her fingers for me to smell. A crude image. Maggie deserved better. But I just couldn't push it away. I saw her stripped

217

and spread, as she had been in Wales, opening herself to me – pink as candy but not so hard on the teeth. Somehow Molly had known about that. Good old e-fucking-vangenical Molly. But that no longer seemed important. That I hadn't said anything to Maggie about Molly wanting to talk to her, that I hadn't created an opportunity for the two of them to speak alone was inconsequential. All I could think of was Maggie. Maggie with her tremors and sighs, Maggie with her humour and willingness to conceal... Maggie with her salt and sorrow.

"Scotch and ice it is, then," she said – and walked away.

Chapter Twelve

The fortnight leading up to Maggie's "Back to Life" party had passed without incident. I worked and generally did my best to keep out of the way whilst Maggie and Ashley discussed what they should do to celebrate Maggie's returning home ("not that I see getting rid of you as cause for celebration, you understand," Ashley quick to point out) – ultimately deciding that it should just be the three of us, the kids and Oliver, Molly bound to put a dampener on the proceedings. The truth was, I wasn't in the mood for any kind of party, and I most assuredly wasn't in the mood for planning one. I felt distant and isolated, I suppose. Oliver was not proving as supportive or contributory as I had hoped, rarely home, his emails tardy and terse, and whilst my overcrowded home had attained a strangely quaint domestic harmony, it seemed to have little to do with me. Maggie hadn't mentioned the bathroom incident again and she and Ashley fit together frighteningly well, one shoring the other up, but I couldn't help feeling, as I turned every corner expecting to see Sheila Mackenzie, that all this was somehow designed to push me further away – and that was something I could only welcome, given my current frame of mind.

The day of the party was cooler than it had been for a good while, and as I stood on the patio, drinking coffee and looking at the neatly described patch of lawn, I thought about the storm of the night before – the way it had beaten down persistently for close on three hours, the temperature dropping with each inch that fell. The thunder and lightning had woken Nadine and Wee Mark, and as Ashley and Maggie had tried to get them settled again, I had looked out of our bedroom window at Sorrow Street. That night, it had seemed aptly named. There had been the promise of grief in the air, an indistinct shift that made me recall the day of Mam and Dad's funerals. It was right that they should have gone together. Theirs had been that sort of relationship; committed and complete – excluding all others quite literally.

Had anyone ever been happy on Sorrow Street, I had wondered. Ashley and I had managed it. Granted, things had not been at their best, of late, but this had been... a minor glitch, something I was sure we would ultimately rise above.

The rain had continued to bounce, and even when Ashley had finally returned to bed, I had remained at the window – watching the amber washed street and counting off the seconds as the storm moved too-slowly east.

Now, breathing in the fresher air, watching a drunken bee tap repeatedly against the facia of the garage as it tried to get over the roof, I couldn't recall just what time I had joined Ashley. A couple of hours had passed, at least, the by then steady rain holding me until the security lights of the house over the road came on – a cat returning home – and the spell had been broken.

Examining my father's lawn, placing my coffee on the wall and squatting down at the edge of the patio, I was both relieved and a little puzzled to see that it was not in the least waterlogged. After the night before I had expected puddles deep and prolific enough to hydrate the Sahara but, in spite of my aborted efforts at fixing the drainage problem, it seemed to be just fine. Back to how it had been in my father's day.

"Penny for them." I turned – pushing myself up and trying on my best smile for my wife. "And don't tell me they aren't worth it. I'm your number one fan, remember. I know what you can do with those stray thoughts of yours."

We'd had far too little time together, of late, and, ironically, it seemed to have helped. I still felt somehow cut off from everything that was going on around me – the organising of Maggie's party, the perpetual herding of Nadine and Wee Mark, all the talk of what Maggie should do if she found herself struggling again – but when Ashley walked over to me and laid her head against my shoulder, I experienced a sense of unity that had eluded me for a very long time. Possibly since my parents had died.

"I was just looking at the lawn," I said, putting my arm around her. "All that rain last night and not a single piddling puddle in sight."

"So your hole did the trick?" Such pride. I felt a disappointing twinge of suspicion.

"I wouldn't be so sure of that," I said, determined not to spoil the mood with my silliness. "I'm not sure I did all that much. Everything I took out, I put back in again."

"Except that tin with the journal in it," she said. "Maybe that was the problem. Maybe it was blocking something and you – "

"Inadvertently released it," I finished for her.

"Yes," she said. "Something like that."

The thought of the journal, buried all those years – somehow waiting for an opportunity that would inexorably come – was not comforting. If what Ned had said were true, my father and others had also seen Sheila Mackenzie. She'd been haunting Sorrow Street long before I'd been born, the journal, I assumed, buried all the while. Also, there was Maggie and Oliver's visits from Jim to factor in. Oliver had seen him *after* I'd unearthed the journal, but Maggie had been "seeing" Jim for a good while before that. If these incidents were part of the same puzzle, it suggested to me that discovering the journal hadn't been the catalyst, after all. It just wasn't that simple.

"Not that simple, at all," I mumbled.

"Maybe not." Ashley shrugged. "But at least it's sorted. One thing less for you to worry about."

I nodded and smiled to myself.

Oliver arrived at seven-thirty and I was surprised and a little disappointed to see him looking quite so cheerful. He filled the living room in a way that he hadn't in a very long time and as I watched him from my place on the settee, where I quietly (and some would say rather ignorantly) read Paul Auster's Oracle Night, I hoped his good humour had something to do with "our little problem". He kissed Maggie and Ashley, immediately set about teasing Nadine and Wee Mark – and barely acknowledged my presence. I'd emailed him a couple of days before to see how his creative explanation was going and, as yet, had received no reply. Similarly, my phone calls and voice mail messages had gone unanswered. I'd even texted him a couple of times, knowing full well that his big thumbs would make tapping out a response rather difficult.

Now I watched as he settled himself in the armchair – Nadine already climbing all over him. He seemed remarkably composed. His face – or what could be seen of it through the now neatly trimmed hair and beard – had regained its usual healthy appearance, flesh pink and ruddy, eyes alert and bold. Had I looked in the mirror, would I have seen that same shade of confidence and contentment, or would I instead have been greeted with a ghoulish visage worthy of the worst Hammer Horror or Amicus movie? I thought of all the old Saturday night horror double bills I had watched with my parents as a child. Boris Karloff, Peter Cushing, Christopher Lee, Lon Chaney Jnr. – they had all been there. A happy time of snacks and contentment, of familial bonds founded on safe scares and embarrassed laughter. I recalled the too numerous horrors I had then witnessed, hugging cushions and keeping my feet well away from the edge of the settee, and wondered which one I would now resemble. Would I be the werewolf or would I be the vampire? A zombie, perhaps, or a ridiculous, taffy-hearted Frankenstein's Monster – stumbling from one tragedy to the next, blithely unaware of its own godless culpability? Whatever, I most assuredly would not resemble the valiant Van Helsing. At best, I would be one of the bumbling peasants that burn the Monster in the castle. A bit player. An extra. Either that or The Blob, doing my damnedest to forestall Steve McQueen's career and regrettably failing. Those boyish good looks. The blue-eyed prick deserved to die.

Oliver was watching me over Nadine's head. I really didn't need him looking at me like that – appraising me, analysing every twitch and turn of the page. He smiled but still didn't speak, merely allowing Nadine to play with his beard whilst Wee Mark stood beside Oliver's armchair and stared at him in attempt to intimidate the big fella.

We had told each other some pretty bizarre stuff, made admissions that, under "normal" circumstances, would have remained unspoken – and it occurred to me as I closed Oracle Night and set it on the arm of the settee that maybe I'd been harsh when I'd checked my email earlier that morning and, finding nothing from Oliver, called him an unresponsive prick.

"You look as if you've been working too hard," he finally said. "You should take some time off, get some sun – stop fretting about stuff so much."

"'Stuff'?" I said.

"Stuff." That bloody smile, again. I suddenly had the crazy notion that Molly had got her hands on him. He had that Born Again look about him. All was well with the world. Everything had its place and purpose. Born Again Christian. Born Again Hetero. A satisfying equality of absurdity.

"That covers a multitude of sins," I said. "Would you care to be more specific?"

I could hear Ashley and Mags laughing in the kitchen, preparing whatever the hell it was that needed preparing. Nadine tickled Olly, sat astride one of his big knees, and Oliver reacted with exaggerated mirth whilst Wee Mark stared on threateningly.

"You know what I'm talking about," Oliver said. "Let it go, Sonny – it's inconsequential."

I had learned to expect many things from Oliver, but such an off-hand dismissal came as something of a shock. Our friendship was founded on an ability to understand each other – an ability to grasp meaning from the most obscure of authorial shorthand – and, so, whilst I was always ready for him to present me with an alternate viewpoint, I certainly didn't believe he would nonchalantly wave away the concerns we had, up until fairly recently, both shared.

Before I could say anything, however, Ashley and Maggie came rolling in – laughing and generally disturbing the peace. They'd both clearly been at the vodka and as I considered and reconsidered that word, *inconsequential*, I thought that perhaps it was not such a good idea for Maggie to drink on top of her medication. I made a mental note to have a word with Ash about rationing her.

"We've had a chat and we are in agreement," Ashley said. "Our dear friend Oliver Montgomery is definitely up to something. He looks like the cat that's got the mouse – "

"Cream," I said, thinking, *inconsequential?*

"Your cat can eat what it wants, mine prefers mice," she told me. "Now, Olly, dearest, what gives?"

He sat smugly staring at Ashley, the light streaming in the window behind him, my beautiful daughter now giving him one of her best cuddles. I thought of a time a couple of years ago when the two of us had escaped the nappies and milky baby sick for the weekend and ran away to "the woods" – a stand of forest just on the edge of the moor. I had camped there with my mates when I'd been a kid, and it had always been somewhere I had wanted to return to, so when Oliver had said he'd wanted to get away from it all for a short while I'd checked that Ashley would be okay with her mother and Mags watching out for her and our new daughter for a night and, when she told me to go for it (a little *too* eagerly), I'd phoned Oliver and told him to get his tent ready – I was taking him to the woods. It had been intended as a back to nature event, something that would help me celebrate the miracle of my shiny new daughter, but as it was, Oliver had insisted on bringing his mobile phone, laptop and spare power packs for the two. He'd also brought a handheld LCD TV and enough tinned food to sink a summer fête. All through that Saturday night, he'd constantly checked his phone and email, and when I'd asked what the hell was going on and why, if he'd wanted to get away from it all, he'd felt the need to bring "it" with him, he'd merely smiled the smile he was now smiling and said, "You'll see. Give it time and you'll see."

As it had turned out, the self-satisfied, secretive mood that he exhibited that weekend hadn't heralded anything all that spectacular. His agent – the infamous and virtually invisible Boots – had been "working" to "secure" him a new contract, seducing the editor in question and guaranteeing in the process that Oliver got a two-book deal with a £35,000 advance against royalties. Not all that incredible, but nevertheless quite impressive for a non-popularist novelist like Oliver.

When he said "You'll see" this time, however, beaming at Ash and Mags like a lighthouse going full tilt, I suspected that this was something rather more impressive.

"You can't just say that," Ashley was telling him. She'd clearly been hitting the voddy pretty hard and when she sat down on the edge of the cushion at the far end of the settee and stared into his eyes like some contemporary Grand Inquisitor, I hoped against hope that it wasn't going to be one her occasional throwing up drunks. I really wasn't in the mood for holding her hair out of the way and telling her that everything was going to be okay and, hey, don't worry, we all overdo it now and then.

"I think you'll find I just can," Oliver told her, stroking Nadine's hair and reaching out his other big hand to tickle under Wee Mark's wee chin. "I can just say what I just want. In a just world, just men just can just say just what they want."

Mags was standing behind me – hand resting against the back of the settee mere inches from my suddenly quite excluded head. The night before I'd walked by the bathroom and, against my better judgment, glanced in to see Mags lovingly bathing Wee Mark. Hands slick and soapy, she had rubbed the gentle curve of his back – splashed water to rinse him off as she sang a song I couldn't name under her breath. It had been a curiously intimate mother-son moment, but one I nevertheless found myself stopping to observe. A glimpse into their private world, Maggie, when she glanced up and saw me watching, had not apparently wished to leave me out of their bathroom ritual; she'd smiled and waved me in to join them – an invitation I'd nevertheless declined.

Now I wished for that inclusion. Even as I once again picked up the Paul Auster novel and fled from my post-modern existence to the post-modern novel (wondering *just* what the hell "post-modern" meant, anyway), I wanted to be a part rather than apart. Maggie Sutherland and Richard shifted around on the periphery of what I knew to be real and somewhere (somehow) Sheila Mackenzie, if that really was her name, invited me to walk with her through the topiary archways so that we might untangle the knot gardens – and whilst it had been a relief to find myself alone over recent days, I now saw the loss and latitude as a threat, a danger that I found far too attractive, even as I acknowledged it.

Whilst Ashley continued to harangue Oliver, Mags sat down on the settee beside me and glanced at the book exaggeratedly. "Good, is it?" she asked, her shoulder nudging against mine like a tug against a leaky old oil tanker.

"Unusual, but strangely readable," I said. "Lucid."

"Lucid?"

"The kind of novel I'd want to write, if he hadn't already written it."

She nodded and made thoughtful noises. I wasn't sure what this was all about, but it was nice to have her sitting beside me. She smelt festive – the booze commingling with the delicate summer perfume and locking her firmly in the here and now.

"I don't know what happened," she said very quietly, "but I want you to know that you can always talk to me – and if it was anything to do with Wales, that's okay. I think about it, too. A lot."

Ashley laughed a little too loudly when Oliver said something about the amount of cleavage she was showing – and I looked at Maggie, not knowing if I had heard her correctly.

"Why wouldn't you come in and help me bathe Mark, last night?" she asked.

"It wasn't my place," I told her, rather flustered.

"Your place is your decision?"

"Occasionally."

"And this time?"

"Probably not."

"So why didn't you come in when I made it perfectly clear you were welcome?"

I was certain that Ashley could have heard our conversation if she had had a mind to. Mere inches from Maggie, it was only the slightly drunken conversation with Oliver that was keeping her from picking up on what we were saying and I didn't like that one little bit. Oliver said something about group dynamics and breast implants and it occurred to me that if I could follow their conversation whilst I talked to Maggie, it was just as likely Ashley could do the same.

"Just leave it," I whispered, and Maggie stiffened somewhat.

"I don't want to leave it," she said – a little more quietly, admittedly. "Too much has been left unsaid, as far as I can see, and I don't think I want to be a party to that."

"So what are you suggesting?"

"Nothing," she said. "I'm just saying, I know something's going on here and... I just want you to know that you and Ashley were there for me, and if you'll let me, I can be there for you, too. If you need to talk, I'll listen, Sonny."

I felt guilty as hell. Again. She didn't deserve my sharpness any more than Old Man Ned had, and I asked myself once more just what it was I was hoping to achieve by pushing away those wanting to help me. It made no sense and, yet, my overwhelming wish right then was simply to retire somewhere quiet with Mister Auster – rebuild the childhood tree house with a fabulous wealth of self-indulgent isolation.

I quietly apologised – aware that Ashley and Oliver's raucous exchange seemed to be drawing to a close and not wanting to prolong this. Nadine was very nearly asleep against Oliver's big chest and Wee Mark looked around for something to wreck. "I don't mean to be a shit," I whispered to Maggie. "It's just that my work's been giving me a few problems and I can't seem to get my head clear, that's all. I get a little seepage and real-life takes on an added dimension. It's best that I keep my distance when I'm like this."

"The Trials of the Contemporary Novelist?" she asked.

"Something like that." I smiled. It was a struggle but by clenching my buttocks really hard, I just about managed it.

"Well," she said, giving my knee a pat, "if that's what you need to tell yourself, fine. But don't let this *whatever it is* get out of hand, Sonny. If you need to talk, you know where I am."

Inconsequential?

The evening passed painfully slowly but I did my best to participate, putting my arm around Ashley when she sat down beside me and gratefully accepting the whisky she brought me. She was concerned, in that way that only the "slightly tipsy" can ever be, that what Oliver had said was true and she was indeed showing too much cleavage, so I tried to reassure her.

"If you were flat-chested and wearing a polo-neck sweater it'd still be too much cleavage for Oliver," I told her – speaking nice and clearly so that Olly could hear. He seemed to have other, *inconsequential* things on his mind, however, staring at the clock on the mantelpiece and smiling that self-satisfied smile, again. "I said," I shouted. "If you were – "

"I heard you the first time," Oliver said. "And, for the record, I don't find cleavage in the least bit objectionable. As long as I don't have look at it whilst I'm partaking of the finger buffet."

"Nice to know you're prepared to be tolerant," Maggie said. She was perched on the arm of his chair – whence she could easily pounce if it looked like Wee Mark was about to do something he shouldn't. In spite of my having had a quiet word with Ashley, Mags was three sheets to the wind and I realised I was going to have to insist she stay another night. There was no way we could in good conscience send her home in this state.

"One does one's best," Oliver said.

Maggie seemed on the verge of saying more. However, just as she was about to open her very capable mouth, the doorbell rang. Oliver looked once again at the clock on the mantelpiece and smiled that intriguingly self-satisfied smile. "That'll be my little surprise," he said – handing a sleepy Nadine to Ashley and getting to his feet.

I stood, letting the Auster fall down the side of the settee as Oliver went out into the hallway and opened the front door. I heard mumbled conversation. Wee Mark stood in the living room doorway, peering out intently at this new development. Maggie pulled him away so that she could have a look herself.

"Oh my giddy aunt," she gasped. "Either I'm more pissed than I thought I was or someone has finally seen sense."

Neither Ashley nor me knew just what the hell she was talking about, but when she stepped aside to let the mystery guest in an air of faultless sobriety fell across the room – a hush so complete that even Wee Mark (who seemed to be getting a summer cold) quit his noisy mouth-breathing.

None of us had seen him for a good eighteen months – at the very least – and it took me a moment to register just what I was seeing. Tall and dark, shoulders broad in a crisp white shirt, hips narrow in the blackest of black jeans I'd ever seen, Donnelly McCrane was the picture of health. His face was delicately tanned and his eyes positively sparkled – and, yet, he nevertheless looked worried and out of place, as if he didn't quite know what kind of reception he would receive.

Oliver followed him in and stood by the window, arms proudly folded – Don left stranded and alone by the far end of the settee. I should have realised. Only one person had ever made Olly look the way he did tonight and, to be fair, I could now go some of the way towards understanding just how Oliver might consider everything else going on in his life inconsequential.

"Don," Ashley said.

"Don," Oliver repeated, nodding and obviously enjoying the moment.

"Don?" Maggie asked.

And Don nodded, smiling. "Don."

Kneeling on the settee, I reached over and shook his hand. "Nice to see you, again, mate," I said.

As Oliver so delicately put it, "the girls" had a lot of catching up to do – so the two of us repaired, as ever, to the back garden with drinks and a mountain of sandwiches.

Sitting together on the stalker wall, each knocking back the whisky and chewing thoughtfully on a ham and pickle bun each, I supposed we looked the epitome of once working-class fellows at rest. We could have just finished mixing darbo, for all anyone seeing us would know – and, yet, there was far more to either of us than that, however reluctant we might be to admit it.

"Inconsequential?" I said, through a mouthful of sandwich.

"That wasn't the best choice of words," he conceded.

"You're telling me."

"But it wasn't exactly the best place or time to get into all that – "

"Inconsequential *stuff*?" I hazarded.

"You aren't going to let it go, are you?" He picked another sandwich from the plate between our feet and opened it to examine its contents – something that irritated me no end.

"I don't expect to hear dismissive shit like that from you," I told him. "Especially after what you saw."

"I didn't see anything," Oliver told me flatly.

"You didn't see anything."

"That's what I said."

"So it was all just a dream, was it?" I asked. "All that *stuff* about seeing Jim. It was all a figment of your imagination?"

"Yes." He sighed and tossed the sandwich back on the plate. "Look, Sonny, I'm not being dismissive, okay? I've thought about it long and hard, and the only possible conclusion I can draw about my experience is that it was personal. It was personal and therefore it spoke *to* me, *about* me."

"Your subconscious trying to tell you something?"

229

"Yes.'"

"And you really think it's that simple?"

"I do, yes." He leant forward and rested his impressive forearms on his knees – hands dangling, head lowered as if fighting a swoon. "I needed to see what was missing," he went on. "Jim... he didn't like what me and Don were... what we *are*. He had love with Mags and we, in Jim's view, should be denied. It was all about having another bloke's dick up your arse to him – he couldn't get beyond that and see that, first and foremost, it was about love."

"And this told you something about yourself?" I said, heavy on the irony.

"Yes. Yes, it told me something about myself, Sonny," he said. "It told me that Maggie and Jim had lost each other through no fault of their own whilst I had thrown it away. I had someone who gave me everything I needed and I was willing to throw that away because Don had made an error of judgment. That was unconscionable – and only by putting that right could I ever guarantee that I wouldn't see Jim again."

Oliver fell silent and I was admittedly at a loss. I could hear Ashley, Mags and Don laughing in the dining room – Nadine joining in hysterically in that way kids do when they so desperately want to convince the adults around them that they get the joke, too – and it seemed a world away from where I was. I watched an ant crawling on the edge of the plate but didn't have the energy or motivation to reach down and flick it away. Oliver had somehow succeeded in getting his life back on track. Don had given him the direction he needed and, it seemed, he was quite happy to rationalise – to *lie to himself* about – everything else.

"So where does that leave me?" I asked him.

His eyes were sombre and vague when he glanced at me – flicking away quickly, not content to rest lest they betray his guilt. "I don't know, Sonny," he said. "All I can assume is that if my experience was personal, then maybe yours is, too."

"It says something *to* me, *about* me?" I sneered and Oliver shook his head dejectedly. "Christ, Olly, do you know just how fucking trite that is?"

"I don't have all the answers," he said, reaching down and flicking the ant away from the sandwiches. He caught it wrong and his big finger mashed it against the plate. How could something so small make so much mess? I tried not to think of what it must have felt like to be that ant, instead listening as Oliver droned on. "I don't have all the answers but I have come to understand that looking for explanations isn't always the way," he said. "It's an insatiable addiction we can well do without, mate. We just have to stop, fix the things that need fixing, and then get on with whatever the hell it is we do. That's all I know for sure."

"So you admit you might be wrong?" I knew that I was quite possibly pushing my luck. I wanted to see Oliver riled. I wanted him to know what it was like, to *remind* him what it was like, to have his reality constantly challenged.

"I'm not doing this, Son," he said – very quietly. "I don't play these kinds of games anymore."

"And now it's a game." I said this with all the energy and passion of a soggy sheet of newspaper – suddenly resigned to my fated solitude.

"You know what I mean."

"Yes – you, as you see it, have solved your part of the problem and you're washing your hands of the whole sorry mess. Very noble of you, I'm sure."

"That isn't fair."

"I don't care."

"I've already helped you," he said. "You just aren't willing to see it."

If my hole had still been there I would have pushed him in and buried the supercilious little prick.

"You've helped me?" I said, incredulously.

"The solution to your problem lies in the example I have set," he told me. *Make that supercilious* didactic *little prick,* I thought. "There were things I needed to put right. Once I did that, everything fell into place. All you have to do is find what's wrong with your life and correct it."

"That simple, eh?"

"I think so, yes," he said. "Look, Sonny – I want to help you, I really do, but I'm just not sure that I can. You know what all this is about. You just have to admit it to yourself and do something about it. Me telling you what I think won't help facilitate that – not while you're still so resistant."

"Why don't you give it a try?"

Big men are as much a victim of their size as are little men, I thought as I watched him squirm. He wanted to be away from here – away from *me* – hiding in some inadequate corner with his eyes tightly closed and his hands clamped over his ears as he sang *la la la* to himself. But he was trapped. Trapped by circumstance and trapped by his own physical nature. Fading into desired oblivion isn't so easy when you're built like a brick shit-house.

"That's what you want?" There was a calmness about him that I didn't really trust. Nevertheless, I nodded. "Fine," he said, getting to his feet and standing with his back to me. "As I see it, you are a fundamentally decent bloke who's tainted his life by making one silly mistake that he's never been able to reconcile. You have a secret, ergo you have guilt. You are 'haunted' by a mystery woman – a woman who walks like a bride going down the aisle, fingers herself, passes right through you even as she, some would say, seeks your help, and has mental health issues."

"Her name's Sheila," I told him.

He looked over his shoulder at me and raised an eyebrow. "No," he said, "her name's Maggie. The two are fully transposable, Sonny. They are one and the same. Stop Maggie haunting you and you stop Sheila haunting you. It really can be that simple. Trust me."

Don was watching us from the doorway. I didn't know how long he'd been there, but when he spoke I felt more vulnerable than ever. "Trust is all we've got," he told me. "Listen to him, Sonny."

I marked the late night silence of the house – the incomplete sense of things desperately trying to fall into place – as I again stood at our bedroom window, looking down on Sorrow Street. Oliver and Don had kindly offered to take Maggie and Wee Mark home, promising that they would stay the night with her, just to be sure that she wasn't too rat-arsed to look after Wee Mark, and I supposed I was grateful. I wanted my home back. I wanted it to be just me, Ashley and Nadine again. But as I watched Old Man Ned walk to the end of his front garden to close the gate, I found myself thinking of Maggie, of her fictional self and the, if Oliver were to be believed, easily transposed Sheila Mackenzie.

"He doesn't know anything," Oliver had said of Don just before they had left. "I didn't tell him anything about the things you thought you saw and he knows nothing of what happened between you and Mags."

I hadn't been convinced. Nevertheless, I had said, "I'm very pleased to hear it – but what about Jim? Did you tell Don what you saw?"

"Of course I did," he'd said – as if this were the most ridiculous question he'd ever heard. "What I *thought* I saw is what brought us back together. I had to tell him."

Something had to be done. Yes. Oliver had strongly suggested that, and I at least accepted that things couldn't continue as they were. But I didn't see that it was quite so straightforward for me. I simply couldn't tell Ashley about the things I had seen because, I supposed, I suspected that Oliver was at least partially right in his assumption that this had something to do with what had happened between Maggie and me in Wales. If I spoke to Ashley about Sheila Mackenzie it would inevitably lead me to Maggie – to Maggie and what we had done to each other all those years ago.

"Every bit the novelist." I turned and saw Ashley standing in the doorway. She was naked and as she walked slowly towards me, I willed her not to touch herself. "You're doing that staring into space thing more than usual just lately – on the brink of a great literary discovery?"

"Not really," I said. "Just that I'm too shagged out to do anything else."

"I'm sorry to hear that." She pressed against me and we kissed. The light was out, but still I felt we were being watched from the street. I glanced down and out and, sure enough, there was Old Man Ned, standing by his garden gate and staring up at our window. He couldn't see us, I was sure, but I nevertheless reached for the cord and closed the blind – still kissing Ashley.

"You taste of vodka," I told her.

"You taste of... actually, you taste a little gamy," she said. "When was the last time you brushed your teeth?"

"This morning, Mum."

"I'd tell you to go do them again," she said, "but I'm in desperate need of a right good fettling. Here, feel." She grabbed my hand and guided my fingers inside her. "Wet or what?"

"Positively sopping, my dear."

"What does it remind you of?" she breathed – squeezing me through my jeans. "Say something literary and sexy."

"McStraw's," I said, and she frowned at me.

"McWhose?"

"McStraw's. The wet fish shop on Brick Street."

Ashley slapped me across the face. It wasn't the playful slap I had anticipated but, rather, a strong and quick contact that brought tears to my eyes. Nevertheless, there was no anger behind it. She smiled and called me a cheeky sod, pushing against my fingers all the harder and slapping my face again. This time I grabbed her wrist, my face burning, but when I saw the look in her eyes and felt myself stiffening, I let go and waited for her to slap me once more.

I am to this place and time what tomorrow is to today. Incongruous, a mere possibility that some would wish to avoid even as others would embrace me – take all they can from me. The Warty Nurse sits in both camps, as much a mystery to me, these days, as I suspect I am to her. She longs for tomorrow even as she dreads what it might bring. She lives to breathe in and taste my humiliation, even as she cleans me – her practical fingers lingering as her uniform crinkles her quivering, ecstatic disgust. Her attentions no longer trouble me. There will be a settling, on that she can count – but in the meantime... in the meantime, I take from it what I can, content to let her make me come even as I number the possible ways of her passing.

She is not the first to use me, but if I have my way, she will be the last. I do not need permission. I do not need the promise of forgiveness. A thought is all I require – the will and the opportunity to bring it to fruition.

I remember the narrow lanes and the steeply inclined streets – the tang of the ocean on the air, the filth in the gutter by my feet. The women in their peculiar bonnets avoided me as though I were plague-ridden and generally foul, knowing of my daughter, Rebecca, and my marriageless state. When I had to, I spoke of widowhood, of the husband lost at sea, but few were convinced by my lies – which were now seemingly less convincing with the Innocent Child in my arms or toddling along at my side. It was as if she robbed me of the capacity to be duplicitous and, so, I gave up my tales and let them believe what they would.

I worked at the inn – a stale and predictable place with sailors and dock labours shouting the odds and orders at all hours of the day and night. It had a familiar feel about it, taking me back to those earlier times of sale and scam, and it was true to say that I felt a degree of comfort in that place – pleasingly cut off from the world with my daughter in our room at the back of the building.

Now I wonder if it ever could have been different. An alignment of stars, the coming and going of a tide – had our lives been set out for us? I think so. I think on the finer details, the things we ignore as mundane and trivial, and now see the refined connections – the web-like tracery waiting for the informative twitch. It all has a place and point, and that was most assuredly the case with my love for my daughter. She deserved so much – all the beauty and grace of a thousand fine cathedrals, the health and vitality of the richest stallion, the intelligence of her mother but without, I could only hope, my poor lack of judgment and my driven need to strike out. I wanted these things and more for her. Dresses from Paris, suitors from the classed and moneyed – the liberty to walk the mews without having to look constantly over her shoulder.

The pay I earned working in the inn put food on our table and clothes on our backs – this much is true – but this was not enough for me. Rebecca was a happy child, easily pleased, her cries quickly silenced with a cuddle from her mother, her laughter quick and generous. She needed little but the love I gave – but I could not imagine this lasting. She would grow and, as a consequence, she would want. There was enough of me in her to all but guarantee that.

I looked for other possible solutions to what was most probably a problem of my own making. I spoke to Susanna, the innkeeper's wife and a sweaty, sympathetic soul, but as she would have it they were already paying me all they could afford. "Laugh while the Lords libate, m'love," I remember her saying with a wink, but only did I *understand more fully when she pulled me into the back room and added, "Don't be telling me it's never crossed your mind, a pretty thing like you. They's got money to throw away on ale, why not let them throw a little extra yours way? Won't get no objections from us."*

Ah, to open my legs and make money with such a simple thing as my cunt! The wheel turns and we find ourselves back where we started – on our backs with a crapulent boor struggling to keep erect long enough to spend himself inside us. It was not a pleasant place to which to return, but it was profitable and, as such, I embraced my notoriety and stacked my counted shillings high – laughing with Rebecca when we toppled them together, the child ignorant of their source and the things they could acquire.

Edwin Mortimer. A man with death in his name. I should have turned him away the minute I set eyes on him – but I saw the twin bulging pouches of his purse and his passion and marked him for the opportunity I imagined him to be.

Susanna did not like him. Nevertheless, she went out of her way to facilitate a meeting – steering me, insisting I take his ale and bread – and, as surely as his Gypsy eyes burned with mayhem and fire, a question was asked.

"How much for your company, lass?"

It should have been different. It is dark here, now, and I struggle to write this by the guttering light of the ward's only candle. I'm sore from my latest humiliation and I want death. My own. That of the Warty Nurse. Death to the ignorant masses.

And, yet, I also want life. I want my daughter with her perpetually parted sweet wine lips, with her budding personality and humour. I want to smell her wholly individual scent – appropriately childlike in its simplicity, beguilingly complex in its effect. She was my saviour and my admittedly ill-formed conscience, and I now rush as the flame sears away the edges of time and see just how significantly I failed her. In my efforts to make a world for her, I destroyed the one she already had – the one she was more than happy with.

Yes, I want her.

And I want him.

She slept, as she always did, on the other side of a heavy curtain. A

236

content child, she seldom stirred – however noisy and demonstrative my "company" might be – and this was how it was the evening I brought Edwin Mortimer to our room. Mortimer pulled the curtain aside a little before I could stop him and glanced in on her, smiling to himself and saying, "Blessed. You must love her very much."

"I do," I whispered, pulling the curtain back in place.

"Now I understand."

"You do?" I did not want a conversation.

"The mother prostitutes herself so that the child need not. Admirable."

My life has brought me into the sphere of many men – all cruel in their own individual ways – but Edwin Mortimer was indeed a cruel man amongst cruel men. That night, he took what he wanted without a care for what was right or good, and when I asked him to kindly pay, he laughed coldly and said, "I think not. I'm not done here yet."

With that, he rose quickly from the bed and pulled aside the curtain that separated my part of the room from Rebecca's. Glancing back at me, he smiled hideously – and in my heart, I knew that all was lost. What was about to happen would change things forever.

"No," I said, pushing myself up.

Mortimer stepped back towards the bed and hit me hard, his thick-skinned knuckles splitting my lip. I tasted blood. I tasted bile. I tasted the filth of all my years, and smelt a return – the familiar surrounding me, sweating its warning and calumny.

"Yes," he insisted. "Call out or try to stop me and she dies. It's that simple, lass."

"I'll kill you."

"I'm sure you will," he said sardonically. "But first I'm going to fuck your little daughter until she bleeds."

He looked back at Rebecca. She slept on, as yet untouched by the drama that was unfolding at her bedside – ignorant of the indignity that was about to be inflicted on her.

"Does it have a name?" Mortimer asked.

"Yes, she does," I told him. I was happy to talk now – anything to delay what was about to happen, anything that would allow me the time I needed to think of a way to stop this. I had no doubt that he would kill Rebecca. If I made a dash for the door he would snap her

fragile neck as if it were a twig for his fire, and I would be alone and adrift – the woman I once was passing through me in an act of heartless reclamation.

"What is it?" he asked, already growing hard again – one hand absently fingering this filthy member.

I didn't want to tell him. It suddenly seemed very important that I withhold something of her from him. When he dreamed of this night in years from now (always assuming he escaped my wrath), I did not want him waking with Rebecca's name on his lips.

"Nadine," I told him. "Her name's Nadine Verity."

He nodded his approval and took a step closer to my daughter. Hesitating, he looked at me again and then walked around to the far side of the bed – keeping me in his line of vision as he pulled down Rebecca's bedclothes and lifted her nightdress. He caressed the pure cleft of her sex, pushing her legs apart as he climbed carefully onto the bed, kneeling between her tiny feet, and I prayed that she wouldn't wake. Sleep through this, my baby child, *I prayed. But God was the contrary, vile creature He so often is – and even before the thought had finished forming, Rebecca opened her eyes and looked up into the face of Edwin Mortimer.*

"Hello, child," Mortimer whispered silkily – and Rebecca looked to me for reassurance.

"It is all right," I told her. "Mama is here. Everything is all right, my darling."

I could push him from the bed. I was sure of that. I could push him from the bed and grab Rebecca. If I made as much noise as I could as I made for the door, we would be safe. Susanna would hear us. She would bring help and my daughter would be safe and Edwin Mortimer would live to die another night – one, I was nevertheless sure, that would be of my choosing.

"It won't work," he told me. "Whatever you're considering, it isn't going to work. I simply won't allow it." He touched her again, parting her lips slightly with his fingers, rubbing spittle into her as his cock twitched like an elder branch in the hands of a dowser. Rebecca flinched and looked at me again – eyes bright with fear and confusion. I felt the rage building, but this wasn't like the other times. There was more at stake here than merely my own life and liberty, certainly more

238

than my ridiculous pride. Rebecca needed my help and protection. I had to do something and, yet, to do something was to possibly place her in even greater danger.

"A neck so fine is easily broken," Mortimer observed. "You'd do well to remember that. Now," he added. "Tell her to relax and cooperate."

"Do want the man wants, my darling," I said, looking around the room for something I could use as a weapon. I still had the hammer I had used so proficiently to kill Chadwick and his whore, but it was at the bottom of my chest. The water jug was on the bedside table, but I couldn't see that a man like Mortimer would be stopped by a prettily patterned piece of pot – however well aimed. Before coming to this place, I would never have allowed myself to be so vulnerable. There would have been a knife under the mattress, a cudgel in a drawer – always something within reach. Even with Chadwick, my sense of self-preservation had been strong. But since coming to this place I had grown complacent.

And now my daughter was going to be the one to suffer.

Always the innocent.

"Just look at mama, darling," I told Rebecca. "Just keep looking at me and everything will be all right, I promise."

"That's good," Mortimer said. "Very good. Just keep it like that and we will have no cause for further suffering."

I have never seen such a look. When Mortimer forced himself into my daughter, her eyes showed only darkness and trust. The pain was nothing because her mama would make it end – would love her and save her and put the world back in its place. She waited for me to do something, but there was nothing I could see to do. Mortimer was a big man and as enraged as I was, I knew that I was powerless. To call out would end this in the most tragic of ways – to attempt to fight him, to find something with which to beat at him and struggle against that which was destined, would bring only more sorrow and my daughter's increased vulnerability. I could do many things, but I was level-headed enough to know that there was nothing I could do to wrench my Rebecca from this pain and humiliation.

"Mama," she pleaded – and all I could do was sit and watch. Mortimer drove deeper and she cried out against the hand he placed

over her mouth. She was a devil, at times, my daughter. She had her mama's temper and some of her father's ingenuity – but she did not bite or struggle as I might have expected; my daughter the compliant child, open to him, almost seeming to welcome his invasive touch.

When she held out her hand, I took it. Mortimer was not there. It was just the two of us, staring through an infinity of space, reaching across a gulf with which no mother and daughter should ever have to contend. Her fingers frail and moist with sweat, I had to lean forward so as not to lose my delicate grip on her when Mortimer violently spent himself. She shuddered and finally the tears started to fall. Mortimer did not move. He remained over her like the shadow of some repugnant bird of prey and then...

... and then he reached down and broke her neck, anyway.

It was a casual act – the arrogant dismissal of the habitual murderer, the total, consciencelessness of the madman. I have seen others like him. In truth, I am surrounded by them, and always have been... in truth... in truth I also saw something of myself in that act. Chadwick and his whore had been despatched with similar efficiency – as had others – but I felt no kinship for this man. Without a care, he had used my child, used her and then killed her with cold heart and swift deed. My one hope had been taken from me. His seed cooled in mother and daughter and yet he couldn't see – he just couldn't see what he had done. He had killed her. He had killed her but it was so much more complicated than that. He had killed her and in so doing, he had removed my one reason for not attempting to kill him.

Her death – mercifully quick but an evil doing nonetheless – brought about the change in me that Mortimer's rape of her could not. I cried out against the unfairness of one lost so young, cried out against my inaction and unaccustomed acceptance – and as I did so, I moved from my place on my bed as if compelled by some unseen force. In a rage during which I saw nothing other than him, the periphery of my vision dimmed and without form or meaning, I leapt at him and took him from my daughter. It didn't now matter that this might not go my way. I cared nought for the possible consequences because there was no longer a consequence worthy of my consideration.

We fell to the floor on the other side of the bed and, for a moment, I thought I heard Rebecca cry. I was mistaken. How could I have been

240

so sure that he had killed her without closer examination? There I was fighting on the floor with Mortimer, unintentionally risking everything that I held dear, and my baby daughter needed me. She was badly hurt, but she was not dead. Not dead.

But when I glanced up I saw only her lifeless eyes staring back at me – willing me on, instructing me in the real meaning of revenge.

Mortimer was laughing. Sat astride him, his impressively recovering member already nudging against my buttock, it seemed I was not, to him, at least, the threat I imagined myself to be. This was no more than a game. As he saw it, I was no more challenging than a game of whist – and only moderately more engaging.

"You killed my little girl," I told him – holding the emotion at bay, for now, as I calculated and conceived. "You raped and killed my three year old daughter, and for that you have to die."

This achieved the desired result; Mortimer laughed all the harder – misled by the melodrama, wholly ignorant of the things of which I was capable.

The fall from the bed and the ensuing struggle had somehow left a deep gash in my thigh, but it had also brought us closer to my trunk. It was unlocked. There was no reason for security when one owned little more than the clothes in which one worked and rested. But the lid was heavy. To lift it and find the hammer and then use it would require speed and strength I just was not sure I possessed. Mortimer was distracted, this was true, but he was not a stupid man. He would read intent on my face as surely as if it were written on paper and that would be an end of it.

And, so, I slowly climbed from him and got to my feet. I turned my back to him and, without so much as a glance at my darling dead daughter, I went to the window and looked out. "It was not meant to be like this," I said.

His laughter stopped. I had his attention.

"I wanted... I wanted to get it right, this time," I continued, "but I am not made for motherhood." Now I looked at him. "For all my tears and claims, I suppose I would be lying were I not to at least admit that you have done me a service. I loved her, that much is true, but love is not always enough and... and caring for her was not always easy. A woman alone and a small child. For me, it was never going to work."

He was not a stupid man. I had known that the very moment I had first met him. To have such appetites and still possess his liberty told me much and I knew that if I was to win, I had to be convincing. I no longer cared what he did to me.

"I did you a service," he said – sounding somewhat disappointed as he tried to make the necessary assessment. He pushed himself up on his elbows so that he could better study me. I looked at him only long enough to see this – not wanting to catch my daughter's dead eye, again, afraid that my resolve would break and he would see through the lie.

"As hard as it is for me to say, yes, I believe you did."

"And you mean to reward this service I have done you?" He was guarded but he was also hopeful. As Chadwick had, Edwin Mortimer saw something familiar in me – something that spoke to him of darker, less inhibited possibilities.

"I don't know what I mean to do, yet," I told him. It is good to build the lie around a truth. The way in which I hovered indecisively by the trunk confirmed what I had just said and I felt him give a little.

"You are an intelligent woman," he told me. "But you are also a woman who has just seen the daughter she loved raped and murdered. Do you honestly expect me to believe that there is a chance I can walk away from this without further, shall we say, inconvenience?"

"What you believe is your business," I said, keeping my back to him as I glanced down at the trunk. I knew exactly where the hammer was, but now was still not the time; whilst he was watching me so avidly, there was no chance for me at all.

"Is it?" he asked – and I knew we were now entering what might well be the most important phase of this conversation. "Or isn't it more accurate to say that what I believe is your business? After all, if you cannot convince me that the death of your daughter was some kind of release for which you are sincerely grateful your business with me will never be done, now, will it?"

"I will never be grateful," I told him – not misguided enough to play into his very obvious trap. "My life, it is true, will possibly be better than it ever would have been, now – but that does not alter the fact that you killed my beautiful daughter. I still mean to see you dead."

"You do?" Faintly amused. A man who falsely believed that he had everything under control.

"I do."

"And just how do you propose to see me dead?"

I waited, staring into the shadows in the corner of the room – wishing that all of this could have been different, that I could have acted sooner... that my darling daughter might still be with me, giggling as she took in the world with her large indigo eyes. I heard Susanna's voice in the distance, and wondered if I could have called for help, after all. Had I judged this all wrong? If I'd shouted and struggled, would Edwin Mortimer have lost courage and let my daughter live? With other men, it would have been more than likely – but not him. If there had been an alternative, that, bitter experience had taught, was not it.

"On that I have not yet decided," I told him. "But when I do decide..."

"I'll be the first to know?"

"You'll be the first to know."

His laughter did not fit comfortably within such a small, solemn space. My daughter's cot-like bed rattled with his basso profundo and I wanted him dead there and then. Waiting no longer seemed an option. This had to happen and it had to happen soon.

My toes nudged against the base of the trunk and my fingers tingled. I fought against myself – my hand straining against my efforts to control it – and willed this to be over. I could endure no more. His laughter mocked my memories, reduced Rebecca to a hollow thing that had never truly lived or taken pleasure from life. I saw my failings. I suffered for my own inadequacies. And only by holding tightly to the memory of my daughter skipping beside me down to the harbour could I stop myself from acting too soon.

"I'll say this for you, lass," he said. "You have more backbone than any man I've ever met."

"I can well believe that," I answered. "I would not imagine a child-killer would have men of courage within his social circle."

The humour had left him. I heard him moving behind me but did not look around to see what he was doing. He could not hurt Rebecca *anymore and if he chose to attack me from behind like the coward he was, so be it.*

"You'd be surprised," he told me, standing close – breathing the words into my ear. "Even men of courage are occasionally fond of the sweeter meat. And for some... cold meat is the greatest of delicacies."

I pulled away from him, disgusted by his smell as much as his vile words. Feigning a stumble, I went down on one knee by the trunk – holding onto it as I now let the tears come. My grief for my daughter was sincere, but I was happy to use it – happy to let him think he had broken me and that I was not a threat worthy of him.

I heard him chuckle as he walked away from me – and when I risked a glance over my shoulder, I saw, as expected, that he was dressing.

... I couldn't remember going to my study. I looked up from the journal and felt the cold air from the open window raise goose pimples on my arms – the recollection of seeing my daughter's name in Sheila Mackenzie's journal making me wish I had burned it, after all, burned it or buried it in the garden where it should have stayed. Sitting back in my chair, I felt the alien, disproportionately distressing soreness of the scratches that Ashley had inflicted on me during what I now remembered to have been an uncharacteristically violent bout of love-making – and I couldn't help connect this to what I had read in the journal. Ashley had cried out and bitten, exhorting me to take her anally and everything had somehow seemed to shift. We became different people. We became the people we had always been. And it was connected. None of it was accidental. Our daughter was a false identity. Where we had hoped for truthfulness when we had chosen her name, we had instead been presented with an alternate name, something once used to cloak – to conceal something that could never be shared. Ashley had talked of our new baby whilst we made love, whispering names and heady plans as she knelt and opened herself to me. I'd heard desperation – a panicky need to make something right – and when she spoke crudely, telling me to fuck her harder, to suck her cunt and bite her tits, I saw nothing unusual with this. I went with her, embraced the fear and abandon, and fell beside her when I was spent – the taste of her blood and juices on my lips.

But still I did not remember coming here – still I did not remember sitting down and taking the journal out of the locked drawer. The screensaver on my PC showed alternating images of an almost naked Ashley and a playful Nadine – and the juxtaposition of the two suddenly seemed somehow obscene. Mother and daughter should never be so closely placed – one sexual, one an innocent product in need of protection, of shielding. I saw them and thought of Rebecca behind that curtain in that room she had shared with her mother and thought for a moment that I heard Nadine call out in her sleep.

Standing in the open doorway, I listened. I heard the strengthening wind against the open window, the latch rattling lightly. I heard the stillness within my home – the home I had known for so many years. I heard the muted bass from a song I didn't know – the questionable entertainment at a party at the end of the street. But I heard nothing else. Nadine slept on, as I assumed my wife did, and when I sat back down, I took some consolation in this. All was not well with our world. Something was spinning uncontrollably to an utterly unforeseeable conclusion. An end, if my fiction was anything to go by, that would only make sense at the price of dissolution. But at least my wife and daughter slept on undisturbed. That could only be a good thing and, turning back the pages of the journal, suddenly convinced that I'd misread it and it hadn't been Nadine Verity's name I had seen there written but something similar and wholly removed from my reality, I experienced a strange moment of peace. I did not see that they had already been touched by the things that I believed were only happening to me. Theirs was a protected world, safe and secure, whilst mine was one of hardship and vertiginous discrepancy. And that, as I saw it, was exactly how it should be. I wanted their contentment. It was only right that none of this should touch them – that this burden should be mine and mine alone.

Oliver had applied Occam's Razor and, I now saw, succeeded only in making himself look ridiculous and narrow minded. To explain the things that were happening to me in such obvious and simplistic terms was beneath him. I'd seen it before, of course. Oliver was a thinker. When he wanted to he could, as I have already said, understand the most complex of philosophies. But he was lazy. I saw that now. Intellectually, he was not prepared to go that extra mile. His mind was as messy as his flat and sometimes he just couldn't be bothered to search amongst the debris for whatever it was he needed.

Something wasn't right. I suppose that was fairly obvious – but this was more specific. I held the journal in my hands, working back through its pages, and its history slipped away from me. The ink faded and, yet, the words became more immediate. I searched for my daughter's name, an oddly appropriate reversal of Sheila's rushing struggle to get the words down before her candle finally died, and found it, finally, just as it washed sleepily from the page.

Chapter Thirteen

They say that a man can accommodate anything, given time and inclination – and whilst there might be an element of truth to that, and however hard I tried to follow Oliver's quite successful example, I'd still had nowhere near enough time to explain away the things that had been happening to me. I worked and "pottered" in the garden, reminded time and again of my father, and sometimes it almost felt bearable even as, for the most part, I felt I was going quietly insane.

"You don't have to avoid me, you know." I was in the front garden – hoeing myself into a mild state of euphoria and silently praying I didn't find any drainage problems. Maggie had dropped by with Wee Mark to have lunch with Ashley and thus far I hadn't said more than a handful of words to her.

"I'm not avoiding you," I insisted.

"Well it certainly seems like you are to me."

I leant my hoe against the wall and looked at her, sighing. "I'm not avoiding you, Mags," I reiterated. "I'm just busy and... I've got a lot on my mind."

"A lot on your mind."

"That's what I said."

I wasn't sure just what it was Maggie wanted from me. She took a step closer and the familiarity was overwhelming. She said my name and put a hand on my arm and my instinct was to pull away – pull away and run from her. But, perhaps against my better judgment, I held my ground and listened to what she had to say.

"I'm not going to go over everything I told you a few weeks, back," she told me – referring to her Back to Life party. "I've said what had to be said and, really, the rest's up to you. But I do want you to know that it's really obvious to me that something's going on that you aren't telling anyone about, and if you do decide that you need to talk... well, I'm always here for you."

"Nothing's going on, Maggie," I insisted.

She looked at me sadly and then shrugged. It seemed the matter had been dismissed. "I saw Molly the other day," she told me. Her voice was unusually breezy. I tensed and took up my hoe again in an attempt to conceal it. "She knows about... you know."

"Do I?"

"Yes – yes, you do, Sonny." She was clearly finding my mood exasperating. She glanced around the corner of the building to make sure Ash hadn't followed her and then added, "She knows about us and I'd like to know how. I didn't tell her and I don't imagine that you told her, so that leaves... who, Sonny? Who else knows about us?"

I concentrated on the rhythm of my hoeing – keeping it regular and tight and finding the repeated sigh of the blade cutting through the moist earth deeply satisfying. "Oliver?" I ventured. "He's the only one that I know of."

"No one else?"

I stopped hoeing and looked at her evenly. "You think – what – I put an announcement in the paper?"

"I'm just trying to figure out who would know. I told no one, Sonny."

"No one? You absolutely sure?"

"I had no one to tell. Ashley was the only one I'd trust with something like that and... well, I wasn't about to tell her, now, was I?"

"So that leaves you, me and Oliver."

"Oliver wouldn't tell her," she said. "He can't abide the woman and, anyway, he's more trustworthy than that."

"I know." I was bored with the conversation. We both knew Molly wasn't about to act on the knowledge and I got the distinct impression that Mags was just using this as a way of reminding me that we were connected – that we had a shared history, a secret that should allow us certain freedoms that we wouldn't otherwise possess. She reminded me of a needy misfit, trying to wheedle her way "in" with the cool kids, and I wondered why I'd never seen that in her before. Wales had merely been a symptom, I realised. The things we had done to each other had had nothing to do with love – physical or otherwise – but were, rather, an expression of something deeper, darker, even. Maggie wanted. Maggie needed. Her world fell apart and she found yet another way of finding inclusion, pulling others into her illusion. It was nothing overt or glaring, of course. Hers was a subtle personality. But, nevertheless, I saw it and understood it and wanted to get away from it.

"Maybe he told Don and *he* let something slip," she ventured, apparently determined to keep this conversation on track – however monosyllabic I might become.

"Don doesn't know anything about us," I told her.

"How do you know?"

"Oliver told me."

She took too long considering this.

"I see," she said.

"I'm not sure you do," I told her. "But either way, I doubt we have anything to worry about. If anyone was going to let the cat out of the bag I'm sure they would have done so by now."

"Unless they're waiting for the right moment," she said.

"Maggie." I sighed and leant against the hoe – wanting space and exclusion.

"Yes?"

"Just leave it, okay?"

One. Two.

"You're not concerned?" she asked.

"Right now my only concern is getting this hoeing done."

In the distance, I heard someone whistling. The tune was familiar and when I recognised it as the Dambusters March I resisted the urge to look down the road to Old Man Ned's. I owed him an apology but I felt I'd left it far too long, and when his whistling faded away, I silently welcomed this further reprieve.

Maggie, meanwhile, leant in close and looked down at the herbaceous border as if I were showing her some new, previously undiscovered genus of flora. Touching my arm, she said, very quietly, "It doesn't just go away, Sonny. None of it does. The things we did, the feelings we shared – they're as real now as they ever were. We're still living the same lives."

Before I could say anything, she turned and walked away – leaving me to ponder and hoe.

Earlier that morning, Ashley had taken a pregnancy test. A week late, she had been certain that our efforts had already paid off and that she had, the beautiful genius that she was, conceived her second baby. I'd joined her in her excitement, sitting on the edge of the bath with her as we'd stared stupidly at the little window. While we'd waited, she'd talked of phoning her parents, who were on holiday in Toronto, to tell them the good news, how pleased her mother would be – what names she'd narrowed it down to and how she wanted a home birth this time.

But it seemed it was not yet meant to be. She'd held out the plastic wand for me to see and her dreams had disappeared. "I'm not," she'd told me.

I recalled the look on Ashley's face as I continued to get the garden ready for winter. I saw false hope, the unfathomable certainty that next time it would be different. I saw the momentary dying of that fiery energy in her eyes, the depression already gaining ground in spite of her best efforts. But, more than anything, she reminded me of the girl she had been when we had first met, funny, brave, intelligent and justifiably tired.

I'd held her, nevertheless afraid that this was the wrong thing to do – that her resolve would crumble like wet sand in my arms and that there would simply be no way of putting her back together again. I thought of Sheila Mackenzie and imagined Ashley with a hammer in her hand, smashing the pregnancy test to pieces before turning her attention to me.

"It was never there," she'd told me. "But I still miss it, Sonny. I miss our baby."

"You can do mine when you're finished there, if you like." I looked up to see Old Man Ned standing on the pavement by the garden gate. "Nice that you keep it up the way you do," he said, nodding at the garden. "So many of the young uns just let everything go to shit. Especially round here. Used to be right lovely but...." He shrugged, hands in the pockets of his dirty chinos. "Well, you'll probably remember it as well as me, having grown up here. Don't need me telling you how it's changed."

"How you doing, Ned?" I asked.

"A little confused, but otherwise fine," he said with a curt nod.

As I walked over to him, I said, "That confusion wouldn't have anything to do with me, would it?"

He chuckled amiably enough. "At the risk of making you think you're the centre of everything, aye, I reckon you could say that. Just not sure what, if anything, I've done wrong. Not even sure it weren't all just in my imagination."

"I've been meaning to apologise for that," I said.

"Been taking your time about it."

"I left it too long and... well, I left it too long."

Ned squinted at me – one eye almost shut. I was down wind of him and it seemed pretty clear from the pissy, musty-paper smell he was giving off and the way his thin, grey hair stuck to his head in greasy clumps that he hadn't been taking care of himself just lately. Right then, I felt sorry for him – even as I wondered if, perhaps, my behaviour hadn't on some level been justified. He was an old man who quite possibly didn't have that long left and I suddenly understood that I should not have left this as long as I had. Ned didn't deserve to die feeling that he had done something wrong when, to all intents and purposes, all he'd ever done (as far as I could then see) was try to help.

"Always best to strike while the iron's hot where apologies are concerned," he agreed. "I'd be a happier old man if I'd learned that while I was still a young man," he added with a sad smile. "And if that isn't the truth, I'm the king of Siam."

"Et cetera, et cetera, et cetera?"

"I'll have you know, my ex-wife always said I had a look of Yul Brynner about me."

I smiled but said only, "I don't remember your ex-wife."

"Ah, well, you wouldn't. Left a long time ago, when you was still a bairn, I'd say. Couldn't put up with my wicked, wicked ways."

"A bit of a one, were you?"

"Oh, I was a one, all right. You might say I was so much of a one I was very nearly a two."

I laughed and, surprisingly, it felt genuine and complete. "Cigarettes and whisky and wild, wild women?"

"And gambling. I went to the dogs, and so did my marriage. But..." he shrugged, "... that's the way it goes, I s'ppose. Got it off my grandfather, by all accounts, but, try as I might, she just wouldn't accept that I was just a victim of my genes."

"Not very charitable of her."

"Well, that's women for you, son," he told me. "Once they get summat in their pretty little heads there's no shifting them. But I'm sure you don't need me to tell you that."

"Sheila Mackenzie?" I asked.

"Among others. It's just the way they are, lad, and we'd all do well to remember that, as I see it."

"I really should be getting on," I said – and Old Man Ned nodded as if this had been just what he had been expecting. The sudden lack of commitment, the swift dismissal.

"Aye, well, I know what you mean," he said. "Have a few things I should be doing myself. If I can still be arsed."

"More Internet research?" I ventured, not wanting to appear too rude.

"Not really." He pulled his chin down into his shirt collar and for the first time I realised just how chilly the day was getting. "I've just about given up on the book," he admitted. "Look back for too long and... well, it just isn't bloody healthy, lad. It never goes away if you live with it for too long."

When we'd said our goodbyes, I went back to my hoeing. The work was finished, but I didn't much fancy heading indoors to be with Ash and Mags – and, also, I wanted to think about what Ned had said. Was it as simple as he, perhaps inadvertently, had made out? Was my fundamental problem merely that I had allowed myself to "live" with these things for far too long? It seemed preposterous and, yet, wholly right. It was a choice. I picked up the journal and I read – and doors both literal and figurative opened up, taking me to places from which it wasn't always easy to return.

Sheila Mackenzie waved from the other side of the road. Naked, remarkably solid – her hair lifting on a growing, chilling breeze. She appeared focused and happy, alert, and when she smiled, I wanted to cry for everything she had lost, all that Fate had inflicted on her. My flesh tightened and the wind cut through me and, instinct crushing me, I glanced to my left and saw Ned in his front garden, staring at the ghost of Sheila Mackenzie.

He turned to me and his mouth opened. He shouted something I didn't hear and pointed. Even at this distance, I could see that his hand shook. A swooping sparrow crossed his line of vision and he blinked, pointing more emphatically and shouting against the seemingly thunderous wind.

I took too long. Something so simple and yet so significant. It could have been different – if only I'd spotted Sheila Mackenzie sooner, registered Ned's urgency a moment earlier.

Nadine was happier that I ever remembered seeing her. She skipped on the spot, waving back at Sheila – the woman I had only moments before felt sorry for – her shoulders seesawing with excitement. I heard her giggle, felt myself moving even as I remained firmly rooted to the spot and marked the potential much too late.

Running out of the gate, Nadine skipped from the curb and out onto the road – still waving, still laughing – and as futile as I knew it was, I threw down my hoe and went after her. Not bothering with the gate, I ran across the lawn and hurdled the low wall, certain I was going to misjudge both the height of the wall and my ability and gracelessly fall flat on my face. But I didn't. I cleared the wall and landed (a little flat-footed, admittedly) on the pavement just as Nadine made the middle of the road.

Sheila was still waving at her, encouraging her on – but I now knew that I would reach Nadine before she in turn reached Sheila. Whatever had been intended would be prevented. My daughter would be all right. I would hold her tight to my chest and Sheila Mackenzie would go back to where she came from and everything would be as it had been. Everything was going to be all right.

That was when I saw the car.

A Ford Ka. Not much bigger than a bump in the road. A curious shade of blue that looked like a bruise in the suddenly poor light. I saw blackness around the edge of my vision – every detail of the Ka suddenly highly defined and specific. Circular scratches in the paintwork on the bonnet, fly-splatters on the grimy windscreen, the troll hanging from the rear view mirror. I saw all of this and more in that split second before I heard the brakes lock on and felt tomorrow turn grey and hopeless.

The car hit my daughter and I stood by and watched her die. I cried out and felt weak arms holding me back as I watched her tiny body crumple into the bumper, her head hitting the bonnet as her legs came up limp and pretty – so painfully pretty. There was grace in the way momentum carried her into the air, and there was horror in the way she came back down.

Her neck was broken. I saw that right away. She lay in the road, metres away from the Ka, and the twisted shape of her, the damage to her skull told me everything I never wanted to know. I smelt her sweet, bedtime smell, and shrugged Ned off me – running to her as, behind me, I was distantly aware of the driver getting out, of Ash screaming a denial as my father said, "It's just an illusion."

"Illusions leave stains, too, dear," Mam said.

There was no place for this in our lives, I saw as I shouted for Ashley and struggled against Ned's surprisingly strong, reapplied grip. Our daughter simply couldn't die like this because nothing had been allocated – nothing had, that I could then see, been moved around to allow for it. People I didn't know ran about me, taking over, doing all the things I should have been doing but simply couldn't, and I pulled back even as I knelt down sobbing beside my broken baby.

Far away, I heard Ashley saying "no, no, no," over and over, but I couldn't go to. Hers had been the name I had called when I had seen Nadine hit the ground – and yet I didn't want to see her. I couldn't comfort her and I couldn't take comfort from her. She was of no consequence to me.

"Don't move her, mate," a man said. I remembered him distantly as a neighbour from the far end of Sorrow Street – but as he reached over my daughter's too-still form he became Jim. His appearance didn't change, but I knew enough to know that appearance was superficial. Reality had nothing to do with the way in which the world appeared; reality had nothing to do with the way in which *people* appeared. The neighbour from the far end of Sorrow Street was Jim as surely as I was Sonuel Moore and as he spoke to me I found a fleeting, inexplicable comfort. "I'm going to take care of her until they get here," Jim said. "I won't let anyone do anything to her that they shouldn't. No one is going to do anything else to hurt her – you have my word, man, okay?"

I nodded and a tear rolled from the tip of my nose and fell against

Nadine's bloody arm. *Blood, sweat and tears,* I thought. *The stuff of life. The stuff of death.*

Gently feeling for a pulse at her neck – possibly the bravest and, yet, most unnecessary act I had ever performed – Jim watched me conscientiously, his eyes never leaving mine as his hand moved slowly to push my wrist away. He knew. I knew. And I didn't doubt that anyone seeing Nadine like that could do anything but know. He knew. I knew. Ned knew. The driver of the innocuous little bump in the road knew.

And somewhere behind me, sobbing in Maggie's arms, my wife knew.

She was pronounced dead at the scene thirty-five minutes later, and such delayed confirmation of what was so clearly obvious – after the Jolly Green Giant paramedics (ho, ho, ho) had shaken their rattles and failed spectacularly in their magic – merely served to underscore the futility and inevitability of all that was to follow that day. Patterns already established took over. We watched the ambulance carry our daughter silently away after kissing her still, cool cheek and as Oliver and Don – quick to respond to Maggie's bugle call, pale and shaken but efficient and invaluable nevertheless – took control, I felt disturbed by the space, aware that there were expectations but not actually sure what they were.

We went to the hospital, Don driving us, where we received further confirmation that Nadine was dead. Statements were taken and I was quick to point out that the driver hadn't seemed to be driving irresponsibly. Nadine had been quick – too quick for me or the driver – and this wasn't about blame, none of it was. It had been an accident and I didn't want my daughter's death sullying with talk of responsibility and culpability. Don nodded at this, but Ashley only stared into space – both her hands clasping my left tightly in her lap, lips thin and bloodless. I wasn't sure how much of this she was taking in, but I suddenly needed her more than I ever had. It felt selfish of me, to expect something of her at a time like this, but I just couldn't help it. I wanted her to nod, as Don had. I had been there and had seen it all happen, and all that talk about the driver not being to blame? It was Ashley's cue to make it known that she didn't blame me – and

255

she didn't respond.

"She's in shock, Sonny," Don said when the constable had finally finished with us. "We all are. Just hold each other and avoid inferences."

Wee Mark greeted us when we arrived home. If Maggie had known we were back I was confident she would have made sure he was well out of the way – but as it was, we walked in through the front door, me trying not to register the clean-up that had taken place outside, Ashley clinging tightly to my arm, and there he was, standing by the stairs, the muck on his face cut through with tear tracks. "It wasn't me," he sobbed – and Ashley finally broke, we both did.

Whilst Don quickly carried Wee Mark off, Ashley and I crumbled. Huddling together at the bottom of the stairs, we cried and, for a while, Ashley screamed loud enough to make her throat bleed. She repeated Nadine's name ceaselessly, an incantation against the permanence of the insubstantial, and I felt anger battling against the shock and loss as I held her and recalled what I had said to the police constable at the hospital. This *was* about blame, I now told myself. My daughter was dead and some fucker had to be held accountable. Right then her beautiful, sweet-smelling form was probably being cut and probed in order to more fully ascertain the exact cause of death (apparently, being hit by a car wasn't a suitable enough explanation) and the only possible way in which that could be balanced, it seemed to me, was if the guilty were made to suffer the same terminal pain and indignity. I wanted agony. It was more than desirable that some *other* should suffer, it was a necessity. If that meant that I had to be the one to suffer, then so be it. I didn't care. Holding Ashley as the screams once again became sobs, I found I no longer cared about the inconsequentiality of form. It didn't even have to *appear* right. My only criterion was that others – *an* other – should suffer as she had done.

That was one of my worst moments. Others inevitably follow, but as it was so early in the whole grieving process, it's one that sticks in my mind with its honesty and sheer, uncompromising weight. Even as I gave Ashley what little comfort I could, rocking with her as my nose ran and my chest spasmed, I considered what it would feel like to just walk back out the front door, past the scrubbed, damp Tarmac, and find someone to take all this out on. I would hit and keep hitting, and when they fell, I would kick until I couldn't stand. I thought of Ned, slow to warn me. I thought of the driver of the Ka, now, to my mind, slow to react. I thought of the paramedics, experts in the art of never being *quite* good enough – my daughter's blood black on their green uniforms.

And I thought of Sheila Mackenzie – feeling the anger leave me as the fear and confusion took over.

When your daughter dies a tragic and untimely death, one's fellow man tends to grip one's shoulder and speak quietly but clearly.

"Sonny?" It was Oliver. His large hand was a comfort, but Ashley and I weren't quite ready for the next stage, yet. I nodded that we were all right (considering) and he backed into the living room, whispering something to Don.

"She's gone," Ashley said.

"Yes."

"Our baby..."

I wanted to be a comfort to her, to hold her and give her the reassurance she needed – but, as helpful as I might have found it to try, I just couldn't. There was nothing left. I felt hopeless and hollow, the words she spoke echoing in my head and taking me places I just didn't want to go. *Our baby,* she had said – and immediately I'd seen the possibilities in those two words and realised that we had set ourselves up for this from the very beginning. Grief and suffering on this scale didn't just arrive, it was invited. That which has never been conceived, it occurred to me as I remembered our ridiculous sense of loss over the negative pregnancy test result of that morning, can never truly die – and I only wished I had understood this sooner.

"Yes," I said – and Ashley fell again, her grip, already tenuous, giving as a fresh torrent of longing, love and unrelenting anguish overtook her.

"It's not right," she managed to stammer a few minutes later. "This shouldn't be happening. It isn't. It can't. It's impossible."

"Nadine's dead, love." Inspired by kindness, this nevertheless felt like the cruellest thing I'd ever said to her. She tried to sit up and pull away from me, but clearly didn't have the strength.

"No," she muttered.

"Yes. I don't want it to be true, either, Ash, but it is. I saw it happen. Our baby's dead."

"No."

I remembered her standing by the road repeating that one word and I saw just how difficult this was going to be for her. This wasn't about being in "denial". It wasn't as simple as that. There was no room for this in her life. It was too big – too impossible.

When Oliver came in to check on us again a few minutes later, we were quieter. I wanted to stay where we were for another minute or two – but I knew that minutes would become hours and hours would become days, and if we didn't move soon archaeologists a couple of thousand years from now would dig us up and conjecture on just why we had been huddled together on the stairs. They would fall back on the word "ritualistic" and would never know. No one would. They couldn't.

"Are you ready to come through?" Olly said, his hand on my shoulder again.

"I'm not sure," I said, looking at Ashley – an emotional sea of tears and snot. "I think so... I don't know.... Ash?"

When she looked at me, I saw Nadine. Until now, I'd never realised just how strong the resemblance between mother and daughter really was. It was in the questing eyes and the tightly pursed, rosebud mouth – but more than anything, it was in her brow and the set of her jaw, in the way she frowned her displeasure and stubbornly prepared herself to resist. It was not a countenance Nadine had often presented, but I recognised it, nevertheless.

"Do you want to go through, now?" I asked.

"I want to go to bed." The best suggestion I had heard in a very long time. Close the curtains, curl up, close your eyes and let it all go. The dreams of Nadine would be sweet and precious – their innate cruelty only apparent upon waking. I didn't want to talk but, more to the point, I didn't want to listen. The idea of having to face Maggie's sympathy and sorrow, of having to "be strong"... I just wasn't sure I could do it.

I started to tell Ashley that that was what we would do, but before I'd got even halfway through what I was saying, Oliver was squatting down in front of us – putting a hand on my left knee and another on

Ashley's right. "Do you think that's a good idea?" he asked. "I don't want to tell either of you what to do, but maybe being alone is something you want to do later? Going to sleep now... well, you have to wake up, you know?"

I could tell he was struggling to find the right thing to say – to do the right thing – and I was grateful. It couldn't have been easy for him. He had adored Nadine, too, and it was beyond doubt that he loved Ashley and me – but I couldn't have him doing this. This was our heartache. This was our suffering. And if we were not allowed to deal with it as we saw fit... well, what was left for us?

"We want to go to bed," I told Oliver – firmly, but with all the kindness I could muster.

"I know, mate, but I just don't think – "

"This isn't about what you think." I swallowed hard, not sure if I could say anymore but determined to try. "This isn't your nightmare. It's ours and we'll – "

Ashley put a hand on my arm. I turned to her, my heart breaking as my wife again became my daughter – my daughter, my wife. Two sorrows for the price of one.

"He's right," she said. "There are things we have to do. For Nadine."

It wasn't what I wanted. Other people, however close and dependable, were an intrusion. Whatever anyone said to the contrary, this was the time for Ashley and me to be alone – to wallow and exclude, to deny, if necessary, the very world that had taken our daughter from us.

But I was too tired and lost to argue. If Nadine's death had, at that point, taught me anything it was that I was not the one in control, here. Like microscopic particles ruled by Brownian motion, we were subject to laws, but there was no real control.

"For Nadine," I repeated, without conviction.

I was surprised to see that Molly was also there with Veronique. She cried when she saw Ashley and the three women held each other – a cabalistic huddle, it seemed, that excluded the rest of us as surely as if they had built a wall around themselves. I smelt coffee and found it somehow reassuring that Maggie appeared sober and in control, and as I left Ashley to be tended to by her and Molly, following Don and Oliver into the kitchen, I thought, albeit it briefly, that maybe we would get through this, after all. For the next week or so, we had purpose and beyond that was another life, one that wasn't yet real or even remotely discoverable. One step at a time, my mother would have said.

Don leant against the sink unit whilst Oliver and I took a chair each at the table. We all sighed within seconds of each other, and I resisted the peculiar urge to laugh. My head hurt but I welcomed it. Anything to hold my focus.

"I'm not going to ask how you're holding up," Oliver said. "But I do want you to know that you don't have to hold anything in, Son. Not with us."

"I know," I told him. "And I appreciate it."

Don nodded and looked as though he was editing his thoughts before speaking. He still felt like something of an outsider, that much was obvious – an old friend who'd been lost and then found again, but who still had to relearn, still had to find his place within the group. In spite of everything that had happened, I found I didn't envy him. He had walked away from his wife and kids, and whilst I didn't condemn him for that, I did see that what had happened to Nadine could only cause him to question his actions.

"There's going to be quite a lot to sort out," he finally said. "People to notify, arrangements to be made et cetera – but you really don't need to worry about that, Sonny. Oliver and I will take care of it. I was just – "

I held up a hand and he stopped. As easy as that. A few hours ago I could do nothing to prevent my daughter's death, and now I could stop a man speaking with a wave of my hand. I had to bite down hard on the bitter anger, closing my eyes and taking a deep breath.

"I appreciate that, Don," I said, "but I really need to do as much of this as I can for myself. Ashley and I have to... it's important that..."

I choked and Oliver reached across the table and gave my arm a squeeze. "Of course," he said. "How about this, then? We'll help when and where you need it, but we won't take over. That okay?"

I nodded and forced a smile. "Actually, there is something you can do for me."

"What's that?" Don asked eagerly. He needed to be "doing" like the rest of us, and I felt another pang of sympathy for him.

"Ashley's parents," I told him. "They're on holiday in Toronto and... I just don't think I can... you know."

He didn't so much as flinch – just nodded determinedly and told me that it wouldn't be a problem. They'd take care of it.

"Make sure you ask to speak to Len," I said. "I don't want Pippa finding out over the phone."

I caught a movement out of the corner of my eye and turned to see the robust but timid Wee Mark and the ever-frail Veronique standing in the living room doorway watching me. I doubted they understood just what was going on, but it was clear from their behaviour that they knew this was serious – and when Veronique smiled uncertainly, I felt myself start to drift, kneeling down before her and taking her delicate form in my arms. I cried and Veronique let me hold her until Oliver and Don separated us – apparently concerned that I was scaring her.

"Why?" The one question no one could answer; the only one that mattered.

"I don't know," Oliver said, holding me to his ursine chest as if we were a twenty-first century Madonna and Child. "I really don't know. It just isn't bloody fair or right."

"I don't... I can't do this."

"You have to, mate."

Pulling away from him as Don herded the kids back into the living room – where Ashley and Maggie were also crying – I spat my reply at him. "No, Oliver – no, I don't *have* to." I saw Nadine, again, in the air, on the ground – the two extremes of human existence – and for only the second time in my life I had to *think* about breathing. I felt dizzy and Oliver guided me back to my chair. He didn't speak, just closed the door into the living room and held me – his strong arms oddly comforting, reminding me of what it had been like to be held by my father, the sense of security and reliability, the misguided belief that he would always be there.

"I'm all right," I said, pulling away from him again.

"No, you're not," he insisted. "You weren't all right before this, even Maggie saw that much, so I really don't see how you can be all right now. I can't pretend to know how you're feeling, Sonny – but I know you're not all right."

Cold and shaky, I hugged myself – leaning forward in my chair. "I just want it to be how it used to be," I said.

Oliver regarded me silently – leaning into the corner formed by the units and clasping his arms before him. He seemed at a loss for something to say, and it occurred to me that at another time I might have taken pleasure from this. I smelt coffee again, and was distantly aware of the others talking in the living room – and none of it felt in any way related to the life I had lived, to the man I had only hours ago been. Oliver breathed deeply and a strange calmness came over me. I could have stayed like that forever. It was the stairs all over again. The exhaustion was complete and when Oliver finally found something to say, I hardly heard him at all.

"What happened, Sonny?" It could have been the most ridiculous question ever, but it wasn't. I stared at the floor and let the words sink in, framing answers I didn't want to share. What *had* happened? My daughter had died and at first glance it appeared that there had been no reason for this. It had been a senseless accident, a tragedy that was all the more difficult to deal with because of its apparently random nature. But there was more to it than that, and only now did I fully acknowledge that.

"Sheila Mackenzie was there," I told Oliver. "She was on the other side of the road, waving at Nadine. Nadine... she laughed and waved back, and then, before I could stop her, she ran to her. She ran to her and – "

"This is the woman from the journal?"

I nodded.

"And you saw her?"

"As clear as day."

"And you're sure you aren't just..." He trailed off when I glanced up at him.

"What?" I asked.

"This isn't an attempt to make sense of what happened?" he asked.

"Nadine saw her, too," I told him. "She would never have run out like that otherwise. She saw her, I saw her, Ned saw her – and nothing you can say is going to change that. That woman... I felt sorry for her, Oliver. I felt *sorry* for her and she *killed* my daughter."

Oliver waited. I imagined him silently counting to ten, and then, when it was clear I wasn't going to say anything else, he said, "Ned saw her?"

"Yes," I said. "Ned saw her."

He glanced at the window, scratching his beard, and then looked back at me.

"You up to paying Ned a visit with me?" he asked.

I had lost so much. Weak and without, as I then saw it, a convincing reason to keep going, I just wanted to be left alone. If Ashley wanted to join me in my dark place, so be it – but what I most assuredly knew I didn't want or need right then was a visit to Old Man Ned's. The mystery and confusion belonged to others now. That Sheila Mackenzie was somehow responsible for Nadine's death was bad. It made me want to hurt and destroy. But nothing could be changed. It was fixed and could not be undone – and if there were questions to be answered, let someone else do it. Sheila Mackenzie had done her worst, but she was a ghost, a shade, and, as such, she was beyond punishment.

In spite of this, I nodded and said, "Yes. Yes, I am."

We were the last people he expected to see, and when he opened the door to let us in I was aware of something about him I hadn't noticed before. There was a caution in the way he spoke – a guarded manner that was either a direct result of my fragile state and all that had happened earlier that day or something I had simply failed to register during my previous conversations with him. He gave my arm a squeeze (a gesture I was already growing tired of) and led us through to the cluttered living room, and whilst there was nothing specific I could put my finger on, I understood that Ned was more uncomfortable than might otherwise have been expected. Uncomfortable and wary.

"I was going to come along and see if there was anything I could do, later," he said, shifting files and newspapers from the settee so we could sit. "Was worried that I might be intruding, though."

Oliver nodded and smiled, but neither of us gave any reply to this. Now that we were here, I wasn't entirely sure what should follow. Ashley had been confused when I had explained that I was going along the street to see Ned – to thank him for being there – but she had accepted that it was apparently something I just had to do. Now, however, I wondered if this was sensible and right.

I'd kissed her goodbye – and I kept flashing on the image, feeling the coolness of her flesh against my lips, her sweet smell commingling with various medical, antiseptic smells and something earthier, something I hadn't wanted to think about. My need to preserve had been strong, and I had forced myself to take in as much as was humanly possible, not looking away until the ambulance had turned the corner at the far end of Sorrow Street, but already the detail was becoming confused – the facts becoming increasingly more obscure as I tried to find ways of justifying leaving my wife in order that – what? – I might prove myself right to Oliver. Nadine had waved, and I wanted to be wrong. Whatever Ned told Oliver, it was too late. I could see all too clearly what the outcome of this would be, whatever was said, and I was resigned to it. At that precise moment, I saw Nadine's death as the beginning of the end for us all – and words of validation would not alter that.

Finally, Oliver broke the silence.

"Sonny tells me you saw what happened," he said, getting straight to the crux of the matter.

"I did, yes," Ned said quietly. He sucked his top lip and blinked rapidly.

"Would you mind telling me about the minutes leading up to the accident?" Oliver asked him. He seemed officious and too removed from the pain the rest of us were suffering and I had to push back a ridiculous surge of anger.

Ned looked at me questioningly, and I indicated that he should continue – breathing hard against sudden, sweaty nausea. I remembered sitting here with Nadine. She had been so patient. Alive with love and possibility. I would never have believed then that Ned would outlive her – it would have been a preposterous proposition and it was one I now found myself dwelling on in the most macabre of ways.

If killing Ned would somehow correct the balance and give my daughter back her life, I thought, I would gladly do it.

"I'd just been along to talk to Sonny here," Ned told Oliver. "And when I got back to my garden, I happened to turn and... well, that was when I saw her, like."

I didn't want to listen to this. To remember it from my own perspective was bad enough, but to have Ned's interpretation added to the confusion of memories was just unthinkable. I tried to block him out and find a way forward through all of this – but my thoughts kept returning to my loss and my loss pushed me ever closer to Ned's words, a thirsty man to water. Maybe I wanted to torture myself, or possibly just find something that, however unlikely, made sense of all this – I really don't know – but one thing was certain; Ned didn't give anything like the response I had been expecting.

"She was so excited," Ned continued. "Jumping up and down and waving her arms in the air. I remember wondering if she'd seen a little friend or someone, but I couldn't see anyone so I suppose she just must have been playing a game or summat – the way little uns do.... Anyway, that was about when I noticed that the gate was open."

"You didn't see anyone?" I said. It had taken a moment to register, but now I was suddenly extremely focused and determined. "You must have, Ned. She was at the other side of the road. You looked right at her."

Ned glanced warily at Oliver – making out like he didn't know quite what was going on here, or just how it should be approached. His fingers picked at the threadbare arm of his chair and I felt his fear – because that was what it was; pure, undiluted fear. This wasn't just a matter of pretending that he didn't know what to say, he was scared to the point of being willing to lie about something that he knew, I was sure, was so very important.

"There was someone there?" he said. "I never saw anyone, lad, but I must admit I was a little preoccupied with the bairn so happen I missed her. It was someone you knew, was it?"

I couldn't quite believe what I was hearing. Ned couldn't have failed to see her. I had been there. I had seen his face and it had been obvious that like Nadine and me, he had spotted Sheila Mackenzie.

"You know who it was," I told him.

"I'm afraid I don't, Sonny," he assured me. "I really wish I did, but can't say I saw anyone other than you and little Nadine."

"But you say it looked like Nadine was waving at someone she

265

knew?" Oliver said – perhaps sensing that this was not heading in a favourable direction. He was clever enough to understand that I needed my reality, however peculiar, propping up right now, not undermining, and I loved him for his efforts at keeping this as pain free as he could.

"Aye, that's how it looked," Ned answered.

"So there could have been someone there? You just didn't see her."

"Well I didn't see that there *wasn't* anybody there, if that helps. Like I say, I was concentrating on the little un and trying to get Sonny's attention, so it's hard to be sure. I looked, but I don't rightly recall the details. I know I didn't see any other children, because that's what I reckon I was looking for, but beyond that... I don't rightly know."

He was getting muddled, starting to come close to contradicting himself. He reminded me of a film I'd once seen. A woman and her family being held captive in their own home. The police call regarding an unrelated incident and she has to talk to them on the doorstep without giving the game away, knowing her family will die if she so much as raises an eyebrow at the wrong time. That was the nature of Ned's fear, and I decided I'd push him. As I saw it, I had nothing to lose.

"You saw her," I said. "Sheila Mackenzie was stark fucking bollocking naked on the other side of the road and *you fucking saw her,* Ned. Don't tell me you didn't."

"I think I'd remember seeing a naked woman, son." His eyes flashed me a warning, or maybe I just imagined it. Either way, he sat forward in his chair, hands dangling between his knees and regarded me gravely. "I can't begin to imagine how you're feeling, but if I thought lying to you and saying that I saw this woman you're talking about would take away some of the pain, then happen I would. But it won't change owt, lad. I didn't see her. Don't even know who you're talking about. Wish I could say different, but I can't."

Oliver wasn't looking at either of us. He stared at the chimneybreast and merely listened as we talked. If he was regretting this (which I was sure he was), he concealed it well – breathing slowly and occasionally scratching his beard.

"You don't know who Sheila Mackenzie is?" I said incredulously. For a moment, I almost forgot that my daughter was dead – and the ensuing grief and guilt almost undid me. I felt the nausea threaten again, breathing hard as pinprick flashes dotted my vision, and only by concentrating on the matter at hand did I get through it.

"Should I?" His eyes were challenging and far too clear for a man of his years. I felt he wanted to hurt me. This was his revenge for my treatment of him. The apology was worthless. It wasn't enough. Ned was a man who surrounded himself with memories – with war histories and local lore – and it suddenly seemed foolish of me to believe that he would let such an insult go so easily.

"You were the one who told me her name," I said. "It was you who told me my father used to see her, too."

"I don't know what you're talking about," he said – his voice hard and unrelenting.

I'd believed I had known Old Man Ned, but I now saw that I understood nothing at all. Like many other aspects of my life, he was unquantifiable and remote – a man with a history of which I knew very little. Only today, I had learned of the wife that had left him and this now served to highlight my ignorance. A man I thought I could trust, it turned out that when I needed him most he let me down – all but thrice denying me – and I saw the pointlessness of arguing.

I got to my feet and left the room – walking out the front door without a backward glance.

Oliver caught up with me just outside my gate. He grabbed my arm, panting, and I turned to face him. I'd expected to see concern, hear inappropriate platitudes and contrived explanations, but what I instead got was anger and the one thing, whatever I felt or believed, that I needed most right then. Belief.

"He was lying," Oliver said. "I didn't believe a fucking word and I told him so, Sonny. I told him. I said, 'I don't know what the fuck you're trying to do to my friend and his family, but you've just made yourself another enemy, you old fuck'. And he has. Because..." He was crying. I'd never, that I could recall, seen Oliver cry and it was extremely disconcerting. I'd never had to comfort someone his size before and the logistics of where to put my arms were beyond me. In the end, I merely squeezed his hard upper arm as he leant against the concrete gatepost.

"I shouldn't have been so dismissive," he finally continued. "If I hadn't been so bloody wrapped up in myself, maybe I could have done something to prevent this."

"Nothing's that simple," I told him, but I wondered just how true that was.

He looked at me – eyes red, snot glistening in his moustache. "Isn't it?" he asked.

"I wish it were."

He paused, and then said, "Maybe it is."

"What do you mean?"

"I'm not sure," he said. "But... maybe – maybe this is just a ghost story. Nothing more, nothing less. Maybe that's what all life is – one big fucking ghost story."

I stood by the bedroom window in the dark, listening to Ashley's gentle, deceptively even breathing as I looked down on Sorrow Street – at the spot where our daughter had died. I could hear Oliver and Don moving about quietly in the spare bedroom. Molly and Mags had left a couple of hours ago, promising they would be back first thing the following day, but Oliver and Don had insisted on staying, and I hadn't felt inclined to argue. Nevertheless, for all intents and purposes, Ashley and I were alone, and as I replayed the accident repeatedly (noting how small the distances seemed from my new vantage point), I tried not the think about what Oliver had said to me by the garden gate.

One big fucking ghost story.

"You need to sleep," Ashley said from the darkness behind me, and I found myself thinking of what it would be like to lose her, as well. Alone. Never the man I could have been. *Nobody in here but us ghosts.*

"So do you," I said softly.

"I need to feel you're still here with me."

And so I joined her and found that, against all the odds, we did indeed find some comfort in each other's arms. Ashley was such a monumental reminder of Nadine – I couldn't look at her now without

268

seeing those lips, that all too familiar countenance – that a part of me had been afraid of getting too close to her since returning from Ned's. I'd hovered in corners and looked at her from a distance, sipping endless cups of tea and wondering how I was going to be able to live with such a constant reflection of the things my daughter had been and the things she might have become. But I need not have worried. If this life was, as Oliver had suggested, nothing but one big fucking ghost story, then so be it.

Some ghosts, however demanding, I would gladly live with.

Ashley was speaking. I had been only distantly aware of her muffled words, the sound oddly prayer-like and soporific, but I now tried to listen more carefully – realising that this was a "conversation" and that I might at some point need to reply.

"I don't know what happened," she whispered. "I should, but I don't. I was there, Sonny. I was there and then I wasn't."

"Where, love?" I asked, thinking that maybe she was on the verge of restless sleep – her mind growing muddled.

"Round the front," she said. "With you."

"I don't understand."

She turned over and faced me, her nose a couple of inches from mine. I breathed in her vinegary breath, reading the day from it, and waited for her to continue. When she took my hand beneath the duvet, I felt how cold she was – cold and clammy, unwashed and oily.

"I brought her round," Ashley told me. "The back gate was locked. Maggie locked it when she came back. I made sure of it. So when Nadine wanted to come and see her daddy, I unlocked the gate and brought her."

I was confused. "You brought her round to the front garden?"

She nodded and gripped my hand more tightly. "I was there," she said solemnly. "I watched you hoeing and then... Nadine started to wave to someone. I couldn't see who but... she was so excited, Sonny. She waved and giggled, and then I was gone."

She wasn't making a whole lot of sense. I was sure I would have seen her if she had been there and, yet, she had clearly seen Nadine waving at Sheila Mackenzie. "What do you mean, and then you were gone, love?" I asked, hoping this might help.

"One minute I was there," she whispered, as if afraid someone might overhear (Oliver or Don, perhaps?). "One minute I was there holding on tightly to Nadine's hand and the next... Sonny, I was on the patio. I was sitting on the sun lounger, cold and shaking and alone. I don't know how I got there but I remember knowing I should have been somewhere else, that what had happened was impossible and that I was probably going mad. Then I heard... it was awful. I was taken away from her. We were taken away from each other."

She was crying again, and as I tried to make sense of what she had just told me, I drew her close and wrapped myself around her. Diminished and once more the vulnerable young woman I had learned to love on the beach all those years ago, I wanted her suffering to end. It didn't matter that I was also breaking under the same grief and pressures – what concerned me at that moment was my wife and how I was going to get her through this.

When she finally fell asleep with her head against my chest, I laid awake – thinking through all the things that had to be done. I wanted to distract myself with formality and preparation, but my mind kept returning to all the unanswered questions, not least, that of what had happened to Ashley.

I had no reason to doubt her. Any lie or fabrication she told me would simply be unnecessary. Since Maggie had been the last one through the gate, she would have been responsible if it had been left open – allowing Nadine to wander round on her own. So if Ashley said she had brought Nadine round to see me, then that, as far as I could see, was what had happened.

So how to explain my not seeing her? I saw all the connections and implications – but I could do nothing with them.

Ashley twitched in her sleep and made a heart-rending whimpering noise in the back of her throat. I stroked her back and stared at the ceiling – pulling the duvet up against her neck. She was my force, now, whatever lay ahead of us and however many times I might forget it in the days and weeks to come. Without her, I was sure, I would head into a tailspin and no amount of skilful piloting on the part of those around me would pull me out of it.

She was all I had left.

"Why didn't I see you?" I whispered.

Chapter Fourteen

Len and Pippa occupied one corner of the living room – sipping coffee and waiting with the rest of us. Since arriving about half an hour earlier, they had done nothing to help with the preparations and had hardly said a single word to their daughter. As I watched, Pippa leant in close and said something to Len. He nodded and glanced reflexively over to me, before staring into his coffee and mumbling a reply. I wanted to know what they were saying – but I suspected it was probably just as well that I didn't.

Since returning from Toronto, Len and Pippa had exhibited clear signs of disapproval towards Ashley and me – Ashley especially. They did their best to hide it, of course, pushing it into the deep fissures of their grief and hoping no one would notice, but I couldn't fail to see it – and if I, far from being their harshest critic, had managed to spot it, then it seemed a given that Ashley had. As far as they were concerned, children didn't just have accidents – they were *allowed* to have them. (This was my interpretation of their attitude, at least, and I didn't think I was too far off the mark). Parents were there to protect and nurture, to bully the child into adulthood, if that was what was required, and they evidently found our failure to grasp even the basics highly disappointing.

My feelings towards my mother- and father-in-law had changed significantly since Ashley had told me of her childhood. Nevertheless, I felt confident that this had little to do with my interpretation of their current behaviour – and I had this confirmed when Oliver came over and said, "I can slap them about a bit, if you think it'll help."

"Who?" I asked, not wanting to make assumptions.

"Desi and Lucy over there," he said, nodding in Len and Pippa's direction. "I thought they were above that kind of behaviour."

"Apparently not."

"So I should slap them?" I knew what he was trying to do and I

271

appreciated it. It was a time, as he saw it, to show solidarity with Ashley and me – to support us in whatever way seemed appropriate at the time – and that Len and Pippa were not subscribing to this view was seriously pissing him off, however well he succeeded in hiding it. I remembered how he had handled Francesca in the hospital waiting room that time, a much more formidable opponent, but didn't worry that he might show the same lack of restraint today. He was bigger than that and, anyway, Don was with him, now.

"Maybe not just yet," I said, and he nodded.

"Have there been problems?" he asked, after a short pause to faff with his tie. "Between Ashley and her folks, I mean."

"There have apparently been underlying tensions for years."

"*Apparently?*"

"Something I've only recently learned about," I told him.

"Ah. Right. So much for writers being perceptive, eh?"

"Whoosh."

"I couldn't have put it better myself."

"Sometimes we just don't look hard enough," I said. "After the iffy early years, we got on okay. They seemed to like and accept me and I was flattered and too comfortable with that. Now... I don't know. I think they saw me as some kind of ally. The sensible older man who'd keep their daughter on the straight and narrow."

"They got you all wrong."

I laughed a little too loudly, hysteria bubbling beneath the surface. Pippa frowned at me. Ashley glanced over from her place on the settee beside Molly and smiled. The past week, we had been good together. We had been tolerant and loving, turning to each other in our pain and anguish and not, as I might have at one time anticipated, pushing each other away and scrapping like feral dogs. It was right and fair that it should be this way – we owed it to our daughter – and it occurred to me that if my wife could smile at my laughter at a time like this, then Pippa had no right looking at me like that.

"I saw him again, you know," Oliver said – so quietly I almost missed it.

"Jim?"

"Yes, Jim."

"Before you got back with Don or after?"

"After."

"Kind of blows your explanation out of the water, doesn't it?"

"You could say that."

"Want to tell me about it later?" I said. "Now isn't really – "

"Of course. I shouldn't have brought it up."

"No, mate, I'm glad you did. I'd suspected as much."

"You had?"

"I had."

Oliver nodded thoughtfully and seemed about to say more. Don came over and interrupted us, however – looking apologetic and just as uncomfortable as he had on the day of Nadine's death. He was a big man, was Don – nowhere near as big as Oliver, but big nonetheless – and, yet, there was an elegant affability about him that belied this. He had grace and charm, and he knew how to get by, however uncomfortably, in just about any social situation. A man who always knew which knife and fork to use, I'd often wondered just what he and Oliver saw in each other (the obvious apart). It wasn't exactly that they were ill matched. I'd known many ill matched couples that'd got along just fine. It was more that they were somehow different in a fundamental sense. They needed different things from life, and I wondered as Don approached us just how they managed their compromises.

"Sorry to interrupt," he said softly. "I wasn't going to bother you with this, but I thought I'd better. It's just that there's a man at the door who'd like a quick word."

"Did he give you his name?" I asked – my immediate thought being that it was Ned, here to cause even more trouble.

Don shook his head. "No," he said. "He didn't need to. I recognised him right away. It's the chap who was driving the car, Sonny."

For a moment, I didn't have a clue what he was talking about. The chap who was driving the car? What chap? What car? I knew of no chaps, of that much I was certain – just as I knew of no cars. Briefly, these were alien concepts. I frowned, about to ask him to be more specific, to explain himself – and then the penny dropped. The man who had been driving the car that had hit and killed Nadine. The man I had wished dead and forgiven a thousand times.

"Send him away," I said.

Don looked about to ask me if I was sure. His mouth opened and he inclined towards me a little, but Oliver gave a quick, barely perceptible shake of his head and, instead, Don merely said, "Of course. I'll do it right away."

I watched him walk away and felt Oliver's brooding presence beside me. He no more knew what to do than I, I realised, and it occurred to me that maybe this was what death was about. Not only did it serve as the cruellest *memento mori*, but it also revealed to us that all the propriety in the world didn't count for a bloody thing. Order. Patterns of behaviour and interaction. These were but constructs in which we foolishly learned to trust. Articles of faith in a godless existence. We shook hands. We spoke softly. Where necessary, we behaved with the utmost tact and diplomacy – but, when all was said and done, we were still the same crass and bumbling creatures we had always been, would *always* be. Sophisticates we would never be, whatever the illusions and delusions said to the contrary, because our primary failing was the one thing that made us who we were.

Our humanity.

I caught up with the young man just as he was about to get back into his friend's car. Don and Oliver remained on the doorstep, and as I approached, the young man faced me – looking anxious and hesitant. I noticed the stubble and the bruises beneath his carved out eyes, but couldn't at that point say whether I felt any sympathy towards him.

He stepped around the back of the car to greet me, offering a hand that I reluctantly shook as he introduced himself as Brian Engells, and we stood in the road like figures in some sleazy twenty-first century duel, each waiting for the other to make his move.

Brian Engells. Judging by the acne blooming in the hollows of his cheeks, he couldn't have been much beyond his eighteenth birthday. He looked frail and unfamiliar with himself – his clothes too self-consciously fashionable, not quite "there" – and his grip when he had shaken my hand had been intended to impress and had predictably failed. The gel in his hair made him look as if his mum had got her "with it" baby ready for the school disco and I knew from his appearance alone that his childhood could not have been an easy one.

He had "victim" stamped across his forehead.

"They told me I shouldn't come," he said – with the slightest hint of a stammer. "But I... I had to. I don't want to make it any harder for you or... or your wife and everyone, but I needed – "

"To let us know you are sorry and that you aren't going to hide away like a criminal," I said.

I'd meant this kindly enough, but Engells apparently didn't know how to take it. He took a step back and his right leg brushed the back bumper of the car. I was aware of his friend watching us as best he could through his mirrors. His friend watched. My friends watched. We all needed friends like that.

"I don't want any trouble," he said uncertainly, and I held up my hands to show that I meant him no harm.

"You're not going to get any," I assured him. "I think... I think that what you've done today is a brave and honourable thing. I appreciate it and... and I want you to know we don't blame you."

"You don't?"

"No." This wasn't completely true – not all of the time, at least – but he didn't need to know that. "I was there, son. I saw what happened. There was nothing you could have done. We all know that."

"There wasn't," he said quietly. "I've thought about it over and over, and I know that but – "

"You wish it were different?"

I wasn't entirely sure why I felt I needed to take this particular tack with him. Maybe it was an extension of what I had felt at the hospital on the day of Nadine's death – that to blame someone was somehow vulgar and insulting to my daughter's memory. But whatever my motivation, the end result was in itself worth it, however fleetingly. To see Engells stand before me with such honesty and gratitude, to know that tonight he would sleep for the first time since the accident – and that this would be my doing – these were life-affirming things, and right then, that was what I needed more than anything.

He nodded and made an odd, grasping movement with his right hand. I watched as he struggled to find the right words, and as much as I wanted to help him further, I knew I couldn't. This was down to him now. I had given him all I could and he was as alone as the rest of us.

"Yes," he said. "I want to change things, but I know that I can't. And I feel guilty. Not just for what happened to... to the little girl."

"Nadine," I said softly.

"Yes. Nadine. I don't just feel guilty about that, I feel guilty because I don't want to feel like this anymore."

I was quite possibly old enough to be Brian Engells' father. It was a peculiar notion, and one that I didn't wish to examine too closely. "That's only natural," I told him. "We none of us want to feel this way anymore."

"I'm sorry," he said again.

I nodded, eyes closed. "I know."

"If I could swap places with her, I would. Really, I would."

"You can't," I told him.

"If I could, though. If I could, I'd do it right away. Without a moment's hesitation."

"I appreciate that," I said, wanting this conversation to be over now.

"I don't want it to be like this anymore." He was repeating himself. Or as near as damn it. I didn't want to interrupt but I had to, for the sake of my own sanity.

"There's something I'd like to ask you," I said.

There were tears in his eyes, now – tears of, I thought, joy that he might be able to do something for me. Like all true penitents, he was committed and zealous. I almost expected him to kneel before me and take my hand. "Anything," he said. "Tell me what I can do and I'll do it."

Go home, I thought. *Go home and take your own life. Cut yourself at the wrists and throat, carve a line from your sternum to your naval and leave me be.*

"Tell me what you saw," I told him.

Brian Engells was puzzled. He'd expected something more. "What I saw?" he said.

"In the moments before you hit my daughter." It seemed simple enough. Brian nevertheless continued to struggle with the notion.

"I'm not sure what – "

I took a step towards him and he flinched, eyes blinking rapidly.

He couldn't account for this sudden change in mood. Neither could I, for that matter.

"I just want to know what you saw," I told him. I still spoke softly, but now the effect was intimidating. "You saw me, you saw my daughter. What else did you see, Brian?"

There must have been some discernable change in my body language – some telltale rigidity and turn. The friend got out of the car and very pointedly asked if everything was all right whilst Oliver and Don strolled purposefully down the garden path to join us.

"Everything's fine," Engells told his friend. "It's okay, really."

"Sonny?" This from Oliver.

"We won't be a minute."

"They're due any time, mate."

"I know." Turning my attention back to Engells, I said. "You better be quick. Tell me what you remember seeing. That's all I want from you."

"She just ran out," he told me, voice clogged with emotion. "There was no reason. I didn't know that at the time because it was all too quick. But it was like... I don't know. It was like she'd seen an ice cream van or something, except there was no ice cream van."

"You didn't see anyone on the other side of the road?"

"No. I only saw you, the little... Nadine, the old man and your wife."

"You saw my wife?"

He thought carefully about this, apparently realising it was important. "Yes," he said. "Yes, I saw your wife."

There was no doubt in my mind that Brian Engells was a good man. My feelings for him altered almost by the minute, but in my heart of hearts, I saw him for what he truly was; a troubled and traumatised innocent who had never been intended for such a complex world. He had little capacity for duplicity, that I could see, and the authority with which he said this convinced me that he was telling the truth. He had not seen Sheila, but he had seen my wife. I, on the other hand, had seen only the naked ghost woman enticing my daughter to her death – and I now saw just how twisted this really was, how perverse and malignant.

Sheila Mackenzie had become more real to me than Ashley. For that moment (and others), she had taken precedence – and the important things had been lost, one temporarily, the other forever.

As Brian Engells' friend drove him away, I realised that I was to blame for all of this. I had "thought" Sheila Mackenzie into existence and, just as surely, I had "thought" Ashley into inexistence. The two could not "be" together, there simply wasn't enough room – physical or emotional. Had I never read the journal, if I had merely glanced at it and resisted the mystery of the world it had promised, all would have been well. But, instead, I had ran to it – hungry for that sense of threat and dark, cancerous sexuality – escaping from Ashley and the too-bright world around me to the sepia stains and tints, that blotchy world of scams, murder, appetite and loss. When I should have been ensuring that my wife and daughter had been all right, I had sat alone in my room and worked my way through those soon-to-fade pages, deciphering the cramped handwriting with increasing ease – forever aware of Sheila Mackenzie's presence in the room without ever truly acknowledging it.

The door had not opened by itself. I understood that now. I had thought it open. Sheila Mackenzie existed because of me. She opened some doors and emphatically closed others, and as the hearse carrying my daughter's corpse came down Sorrow Street towards me, Oliver taking my arm and trying to lead me away, I was sickened that I had not seen this so clearly before. The knowledge had been there all along, but only now did I dare look at it – only now did I see it for what it was.

The coffin was larger than I would have expected. Like us all, I had watched the funerals of children on television too many times – sweet victims of socio-sexual deviance and ineptitude – and banally commented along with the rest on just how small the coffins appeared, how it wasn't meant to be this way. But Nadine's coffin didn't inspire such predictability in me. Simple oak, beautifully crafted with high-polish brass handles, it possessed a certain dignity and, even, maturity that seemed perfectly placed. My baby girl was no longer a baby girl. In death, she had lost one thing and gained something else.

Her toys were discarded.

She had no need of them now.

It wasn't raining. The forecast had predicted showers, growing heavier through the afternoon, but as we stood by the graveside, waiting for Nadine to be lowered into the ground, I glanced at the clearing sky and thought that this was somehow right. Nadine had loved the sunshine. Sunshine for her had meant play and laughter, long days followed by nights of solid slumber, and the thought that it might rain on this day of all days, *her* day, had taken me lower than I'd been since the day of her death.

Ashley had brought Nadine's favourite Action Man with her – apparently feeling that, contrary to what I believed, Nadine would still need such a childish emblem. Spiky hair and beard. Blue polo-neck sweater. Real gripping hands. "I want him to go with her," she had told me in the car. "She won't be alone and... he was yours. He'll take good care of her."

I'd always called him Jack. I'd shared secrets with him and together we had saved the world during the week and pulled slanty-eyed girls in low-life Asian bars at the weekend. He'd been a companion and a confidant. He'd also been one of the first fictions that I'd truly brought to life in my imagination. Jack had lived, just as I lived, just as Ashley lived – just as Sheila Mackenzie lived – and the thought of him spending all eternity with my daughter was an extremely comforting one.

Ashley held the action figure in front of her – her left arm linked through my right, Oliver on her other side, ever attentive and alert to the dangers. She ran her thumb repeatedly over the prickly hair as the vicar droned on ceaselessly.

We'd opted for a fairly standard Church of England funeral – short service in the crematorium chapel (we drew the line at a full church service) followed by burial – feeling that it was somehow wrong to take the Humanist path. It had not been an easy decision. Our whole approach to the matter of Nadine's faith had been to wait until she was old enough to understand all the options and then let her decide. Her predeceasing us had not been something we had accounted for and, in the event, superstition had taken over.

"When do I put it in?" Ashley asked me in a whisper. She held the Action Man up. "When do I put him in with her."

"Whenever you feel it's right," I told her. She felt heavy against me. I gave Oliver an anxious glance, and he nodded reassuringly. He had everything under control. If she fell, he would catch her.

He would catch us both.

This had all started with a hole, I thought as Ashley leant forward and dropped Jack onto the lid of our daughter's coffin. It seemed only fitting that it – that *I* – should end in a similar hole. There was a pleasing symmetry to it, a spiritual balance that made me think that this had been the underlying point. In order to understand, all I had to do was look. No complex philosophical arguments were required, no convoluted computation. All I had to do was open my eyes and *see* – take in the not-so-subtle layering and meaning and *walk with it.* Nothing more was required of me other than commitment. The grave waited. Nadine and Jack waited. I tossed earth and felt how easy it would be to just let go, take that extra step and leave it behind, complete the crudely delineated cycle.

I glanced up into the faces of the people crowding round the other side of the grave. Friends and neighbours, family I hadn't seen for years. Their eyes held pity; some reflected their love for Nadine, for Ashley and me – all revealed ill-concealed fascination and relief. People, on the whole, were not callous. This much I knew. They behaved cruelly, without thought, but in essence most people were decent and considerate. And, yet, today, at least, we were a show – a reason to breathe a sigh and give thanks.

Don was at my side. He tossed some soil and then the two of us stepped back. He whispered something to me I didn't quite catch, something about Ashley, and I looked up, sensing a movement, knowing that there was something I had to see – something very deliberately placed.

A plot device.

At first, I thought it was Sheila Mackenzie. The woman looked at me very directly. Wearing black jeans, a crisp white blouse and a black jacket that looked a size too big, she seemed vulnerable and unsure of herself, and it took me a moment to recognise her as Polly – our eavesdropping friend from the pub. Her smile was uncertain. I remembered the slip of paper she had given me, the expressed need to speak to me, and walked over to her as the mourners started to disperse.

"Sonny?" Oliver said.

"One minute." I paused and held Ashley, kissing her on the forehead – telling her that I loved her and that I wouldn't be long.

"Don't ever leave me," she whispered.

"I won't." I couldn't. Not ever. I needed her as much as she needed me and however neglectful and arrogant I was sure I had been towards her in the past, I was now determined that I would find a way of making this right – for myself and Ashley, and for Nadine.

Polly met me halfway. We stood apart from the main body of mourners, the sun surprisingly hot on the side of my face, and she offered her condolences before becoming embarrassed and apologetic.

"It's all right," I said, surprised by her sudden, uncertain tears. "It's appreciated, Polly, thank you."

"I heard about it on the news and I knew it was your little girl right away," she said, dabbing at her eyes with a crumpled tissue. "I had to come. I know I'm just... I had to come."

"It helps, believe me," I lied. "Knowing that people are thinking of us, that we aren't alone."

"Does it?"

I smiled sadly. "Not really, no. But it's still nice that you took the time to come."

"It was important that I came," she said. "I had to because – "

But before she could say anymore, I heard my name being called. Oliver. With an urgency that made my head throb and my vision blur. I turned away from Polly with only the most cursory of apologies, dreading what I would see – imagining them dragging Ashley, muddy and hysterical, out of the grave, suddenly quite sure that tragedy could only be followed by further tragedy.

Ashley was nose to nose with Pippa. Oliver carefully held Ashley back, Len doing his best to lead a tearful Pippa away. I heard Ashley say, "But it wasn't. Whatever you think, it wasn't and – *stop looking at me like that!* It wasn't my fault. I didn't... I didn't, Mam."

She sagged as I got to her and fell into my arms, Oliver and Don standing by in case her dead weight was too much for me. She smelt damp and a little sweet, and I wanted her away from all this – I wanted her home where I could take care of her, where I could close the doors and blinds against the intrusive stares and shallow, pitying asides. If we were to break, it was only right that we should break alone, together, within the privacy of our own home. I didn't want these people – family, friends and neighbours alike – witnessing this. It wasn't right. They were not worthy.

"Come on," I said soothingly. "Let's get you to the car."

"She's hardly spoken to me, Sonny," Ashley said, her breath catching. She burped quietly and I smelt vomit and bile. "She just kept looking over at me and... it was *never* my fault. Nothing was."

"I know, love."

"Do you?"

"Of course.

"And you believe me?"

I pressed my forehead to hers, holding her face in my hands as I said, "I believe you, Ash."

It no longer felt like my home. When I looked at the aunts and uncles I hadn't seen, if I remembered correctly, since my parent's funerals, huddled in corners with drinks and sandwiches in their hands, it was virtually impossible for me to imagine Nadine occupying the same space – or, for that matter, my mother and father, sitting hand in hand on the settee in front of the fire, watching the old GEC television in the corner and quietly talking. Our home had been taken over, invaded, and, politely shaking hands and thanking the alcoholic second cousin whose name I couldn't remember (and didn't particularly care to) for coming, I saw now that this had not been a good idea. A traditional working-class wake – which was what this was, however I tried to dress it up – was not appropriate for the death of a child. Such an event required a life to be celebrated, anecdotes and drunken reverie flowing with the beer – but with a child, that just wasn't possible and the living room already had an uncomfortable air about it.

I made sure Ashley was all right, finding her a relatively quiet place with Molly and Mags in the kitchen. She was still a little uncommunicative after the episode with her mother but she smiled and nuzzled into me when I told her that I was proud of her – that I loved her and that this would be over as soon as was humanly possible.

"I only agreed to it because she suggested it," she said – meaning the wake and her mother. "I didn't want her to feel left out. Wish I'd never bothered, now."

"You don't mean that," I said.

"Oh I think I do. Why's she being like that, Sonny?"

"I don't know, love. Grief, I guess."

"Grief?" It was good to hear the ironic, slightly mocking tone. She was alive, in spite of everything. It surprised me – and, on another level, depressed me a little – to think that we could continue like this. Everything we had lived and worked for had been taken away from us, oh so cruelly destroyed right before our eyes, and still we walked through rooms where she had once played and talked of things unrelated and mundane. It was obscene. It was right. "You think she knows what grief is?"

"Yes, I do," I said quietly. "And so do you, love. Whatever you like to tell yourself to the contrary, you know she's no monster."

"He's right," Mags said. "We're all a mess right now, Ash, your mum included. Don't let this come between you both, love. It happens too quickly and then..." She shrugged. "Well, you know."

"I do," she said, grabbing Maggie's hand and giving it a squeeze. "But she needs to be willing, too. She's been just awful to me today and... I don't deserve it. One time I might have thought I did, but I don't." She glanced up at me. "Do I?"

"No," I said. "You don't. Just give her time to cool down and I'll have a word," I added. "See if we can get this sorted out."

After telling Oliver where I was going and that I wouldn't be long – just in case Ash needed me– I went up to our bedroom, removing my tie and jacket and throwing them on the bed.

Since returning home, something had been bothering me. What with the additional upset of the incident between Ashley and Pippa it had taken me a little longer than it otherwise would have, but once I had Ashley fairly settled with Molly and Mags, it occurred to me that I hadn't said a proper goodbye to Polly – and that she had seemed on the verge of telling me something.

I couldn't remember what I had done with her telephone number. I seemed to recall putting it in the pocket of my jeans – or possibly my shirt – but I couldn't remember which particular pair and so ended up searching through all of them, to no avail. It was more than likely that Ashley had washed the clothes I'd been wearing that day, but she was fastidious about checking pockets and if she had found it I was fairly confidant she would have mentioned it. I hadn't taken it out and put it somewhere safe, of that much I was certain, so that only left... what? Either it had managed to get past Ashley and disintegrated in the washing machine, or I had somehow lost it – the latter seeming increasingly more likely when I considered that it hadn't been something I'd thought all thought important (it wasn't like I'd ever intended on actually calling her).

I sat on the edge of the bed, the wardrobe a mess, and listened to the steady hum of the still quite decorous wake downstairs. That was where I should have been. In the kitchen with my wife, making sure she was all right. But, instead, as was all too frequently my way, I was up here alone – thinking about a woman I hardly knew and wondering what she had wanted to say to me.

Whatever it was, I decided it would have to wait. When everything was back on a more even keel I might catch her at the pub – but for now, there were more important things to attend to.

As I stood, my hand caught my discarded tie and it fell to the floor. I would have left it there for later, now wanting to get back downstairs to my wife, but the thought of Ashley coming up before me and having to tidy up after me was not particularly appealing. So I first hung up my jacket, smoothing down the creases haphazardly, and then bent for the tie – feeling an increasingly familiar twinge in my lower back, a soreness in my neck that made me think back to the night I had slept in the back garden. Today was not the day for such thoughts. I didn't want Sheila Mackenzie intruding further on our lives. And so I exiled them for another time, grabbed the tie...

... and stopped.

The wardrobe door was still open. I'd intended to hang up the tie and now, bent at this slightly precarious angle, I saw into the wardrobe from this new perspective and spotted immediately the crumpled piece of paper in the far corner.

I knew what it was right away, of course. Nevertheless, I sat for a moment on the edge of the bed – suddenly not sure if this was something I actually wanted to do. For me, Polly sang of numerous possibilities. She was someone from another life, a fan with God only knew what on her mind. I'd met women like her before (or so I then thought) at signing sessions and writers' conferences and I knew it was possibly quite dangerous to do anything that could even remotely be misinterpreted as "showing an interest". Nevertheless, I got down on my hands and knees and fished out the scrap of paper – holding it tightly in my palm as I knelt on the floor before the wardrobe trying to decide on the best course of action.

By the window, my mobile in one hand, the number in the other, I looked down on Sorrow Street – packed with more cars than usual and locked within the unusual appropriateness of its own meaning – knowing what I was going to do now but still hesitant. I wanted only to do what was right. I was not in the least concerned that Polly might pose some kind of threat to my marriage. That was never going to happen. But I felt the inexplicable need to be cautious. I was merely calling to thank her once more for attending the funeral and to apologise for having to dash off the way I had, and, yet, I couldn't help feeling that there was more going on here. Polly had had something she had wanted to tell me, that much had been fairly obvious. What nature of a "something" that might have been, however, I could only begin to imagine – and it was this that caused me to pause before thumbing in the number and dialling.

Polly picked up immediately – her "yes" efficient and with a too-sensitive awareness of the possible need for urgency. I waited a beat before speaking, framing my thoughts.

"Hello?" Polly said, clearly growing impatient. "Look, I'm very busy. If you've got something you want to say to me could you please just get the fuck on with it?"

"Polly?" I said. "It's Sonny Moore."

Now it was her turn to be silent. I heard her breathing – shallow and a little asthmatic – and in the background voices and the occasional chink of glasses. She was working. Probably still wearing the un-Pollylike clothes she had worn to the funeral. Uncomfortable and preoccupied, a woman on unfamiliar ground.

"Sonny." Again a pause. "You kept my number."

"Yes," I said. "Although I must admit, it took some finding." Best not to let her get too carried away. "I just wanted to thank you again for coming to the funeral, and to apologise for having to rush off the way I did."   -

"You really have nothing to apologise for," she said.

"Nevertheless, it was nice of you and – "

"I still need to speak to you." She cut through my attempt at small talk. "I know it might not be something you're all that comfortable with, but it can't really wait, Sonny."

"Polly, I'm sure you're a lovely woman but – "

"For Christ's sake, Sonny. I'm not coming on to you. This is important. I have something to tell you about that bloke that lives a few doors along from you. Ned Mortimer."

My knees almost buckled. I leant against the wall at the side of the window and closed my eyes, breathing out through my mouth and smelling the same odour of bile and vomit I'd smelt on Ashley's breath earlier. "What about him?" I asked.

I heard someone call her name – a gruff, impatient voice. "Listen," she said. "I can't talk now, and I don't like doing this on the phone.... Do you know Robertson Park?"

"Of course I do, but – "

"Meet me there tomorrow."

I agreed to meet Polly in Robertson Park, "by the knot gardens", bright and early the following morning. I tried to imagine just what it was she might have to tell me – what further sickening twist she might reveal – but all this served to do was heighten my sense of unease and dislocation. I glanced out of the window and watched a number of our guests leaving and briefly wondered if now was the time for a confrontation. Why wait until tomorrow? Why not merely march down Sorrow Street, hammer on Ned's door and demand a full explanation?

There was a gentle tap at the bedroom door. I turned, expecting to see Nadine – pretty and playful, quietly assessing – and felt everything shift to the left before settling back into place as Pippa tentatively stepped into the room.

"Can I have a word?" she asked.

I really wasn't in the mood for her but I nevertheless nodded and gestured for her to sit on the bed. She remained standing just inside of the doorway, however, whilst I stayed by my window – my bum resting against the radiator that my daughter had "helped" paint.

"I'm not sure what's wrong with me," she said quietly.

"What do you mean?" I didn't want to do or say any more than was absolutely required of me. Making her life easier was not high up on my list of priorities.

"I should be better at this by now, but I'm not."

"Better at what?"

"Being a mother." She sighed and finally took up the offer of a seat, perching on the end of the bed and staring into the still open wardrobe. In a Chanel-like little black dress, she could have passed for Ashley's sister, had it not been for the deep-cut lines of worry around her thinning lips and across her brow. I was tempted to take pity on her, but I'd learned my lesson; I didn't want to risk Ashley overhearing us talking about her.

"I really don't think I'm the one you should be discussing this with," I told her.

"Ashley won't talk to me, Sonny."

"Have you tried?"

"You saw what she was like at the cemetery." She glanced at me and then looked away, frowning.

"Her behaviour was reactive, Pippa," I warned. "Don't try pinning this one on her."

"She's grieving, I know – and I made allowances for that, I really did, but – "

"That's not what I meant." I let this hang ominously in the air between us for a short while and then added, "I saw the looks you were giving her, and me for that matter. We all did."

"I don't – "

"You know *exactly* what I'm talking about." I had to relax and consciously unclench my fists. I was the reasonable one, here. The lamentable grieving father, I nevertheless had to hold on tight to the reins and not let this one get away from me. "She needed you like she's never needed anyone before, Pippa, and not only were you not there for her, but you seemed to actively go out of your way to make it more difficult for her."

"That isn't true," she said. "It wasn't like that at all."

"Then how do you explain your behaviour?" I spoke softly, now – not wanting to bully her, knowing she would only respond with obstinacy and misdirection if I did.

She shook her head. Her tears didn't work quite as well as they should have; I felt no real sympathy towards her.

"I'm just not a good mother," she repeated. "I love Ashley – I love you all, and I honestly don't judge, truly I don't, but... she was precious and I miss her and I just don't know how to do this."

Sitting on the bed beside her, I saw she still wasn't the woman I had once imagined her to be. There were things going on in her head that I would never understand. Pippa was not evil. Compared to Maggie's mother, she was a saint. But her problems were not ours to fix or endure. We had more than enough to contend with.

Nevertheless, I spoke to her as kindly as I could. "Just hold her. It's really that simple."

At ten-fifteen that night, I finally gave in and had my first drink of the day. Stomach empty, and already feeling light-headed and shaky, it hit hard – sensation quickly folding in on itself as I sat on the stalker wall beside a drunken, dishevelled Oliver and wondered why the cold night air didn't seem to *mean* anything anymore. The house was quiet – only Maggie and Don remaining to keep a coping Ashley company – but every once in a while I thought I heard childish laughter, as distant and hollow as an early Elvis Sun demo. It held me in place and I was not disturbed by it.

"You okay?" Oliver asked me, and I nodded, swirling the whisky around in the glass as I tried not to think of all the other times I'd sat here – happier times, by and large, and, yet, far more difficult to recall in any real detail. Nadine was dead. I had to keep telling myself that. It was too easy to think of this as just any night, the epilogue to a late summer party, the drunken wind-down before bed.

"It was good to see Ashley and Pippa getting on again." Oliver sounded as though he was trying to delay the inevitable and it took me a short while to work out just what this meant. "I was really concerned about that, we all were. The two of you don't need something like that. Not today of all days."

"The older I get, the less I understand people," I told him.

"Her behaviour didn't make a lot of sense," he agreed, then fell silent.

I didn't know whether that was true or not. As I saw it, drunk and lost, nothing made that much sense anymore – but that didn't mean that there wasn't something there just waiting to be understood, something beneath the surface that would make everything fall into place. Maybe Pippa had been intended to behave that way. Perhaps on some unknown level her behaviour had the simplest, most perfect explanation that we were just incapable of grasping. I heard a noise overhead – leathery, faint and frantic – and looked up into the darkness, knowing what I'd heard but nevertheless questioning it. Weakened by the light pollution, I saw only stars.

"You up to hearing about Jim, now? Oliver asked.

At first, I didn't know what he was talking about – but then I remembered our conversation of earlier that day and nodded, telling him that now was as good a time as any.

"You're sure?"

"Absolutely," I said, filling our glasses from the bottle we'd brought out with us.

"I don't know where to start." He picked something out of his glass with his middle finger – wiping it on his trousers. "He was nice, Sonny. Can you believe that? I'm now being haunted by a nice ghost. I mean, don't get me wrong, he's no Casper, but... he's not like the Jim I remember. Not one jot."

"Nice in what way?" I asked him.

"Well, he... I don't know. It's just the things he says. He expresses regret and... it's almost like he wants to put things right."

"Between him and Mags?"

"Possibly. Yes. But there's more to it than that." Oliver stood up and faced away from me. He sighed and necked his whisky. "From the beginning," he said.

I wasn't sure I liked beginnings anymore. Endings were suddenly preferable. Conclusions drawn, pages finally closed. Nevertheless, I repeated the phrase in whispered prayer and waited for him to start.

"Don had taken his kids to the pictures for the evening," he told me. "We'd been back together for, I don't know, about a month or so and I was feeling pretty fucking smug. I was right. My work was going well, Don was back with me, my flat was clean and tidy and it seemed ludicrous to think that it had ever been any other way. As far as I was concerned, some things were just meant to be – and if we only knew enough to recognise and follow the clues when they were presented to us, then all would be well."

"Clues," I said ruminatively.

He glanced over his shoulder to see if I was mocking him. When he was satisfied that I wasn't, he turned away again and said, "Universal Clues. If you're open to them, they're everywhere – guiding us, presenting options and stating preferences."

"Like a god?"

He shrugged. "No. I don't think so. It doesn't matter, anyway. That was what I thought then. All I had to do was look honestly at the world around me, the world *within* me, and divine which paths to take. That was all there was to it. As easy as pie."

"But Jim changed all that."

"You could say that, yes." Sitting down on the lawn facing me, a few feet from where my hole had been, he crossed his legs – setting the empty glass on the grass beside him. "I'd just finished working for the evening," he said. "Like I say, I was feeling pretty bloody smug and, well, a little hyper. I'd written flat out for two and a half hours and had a couple of thousand words in the bag, but I knew I had to wind down before Don got back or I'd drive the poor love nuts with all my nervous energy. I thought about going for a walk, but I didn't know what time he'd be getting back and I didn't want him coming home to an empty flat. Especially if his ex had given him shit when he'd dropped the kids off. For the same reason, the gym was out of the question. So... you have to remember, I wasn't really feeling myself. I was euphoric and buzzing and I just didn't care. So I stuck Elvis in the DVD – the '68 Comeback Special – sat myself down with a large scotch and just let fucking rip. I was there, Sonny, and I was fucking amazing, if I do say so myself. You've heard me sing, right?"

"For my sins."

"Exactly. As a rule, I'm flat as a fart. But that night, I was *good*. I brought the bloody house down and then some."

Oliver was trying to communicate something singular and, to him, at least, somehow explanatory – but I didn't get it one little bit. I battled with emotion and memory, the effects of the alcohol, and tried to let his meandering monologue sink in, but try as I might I found myself drifting time and again until, leaning forward with his elbows on his knees and a strangely zealous look in his eyes, he said:

"I wasn't there anymore."

My eyes locked with his and he nodded. "I was gone, man, like totally gone," he added with a chuckle. "I sang and it was as if the flat just melted away. It was still there, or something resembling it was, but for all intents and purposes I was somewhere else. I was Elvis, sitting on that little square stage with his old band mates and those backcombed babes staring up at him, moonstruck and dripping – and then I wasn't. Then I was just some guy, watching and waiting, stalking, if you like. That bit was especially weird. I had a very definite sense of being outside. The flat was still there, stinking of polish and those fucking plug-in air fresheners that Don loves so much, but at the same time, it wasn't. I felt the breeze against my skin, heard it whispering in the trees overhead, and sang under my breath."

He paused, possibly for dramatic effect, and then belted out a few lines from *Trying to Get to You*.

When he'd finished, he seemed to sag. His voice had been quite unlike the one to which I had grown accustomed over the years – rich and mellifluous, with just a hint of the gutter growl. He leant back on his elbows, stretching his legs and inadvertently kicking the glass to the edge of the lawn in the process. Seeming suddenly quite exhausted, he went on.

"I could see someone," he told me. "Not Jim. Not yet. This was someone else entirely. Someone I'd never seen before."

"There in your flat?"

He shook his head. "Yes."

He nodded. "No."

I didn't need further explanation. I understood.

"She was young," he continued. "In some ways, she reminded me of Glenda – the girl I lost my virginity to. There was this... she wanted to please. I watched her and she faced me. She undressed and she smelt like a seaside rock shop – that sweet, high-pitched smell that makes your teeth ache just thinking about it. When she spoke... I don't know what she said, but something changed. We were no longer in her garden."

"Garden?" This was all becoming far too familiar.

"Yes, garden," he said. "Secluded. Alone. Needy. Garden."

"It all starts in a garden."

"A little too biblical for my liking," he said, "but I guess so."

I retrieved his glass from the edge of the lawn, shook a little dirt out of it and topped us both up.

"Go on," I said, handing him his glass.

"I was still in my flat," he said. "You have to remember that. I was still in my flat and, yet, I was also wandering the streets with this beautiful young woman – protecting her, teaching her, learning from her. She knew who I was, but she didn't. Don't ask me to explain that. I can't. Elvis was still playing in the background. *If I Can Dream*. I could hear it and because I could hear it – "

"She could hear it."

He sipped his whisky. Oliver now had no desire to rush anything.

"Yes," he said, oh so slowly. "Yes, she could hear it. For years, it seemed, I sat there in my flat as I wandered the streets with her and eventually the inevitable happened. She met him and... we drifted. I'd served my purpose."

"Him?" I thought I already knew the answer.

"Jim."

It was minutes since either of us had spoken. I once more heard childish laughter and tried to cling to it as I struggled to work out where this fit, always assuming it fit, at all. Oliver studied me, watching for signs and cues – and somewhere far off I heard car tyres screeching. A fatal sound and, yet, one that nevertheless helped me from my reverie.

"Maggie's Jim?" I said.

"Is there any other?"

"Actually, yes, there is."

"The Jim from your Elvis story?"

"Yes."

"But isn't he Maggie's Jim, too?"

"Yes," I said. "But not in any real sense."

Oliver looked vaguely amused. He squinted, his eyes catching some remnant of light and twinkling merrily, and his chin dropped as he made a huffing noise through his nose. Now was not the time for humour, I thought. Especially if it was at my expense. "You still think it's that simple?" he asked.

"What do you mean?" I wandered with my daughter. Following her through coniferous mazes, I struggled to keep up – forever just beyond reach, imprisoned within conflict and confusion, grief and ingratitude. Shapes shifted, as shapes are wont to do, and meaning became a mere path of disassociation. I listened to my friend talk, perhaps one of the most well-meaning men I had ever had the good fortune to know, and fought to find a way to make it different. I wanted solidity. I yearned for it in the same way that I yearned for my daughter's return – for my fingers to brush the back of her T-shirt and, miraculously, find purchase. Oliver continued talking and I listened, where necessary I even replied, but I nevertheless wished for other ways.

In the darkness, my tears fell into my scotch – unnoticed by Oliver as he said, "You still think of things as being 'real' and 'unreal'. After all that you've seen and been through."

"And that's wrong?"

"Not if you can distinguish between the two."

"Which you don't think I can anymore."

"That's not what I'm saying."

"Then what are you saying?"

When dialogue is so keenly paced, it all too quickly has a habit of becoming adversarial. Oliver knew this as well as I and therefore paused for the count of three before going on.

"It's no longer about being able to distinguish between what's real and what isn't," he said. "Our experiences have gone way beyond that. It's time for us to redefine our terms – that one term, 'real', in particular."

"Both Jims are as real as the other?"

"Exactly." He sat forward eagerly, rolling the glass between his palms. "They touch us, Sonny. They affect the way we assess and act – all of them, our ghosts and our fictions. They seek wisdom and they impart it. They create as they are created, destroy as they are destroyed. We fail to satisfy their hunger as they fail to satisfy ours.

Such utterly fucking paltry terms as 'real' don't even begin to come into it. What we call this just doesn't matter – how we think of it is inconsequential. What should concern us is that, however unlikely they might seem to be, these events are happening. Histories and fictions are having a very solid effect on our present and these ghosts or whatever the fuck you want to call them... these ghosts... they just might well be as haunted as we are."

I rocked back against this deluge, almost losing my balance in my inebriated state and very nearly toppling from the wall.

"My parents," I said, nodding quickly, and Oliver tilted his head questioningly. "My mam and dad," I said, just in case "parents" was too difficult a concept for him to grasp. "They never went away. When they died. Things they said. Things we did together. They still guide me, help me find a way forward – like with Polly, earlier."

"Polly?"

"Our favourite eavesdropper."

"Ah, yes. So what about her?"

I told him all about her being at the funeral and the following phone call. He sat up a little straighter when I mentioned what she had said about having something to tell me about Ned and how I was meeting her at Robertson Park the following day. Getting to his feet quickly, or as quickly as a moderately pissed twenty-three stone powerlifting novelist can, he sat eagerly on the wall beside me – hands on his knees like a good little boy awaiting his pudding.

"I'm coming with you," he said.

"I'd rather do it alone," I told him. This wasn't true, of course; making it easy for Oliver just didn't seem appropriate.

"I'm a part of this," he reminded me. "This is my problem as well as yours, mate. And Jim would want me to, I'm sure."

I'd almost forgotten that he hadn't finished the story of his latest Jim encounter. The nice Jim. The Jim of lingering fact and fiction.

"What did he say?" I asked – a little wearily.

Oliver started to stand again, but I reached up and put a hand on his shoulder, shaking my head. Reluctantly making himself as comfortable on the wall as he could, he sniffed and then said:

"I was still there, right? I was still in the flat but I wasn't still in the flat. I had this notion, when it was all over, that if Don had returned whilst it had been happening he would have found a semi-transparent me sitting in my favourite armchair singing along to Guitar Man. That's what it was like, or as close as I can get, anyway."

"A foot in either world."

"Yes. And no. I don't know, Sonny – but what I do know is that while I sat there singing along with Elvis, I watched her walk away from me. Jim took her and then he sat down and talked to me. I didn't fight any of it. It was too well scripted."

Oliver stopped and looked past me to the house. I glanced to my right and sure enough, there was Don, standing on the back doorstep watching us – checking that we were all right, I liked to think, or maybe just wishing to be included. What would he say? I wondered. If he knew of all that had happened to Oliver and me, would he still want to be involved or would he run a mile? To be ignorant truly could be a blessing, I saw that, now. To find a corner of the world, remote and untouched by rumour, and just cut off, sit and stare at the sky and never have to contemplate such complexity and confusion. Don would wish for that, if he knew what we knew. He would wish it for us all.

"Ash has gone up," he said quietly. "She asked me to tell you not to be too long."

I nodded. "Is she alone?"

"No, Maggie's keeping an eye on her."

"We'll only be another few minutes," Oliver told him – and Don took this as the gentle dismissal it had been intended, retreating into the kitchen and letting the door ease to behind him.

"He knows something's going on," I said.

"I doubt it. He'll draw the obvious conclusions, Sonny. Don't worry about that, yet."

He was speaking more quietly, now – almost in a whisper – and this made what he had to say sound even more ominous. The words crept out, whispering through his beard, and I felt them heavy about me in the chill night air. A moth brushed against the side of my face, the most gentle and distressing of somnolent kisses, and I slapped it away, waiting for Oliver to go on so that this could be over – so that I could finally lie down beside Ashley and let it all fall away.

"He was in my living room," Oliver continued. "He sat on the edge of the settee and grinned at me as I finished singing Guitar Man, and then he just started talking as if this were the most natural thing in the world, like it was something we did every day of the fucking week – like it was something we'd *always* done. He talked about the weather; he talked about the football and who'd won Big Fucking Brother this year. It was really that mundane, for a while."

"Spectral small talk."

Oliver smiled. "If you like." He shifted his position, desperate to stand but knowing that I... well, wouldn't stand for it – and then continued.

"It wasn't like that for long, though," he said. "He started talking about the person he had been, the mistakes he had made. He was sincere, something I don't ever recall seeing in him when he was alive, but more than anything he seemed... this is going to sound bloody odd but he seemed wise. There was this air about him. A confidence and ease. I even got an apology for the way he had been with me over the years – if you can believe that."

"Right now, I think I can believe just about anything," I said. *And nothing.*

He smiled kindly and did his best to bring his story to its point. "Anyway," he said, "Jim apologised and made himself even more comfortable on my settee – putting his feet up after first kicking off his shoes and heaping cushions around him. It was as if such simple luxury had been denied him for a very long time and I have to admit, I could have sat there and looked at the bloody big stupid grin all day. He got himself settled, and then he just grinned at me like that for a bit before saying, 'I got it all wrong with my Maggie' – something like that. I didn't know what he meant, at first, of course, but as he went on, it became much, much clearer.

"He told me that he'd wanted her with him. That's why he'd done what he'd done – following her, harassing in the way he had. Knowing what he knew, he said he'd initially thought it ridiculous that loved ones should remain apart when there was such a simple, permanent way of their being together. The way he saw it, the natural course was pointless, a needless torture. Once she was with him, he said, he'd thought he'd be able to make everything right. He would dance with her, show her all the beauty of 'being without being', as he put it – but he'd been naïve and selfish. He apparently saw that now.

"Did you ever catch Jim when he was well into his cups but hadn't quite reached the bolshy, eat-shit-and-die stage?" Oliver suddenly asked.

"The Tangerine Dream Drunk."

Oliver chuckled and shook his head at the memory. "So you did?"

"Once or twice."

"Well that was what he was like. All loved up and philosophical. He had regrets aplenty, but he only saw how truly wrong he'd been when he started to look around him a bit more."

At this point, Oliver grew more serious. His words considered and reluctant. I thought of Ashley, waiting for me, but resisted the urge to rush him.

"There is no perfect state," Oliver said. "That's what he told me. He said something was going to happen, there was no stopping it – he insisted that, when the time was right, I tell you this. Then he said something about what he would say to you on the day?"

I remembered the neighbour, kneeling over Nadine's body with me – how he had become Jim. *I won't let anyone do anything to her that they shouldn't,* he had said. *No one is going to do anything else to hurt her – you have my word, man, okay?*

Oliver nodded thoughtfully when I told him about this. We sat for a while just staring at the garden – the darkness a little too complete around us now. I felt I should say more. I wanted to question why Oliver hadn't told me this earlier, but I already knew all the possible answers and so didn't bother. Far off, I heard the ululating sound of a police siren. A sound that could never enchant – a warning misnamed, a travesty against mythology and romanticism. It sang out through the night and repelled. People fled from it, this cruel embodiment of all that was modern, all that was real. And Oliver and I sat on our wall and listened beyond it to the subtle sound of a world being carefully ripped apart.

"They're everywhere," he finally said, and I nodded. "They never go away."

"They can't" I told him. "Even if they wanted to, we wouldn't let them."

Chapter Fifteen

An Indian summer was promised, and when I woke the following morning – Ashley a damp, knotted and twisted mass amongst the sheets beside me – I felt the effects of the previous day's stress, sorrow and alcohol multiplied. My head throbbed relentlessly and my stomach burned, my tongue sticking to the roof of my mouth. I heard Oliver and Don moving about downstairs and my first thought was that I must tell them to be more quiet in future, so's not to wake Nadine. The realisation that followed was as harsh as ever, but it was softened slightly when Ashley turned over and looked at me.

She still wore the light make-up Maggie had helped her apply for the funeral – Maggie telling her that Nadine wouldn't want her mum going out looking *too* scary – and it now gave her a sleazy, panda-eyed look that at another time would have aroused me. Her smile was uncertain, laboured and brave, but her puffy face spoke of a hundred miseries, all stemming from that one unalterable event.

"You look dreadful," she said softly.

"You are too kind." I kissed her on the end of the nose and smelled the aftermath of grief; sweat and stale tea, salty seas and the heat of dying rage.

"You should have come up earlier last night," she said. There was no accusation to this and I merely nodded in reply. "We need to look after ourselves. It just won't do for us to let ourselves go."

"I agree," I said, rearranging my arms so that she could snuggle in. The damp sheet shifted and I saw she was naked, felt she was naked. Her skin had that clammy, post-fever chill about it and I tightly wrapped my arms around her.

"I had a nice dream last night," she told me. We'd been laying together in silence, just holding each other, for a good five minutes. "Want me to tell you about it?"

I'd had dreams of my own, most of them featuring Nadine in some way – if only in the symbolism of spaces that could never again be filled. Some had been a delight, others harrowing, but one thing they had all had in common had been the way in which they had torn me afresh upon waking. I wasn't sure that I could cope with Ashley's dream on top of that but, nevertheless, I said as brushed the hair back from her face, "Yes, I'd love to hear about it."

"It's a bit silly," she warned.

"Silly is good. I could do with a bit of silly right now."

She craned her neck and looked me in the face. "You're okay, though, right?"

"I will be," I said. "In time. You?"

"I think so. We've got to be, haven't we?"

"Not really," I said, "but it'll be much better if we are."

She nodded thoughtfully and settled her head back on the pillow, pressing her back into me. "Nadine was in the dream," she told me. "Except she was grown up – tall and intelligent like her dad and so full of wisdom she practically glowed. We were at the beach. In the sand dunes where you and I... you know, that first time."

"Made love," I said.

She nodded. "Yes. Made love. We were both there with her and... she pointed at the sand where you and I had been and told us that that was where she had been conceived."

"Except it wasn't," I said.

"That's what I told her. I said she was conceived much later, but she wasn't having any of it. She was insistent. For all intents and purposes, that was where she was conceived. That was where the idea of her came from."

"The idea."

"The idea. Yes. She said that that was the most important part. The idea of who she would become. She said that never dies, Sonny. That's what she told me. The idea never dies."

I had to admit that it was a far better dream than any of the ones I'd had. Ashley had clearly been lifted by it, and as I laid there with her – sharing her warmth and listening to Oliver and Don clank about in the kitchen – I thought how clever our daughter must be to visit her mum in such a revealing dream. It was beautiful. It was kind. The familiar, nostalgic imagery gave it substance – and I couldn't help marvelling at the deliberateness of it all. Dreams such as that were never accidental. They simply couldn't be.

"What you doing today?" she asked a few minutes later, moving her head on the pillow, nudging her hips against mine.

"I'm not sure," I lied. "I have a few things to sort out with Oliver and then... I don't know. Back here to spoil my woman, I guess."

"You don't need to watch me all the time, you know," she said softly. "I will be all right, Sonny."

"I know, love. I just need us to be together more right now. It's easier that way."

"Is it?"

"Well for me it is, but if – "

"Where are you and Oliver going?" The question came out of the blue and I had to struggle not to stiffen beside her. I wanted to tell her about Polly – about everything that had been happening – but the thought of how she would react was not an appealing one.

Without a halfway decent alternate response, however, I was left floundering, somewhat. I started to tell her that it was some left over business regarding Nadine's death – last minute formalities – but stopped myself just in time, knowing full well that, however distraught she had been during the past week, Ashley had nevertheless insisted on being kept in the loop. She knew as well as I that everything that had had to be done had already been taken care of.

"The truth?" I said, thinking on my feet.

"Of course." She frowned at me and I knew this wasn't going to be easy. "Sonny – what is it?"

"Oliver," I told her.

"What about him?"

"That's just it. I don't know. All he's told me is that he wants to speak to me. Away from Don."

"Away from Don." She said this as if it were a particularly challenging delicacy to be rolled and considered on the tongue. "That doesn't make sense."

"These things never do when viewed from the outside," I told her.

"This is different." She rolled onto her back and stared at the ceiling. I heard her stomach rumble, watched the painful frown – nigh on addicted to the drawn out silence as I waited for her to continue.

"The implication is that something's wrong between them and it's patently obvious that nothing is."

"But we can't know that," I insisted – a little too desperately. "We only see what they want us to see, pet."

"That's rubbish, and you bloody well know it. Oliver is an open book where Don is concerned." She looked at me, again, and I felt a chill. An Indian summer suddenly seemed much less likely. "No," she said. "If Oliver implied there's something wrong between him and Don, he's lying. There's something else going on. Either that or you're the one doing the lying."

"That'll be it, then," I said, trying to joke my way out of this. "

"I'm not stupid, Sonny," she said.

"I never thought for one minute you were."

"Then don't treat me as if I am." This came out more forcefully than she had apparently intended. She repeated it, this time more softly, and then added, "I know something's wrong. I've spoken to Maggie." My heart skipped a beat. I started to ask her what she meant but she put a finger against my lips and said, "I've spoken to Maggie and she agrees that you weren't yourself even before Nadine died, darling. I'm not saying you're lying to me, exactly, but I know there are things you aren't telling me."

"I don't know what you're talking about," I said.

I was a writer. If not a creative genius, at least a creative natural. Though recent work suggested otherwise. I wrote approximately two hundred thousand words a year, on average.

Nevertheless, this was the best reply I could come up with.

Ashley studied me. "We imagined it?" she asked, her voice suddenly rich with velveteen sadness. "Don't tell me that, Sonny. I know it isn't true and if you continue to say it is... I don't want that. I don't want us being that way. Especially not now. We... we *can't*."

It was no good. Maybe I couldn't tell her the truth – not then – but by the same token, I knew that I simply couldn't go on denying that I was keeping something from her. We'd been through too much to risk what we still, amazingly, had together, and, so, I said, "I can't tell you about it now, but I promise I will tell you about it soon, love. Something is going on. You and Maggie are right. Something's going on and Oliver's helping me try to get to the bottom of it."

"It's something to do with that morning I found you asleep in the garden, isn't it?"

If I discussed this with her for too long I knew I would end up telling her everything. It would all come out. The story of everything that had been happening to Oliver and me would pour out in a jumbled confusion and Ashley would stare on in disbelief, struggling as I struggled – ultimately, nothing constructive coming of our efforts. I could already see that look of bemused realisation on her face, hear the tears in her voice as she asked what all this meant, and I wanted desperately to put that moment off for as long as possible, hopefully until I had something conclusive to share.

And so I spoke very carefully, determined not to be drawn. "Yes, it is," I told her. "But please don't ask me anymore about it, yet, Ash. There are things even I don't understand, right now, and I can't even begin to explain it to you until I know what's going on myself."

"Is it dangerous?"

"No. No, I don't think so."

"And you promise me you'll tell me as soon as you can?"

"Of course."

"I don't like us having secrets," she said. There seemed something pointed in the way in which she said this and I briefly entertained the notion of Ashley and Maggie sitting down together discussing this over coffee. They'd talked about me. Under normal circumstances, that wouldn't have troubled me – but these weren't normal circumstances, and I couldn't help but wonder what other topics they might have touched upon. Was it possible that Ashley suspected that something had happened between Maggie and me? And if so, how much did she actually know?

"Me neither," I said.

Sometimes, even before Nadine died, I would find myself in a place – geographically mundane and dependable – where the commonplace would speak of incalculable mystery. The simplest thing would become loaded with meaning – the lamppost suggesting lost and forgotten civilisations, a sewer grate the most impenetrable future of decay and deliberation – and I would find myself hurrying home so that I might quickly jot down these insights before they disappeared into the ether.

Today, however, was not such a day.

Oliver and I walked through the gates into Robertson Park, and even though it was a place heavy with memories of my own and Nadine's childhood, the trees whispering our histories to each other as we walked beneath their beneficent canopy, it today felt somehow featureless and deserted – a soulless place without texture or sparkle. During our walk to the park, we had largely remained silent, neither of us feeling the need to talk, content not to plan or speculate. It had been a comfortable state, and not one either of us had seemed inclined to change. Only when we stepped into the park grounds did we feel the need to speak – the oppressive sense of forced function and curious hopelessness prompting us to latch onto the first subject that came to mind; bizarrely, the park itself.

"I've never liked this place," Oliver whispered, as though fearing the picnic benches might overhear him. "It's always felt so bloody artificial."

"I always liked it when I was a kid," I told him. "Me and Dad used to come here fishing."

"In the lake?"

"No, in the Bunny Retirement Home – of course in the lake, Oliver. Where the fuck else?"

"I thought heterosexuals might do it differently," he said, grinning his much-missed, hairy grin.

"With fishing, the missionary position is all there is, mate. No room for deviancy."

"Were you monogamous, or did you fish other lakes, too?"

"Strictly a one lake guy." Something like this would have normally been his cue to say something about Welsh Wales and Maggie, but blessedly he held his tongue and after a minute or two, I said, "I'm glad I let you come along."

"You are?" He sounded more than a little incredulous.

"I am. I can't remember the way to the knot gardens."

We were standing at a fork in the path. A few yards away a distracted-looking old woman in wobbly carpet slippers was walking a snuffling terrier. Oliver glanced left, then right, then left again. "I hate to so quickly prove a disappointment," he said, "but neither can I."

I suggested we ask the old woman, but Oliver took one look at her and vetoed the idea. "I'd rather trust to luck," he said. "And, anyway, it's not like the odds are stacked against us." He tossed an imaginary coin in the air and slapped it skilfully onto the back of his right hands. "Heads we go left, tails we go right." Uncovering the coin, he said, "Heads", and marched off, typically, along the right hand fork.

However questionable the method, it worked. We came over a slight rise in the path, down through a wooded area that had been here long before the park had been a park, and passed beneath a topiary archway into the painfully quiet knot garden.

As a boy, this place had always bored me into a monosyllabic grump. It was not a place for little boys (unless they'd remembered to bring their bikes or skateboards so that they could race along the narrow pathways scaring seven shades of shite out of the perambulating pensioners) but my parents had never missed an opportunity to stroll these carefully tended gardens, and I now thought I could see the attraction.

Dad would have loved the order and discipline, that much was obvious, whilst Mam would have found the symmetry and beauty soothing – a confirmation and gentle blessing of all that she'd held dear. I stood beside Oliver and surveyed the low-lying display, feeling their calm approval and gentle assurances as they quietly encouraged me on. What Oliver and I had discussed the night before was true, I now saw; they never go away, and even if they wanted to, we wouldn't let them.

"There she is," Oliver said, pointing to a lone figure on a bench at the far side of the knot garden. She spotted us at the same instant and waved – looking a little chilly in a short, ruffled green plaid skirt that seemed a distant cousin of the ra-ra skirts I so fondly remembered from my youth. Her blousy T-shirt had something written across the front that I couldn't quite make out, and as we walked towards her, I studied it, my eyes therefore focused on her breasts rather than her face.

Her T-shirt said "bitch", but when I looked up, her simple sad smile told me she was anything but.

It was fairly obvious that Polly had been crying. Her dark make-up had run a little and there was a crumpled tissue in her left hand. She sniffed and dabbed at her nose as we greeted her, and before I could say anything, Oliver asked her if she was all right.

Polly waved a hand dismissively and moved to one end of the bench so that we could both sit on her left – me closest to her. "I'm fine," she said. "It's nothing that a new job won't fix."

"Eddie giving you a hard time?" Oliver asked. Eddie was the pub landlord. I'd had very little to do with him over the years, preferring to order from his prettier bar staff, but I knew Oliver didn't much care for the bloke.

"You could say that," she said. "The little shit fired me."

"Really?" I said – admittedly sounding a little dim.

"Really." She gave an impressively snotty sniff and then added, "Apparently, I have a tendency to eavesdrop. Not sure where the fuck he got that idea but..." she shrugged and smiled, "... there you go. I suppose I deserved it, really. It wasn't as if I hadn't been warned, and there had been complaints. You know what people are like."

"Not as accepting as some of us," I said with a sympathetic smile.

"You two were harder to resist than most," she said. She chuckled and there was something pleasantly throaty and suggestive of forty fags a day about it. "You had some of the strangest conversations I've ever had the pleasure of overhearing. Especially when you'd both had a few. If I hadn't known you were writers I just might have sent for the men in white coats. Had you both locked up."

"Insanity's acceptable when you're a writer?" I asked.

"No, just a little easier to understand."

Polly truly was a lovely young woman. Intelligent and easy on the eye, I could have chatted like this with her all day – but as Oliver was quick to point out, we were here for a very specific reason, and as pleasant as the conversation admittedly was, we were wasting time.

"Yes," she said. "Yes, you are quite right." She dabbed at her nose with the tissue again and I warned Oliver with a glance not to start all that stern, pompous shit. There was no immediate rush, though it was certainly true that I was anxious to hear whatever it was she had to tell us. "I'm glad you could come," she continued. She spoke more quietly now, and we had to lean in to hear her properly. "I don't pretend to ever understand all the things I hear, but I do know when something isn't right."

"What do you mean?" Oliver asked.

Polly stared out over the seemingly expansive knot gardens and shrugged. She was telling this her way, I realised, and no amount of interruptions was going to change that. "When I gave you my number," she said. "I had nothing I wanted to talk to you about. Not really. I just... you know. I'm a fan and I wanted to see how easy it was."

"To write a novel?" I said kindly.

"Yes. Or live one." She shook her head and started shredding the tissue between her fingers. "It would have been silly and irresponsible, and, whether you believe it or not, I'd actually decided that even if you called me, I wouldn't go through with it. I just did my work, listened in on my customers' conversations and when you didn't phone, that was just fine.

"Then your little girl died and... I couldn't shake the feeling that there was something I knew that could help you, somehow." Normally a woman with good posture and a confidant air about her, Polly hunched over her fiddling fingers – crone shoulders rising and falling as she breathed rather too quickly.

"And this was to do with Ned?" I said, wanting to help.

"I didn't know it immediately," she told me. "Up until a couple of nights before the funeral I just didn't have a clue what it was that was bugging me. Then... he came in for a couple of pints and I remembered."

This was it. It seemed everything had been building up to this moment – and now that it was here, there was no doubt in my mind; whatever it was that Polly had to say, I wanted to hear it. Ashley had been right all along. Ned was not a good man. And I was wholly convinced that what Polly was about to tell Oliver and me would somehow underscore that.

"I quizzed him while I served him, just to be sure he knew you," she said. "He said he lives a few doors along from you, had seen the accident and everything. So sad, that's what he said, but I'd heard him, you see, Sonny. I'd heard what he'd said before and nothing he said about how sad and tragic your daughter's death was convincing. Because I'd *heard* him."

"What did you hear?" Oliver asked with surprising compassion.

On the far side of the knot garden, beside a tree at its entrance, I thought I saw someone studying us. I watched as Polly continued speaking – seeing movement but managing to separate nothing from the peculiarly dense shadow. The breeze picked up, rustling discarded sweet wrappers and raising goosebumps on Polly's legs and arms. Her words made sense. They fitted with some inner scheme that I'd never quite been able to articulate, but the crisply-trimmed reality about us, the shape and shadow, nevertheless threatened to distract me – because that was how instinct, some remnant of a primitive flee psychology, told me it should be. Sense was suddenly to be avoided. Explanation could almost have been the enemy.

"He came in quite a lot," Polly was saying. "You have to remember that. And after you two he was probably the oddest customer we had. The oddest and most interesting. He was a lonely, troubled old man. That's what I thought. Sad, you know? He'd come in and get himself a booth every Sunday lunch time and just sit there, eating and drinking and chattering away to himself... except it wasn't like he was talking to himself. It was more as though there was someone there with him. He talked about the past all the time – about boys he'd played with when he was little, about wars and the need for rest. That was one of his common themes, the need for rest. He wanted 'it' to end, and for a long time I thought he had a loved one dying of cancer, something like that – but then I realised he was talking about himself. He wanted it all, life I suppose, to be over, but it was almost as if he didn't see any comfort or release for himself in the afterlife, either. 'Death won't change owt for me,' he said one day. 'Not the way things are'. I always felt depressed after listening to him, but I couldn't stop myself – and over a period of about four or five weeks I got a slightly clearer picture of just what it was he imagined was troubling him."

She paused at this point to reach into a bag that I hadn't noticed tucked away behind her feet under the bench. She pulled out a pack of cigarettes and a lighter – lighting up before offering them around. Oliver and I declined (Oliver had never smoked and I'd only ever partaken occasionally back in sixth form college), and she shrugged as she put the pack and the lighter back in her bag, drawing deeply.

After a couple of hits, she was more able to continue. "He was being made to do something he didn't want to do," she said, before thinking better of it and adding, "No. No, that isn't quite accurate. His own need for peace, for *rest*, was making him *allow* something to happen that he would, under different circumstances, have stopped. The last conversation I heard him have before Nadine died didn't make a whole lot of sense at the time – but later..." she shook her head and took another long pull on her cigarette. For all my sixth form posturing, I'd never really understood cigarettes. Today, however, as Polly flicked ash and exhaled through her nose, I did.

"He seemed more distracted than usual," she continued. "It was hot and humid, and I wasn't on especially good form myself. I'd had a pretty wild night the night before and only had a couple of hours' sleep. Consequently, I very nearly didn't bother listening in on what he was saying. It was pretty quiet so I thought I'd go hide out in the back room for a bit. Sit in front of the fan, smoke a few ciggies and read some TC Boyle."

"TC Boyle on a hot and humid day?" Oliver asked.

"That's what put me off the idea, actually," she said. "Boyle's a nice enough bloke – "

"You've met him?" This from Oliver, again.

"We've chatted online a few times." I wasn't surprised, somehow. "His coyote-fighting dog died. It was kinda sad."

"So Boyle put you off skiving in the back room," I said, trying to steer the conversation back on course.

She nodded and exhaled more smoke. "Like I say," she said, "he's a lovely bloke, but he does tend to go on a bit. So I stuck around and made a pretence of cleaning a few tables, but in the end I just sat myself down for my break in the booth next to his and listened.

"He was mumbling a lot, to begin with," she told me, dropping what remained of her cigarette and twisting it out with the sole of her shoe. On the periphery of my vision, shadows became nothing more than shadows. Reality reinforced itself, however bizarre and destructive the circumstances, and I listened. I had no choice.

"He mumbled, but then he started speaking more clearly, with more... with more purpose. I heard him mention 'the little lass', how it was wrong that she had to die. He didn't want that. Children shouldn't die and she should know that better than anyone.'"

"'She'?" Oliver asked.

"He didn't say her name, but it was definitely a woman he imagined himself talking to. He said she was a mother and must know that it was wrong. Then... he sort of flinched. It wasn't as if he'd been struck, or anything – but it was as if someone was right in his face, really yelling at him. He mumbled something else. And then he said... hold on, I wrote this bit down." She reached into the bag again and pulled out a notebook. Flicking to the right page, she read, "'He's a friend.... I can't.... You promise me?... I'll be free of you.... Then it has to happen.'" She closed the notebook and set it on the bench beside her. "Like I say, it didn't make a whole lot of sense when I first heard him. He was just a dotty old bloke, probably reliving some ancient tragedy, as I saw it. Then I spoke to him about Nadine's accident and I just knew I had to speak to you."

Polly had little more to tell us. The conversation quickly became stilted and unnatural, Polly wanting to know what all this meant, Oliver and I wanting to avoid the subject until we were well out of her company. I looked for some excuse or reason to get away from her, needing to think and figure out the next move, but Polly lit up another cigarette and asked what was perhaps the one question I didn't want to hear:

"Are you going to confront him?"

We left Polly without answering the question, though I think she knew the answer. Walking away in the direction of the lake, I glanced back over my shoulder once – feeling unusually guilty for leaving her alone like that – and watched as she lit up another cigarette. I felt I owed her something, if only consideration. She had put herself out for me. What she had done had quite possibly contributed considerably to her dismissal, and yet I saw no way in which I could make this any easier for her. My concern now was for my family – or what was left of it.

"He knew all along," Oliver said as we headed out of the knot garden's south gate – the lake with all its childhood memories still far off in the distance. "The son of a bitch knew what she was planning all along and he did fuck all about it."

"What could he have done?" I asked, oddly resigned to the choices Ned had made whilst also unwilling to accept that he had been

309

innocent in all of this. "Called the police?"

"He could have warned you," Oliver said, his words flat with emphasis.

"'A mad ghost woman is going to lure your daughter to her death'. Oh, yes, that would have worked a treat."

"Sonny."

"What?"

"Just fucking stop it, okay? Don't lessen his involvement with sarcasm. He could have prevented this and he didn't. He's culpable."

"I know that." I paused beneath an old willow, looking up into its drooping, sorrowful branches. Yearning for simpler times, I imagined myself climbing into its midst and never leaving it. Like some dreaded eco-warrior, it would be my charge and my champion – my very being – and for me there would never again be the need for the material and commonplace. My life would be a spiritual, philosophical harmony. It would make sense. *I* would make sense. And when I was bored, I would talk to my daughter.

"Good," Oliver said. "But now the question is; what are we going to do about it?" It was a variation on what Polly had asked us, and I still didn't want to think about it.

"I don't know." We were both leaning with a shoulder against the willow, now, as if trying to push it over (which Oliver could no doubt have done, had he set his mind to it). Oliver stared at me. I stared at my shoes.

"Yes you do," he told me. "There's only one thing we can do. You know it, I know it – even Polly knew it."

"Confront him."

"What other option is there?"

"None, I guess. I just... I'm not sure that I'm up to it, mate."

It hadn't occurred to him that I might not be emotionally strong enough to deal with something like this. His lips curled into his beard and he nodded thoughtfully, exhaling long and hard through his nose.

"Of course," he said. "Understandably." He thought some more and then continued. "We could leave it until you feel fit enough," he said. "Or, if you prefer, Don and I can go round there and have a word with him. It's up to you, Sonny. We'll play this whichever way you think best."

310

That was the problem – right then I didn't even feel that I was up to *thinking*. I knew what had to be done. We had left Polly alone back there on the bench in the far too orderly knot garden because we had purpose, because, however reluctant I might be, there were things that just had to be done. I saw this as clearly as I now saw the lake in the distance and –

"No," I said to Oliver, before I had time to reconsider. "We'll do it now. You and me. We'll do it together."

We knew we were being watched, but we didn't hesitate. Their eyes were on us as we walked right past my house and strode purposefully on to Ned's. It wasn't easy. I so desperately wanted to reassure Ashley and, in turn, be reassured by her – but that was something I just couldn't risk. To see her eyes, even through two layers of reinforced glass, would be to see Nadine – Nadine and Ashley together, lost and longing – and that was something I knew myself incapable of resisting.

"You can still change your mind," Oliver said when we reached Ned's gate. "Don and I can easily take care of it."

"That would mean telling Don first," I pointed out.

"Ah, yes."

"I'm doing this Oliver. With you there, I can do this."

"As long as you're sure."

It had never really occurred to me before, but Ned's house was essentially a mirror image of my own. At the side of the house, a path damp within the shadow of two gable ends ran straight as a Roman road to the back garden – and, rather than stand at the front door and knock where everyone could see us, it was this very path we took, preferring the relative seclusion of the back door. I felt the chill of the shade immediately, and considered the significance of this. A wholly natural phenomenon, and, yet, it seemed to communicate so much. The cool air cautioned, the gloomy light resisting us in the only way it knew how. The concrete beneath my feet was unusually gritty, and I concentrated on very deliberately picking up my feet – the scuffing sound going through me like fingernails down a blackboard. When Oliver said something to me about the stench wafting around from the back garden, both his words and the smell barely registered. We walked deeper into shadow and all I could think about was what Polly had told us of the "conversation" Ned had had. He had known. He had sat there on his couch with Nadine beside him and *he had known.* Maybe her ultimate fate could not have been altered, as Jim had stated, but what kind of man wouldn't at least *try?* His own freedom and peace had, it seemed, been an issue – this somehow dependent on my daughter's death – and he had put this before all other considerations. He'd had a lifetime, over eighty years to make his mistakes and learn his lessons, to enjoy the many pleasures he would all too frequently encounter, whilst Nadine had known little of life. Three short years of food, warmth, love, sleep and play. The shadows pushed against the back of my neck and I again thought of the dream Ashley had had. To see Nadine as a young woman was something I now yearned for more than ever. She would walk around corners like the one before us with confidence and grace. Bright and direct, she would command with her beauty and intellect. But she would always be humble – always have enough class to know when to lower her chin and blush. She would indeed be a rare creature... all the rarer because her father would never have the pleasure of seeing her... and as we stepped out of the frigid shade into the comparative brightness of the back garden, I felt tears of both love and rage welling. I didn't care how responsible Ned might or might not be. Someone had to pay for what we had all been denied – and if it couldn't be Sheila Mackenzie, then he was most assuredly the next best thing.

The back garden was an eyesore. It reminded me of the "before" shots for one of those horrendous garden makeover programmes. There was a mound of dirt and rubbish in the south-west corner, up against the dilapidated fence – the mound paradoxically seeming to lend the immediate panels a little stability – and a soggy, stained mattress had been placed very precisely on the ill-kept back lawn. Grass grew around it as if it were a Tate Modern exhibit, and birds shat on it indiscriminately.

More offensive than this, however, was the smell Oliver had already mentioned. It seemed an exaggeration of the vague, difficult to define odour I'd smelt around Ned before – something that now seemed organic and gaseous, and which was strong enough to make me want to retch.

Oliver pointed to the rubbish heap. "Rotting food and Christ knows what else," he said. "I'm surprised someone hasn't had the environmental health onto him. It's a wonder your place isn't wick with rats."

I nodded dispassionately and turned to the back door. We should have tried the front way first, but like most of us in the area, Ned favoured the back door, and its state reflected this. Burgundy paint blistered and peeling, gangrenous rot pitting the surface in places, it had the look of too many leaky winters and warped summers – and knocking on it struck me as a potentially rather risky business.

Knock, however, I nevertheless did – cautiously, at first, then with more force when it became evident that the door wasn't about to cave in on itself.

After a minute or two, Oliver said what I'd been thinking – but didn't particularly want to acknowledge. "Doesn't look like he's in," he said.

"He's always in," I said, a little petulantly. I took a couple of steps back and looked up at the bedroom windows; the curtains were open – he wasn't having a lie in.

"Not today he ain't."

I sighed heavily, pushing my fingers through my hair before kicking the wall in frustration – the tears starting to come now. I looked at the door again, blurry with sorrow and anger, and pounded my fist into it three times before Oliver managed to restrain me. It held up remarkably well, I noted with some disappointment, as Oliver held me whilst I sobbed and struggled. It should have crumbled – it should have broken and crumbled in the very same way I was sure I would soon break and crumble. But it held firm and taunted me.

"Hey, come on, now," Oliver was saying quietly in my ear, his arms around me in a bear hug. "Calm down, mate. It's okay. It's going to be okay. We'll catch him the minute he comes in, I promise you."

"It should have fucking crumbled," I sobbed. "It should have fallen a-fucking-part, Olly."

"What should have?" he softly asked.

"The door. The fucking door. It should have crumbled. It shouldn't be stronger than me!"

Without Oliver's strength, I didn't know what might have become of me at that moment. I saw no hope or way forward, only the overwhelming certainty that everything was against me – that everything had the capacity to resist me. Nadine's death was a thing of abstraction, something I still couldn't quite get a grip on, and yet it was so solid and real, so destructive and disarming in its power and totality. The door refused to succumb and the world continued to revolve, and these offences weighed so heavily on me that any meagre hope I'd had dissipated, draining away with my energy and wit. I blubbed and hiccupped, and Oliver knelt on the floor with me – holding me, supporting me, whispering words whose meanings I couldn't grasp but whose tone helped moderate my hysteria. The smell of Ned's garden seemed to grow stronger, and as I hiccupped, I dry-retched, repulsed not only by the stench but, also, my all too obvious inadequacies. My knees hurt from kneeling and my knuckles burned and bled from where I'd thumped the door, but none of this really registered. I felt myself being pulled down to some place I didn't want to be but which I nevertheless found attractive in its isolation and severed calm, and although Oliver's voice grew stronger and more meaningful, I had to fight not to succumb. Whispering Ashley's name like a mantra, I held on to the remnant of that purpose I had only moments before had, feeling it pull away from me in a way that was very physical and driven. It didn't have to be like this. I saw that very clearly. I could break down doors. I could make things right again – but first I needed to sleep, to shut down and think only of the darkness on the edge of the world I thought I knew.

"You're okay, mate," Oliver was still saying. "We'll get there, I promise you. Just try to breathe, man. Breathe slow and deep."

"I'm not going home," I told him. This suddenly seemed important. "I'm staying here until he comes back. I'm staying here and I'm going to put it right. I'm going to do whatever it fucking takes, but I'm putting it right."

Oliver was running on empty. He'd said all that could reasonably be said, and now all he apparently could do for me was to nod and offer me the handkerchief. Eyes downcast, he helped me stand – propping me against the wall like a complacent extension ladder and rolling his head from side to side, stretching his neck and arching his back.

"There's nothing we can do here, now," he finally said. "I think we should be getting back, Sonny. We can keep an eye out for him and, like I say, catch him when he gets back."

"I'm staying here, Oliver," I said, wiping my face with his blessedly clean handkerchief (this no doubt one of Don's influences). "I want to be here when he gets back. I want to see the look in his eye when he sees me."

"I understand that but – "

"No," I said, with newfound resolve, holding up my hand and stepping away from the wall. "I'm not discussing it further. This is where I need to be right now, and this is where I'm staying." I felt his eyes on me as I walked past him, down the garden, beyond the corrupting mattress to the mouldering rubbish heap. I was within, again, looking into that well of loss and anger. I realised, now, just what form my earlier sense of purpose had taken and I thought that maybe, just *maybe*, Ned's not being in had been for the best, after all. As it was, I had only kicked his wall and thumped his back door. It could have been so much worse.

With rather more composure, I gestured at the rubbish heap. "Would you look at this?" I said. "The guy's got a fucking screw loose."

Oliver walked over and stood beside me, hands in his pockets. The rubbish heap didn't just consist of garden cuttings and household waste, as we had originally thought. As we studied it, we spotted DVDs, half-burned books, what looked like a torched manuscript and more CDs than I could count. At a rough guess, it looked to me as if Ned had thrown away a couple of hundred quids' worth of stuff – and this made me wonder.

"He's not coming back," I said.

"He'll be back," Oliver nevertheless insisted. "Maybe not tonight, but he'll be back."

"I'm not so sure."

Oliver edged closer to the fence. A hydrangea obscuring something he was looking at. He pushed it to one side, as best he could, and reached down to pull something I couldn't yet see off the rubbish heap.

"Either he's fucking loaded or, like you say, well and truly loopy,"

Oliver said, holding Ned's dirty but apparently undamaged laptop out before him. "It looks practically brand new."

"It is," I said, taking it off him. "I helped him set it up."

I didn't understand any of this. Ned had paid over the odds for the laptop, and bought an extortionate extended warranty – so why on earth would he just throw it away? The whole point of a laptop was that you could take it with you wherever the hell you went, so it seemed ludicrous that –

"It's obviously served its purpose," Oliver said casually, and I nodded, seeing just how right he was. "Did he give you any idea what he'd wanted it for?"

"He was writing a book, he said. Local history. Last I heard, he'd given up on it."

"That explains it, then."

"Maybe."

"What do you mean?"

"I don't know. Just maybe."

I saw vague lines of connection, but I could no more explain them than I could bring my daughter back – and, so, I simply shrugged, tucked the laptop under my arm and started walking back down the garden to the path at the side of the house... the path with its cool shadows and its space to think.

Oliver placed a hand on my shoulder, however, and I turned to face him. He pointed at the laptop and I asked me what I thought I was doing.

"He's thrown it away," I said.

"It's still on his property. Whether he wants it or not isn't the issue. Technically, it's still theft."

"I'm prepared to take my chances," I told him. My tone was a little off, so, after first taking a deep breath, I moderated it somewhat and added, "It's gone beyond that, mate. As I see it this... maybe it's an unusable piece of junk. Who's to say? It'll probably tell us nothing of any use. But... who knows? It could well contain all the answers we need."

"Need?"

"To make sense of all this."

316

Ashley and Maggie were waiting for us when we stepped into the slightly stuffy living room. We could hear Don playing noisily in the back garden with Wee Mark – their giggles and laughter filling me with that peculiar brand of hope that was always, allowed to run its course, something of a let-down – and, consequently, I wasn't really prepared for the stern looks and folded arms with which we were greeted.

Oliver and I exchanged a glance. Ashley and Maggie stood by the fireplace and continued to stare at us. Don laughed loudly, whilst Wee Mark giggled uncontrollably. We had been watched – that much I already knew. Ashley and Maggie had stood at the window and watched us walk right on by to Old Man Ned's and now, as sure as the sun rose in the east and set in the west, there would be questions.

I set the laptop on the floor behind the settee and Oliver waited by the door. I could hear a clock ticking, but didn't remember our having a clock that *did* tick (at least not so audibly), and found myself marking off the various ways in which Ashley and Maggie's intolerable silence could be brought to an end. Walk away. Make small talk. Tell them exactly what we'd been doing. *Run* away. Make the excuse of desperately needing the toilet and leave Oliver to deal with it. Vomit on the hearth rug. Hold my breath until I passed out. I remembered the Just William books Dad had loved so much, and thought of Violet Elizabeth thcreaming and thcreaming until she was thick and wondered at the genius of such a simple and yet effective tactic. I could thcream. I knew that. I could feel it locked in my chest, just waiting to be given vent. It would be easy. All I would have to do would be to –

"I think it's time, don't you?" Ashley said and, in spite of what I felt and thought was best, I nodded and sat down on the armchair by the living room window.

Somehow sensing that something important was occurring, Don joined us – carrying a worn-out Wee Mark, whom he now placed beside Maggie as she made herself comfortable on the settee, apparently expecting this to be a long and demanding exposition. Oliver sat on the floor beside my armchair, legs outstretched, whilst Ashley – looking striking and in control – sat in the armchair on the opposite side of the fireplace. Only Don remained standing. Behind the settee, he leant back against the wall – one of us and, yet, somehow separate. I felt for him. I felt for his uncertainty and need. Even as I admired the bravery of his choices, I wondered how a man could leave so much behind for the love of another man.

"I don't know where to start," I told Ashley. For the time being, it was just the two of us. The others were merely our audience.

"Old Man Ned," she said. "Why did you need to see him so urgently?"

"Because he's a fundamental part of everything that's been going on." I glanced at Oliver, but he wasn't yet ready to offer any additional insight or explanation. "We learned something else about him today and we needed to speak to him."

"He left about an hour ago. In a taxi. He took two cases and a bag with him and he kept glancing over here as if he expected you to go out and clock him one."

"If I'd been here I just might have," I admitted.

"You'd have hit an old man?" She was looking at me as if she didn't know me. I wasn't sure that she did. The truth be known, I wasn't that sure I knew myself – and I certainly didn't know just what I was or was not capable of. Different rules and completely removed physical laws seemed to apply now, and for all I knew I might start walking ghost-like through walls at any moment.

"I don't know," I said. "Probably."

"It's that bad?"

"Yes, love. It's that bad."

There were no immediate interruptions. I started at the very beginning, with the day I found the journal, adding that it had been around the time Maggie had told us about her stalker. Carefully highlighting my growing obsession with the journal and the woman I would ultimately come to know as Sheila Mackenzie, I explained that, at the time, it had seemed perfectly healthy but that, in retrospect, it now seemed the thin edge of the wedge – the open door that had finally let her in. I kept my eyes on Ashley, she my only real concern in all of this, and walked her with care through the various encounters and incidents, the attempts Oliver and I had made at understanding just what it was that was going on here, and explained Ned's involvement – how he had already known about Sheila Mackenzie and

318

what Polly had told us about him. After telling them about Oliver's encounters with Jim and a rather upsetting, initially accusatory conversation with Mags, I told them more about the journal – the name Sheila Mackenzie had used to help protect her daughter's identity from Edwin Mortimer, how the ink had faded from the pages, leaving me with little more than my memory of it.

"I wanted to understand this more before I told you," I said to Ashley. "I wanted to be able to explain it all and make some kind of sense of it for you, but I can't. All I know is that, for whatever reason, this Sheila Mackenzie – this fucking *dead woman* – took our baby away from us and Ned somehow knew about it."

"She's a... a what?" Ash said. She'd been crying steadily ever since I'd told her about Nadine Verity's name being in the journal; a tear hung briefly from her chin and then dropped onto the back of the hand resting in her lap. "She's a what? A *ghost*? Is that what you're telling me?"

"I don't know what she is but... yes, 'ghost' is the closest I've come to describing her to myself."

"You should have told me, Sonny."

"I know," I said, eyes downcast. "But it really wasn't that simple, love. It wasn't obvious that something strange was happening, to begin with, and by the time it was, it was too late. Events had already started to take over."

I realised right away that this was a mistake.

"Events being?" she asked.

"Ashley..."

"She needn't have died, Sonny. This could have been prevented – if only you'd included the rest of us in this. If you'd – "

"Don't even think of going there, love." Oliver clumsily pulled his legs under him and knelt – apparently wanting a bit more height for this. "Just don't, Ash. This isn't Sonny's fault and it isn't mine. We did the best we could under what were bloody unusual and difficult conditions."

"But *we could have stopped it happening!*"

She was red in the face, now, and I watched as her fists slowly unclenched. There would be an explosion. It was written. Tears would fall and her anger and anguish would bounce off the walls. Holding her wouldn't help. She would push herself away, grab and clutch, push again – claw at whatever in the least offended her. And nothing any of us could do would alter that. To speak to her would be futile. But she merely continued to stare at the fire hearth – lost in her own little world of realisation and question.

"If you believe any part of this story," Oliver told her, ever so calmly, "then you have to believe all of it." His authority was incontrovertible. Her mouth hung open as she reconsidered her argument, and then her head tilted questioningly to her right. "The Jim part, too," Oliver continued, very softly. Maggie regarded him. Such hope. From attempted suicide to this... *this what?* I thought. A straw to grasp, or real meaning? "You have to believe what he told me, Ash. If you believe any of it... you can't pick or choose. It's all or nothing."

"It couldn't have been stopped?" she said, this barely a whisper – her hands clenching again.

"That's right. That's what he told me, and, for what it's worth, I believe him. Nothing any of us could have done would have saved Nadine."

I expected more tears as the reality of this hit home – but, instead, her attention snapped back to me and she asked, "So why were you so concerned with going after Old Man Ned? If we couldn't have stopped this, what makes you think he could?"

"I want explanations."

"You want to make him pay. You can't get to this sick bitch of a ghost woman or whatever the fuck she is and, so, you want to take it out on him."

I remembered how I had kicked the wall and thumped the back door, and nodded. "That's part of it," I said. "Yes."

"Good." She sat back in the chair and all the fight and energy seemed to drain out of her. Even her hair looked suddenly lifeless, sticking to her head like a greasy sickbed cap. "Good, because... I want him to know. I want him to know what he's done. *Feel* it. If I understand any of this, I understand that. Maybe he couldn't have changed anything, but... he didn't even try. The bastard put himself first."

I held her as the others looked on in silence.

Chapter Sixteen

There was unexpected noise and movement – the subtlest shifting and settling. His hand was suddenly in hers, wrapped in it, become it, and he tried to pull away from both the sound and Maggie herself. The movement stopped, and somehow this was even more ominous – a suggestion of what was to come, the interminable purgatory that they would never face together, destined like every other man, woman and child to endure it alone. A sigh, light on the breeze, hopeless as dying embers – the sound of resignation and resolve. The man knew what had to be done, and he was accepting of it, if not exactly overjoyed.

Like the child he essentially was, Richard closed his eyes and wished the man into inexistence. If he couldn't see him, this Elvis man, he wasn't there. He had never been there. He was a myth. A legend. A game. They played, he and Sheila, and even if she didn't realise it, that was all it was. Rich men did not fake their own deaths in order to achieve more privacy; to do so was to merely build bigger walls, apply tighter constraints. Even he could see that. This was a man like any other. A villager who had been talking to his reflection in the window, not his long dead twin brother. A man who Richard had probably seen "around" more times than he could count, without so much as registering his existence... and here they were hiding behind the bushes at the bottom of his garden – hiding and, yes, trespassing. So suspicious was their predicament, it was difficult to believe that the man hadn't already called the police. He could so easily imagine him standing there, telephone still in his hand, waiting for the cavalry to come charging up his drive on its bicycle before making his move. And then... then it would simply be a fairly standard case of heroics and self-righteous indignation, men throwing their weight about, just like his father – expressing disgust, giving threatening accounts of what would happen to Richard if he didn't cooperate fully, pushing him, pushing him, pushing him into a corner until he finally told them what they wanted to hear.

Opening his eyes, he looked at Maggie – her hand still firmly clenching his. Mouth open, her face suggested euphoria. It was difficult to be completely sure in the poor light, but he thought she was crying. She had said that she had given birth to this man's sons – twin sons, just like Elvis and Jesse – but how on earth could any of that be true? This was just a man like any other, a stranger picked out of the crowd. Richard could not see him now, dared not move to get a better look, but he'd seen him clearly enough when he'd been standing at the window and he was sure that all the plastic surgery in the world could not have made so radical a difference. Nevertheless, Maggie was almost... almost exultant with the possibility of coming face to face with him. He could feel it in her hand – a thrumming energy, charged and potentially dangerous. He wanted to pull away from where he knew the man to be, but that would mean moving closer to Maggie... closer to that humming substation that could take even as it gave.

"He is because I say he is," Maggie whispered, putting her face close to his. He could smell the staleness of her breath – overripe with the wine they had shared earlier – and the heat from her body, that musty, salty promise he had fallen into so many times. "It's really very simple. I don't even have to think about it anymore. I know how it sounds. I've always known how it sounds. That's why you're the first person I've ever told. It just is. All of this. It is and... I trust you with it. Whatever you make of it, you've got to understand that my telling you is based in a willingness to trust you like I've never trusted anyone before."

Richard wanted her. He was hard again and quite suddenly the consequences didn't matter. They could haul him off to a cell, it was of no concern – as long as he could do whatever it was that Maggie needed him to do. A significant part of him still wanted to run from her, would always want to run from her, but he believed that he never would. She needed him too much... and, he realised, it was no different for him. She had opened doors for him that would have otherwise remained closed, allowed him to breathe as he went down on her, parting the lips of her cunt so that he might taste her deepest accessible point – and he wanted to hold fast to that. No one was going to take that away from him. Not his father, not this man that was clearly not and never had been Elvis, and certainly not some jumped up little village bobby who didn't know his arse from his elbow.

"I knew it that day on the bench," she told him quietly. "I knew it the first time I saw you following me. I saw right away that you had imagination – that you'd be gentle with my past and the things I just know *are* true. That's why we're here. Because you allowed it. You brought us here. You understood what I wanted immediately *and right away you set about seeing that I got it. You did this for me, and I will always be grateful."

Richard was about to tell her that he'd done nothing – nothing except take what she had offered – but it was too late for that. A light came on, harsh and precisely aimed at their faces, and a gruff, impatient voice said, "Get the fuck out here where I can see you."

Maggie laughed and brushed away a tear. "And he didn't even bother saying please," she said. "What is the world coming to?"

"You helped me find my way," Maggie was saying. The man had lowered the torch a little and Richard could just make out a dense black beard, a thick column of neck that seemed a little overdeveloped. This was no man in his seventies. As far as Richard could see, he was no older than forty – forty-five at the very most... forty-five and a lot more patient than might otherwise have been expected.

"I've never seen you before in my life," the man told her.

"You don't have to see someone to change their lives," she replied, squeezing Richard's hand. He didn't know if this was some kind of signal or if she was trying to reassure him. Either way, it meant very little. He didn't try to interpret it and he didn't worry that he might be missing something. He listened to the strange exchanged and wondered how he had got here. Nothing had changed, not really. Maggie was still his lover and a significant part of him still wanted to do all he could to make her happy – to help her. But... this wasn't right. This wasn't how it should be, at all. She was caught up in some delusion he didn't rightly understand, and he had encouraged it – wallowed with her in it and convinced himself that it was little more than a game, a highly creative form of foreplay (which, in truth, was how he saw most things, these days). When she took a step closer to the man – to, as she would have it, Elvis – her hip brushed against his and he felt the old, familiar charge. That was still what this was about, for him. He allowed her the freedoms she believed she needed, and in return he was rewarded with just about everything he had ever wished for.

He squeezed her hand in return and hoped he was doing the right thing.

The man seemed intrigued. He no longer considered them a threat – that much was obvious. He kept the torch beam low and Richard thought he caught a look of crinkled, far too patient amusement around the eyes. The man was prepared to humour Maggie Sutherland – but, Richard suspected, only until he grew bored.

"That's true," he said. "But I still find it difficult to believe that I could have such a profound effect on someone I've never met before."

"Difficult," Maggie told him, her smile too intimate. Much more of this and she would really start to scare the man. "Difficult, but not impossible. Yes?"

He wasn't foolish enough to be drawn into that one. Richard felt a moment of fleeting admiration and then, quite unexpectedly, a surge of outright jealousy. This man could take her away from him. Possibly already had. And all he could do about it was to stand here squeezing Maggie's hand whilst he jumped from one bloody stupid thought to the next. He took a breath and tried not to think. Watch and listen, he told himself. That was where his real strength lay. Always had.

"I'm not qualified to say."

"You've lived, haven't you?"

"After a fashion."

"Then you are qualified to say."

He shook his head at her persistence and Richard thought (hoped) he might be growing bored with all this. "I find it difficult to believe," he reiterated, just as stubbornly.

"So you don't remember me, at all?" Maggie asked.

The man shook his head. "Should I?"

"I had your twin sons," she told him – and Richard saw any trace of patient amusement drop from the man's face. They would be leaving soon. Maggie had taken this too far and their presence would no longer be tolerated. The man would lift his arm and point, tell them *yet again, with an underscoring flick of the torch, to get the fuck off his property – and whatever upset might follow, it would be for the best. The game would be over and they would be able to go back to how it had been just after they had started fucking and even if it wasn't* exactly *like it had been before, it would still be better than this because –*

"I don't have twin sons," the man said – but it was obvious from the note of dread in his voice that he did. He had twin sons just as surely as Richard's crapulent sponge of a father took great delight in pissing the bed.

"You don't?"

"No – no, I don't and I really think now would be a good time for – "

"You took them away from me," Maggie told him. "You took them away from me and you put them in that hospital. That place. *You put them there because they weren't how you thought they should be. They looked different. They would never walk or talk. So you blamed the drugs and you took them away. Our sons. Our babies.* My *babies."*

He flicked the torch up – getting a better look at Maggie's face; the beam shook noticeably. "That wasn't you," he said, and then seemed to think better of it. "I don't know what you mean. Get the fuck out of here before I call the police."

"People change," she told him.

"Not that much."

"Oh yes that much. That much and more. You took my babies and I changed. How could I not?"

The man was quickly losing patience. Whether he knew Maggie or not, it was clear that she had hit on a nerve – and what concerned Richard more than anything was where this might lead, and just what was expected of him. He was no match for the man before him. It was true that, for his age, he was fairly tall and well-toned, but, at heart, he was still a boy – a boy who had already taken too many adult punches.

Thankfully, the bearded hulk before Maggie and him was apparently not the fighting type. His eyes closed, and Richard could almost hear him counting to himself. He curled his lips into his mouth, and the torch waved about aimlessly, pulsing with suppressed rage.

And then he opened his eyes and started walking back to the house. Without looking at them again, he said into the darkness, "You have five minutes to leave. I'll be watching. If you haven't gone in that time, I'm calling the police."

They returned to Maggie's house feeling dejected and not yet ready for conversation. Richard wanted to know more – to have her lay naked beside him on the bed and explain just where it all had come from, how much of it was true. But he couldn't ask her about it. This had to be something she volunteered. For him to pry would be to run the risk of alienating her, of making her feel somehow attacked and therefore, by necessity, more defensive. And so he quietly followed her upstairs, smelling the dank night air on her clothes and trying to still his hectic thoughts.

On the landing, she stopped – staring blankly at the wall as her lips worked silently. Richard moved carefully around her, watching her, concerned but also fascinated. When he waved a hand in front of her eyes, she smiled and focused on him – not what he had expected, at all – apparently amused by his reaction.

"I'm not completely gone, yet," she told him, leaning in and kissing him hard on the lips – her tongue languorous and acidic. "Don't worry, love. I know how it looks but... I'm still here."

Richard tried to find something suitably adult with which to respond – something that would help her and, perhaps more to the point, help him – but he was a boy again and, in this respect, at least, largely impotent. He mumbled something about how he wanted to help her and she placed an icy finger to his lips.

"Stop," she said. "Just be for me. That's all I need you to do. Words... they build all we have, it's true. They give the illusion of sense that most people need but... I don't want that anymore, Richard, sweetheart. I want what is, however difficult it is to explain, because, at the end of the day, that's all I've got."

"You've got me." Almost sulkily.

"Of course," she said, touching his face lightly. "That goes without saying, darling. You are a fundamental part of what is. Without you, tonight would never have happened and – "

"Would that have been such a bad thing?"

Again that vacant look.

"Yes," she said after a moment's consideration. "Yes, it would have been such a bad thing, Richard. I know it's difficult for you to understand, love – and even more difficult for me to explain – but everything I've told you is true. Everything I said tonight is true, on some level, at least. I can tell you things about that man that no one else knows because I've been places and done things with him. He was the man I said, because I said it, but that doesn't make it fantasy. It just makes it another part of the things we've yet to learn to accept."

"He really did that with the twins, didn't he?"

She nodded.

"But he genuinely didn't recognise you."

"Who says he should?"

"You had his twin sons."

"I did."

"But he – "

Once more she placed that cold, cold finger to his lips. "Shush, love," she said. "You're just going to keep going round and round in circles."

"But it's important that I understand.*"*

"No. No, it isn't Richard. It isn't important. Not at all." Colour rose in her cheeks and she closed her eyes briefly, making him think of the man in the garden, again. She sighed and looked at him, squeezing his upper arm, rubbing it, smoothing *it. "Love," she said. "Tell me. Why did you start following me?"*

Richard hadn't expected this. He opened his mouth to speak, and then merely shrugged.

"Come on," she said, smiling encouragingly. "You can do better than that." She kissed him again, and then breathed in his ear. "I know you, don't forget. I know what you're capable of. So don't play the inarticulate little boy with me, love. It doesn't wash."

There was no real venom in her words. If anything, they were playful – in spite of their apparent harshness. She kissed him once more and he felt himself growing hard as he struggled to find a way to express how it had been for him. Rubbing her crotch against his thigh, she hiccupped and giggled into his mouth and finally said, "Well? I'm waiting."

Maggie Sutherland stepped quickly back from him. She was crying, again. Crying even as she smiled.

"I wanted to possess you, I suppose," he said, a little desperately.

"Not good enough! Try again."

"You..." he faltered, and seized on the first thing that came to mind. "You had more possibilities than any of the others," he said.

Maggie nodded, still crying and smiling. "I had the possibility of being *for you," she said. "You could make me* be*, Richard. Just like I made him be."*

Richard wasn't sure he understood – but if what Maggie had said was true, it didn't matter. What did *matter now, however, was that she was holding him, leading him to the bedroom – undressing and, in the eyes of the world, abusing him.*

On the bed, she knelt beside him, naked, clawing at her cunt desperately as she let him know all the things she wanted him to do to her. She told him again of the "in-between" years, the times she had wandered the "highways and byways", pissing and shitting amongst the discarded hypodermics in underpasses and forgotten and forbidden parks. And as she did so, she slapped at herself methodically, scratched frantically at the pimply flesh beneath her breasts – pausing only to occasionally touch his cock, treating it with a care she didn't afford herself.

"He shouldn't have been like that," she said. "He should have welcomed me. That was how it was supposed to be. He should have recognised me – invited me in and apologised for what he did to our boys. That was what had been meant to happen."

"He isn't worth it," Richard said. He couldn't think of anything else to say. "Don't let him worry you." Pathetic. After all the hours he had spent with her in this bed, he should have been able to come up with something better than that.

She smiled down at him, still playing cruelly with her cunt – drawing blood, now. "You're right," she said. "Of course, you're right. But he's in my head, now, Richard. You must know what that's like. He's in my head and if I stop thinking about him... if I stop thinking about him, he dies again – and I don't want that. I really don't want that."

Sitting astride him, she bent and kissed him – guiding his hard and urgent cock inside her. He gasped as she pushed down onto him, covering his body with hers, biting his lip playfully as he let the movement steadily grow. Her mouth against his ear, she whispered breathless encouragement, telling him over and over that he was the only one she could depend on – that he was the only one she now wanted or needed. At the beginning of their relationship, he wouldn't have been able to do this. He would have shot his load the minute he smelt the salty tang of her cunt. But now it was different. Now he was her match, in this if nothing else.

Rolling her onto her back, he pinned her hands against the headboard. She pulled a hand free and dug her fingernails into her breast – encouraging him to bite and taste her, screaming at him, with him, finding the abyss they both needed.

As he came, Richard rolled his eyes to his right and saw a figure watching them from the corner of the room. Initially (and possibly quite foolishly), he thought it was the man from the garden – the not-Elvis man. Somehow, he had followed them back here and broken in and now... now he was going to do God only knew what to them. As his eyes adjusted to the shadows, however, he saw his mistake. This was someone else entirely. Slender and clean-shaven, the man was familiar. Richard was sure he had never seen him before in his life and, yet, he was familiar.

Maggie was still in a world of her own, still rocking with the force of her orgasms as he rolled off her and studied the figure watching them. Oddly, he didn't feel afraid. There was something natural about this. He knew the man, on some level, at least – and this wasn't a threatening situation. If anything, there was something gentle and touching about the way in which the man's shoulders slumped as he stepped forward, something battered and forlorn.

"In the shed," the man said, and Richard knew. Something shifted, Maggie readjusting herself beside him, and the man fell back into the shadows – becoming them as they became him – and Richard knew.

When Maggie finally fell asleep, Richard dressed and left the room, going down to the garden shed.

Just as Jim Sutherland had suggested he should.

***

329

He stood for a moment, letting his eyes adjust and breathing in the steady, reassuring night air. Overhead, he heard a frantic, leathery sound – more of a presence than anything else – and even though his instinct was to flinch from it, he didn't. None of this was preordained. It was far more complex than that. Tonight was not written. It was a life inside an idea. That was what Maggie had meant. He saw it, now. They lived inside the idea. They fashioned it and, in turn, were fashioned by it – and all the denial in the world wouldn't change a bloody thing.

Acceptance was the key. Maggie had more or less said as much and he understood that now. Take things at face value and deal with them. It was an unusually street savvy philosophy, one for which the word and phrase "whatever" and "get over it" seemed to have been invented, and as he closed his eyes and breathed deeply, Richard found himself warming to it. What awaited him in the shed didn't concern him. Not now. If he wished, he could walk away – forget the vision of Jim and climb back in bed with Maggie, slide into his familiar position with her and slowly fuck her up the arse. He didn't have to take the next step because... well, there was no next step, not until he decided to take it – and at that point it became whatever the hell he wanted it to be.

My mother would never have made the choices I was to make, *Maggie had once told him.* It simply... they simply weren't a part of her vocabulary. If you can't articulate it, Richard, it can never be. *She'd been holding a book –* Oracle Night *by Paul Auster, he remembered that, now. She'd been holding it and had shaken it under his nose with didactic glee.* That's why these things are so bloody important, *she had told him.* They open doors – or, rather, we open doors by reading them. They show us all the ways in which a world can be made and allow us to seek out new possibilities for ourselves that wouldn't otherwise exist. My mother didn't understand that, thankfully. She didn't see that by keeping me there alone and bringing me all the books I asked for she was actually helping me build my very own escape tunnel. The fantasies alone were good enough. It was such a relief to curl up in my bed at night with a book and my own idea of the man that should have been beside me. It was the purest form of comfort, and one to which I still occasionally retreat when times are really bad. I'm sure you have your own place like that, a favoured fantasy to keep you warm when you are alone and suffering. We all do, whether we admit to it or not. It's a mark of sanity – a primitive instinct that few know how to develop. And, like I say, these places – these *fantasies* – they're good enough. With them, I'm confident I could have continued living that way, if I'd had to. But their natural extension, the real freedom they afforded me, was so much better. Never underestimate the value of an idea, Richard. It can make a life.

Opening his eyes, he started walking along the narrow and overgrown path – feeling the stones and grit against the soles of his trainers setting his teeth on edge. It was only a few yards from the back door to the shed and, yet, the walk seemed to take forever. As long as he wanted it to take. An age. A universal lifetime. The blinking of an eye.

Pausing by the shed door, he looked out across the field to the place he had once thought of as home. It was so far removed from what he now was. His father no longer dictated – all but accepting his son's absences. Still very much the boy – prone to fear and uncertainty, the strangling grip of the things he couldn't yet articulate – he had nevertheless found a place for himself... made *a place for himself, if Maggie was to be believed... and, just like Maggie's mother, he knew his father would never have made the choices he had made. He simply wasn't capable.*

The shed door was padlocked – but the wood was so rotten and the latch so inexpertly fitted that, within the space of a few minutes, he had the door open and was stepping over the threshold into the musty interior.

It could have been a sanctuary. He saw that immediately. It could have been his and Maggie's world – a childhood escape that could have sustained them through all the years. Cave-like and intimate, it would remind her of her "place", just as it reminded him of his.

"This is where we could really fucking be,*" he said to himself – remembering what it had been like in the not-Elvis man's garden, how he had doubted and been afraid, whilst at the same time relishing the closeness and complicity inherent in the voyeuristic act. He had doubted her sanity, he remembered. But what the fuck was sanity,*

anyway, other than another peg for the dim-witted masses to hang you on? What did they know? What did any of them know?

The shed was empty except for a stained sleeping bag rolled up in one corner and a worn and dented biscuit tin on the floor beside it. Richard gently closed the door behind him – so that the breeze wouldn't catch it and make it clatter against its frame. Squatting down, he first touched the sleeping bag and then, ever so carefully, the tin. There were stories, here – more than he would ever know. He imagined Maggie curled up in the sleeping bag in some grotty, god-forsaken place, and he wished he could have been with her. It should have been him. All this shit about this Elvis bloke, it just shouldn't have happened. He was the one and he hoped Maggie realised that, now. The others, whoever they might be, would let her down time and time again. But not him. If need be, he now saw, he would curl up with her in that sleeping bag and tell the world to go fuck itself. It was of no value to him, not anymore.

Once more, he ran his fingers over the sleeping bag's filthy fabric before lifting the tin and prising off the lid.

It was dark in the shed, but there was just enough moonlight from the single grimy window for him to see by. The smell hit him first, however; old paper and that curiously sharp odour of rusty metal – a smell that always made him think of blood. Flicking carefully through the papers he found within – old letters from people he'd never heard of, bills and receipts, a few old photos of Maggie when she had been a girl, taken in that *garden and wearing* that *bikini – he didn't feel like he was intruding. It was almost as if this had been meant to be... meant to be because he had made certain choices... meant to be because he had listened to the voice of a ghost... because he had walked down the path that had led to this place, leaving a cooling space in the bed beside Maggie.*

Spreading out the sleeping bag, he made himself more comfortable – leafing through the letters, catching snatches of lives and loves that seemed far removed from the woman he believed he knew. The more he disturbed, the stronger the smell became, and pretty soon he was sneezing uncontrollably, tears blurring his vision.

He stopped to wipe his eyes on his shirtsleeve, and then continued. More bills, a receipt for a television, a letter from someone called

Paula telling Maggie that she was happy now and didn't want anything else to do with her, a to-do list that included a reminder to write to her mother and buy some bleach... it was all pretty tedious and unremarkable, and Richard was just on the point of putting everything back in its place and returning to bed when he found, right at the bottom of the tin, Maggie's passport.

It was hardly used, one trip to France in 1992, and well out of date, but the photo was moderately amusing and he found himself staring at it and chuckling at the large glasses and the spiral perm. Had it ever been fashionable to look like that? he wondered. Or had it just been rehab chic – the best she could hope for under the pretty dire circumstances? Whatever, it was a desperate image and he just knew he would have to find a way to rib her about it. It was his duty.

He tossed the passport down on the sleeping bag beside him... and then stopped. Something wasn't right. He glanced at the letters and bills, but that wasn't it. Nor was it the garden photos he had found of her. Richard looked up at the window, the night sky heavy with grease and watermarks. The light had changed, but that wasn't it, either.

Picking up the passport, he looked first at Maggie's photograph and then the name on the front.

Sheila Mackenzie.

He wasn't surprised when the shed door opened. Looking down at him, naked and unafraid, the woman he had always thought of as Maggie Sutherland touched herself experimentally and said, "One day you'll understand. It's never enough, Richard. Never."

The next three days saw us pulling together in ways I would at one time have thought impossible. We worked through all the things we knew, taking them apart and putting them back together again – drawing on each other for support and finding an acceptance of events that I can now only partially relate to. It grew much colder very quickly, rain pelting at the windows and bruise-blue clouds sitting just above the rooftops, but as the five of us sat up late into the night – drinking and talking and, more often than not, crying – we didn't feel this change, not in any real way. We turned the heating up, put another bar on the fire and continued and continued and continued.

During that time, I don't think any of us seriously expected Old

Man Ned to return – but it was really only on the evening of the third day of his absence that we truly accepted this.

Wee Mark was asleep upstairs and Maggie had just joined us in front of the fire. I was on the settee beside Ashley – my arm around her as she snuggled in. Since the funeral and mine and Oliver's little disclosure, it had been getting steadily more difficult for her. She clung to me in a way that she never had before, and all I could think to do was to let her. We were better than we'd ever been, it was true – much more of a unit – but as much as I welcomed this, I couldn't at times help but wonder if it was entirely healthy. Ashley wasn't exactly afraid of this world without Nadine Verity; she just didn't like it much.

Don was on the floor at the side of the fire, nursing a large brandy. He looked up when Maggie sat down and said, "I think it's time we stopped beating about the bush. Ned's not coming back, and if we want to speak to him... well, we're going to have to find him first."

Since the events of a few days ago, it was fair to say that Don had really come into his own. The minute we took him into our confidence along with Ashley and Maggie, his pragmatism and confidence became far more obvious. He was a part of us. When he and Oliver stood beside each other, there was a greater sense of equality – a greater sense of their being a balanced and uncompromised couple. I welcomed this change, as I'm confident everyone else did. It provided something I needed, that additional voice that could only serve to make it more difficult to miss something vital and follow the wrong course. Oliver was the voice of reason; Don was his conscience and crutch, his checking mechanism and our friend.

"Do we know that?" Oliver wanted to know.

"For certain?" Don asked. "No. We've come far enough to realise that we know nothing for certain. But what we do know is that the man we feel we need to talk to isn't where he should be. Now, as I see it, this leaves us with two options. We can either sit here on our butts waiting in the vain hope that he might return and magically appear on our doorstep, or..."

"Or we can go after him," Oliver said. He was seated on the other side of the fireplace to Don, hugging his knees. The two of them reminded me of the wooden ornamental horses my gran had kept on either side of her fireplace. Just as self-possessed and elegant, but bigger and not as glossy. Don nodded and something passed between them – something the rest of us would never be able to interpret, a recognition of things shared in the night's dead embrace, perhaps, or maybe just inappropriate need quickly quelled.

"That just about sums it up from where I'm sitting," Don said. He glanced up at Ashley and me. "What do you two think?"

"That it'll be like looking for a very old and blunt needle in the mother of all haystacks," I said. Ashley's right hand rested on my stomach. It rose and fell as I breathed. I squeezed her more tightly, wishing that it were just the two of us – that it were just the two of us and that we didn't have to contend with questions like this.

"You don't want to do it?" Oliver asked.

"I didn't say that," I told him.

"No, but you don't exactly sound enthusiastic."

"You'll have to forgive me," I said. "I've had a few things on my mind just recently."

"Sonny." Ashley's hand moved to my chest now. I looked at her questioningly. The inner rim of her lower eyelids looked sore. "Don't," she said. The hand circled soothingly and I nodded.

"I'm sorry, mate," I said, and Oliver shrugged; we were united, but we were none of us infallible.

"Forget it," he told me, smiling. "Anyway," he continued. "The real question now seems to be, do we let Sonny's lack of enthusiasm get in the way, or do we try to find Ned?"

Don rolled his eyes and, in spite of my wish to be alone with Ash, I smiled. Oliver was one of the few people who could get away with doing this to me. He knew it, I knew it – we all knew it. He was just so fucking *big*.

"Well, if you want to know what I think," Maggie said, "I reckon we should at least try to find him."

"Even if we do manage to find him," I pointed out, "there's no guarantee that we'll get any answers. Ned is... well, he's a piece of shit, but apart from that, he knows how to play his cards close to his chest."

"He ran," Oliver pointed out. "He's scared."

"We're assuming he ran. Our belief that he's scared is based on an assumption. For all we know, he might be off on a package holiday he booked months ago."

"He looked scared to me," Ashley said – her words rumbling in my chest. "Anxious, at the very least." She shifted so that she could better observe me. "He really didn't look as if he was going on any holiday, Sonny. He... he looked like he wanted to get away from here before anyone had chance to stop him. That wasn't a man planning on coming back any time soon."

I couldn't doubt or contradict her. Ned was out there, somewhere, doing god alone knew what.

"OK," I said. "So where do we start?"

She stopped me at the bottom of the stairs, putting a hand on my arm as I placed my foot on the first riser. Fragile and soft around the eyes, I again imagined that it was just the two of us – that we were together in a place where no one else could reach. She sniffed and smiled, her fingers feeling damp through my shirtsleeve. It was all so familiar. I had never before experienced anything like this – neither of us had. My parent's deaths had been hard, as much of a shock and just as painful, but it had been nothing like this. Nadine's death and its confusing aftermath brought with it a frightening freshness – a new awareness that anything could and probably would happen. I looked at the faces of the people around me, the people closest to me, and it was as if their old selves had been peeled away to be replaced by these newly-wise, semi-tragic figures that I loved even as I resented the reflection they presented. And, yet, I couldn't help feeling that I'd somehow experienced all this before. The damp feeling of Ashley's hand on my arm was nothing new, the torn look of anguish on her face I'd seen before – and even though I realised it was complete nonsense, I knew that if I put my arm around her and touched the small of her back beneath her blouse, I would feel a blister-like spot there... one that most definitely hadn't been there that morning but which would have grown in that time into something sore and ready to pop. A suitable expression of the way in which she was no doubt feeling. It was a familiarity and awareness that could so easily have pushed me away, disturbing and ineffable as it was, but it didn't, because I understood it for what it was – a symptom, the syntax of complex grief – so instead I embraced it as I might embrace Ashley, my world of multi-layered character.

I smiled at her and she said, "I don't want to push you into this. If you don't want to do it, you just have to say."

"I know that," I said, stepping down and kissing her on the cheek. "I think it's the right thing to do, though. For all of us.... Unless..."

"What?"

"It is what you want, isn't it?"

She nodded slowly, eyes closed. I reached around her and drew her close, touching the small of her back in the process. Sure enough, the spot was there – in all its pustulant glory.

"It might not help," she admitted. "I don't know. But we have to try, don't we? We can't just sit around here waiting for things to happen. It... it wouldn't be fair on... it just wouldn't be fair."

On the way up the stairs, having decided to find the slip of paper with Polly's number on it and call her, I was acutely aware of Ashley standing at the bottom watching me go. The polarity had flipped. We were so far from where we had begun. But, nevertheless, we remained stubbornly locked in place.

"Marry me." It had perhaps been the easiest thing I had ever said. I had not knelt, not arranged some gauche but well-intentioned candlelit meal. It had been impulsive – more of an instruction than a question – and I now paused at the top of the stairs to look down at her, remembering that evening so long ago.

In retrospect, it was all too easy to colour that before-time with rosy hues and soft washes. We had neither of us known what real heartache was – although we had liked to think ourselves world-weary and fashionably angst-ridden. I had freedom, Ashley was just finding hers – individual and bright, pushing herself educationally as she tested boundaries and reassessed her place in the world. There had been excitement, but there had also been fear, and I had seen those peculiar fuck buddies reflected in her eyes when I said those two words to her.

As she stared up at me from the foot of the stairs, I wondered just what she had felt that night. Where had the fear come from? Had it been endogenous, or had she perhaps understood something that, at the time, I never would have?

In the bedroom, I quickly found Polly's number. I'd been careful, this time, to put it away between the pages of an old address book until I had time to enter it properly. Slipping it into my pocket, I started heading out of the room again – but stopped by the door, certain that something was out of place, or that I had somehow forgotten something.

I turned and half-expected to see Sheila Mackenzie standing by the window – naked and smug, silently taunting me as she stared into space and languorously pleasured herself. But this, at least, I was spared. The room was how it always was, how it had been when I had finished helping Ash make the bed that morning. The light from the window was cool and steady, twilit and tasteful, fixed by the moment, and everything was as it should have been. Nothing had been moved and nothing was forgotten.

Or so I initially reasoned.

Ned's laptop was on the floor by the wardrobe. I'd brought it up here the evening of his departure and hadn't given it a second thought since. Now it seemed ridiculous that we had talked about the man so much without my once thinking to bring the laptop down and search it for clues to his whereabouts, so I quickly grabbed it and headed down the stairs as fast as my little legs would carry me – bursting into the living with a premature look of victory on my face.

The living room was empty. I stood in the doorway, feeling ridiculous and curiously let down, and scanned the empty chairs and settee – listening to the hiss of the gas fire, wondering why I couldn't hear anything else... no voices, no cars on the road outside... no children playing out beyond their bedtime. I glanced out of the window to my right at the street. It was beginning to get dark. Another half an hour and the light would be gone completely. Darkness. Silence. The shifting sounds of the house, familiar and, yet, a world apart from everything I knew. I didn't want that. I wanted my wife and friends by my side, around me – watching my back and ensuring that I didn't come to any harm. I remembered that Wee Mark was still asleep upstairs and my first concern was not that I should search for his mother and the rest of our little "family", but rather that I should check on him. It was vitally important that he was all right – that he was comforted and secure – but before I could follow this unexpected instinct, I spotted her in the corner of the room, standing by the curtain... as naked as she'd ever been.

There was now nothing shocking about the appearance of Sheila Mackenzie. I didn't start or step back in horror. I'd seen her enough times to know that, yes, she was a woman who could influence and hurt, but she was also someone that I believed couldn't directly touch me. She hurt by taking away. I saw that, now. She could subtract the most precious elements of my life and leave me a blubbering mass of lost hope and truth – but that was all she could do. It was all too easy for her to remove my daughter (and my wife and friends?) from my life, but if she tried to touch me, she would pass through me as surely as she had that night in the garden.

And, so, I stood quite calmly – leaning the laptop against the side of the settee and waiting to see what would happen next.

Sheila Mackenzie slowly walked around the armchair and stood by the fire, looking at me. Her eyes were more direct than they had been before – cold and astute, as though laughing at me... mocking me. I smelt her damp, summer storm smell – something which I hadn't noticed before but which had, I was sure, nevertheless been there – and felt the air move around me, a desperate struggle, turmoil, an inversion, the storm within the calm.

I had been wrong about her not being able to touch me. She reached out a hand and her grubby fingers – slick and granular, tacky as flypaper – gently caressed the side of my face. I looked down at her, at breasts abused by time, at the slight swell of her belly and the hirsute, seemingly swollen vulva. Her fingers lingered and she took a step closer, breathing dead air in my face, subtracting my warmth... true to type... and when she touched me through my trousers, I responded in the only way I knew how.

I saw my wife and the cruel indignity I had, all those years ago, inflicted on her with Maggie in Wales. So trusting – so undeserving of such intolerable treatment. Sheila Mackenzie took my hand and guided my fingers into the dead, papery husk of her sex and I felt myself retract – pushing her away with my free hand and stepping back. She laughed in my face and I raised a hand to slap her, something I'd never done to a woman before but this, after all, was the evil fucking *dead woman* who'd killed my daughter and so this didn't count and, anyway, what was I supposed to do when she was touching me and making me touch her and...

She waited for the blow to come – daring me with a look – but I couldn't. It wasn't a matter of moral rectitude. I didn't believe myself somehow "bigger" than all that. I just couldn't. The strength drained out of me and my arm dropped and Sheila Mackenzie took another step towards me.

Her teeth were rotten and crooked. Her tongue appeared as dry and rough as her sex. I tried not to breathe in as she opened her mouth to speak.

"The father lives that the daughter might die," she said, and then kissed me on the mouth.

The night fell on me hard and swift. I suffocated and struggled, pushing it away as I lost all sense of the things I would normally take for granted – awareness of location, concepts of time and ego... little things like knowing that it was just as important to exhale as inhale. Everything became muffled and fuzzy, my mind racing urgently as I tried to work out the best way to function under such circumstances. Sheila Mackenzie's words bounced off the walls – flew at me like crazed bats, tangling themselves in my hair and biting and clawing at my scalp. I no longer had the ability to wonder where Ashley and the others were, or to worry about checking on Wee Mark. My only concern was that I should get rid of those bats – forget forever the obscenity that Sheila Mackenzie had spoken. Huddled on the floor, my very existence a weight I no longer felt I could bear, it slipped away from me... I slipped away from myself.

My fingers had been inside her – and, just as surely, her fingers had been inside me... clawing away at who I was, the things that were important to me. It didn't matter what her purpose was, only that she did it, and as I struggled to push myself up, away, out, I heard those words again – echoing, stripping me of reason and comprehension.

The father lives that the daughter might die.

Sheila Mackenzie was gone. The most brittle of moments followed. I saw the room about me for what it was – the carapace of a life beyond reason and understanding, crazed and flaking, as impermanent as it was insubstantial. Sickness and vertigo came and went, the two oddly independent of one another, and I grasped at the arm of the settee – trying to pull myself up as common sense told me to stay down. The softest of brushing sounds came to me, a mournful jazz percussion, but I couldn't open my eyes to find the source. I had to get up. I had to stay down. Sheila Mackenzie might still be there, waiting for me to do something wrong, something *particular* – she had to be – but even as I tried to stand, I found that I was fighting with myself. It just wasn't possible for me to stay like this, huddled and dislocated on the floor. I had to move. I had to find the others and tell them that I had seen her again. It was especially important that I –

I could almost have written it.

A hand touched my shoulder and everything stopped. The strange percussion drifted away, became the shushing of a dying tide, and an overwhelming silence overtook me. I felt warmth and was aware of the fading light – safe and comforting, a lullaby of sensation.

And then I heard their voices, concerned and hushed – closing in on me as they touched, caressed, gently lifted me onto the settee and placed too-thick cushions under my head, my chin pushed onto my chest. The vertigo slipped away as I settled into the familiar warmth of that shape, the sprung base shifting with my weight, but the nausea returned and I thought for a moment that I would have to vomit, that there would be no holding it back. It would come as surely as Sheila Mackenzie had come – taunting and crippling, ripping from me as if intending to kill.

When I finally opened my eyes, Ashley and the others were leaning over me. Ashley knelt on the floor beside the settee, her cool hand on my brow – eyes soft with fear and concern. She shifted, moving in closer. I could feel her breath against my face – irregular and swift, panicked and broken – and I wanted more than anything to reassure her. We needed each other to be all right. Whether this would ever be enough, only time would tell – but as Ashley opened her mouth to speak, I thought I saw our future together in the resolute set of her jaw and the unhesitant blink of her eyes.

"She was here again, wasn't she?" Ashley said.

I nodded, trying not to be sick.

"What happened?"

"I came downstairs and you weren't here," I told her, my voice weak and shaky. "None of you was. The room was empty but it wasn't... it wasn't.... Didn't you see her?"

Oliver and Don were behind the settee, looking down at me. Mags was down by my feet somewhere. They all shook their heads and Oliver said, "No, mate. We only saw you. One minute, you weren't there – the next you were huddled on the floor." He shrugged, obviously wishing there was more he could tell me, if only for the sake of story.

"Just you and this," Maggie said, lifting the laptop from the floor and showing it to me.

"Did she say anything?" Ashley said, ignoring Mags. I caught a whiff of her optimism and felt my heart knot. Such things were physical, I now saw. The emotional touched us in ways that were altogether too real, making us limp and stoop under the collective burden, and all we could ever do, it seemed, was grasp at whatever meagre hope and consolation we could find. "Did she say anything... did she say anything about Nadine? Is she all right, Sonny?"

I could have lied to her. I *wanted* to lie to her. But I couldn't.

"She didn't say, love," I said. "I wish I could say she had but..."

"Then what *did* she say?" Ashley asked. "She must have said something, otherwise why would she bother... you know."

"Manifesting," Oliver said.

I felt sick to my stomach. My head was spinning with too many mysteries and possibilities. I'd had my heart ripped out and clumsily replaced the day my daughter had died. Nevertheless, I found myself laughing at this – seeing my old friend Oliver standing gravely in the darkened rooms of a hundred horror movie haunted houses, uttering that one word repeatedly and with the kind of authority that suggested a hardened, long-in-the-tooth ghost hunter. Usually one who chose to subvert genre, he today opted to stick to the familiar, tried and tested formula – and a funnier sight I'd never seen.

When the fit had passed, I apologised to the slightly bemused gathering and then turned my attention back to Ashley.

"She did say something, love," I told her. "I don't understand it but, yes, she did."

"What? What did she say, Sonny?"

It was true, I didn't understand it. Now, however, I realised that it was very probably something I would never *want* to understand. For all its cryptic nature, it was clear enough, and this was something I just didn't want to inflict on Ash.

Nevertheless, I said, "It was... like I say, I don't understand it but she said something about the father living so that the daughter might die."

"The father...?"

"Yes."

"And nothing else?"

"No."

After calling Polly and getting no further – her knowledge of Ned apparently limited to what she had already told us – Mags handed me the laptop and the five of us huddled around it whilst I painstakingly clicked through Ned's documents. I found his cack-handed attempts at transcribing the local history he had been working on and a few notes on the possibility of using it as the background for a novel "like what that lad down the road does", but little else. A look at his Internet history told me that, a little unexpectedly, he wasn't as keen on porn as I might have expected. He seemed to favour news sites, history databases and anything that even remotely touched upon parapsychology and metaphysics. I noticed that he appeared to have read up a little on Leibnitz and asked Oliver what he thought that might mean. He shook his head and shrugged, not even prepared to hazard a guess.

Finally, I opened Outlook Express and checked his email activity – not once considering just how grossly intrusive this actually was.

"What's that?" Ashley asked, pointing to the subject field of one incoming email in particular. It appeared to be a fairly standard piece of spam promising Ned and a million others that, yes, he too could pleasure his woman for hours on end – and all for the small sum of $26.94.

"Junk," I told her. "Trying to sell him Viagra or something similar."

"Oh." She sighed and rotated her neck. "So there isn't an actual woman we should be looking for or anything?"

"I wouldn't have thought so, no," I said. "We'll know better when

I've had a proper look through the rest of his emails, but from what I can see, he was mainly concerned with chatting to relative strangers about various wars and the development of this little town of ours."

"No personal stuff?" Don asked.

"Not that I can see. It's all very... stiff. In some cases – with this bloke called Dave, for example – he seems concerned only with the subject they're discussing, even though the guy is clearly trying to offer the hand of friendship. Dave says he'll be happy to lend Ned some of the literature he has on the subject, and Ned very formally says no thank you – telling him that he's managed to find and order copies online."

"Address book?" This from Oliver.

"A few email addresses but no other contact info. These people are strangers." I closed the laptop and sat back on the settee beside Ashley. "He wouldn't have told them anything."

"So where does that leave us?" Maggie asked.

"Right back where we started. None the bloody wiser." Ashley linked my arm and squeezed in against me. We just sit and wait, I suppose," I said, finally. "Hope and pray he comes back."

"Hoping, I can just about manage," Oliver said. "But if you want prayers, you'll have to get Molly round."

"And if you get Molly round," Don said with a smile, "me and him is off home. Right, love?"

"Right," Oliver said, though with little real enthusiasm. He stretched a leg and wiggled a big toe – the black sock thinning at the heel. "You know what I can't stop thinking about?" he suddenly asked. "Ned's garden. That rubbish heap where we found the laptop – there were all kinds of crap there."

"You aren't – "

"Short of breaking into his place, are there any other options?"

"You want to go searching through a garden rubbish heap," Don said incredulously.

"I don't *want* to. But what other option is there?"

"We could always have a word with some of the other neighbours," Mags suggested. "See if he told any of them where he might be going."

"He wouldn't do that," I pointed out. "Not if he wanted to be certain that we wouldn't be able to find him."

Oliver looked at me. That tiredness I had seen a few weeks ago had once more marked the flesh around his eyes – but his smile was broad and mischievous. "So," he said. "Are we going to do it, then, or what?"

If we'd wanted to look anymore suspicious, I was sure we couldn't have.

Almost fully dark by this time, we took torches with us – just in case we needed them – and had briefly considered wearing something in an appropriate shade of black, only Ashley tactfully suggesting that this might be a *little* over the top. As we walked from our house to Ned's, we glanced over our shoulders repeatedly, doing our level best to ensure that we weren't being watched and no doubt inadvertently guaranteeing that we would draw attention to ourselves. I was reminded of the day we had followed Maggie and her "stalker" – two men working together to achieve a very specific and unusual goal, the most specialist of collaborations. If I had to have anyone at my side during these strange little adventures, Oliver was the natural candidate after Ashley. His sheer bulk was in and of itself comforting, but it was more than that. He was like a brother to me. It wasn't something I'd ever acknowledged before, but it really was that simple – that perfect. All but estranged from his own family, an only child like all of us except Don, he had connected with us in a way that he could have with no one else. There had been no invitation, there had been no request. Oliver had simply *grown* into our lives just as we had *grown* into his. And it had been right. Even when my parents had been alive and I had still been living at home, it had been happening – Mam always making that little bit extra at meal times, on the off chance that Olly would drop by. And I couldn't help wondering if it had somehow been meant to be this way. I wouldn't say that I was exactly beginning to believe in Molly's idea of a "god", but patterns were certainly starting to suggest themselves and those patterns in turn seemed to imply a "creative force", a deliberateness that went beyond mere chance.

Pausing before we headed along the by now extremely chilly path at the side of the house, Oliver checked his torch – flashing it under his chin a couple of times, eyes wide and grinning stupidly. I didn't know quite what had got into him, but it was a relief to be out of the house.

"Don't use that unless you really have to," I told him. "If there's one thing guaranteed to make us look like we're up to no good it's a bloody torch."

"We need a cover story," he said. "Just in case we get caught."

"We aren't going to get caught," I emphatically told him.

He was smiling that inane grin, again – this time thankfully with the torch off – and in spite of the seriousness of what we were doing, of what we were hoping to discover and understand, I found myself smiling and shaking my head. Like Oliver, I saw the absurdity of it all. And, yet, I couldn't escape the feeling that all this was necessary. I thought of patterns, again, of Oliver's supportive role in the whole scheme, and I understood implicitly that there simply was no other way for us to get through this. Sitting down and doing nothing just wasn't an option. However futile our efforts might be, they were efforts nonetheless – and to laugh at that futility as Oliver had done was perhaps the best antidote to its subtle poison.

"Come on," I said, slapping his shoulder and this time leading the way into the unforgiving darkness cast by the gable end.

It wasn't like it had been a few days before. Then I had been at least partially cut off from the place by thought and emotion, wrapped in a cocoon of grief, anger and confusion. This evening, however, I felt wholly *there*. I smelt the foul odour immediately, felt the dampness pressing against me like a slick, sickly fabric – layered with filth and fetid water, pushing itself into my nostrils and clogging my lungs. I heard Oliver mouth breathing behind me and saw his torch flicker on, briefly but reassuringly. The silt grated beneath my shoes and –

A light came on in the landing window of the neighbouring house – high on the gable end. Oliver and I pushed ourselves against the wall, instinct taking over. I heard Oliver chuckling to himself when the light went out, and then we were moving again – Oliver pushing me ahead of him. He bore down a little too hard and I almost lost my balance. His hand on my shoulder steadied me.

The back garden was remarkably well lit. Ned being Ned, he had not followed the example of his neighbours and had security lights installed – and now I could see why. He just didn't need them. Whatever else could be said about him, he had at least been shrewd enough to realise that light does not respect boundaries, and the "spillage" from his immediate neighbours was more than adequate for his needs.

Oliver marched straight over to the rubbish heap, needlessly switched on his torch and started scanning back and forth for something interesting.

I joined him, bending down and picking up what looked like a page of manuscript but which turned out to be a series of small pencil sketches – minutely detailed military horses and Second World War soldiers. The quality was impressive and spoke of firsthand experience – prompting me to, at least momentarily, rethink my appraisal of Old Man Ned. Did I know him? Could I ever conceive of the things he had been through and, if not, what right did I ultimately have to judge him? These thoughts, of course, were naturally followed by thoughts of my daughter – those striking indigo eyes, the pouting lips and the indefinable intelligence that always made me feel as if she had understood every word I had said to her. I wished I'd spent more time with her – just holding her, listening to the peculiar little sounds she had always made, smelling the top of her head and feeling time pass as she fell asleep in my arms. In my pursuit of purpose and an ordered, fulfilling life I had, like so many, deprived myself of the fleeting moments that made sense of everything else.

There were no second chances.

I crumpled the drawing into a ball and threw it back on the rubbish heap.

"This is fucking futile," Oliver said after a further five minutes of randomly picking bits of paper, books, files and photographs off the pile. "If we wanted to commit identity theft, we could have a bloody field day – but other than that..." He shrugged.

"It is just what it appears to be?" I said.

He nodded. "A load of old rubbish."

I squatted down and picked up one of the discarded DVDs, turning it over in my hands. Kill Bill Volume One. This I didn't understand. Relatively new, like so much of the stuff he had thrown away. If he didn't like these things, or had no further use for them, why just throw them on the rubbish heap like this – why not sell them or at least give them to the local charity shop?

"He's not behaving rationally," Oliver said – as if reading my mind. "We can't explain his behaviour using familiarly defined terms. It's gone too far beyond that."

"So there's no hidden meaning to all of this? This isn't a *clue*?" I was being ironic. The actions of a desperate man.

"Probably not in any obvious way." I hated it when he took an ironic question at face value. "But it at least gives some indication of just how deeply affected he's been by all of this."

"You know this for a fact, or it's just something you've assumed?"

"It's a reasonable indication, Sonny. Maybe the evidence isn't incontrovertible, but I think it's fairly safe to say that – "

We heard a movement behind us and turned together to face its source. A part of me expected to see Sheila Mackenzie, again. She was such a part of my "reality", now, that nothing would surprise me. I was, however, relieved to see that it was not her. The neighbouring landing light was on again. The window was open, an old woman peering down at us.

"What do you think you're doing?" she called, hesitant but querulous. "My sister's about to phone the police – so no funny business, now. Just give me an explanation or get out of here."

I'd seen her around but – this being about as close knit as it seemed a twenty-first century community could get – I didn't have a bloody clue what her name was. I knew she was widowed, lived with her housebound sister and that she had a cat that seemed to delight in "scratting" (as my dad used to put it) in my flowerbeds. Beyond that, she was a stranger that I occasionally nodded to.

"It's okay, love," I said, holding up my hands to show that we meant no one any harm. "It's Sonny Moore from down the road."

"Sonny who?"

"Moore? The writer?"

"The writer..." she said, thoughtfully. "Yes. Your little lass got run down and died."

She said it like it should be news to me.

"Yes."

"I was sorry about that."

"Thank you."

"And the big lad?"

"Sorry?"

"You're friend. Who is he?"

I glanced at "the big lad". He smirked and muttered something about being whoever she wanted him to be.

"This is Oliver," I told her. "My... my friend."

"I'm the torch bearer," he offered, bearing the torch by way of proof.

"And you brought a torch why?" the old widow woman asked.

"Interesting sentence structure," Oliver mumbled, before saying very clearly, "We thought it might be dark."

Quickly, I stepped in – hoping to steer the conversation in a more sensible direction. "We've been looking for Ned and – "

"Don't think you'll find him there, pet," she said, frustrating me further.

"No... no, I realise that." I sighed and started again, much to Oliver's amusement. "What I mean is, we've dropped by a couple of times to have a word with him but he seems to have gone away."

"Aye, well, people do that, I suppose. Not that I have much time for holidays and such, what with looking after my sister and everything. I was just saying – "

"He didn't happen to tell you where he might be going, did he?" Oliver asked. "It's actually very important that we speak to him."

She folded her arms and leant on the sill. "We don't have nothing to do with Ned no more," she said. "Not since he hit my pussy with a big stick." I took the precaution of dealing Oliver a swift sideways kick to the lower leg. "He was bad enough before his wife left him, if you ask me – but once she saw sense and ran off he just got worse." She put a finger to her temple. "Bit tapped, you know. Talks to himself all the time."

"And you have no idea where he might be?" I asked, determined not to let the conversation get bogged down.

The old woman gave a shrug that as much said "no" as it said "maybe". She seemed to consider it for a moment, and then shook her head emphatically. "Can't say I do, pet," she said. "But his sister might know, I suppose."

"He has a sister?" This was news to me – and welcome news, at that.

"As far as I know. Spinster, last time I heard. Probably took one look at her brother and thought better of marriage. Can't say I blame her, either."

"Do you know where she lives?" Oliver asked – all seriousness, now.

"I only know he has a sister and that she isn't married," she said, sounding rather impatient. "Now, if that's all, I think it might be a good idea if the two of you left. Ned might be an old nuisance but I don't think he'd much appreciate the two of you prowling around in his back garden at this time of night, now, do you?"

I thought about telling her that I didn't much care what Ned might or might not like – that as far as I was concerned he could rot in hell – but she had provided us with our first real clue to Ned's possible whereabouts, and, as such, that just didn't seem appropriate.

"But you didn't get an address?" Maggie asked.

Our arrival back home had been greeted with scepticism and apathy. Maggie, Don and Ashley huddled around the fire, the television playing quietly to itself in the background, looking tired and disinterested. Whilst Oliver and I had been on our "little adventure", it seemed that any enthusiasm they might have had for this had somehow slipped away. My instinct was to take hold of each of them in turn and give them all a bloody good shake.

Oliver had other ideas, however. He walked over to the hearth and stood with his back to the fire – the torch still clasped in his hands before him. He exuded authority and when he glanced at me, even I had to sit down.

"We discovered something that might be really useful tonight," he said. "We found out that Ned has a sister – not only that, but a *spinster* sister... unmarried and therefore still with the same surname as Ned, yes?"

Maggie sat up a little straighter with an "ah" of recognition. She nodded and gave Ashley an encouraging smile, and I thought that just maybe Oliver had saved the day – had taken the first step towards rebuilding whatever had been lost whilst we had been gone.

"So as long as we know Ned's surname, and as long as she isn't ex-directory, we should be able to look her up in the phone book," Maggie said.

"It doesn't matter if she is ex-directory," I pointed out. "As long as she's on the electoral register – or has been recently."

Maggie didn't seem to understand what I was saying. "It's available online," Oliver told her.

"It is?"

"Yes. Most everything is."

She looked at me. "And we know Ned's surname?"

I nodded. "Mortimer," I said – and felt all the strength drain out of me as realisation suddenly took hold.

I couldn't believe that I hadn't picked up on it earlier. I sat back in the armchair, closing my eyes as I felt all the warmth and drive leave me. My hand shook as I swore under my breath and pushed my oily hair back from my brow – and even though my eyes were closed, I knew Ashley, Don, Mags and Oliver were staring at me.

"What is it?" Oliver quietly asked.

"Mortimer," I answered, without opening my eyes.

"What about it? It's Ned's surname."

"Not just Ned's."

"No. It's his sister's surname, too."

I shook my head and sat forward – the world reacting oddly to this sudden movement, swimming and rocking on the periphery, the visual lag unsettling but not in any way restrictive. "Not just hers," I said. I didn't want to blurt it out. This was important information. It could make all the difference to us – the difference between going through the rest of our lives ignorant or finding some grace, some peace and belonging. I had to introduce them to this new fact with care, with the reverence and skill that this kind of revelation deserved. So it wasn't Divine. So it hadn't been handed down from On High. What did that matter? As far as I was concerned, it was The Holy Fucking Grail and it should be treated as such.

Oliver waited. Ashley waited. Don and Maggie stared at me expectantly. I was aware only of the hissing noise of the gas fire – the world outside silent and still, waiting with us, the cycle lost, the breath incapable of being released. I remembered being alone in my room all those times – reading the journal, lost in it, the words and names moving beyond meaning, becoming something else... something that touched even as it remained just on the edge of perception, shaping with insinuation whilst always remaining perplexingly removed. I had been enchanted. The warnings had been there, in that room, in that time – but I had initially seen nothing beyond story and the possibility of more story. I had missed the detail, maybe even ignored it, and whilst it might indeed have been true that this new fact could not have changed anything, I couldn't help but feel responsible.

"Edwin," I said. "The man who killed Sheila Mackenzie's daughter. His name was Edwin Mortimer."

Chapter Seventeen

Faced with having to decide whether or not we should leave it until morning, we arrived at the only conclusion we felt we could live with and left quickly in Don's Grand Scenic – the printout of Charlotte Mortimer's address tucked safely into the inside pocket of my jacket.

Estby Bay. That place of childhood remembrance and the glorious awakenings of early adulthood. It resided fondly in a part of me I could not name, a deep recess seamed with rich emotion and, as I remembered it, subtle hope. Standing a mere few hundred yards from the shelter where Ashley and I had first met, I felt it all again – how my shirt had clung damply to me, relief at being away from the caravan, regret at ever allowing myself to be persuaded to come along in the first place... that swelling in my chest when Ashley had first spoken to me. Joseph Heller. She had been reading Joseph Heller and those had most assuredly been simpler times. We had had a future that we could never have then envisaged – times when we would laugh, times, as now, when we would cry... times when we would struggle to keep a balance, a shape, a clarity that could only ever be peripheral – and now we had a past that seemed equally ephemeral. So far removed from what we were.

"It's ten forty-five," Oliver said as we stood with our backs to the sea wall, looking over the road at the tall, thin house belonging to Charlotte Mortimer. Three storeys, the building little more than one room wide – squeezed in between a condensated café called, ironically, the Ritz and a souvenir shop, its façade pebbledashed and dirty... I didn't want to imagine what it must be like to live there. Bad in season – noisy, the pavement outside slick with dropped chips – worse out of season. Sad and bleak, the walls too close, the light as grey and insipid as the pebbledashing. "Do you really think we should be calling on an old lady at this time of night?"

"If Ned isn't there, she'll at least understand," I said – feeling that this wasn't what I really wanted to say, but utterly unable to frame my thoughts more clearly.

"Will she?"

"Yes."

Don touched Oliver's arm and shook his head as if to say it was too late now. We had all made the decision together. Sleeping on it just hadn't been an option.

"It looks so sad," Maggie said, and we all nodded. A sleeping Wee Mark was mounted on her hip, his head resting in the hollow between her neck and shoulder – dribbling on her sweatshirt. I felt guilty about allowing her to bring him along with us. She should have stayed behind, taken care of her little boy... but it hadn't been that simple. Maggie was on a quest of her own. She needed to complete the picture now that she understood that her "stalker" had been real – and that he now regretted what he had done.

"He's not in there," Ashley said. I shook my head in agreement – not knowing how either of us knew this, but not about to question it. The wind came off the sea, cold against the back of my neck, and I imagined I could feel the sea-salt drying into the cracks and crevices of my face – that unforgiving, unknowable depth so close, so personal and accusatory. The tide out, the sea-sounds distantly soporific, I more felt than saw the wash of the gibbous moon, the milky cataract a breath against my skin – and, coupled with our sure knowledge of Ned's absence, this prompted me to move closer to Ashley, to put my arm around her and draw her close.

"Do we all go?" Don said. "Or do you think it would be wiser if some of us hung back a bit?"

I knew what he was doing. It was what we were all doing. Stalling. Putting off the moment when we would have to cross the road and face whatever disappointment fate had in store for us.

"It won't make any difference," I said. "As long as Maggie's there with Wee Mark, everything'll be okay." I didn't know this for a fact; it just seemed logical that an old woman seeing a mother and child would conclude that the rest of the group with them would not pose a threat. Maybe Wee Mark and Maggie had been intended to come along, after all.

On the other side of the road, I glanced at Ashley and each of my friends in turn before finally reaching out and ringing the doorbell.

Charlotte Mortimer answered the door promptly – swinging it wide and standing on the step as if challenging the world to cross her. I smelt basil and garlic.

Charlotte Mortimer wore a pair of jeans and an old, plaid work shirt. Staring down at us, she looked as though the word "formidable" had been invented specifically for her. In her early seventies, I believed, her arms nevertheless looked strong – her face intelligent and alert. There was a dark smudge on the side of her face and a pair of ancient secateurs in her right hand. The frames of the glasses she wore were bent out of shape. All in all, she struck me as someone who would not suffer fools gladly. She had an impatient air about her – a need to "get on" and "make a difference".

"I knew he'd been up to no good," she said by way of a greeting. "You'd better come in."

The corridor she led us along to the back of the house was as narrow and long as I had imagined. At one point, we all but had to squeeze past the stairway on our right as the wall of the room on our left jutted out to confine the space even further. Wee Mark had woken up – looking dazed and a little afraid, however much Mags reassured him – and as he stared over Maggie's shoulder at me I couldn't help but feel again that we shouldn't be putting him through this.

At the back of the house, we found ourselves in a large conservatory cum greenhouse. It was a dirty place – what furniture there was sagging and threadbare, the plants unnameable and wild, vine-like and scrawny – but with the darkness outside and the weak lighting, it was improbably soothing and otherworldly. There was that pungent smell in the air that spoke of plant decay, a rich, underlying theme that slowed me, made me stop and look about with greater care, and I understood implicitly that this was Charlotte Mortimer's world, that she had made it for herself in order to escape I didn't know what.

Standing by a bench containing half-dead roses and a couple of shitty-looking seed trays, she turned to face us – clattering the secateurs down on the bench and clasping her hands together at her waist.

"You *are* here about Ned, I take it?" she finally asked.

"Yes," I said. "We really need to talk to him. Is he here?"

Charlotte Mortimer smiled and closed her puffy eyes, her face wrinkling with the apparent absurdity of my question. Shaking her head, she said, "No – no, I'm sorry to say he isn't... actually, no, I'm not in the least bit sorry. I'm glad. I'm more than glad; I'm ecstatic. I don't want that man in this house ever again."

"So you haven't seen him?" Ashley asked.

"I didn't say that, pet." She sighed and gestured for us to sit down. There were not enough chairs for us all, so Ashley, Mags and Wee Mark took what were available and Oliver, Don and I just stood around looking beautiful. "I've seen him all right," she continued. "He was here a couple of days ago. That's why I wasn't surprised to see all of you on my doorstep. You can bet your bottom dollar that if Ned 'drops by' it's because he's been up to no good and has got himself into a bit of a tight spot, again. Some things never change."

"Did he say anything about where he planned on staying?" Oliver asked.

"Oh, yes," she said with a low chuckle. "He expected to stay here. He just turned up on my doorstep, grinning like butter wouldn't melt, and said, 'Here I am – I've come for a visit.' I said, 'On your bike, Ned, you're not setting so much of a toenail over this doorstep', and shut the door in his face. I wasn't about to have any of his nonsense. I've never had time for him – for any of them, for that matter."

"Any of them?" I asked.

"Anyone with the misfortune to be named Mortimer," Charlotte said. "Apart from our Bert. Bloody rabble, at best, the rest of them. I haven't had anything to do with any of them for as long as I can remember. Shifty lot – which isn't surprising, I suppose, when you look at what they came from."

"Edwin Mortimer," I said.

"Ah, you know about him, then. Granddad Edwin, just about the sickest man you were ever likely to meet. Him and Gran brought Ned up, for a while, you know.... Could have been a lot worse, I suppose.... Ned... well, deep down, he has a good heart. Right selfish bugger but he's not evil like Granddad Edwin was. He can be nasty of course, but I don't believe he'd do anything as bad as what Edwin did." She glanced over at me – her plaintive eyes telling me so much more. "This isn't where you contradict me, is it?" she asked.

It would have taken too long to tell her the whole story – and even if we had taken the time to tell her, I seriously doubted that she would believe half of what we had to say. Essentially, I believed she was right. Ned was selfish, with a definite capacity for nastiness, but I didn't believe he was evil.

And so I simply shook my head and said, "No. No, this isn't where we contradict you."

I wasn't sure she entirely believed me, but she nodded nevertheless and said, "Like I say, I have no time for him. But if you have a problem with him... well, it's only right and fair that you know that he's never exactly had it easy. His childhood with Edwin was bad and it's a miracle that man didn't mark him more than he evidently did."

We none of us particularly wanted to hear this. Whilst we understood that Ned wasn't entirely to blame, that something was occurring here that was beyond his control, it was equally true that any sob story Charlotte Mortimer might have to tell about him didn't really interest us. Ned had run. That was what now first and foremost struck me. Whatever regrets he might have (and that he had any was certainly debatable), he had not been man enough to stick around and face whatever he had coming to him. Any sympathy I might have had for him was heavily diluted by this.

Oliver, however, was intrigued. "It was that bad?" he asked.

Charlotte nodded. "Times weren't like what they are today," she said. "I suppose that goes without saying, but it was especially true for us – for Ned more so." She sighed and looked at her reflection in the black, filthy window. "Ned was around Edwin for a year or so. He must have only been about four or five. I don't recall this, you understand, because I hadn't yet been born. It's only what Ned and others have told me... and what I've managed to work out for myself. Not exactly the easiest story to piece together, but from what I can tell our mam had been having a tough old time of it. She wasn't the most well adjusted of women, but Dad didn't exactly help matters. He was Edwin's only son and he... he was a sensitive chap, utterly unlike Edwin. The type of man whose lip quivers if he has to speak in front of more than three or four people at a time. Edwin loved nothing more than to give him a hard time. Taunting him whenever the opportunity arose and, more to the point, convincing him that Ned wasn't his...

"That was about the cruellest thing he did to his own family – he did far, far worse to others, as you probably already know, but as far as we were concerned...

"As Edwin would have it, Ned was his son, not his grandson. He repeated the claim time and time again – to just about everyone he met – and even though Dad knew it was utter rubbish, it nevertheless started to take its toll on his relationship with Mam. Our older brother, Bert, may he rest in peace, saw it all. The arguments, the insidiousness of Edwin's claims – the complete dissolution of a once happy relationship. Edwin said so much, you see, that some of it couldn't fail to hit the mark. And that's all Dad could hear, after a while – the comments that rang true. It didn't matter that ninety-nine percent of what Edwin said was pure Tommyrot, all Dad could focus on was the lucky hits. It just ate away at him. He worked, then came home and gave Mam hell. This from a man who previously wouldn't say boo to a goose. Used to scare our Bert and Ned silly, but Bert was nevertheless always there at the top of the stairs – watching and listening.

"Things got worse really quickly, and, as Bert used to tell it, one night in particular, Dad stepped right over the edge and took a swing at Mam. Gave her a right clip around the ear and she went down like a sack of spuds. Fell and hit her head on the fire hearth..." Charlotte shook her head and smiled sadly. "Right out of a bloody Catherine Cookson novel, isn't it?"

Oliver gave her a weak smile – no doubt wishing he'd kept his mouth shut. For my part, I was concerned about Ashley, Mags and Wee Mark. I therefore took the opportunity to see that they were all right – touching Ashley on the shoulder. She looked up at me and nodded. Mags smiled, a sleeping Wee Mark cuddling into her. They were fine. They would be fine.

"Dad was mortified," Charlotte was saying. "He'd never done anything like that to her in his life and once he'd made sure she... you know – once he'd made sure the bang on the head hadn't killed her, he packed a few things into his kit bag and, well, he just went. Told our Bert that he had to go away to get himself right in the head again, but he'd be back as soon as he could and until then it was up to him to see that Mam was taken care of. Broke our Bert's heart, seeing his dad go like that. He knew, you see. He knew Dad wasn't a bad man, whatever he might have done to Mam. Dad felt too deeply. That's what Edwin preyed on."

Charlotte struck me as an articulate and lonely old woman. It was all too easy for me to imagine her in this greenhouse, talking to her flowers and growing ever more reclusive as the concept of company grew increasingly alien. As ridiculous as it might seem, I think a significant part of me envied her; her life may not have been full of lively conversation with interesting friends, but it was, at least, relatively comfortable and secure. Her worldview would not, I was sure, be challenged every five minutes – her periods of mourning would be few and far between. Charlotte Mortimer would talk to her ailing plants and try not to think of bygone times, her past of hardship and struggle. Well spoken, I saw her as self-educated and determined. She had made her life this way. Accidents had happened along the way, as they all too often do, but, by and large, she had arrived pretty much where she had expected. I wondered, briefly, why she hadn't married – and then I remembered the family's history.

"Mam went to pieces," she was saying. "All she wanted was for Dad to come back so that she could tell him that it was all right – everything would be just fine and she didn't hold any of it against him. Mam was a loving woman, you see. And she knew Dad was right for her. She would never have done anything to hurt him, and I suppose deep down Dad knew that. But Edwin got into his head and that was that. Dad left and Mam just went to pieces. As Bert used to tell it, she hit the sauce for a while but that just used to make her feel ill so she gave it up as a bad job and, instead, stopped eating. She had two little boys to look after but she just couldn't do it. She was too weak from hunger, but still she wouldn't eat. Bert would force her, best he could – and she did manage to keep enough down to survive – but she was a right state. The house went to pot, Ned was neglected… however hard Bert tried to keep it together, he was just a bairn himself and he had no real idea what needed to be done, however bright he was.

"The neighbours started getting concerned fairly quickly. Bert reckoned the house started smelling pretty bad and Ned was running around like a little urchin with no arse in his trousers. They tried to help – folk were like that, then, always willing to rally round and band together – but Mam was a proud woman and she wouldn't let them anywhere near. As far as she was concerned, what with the state she was in and everything, they were just interfering busybodies on the lookout for some juicy gossip. Maybe they were – I don't know – but some of them, at least, were genuinely concerned. Concerned enough about Bert and Ned to do the one thing they… well, they knew what he was like. They must have considered it a last resort."

"They told Edwin," Oliver said.

"They did, indeed. He came round, told Mam that Dad was nothing better than a wank rag and that she, if she couldn't keep such a weak man, was far, far worse. Bert always told it that Edwin stood over her whilst she cowered on the floor in the corner of the living room and when he, Bert, tried to get between them, to protect his mam, Edwin just picked him up by the back of his shirt and set him aside – nothing more than a minor inconvenience.

"There was nothing else Bert could do except keep Ned out of the way," she told us, after a short pause to roll back the cuffs of her shirt. "Edwin kept on shouting at and taunting Mam for a good ten minutes and then, finally, he left her there and came through to the kitchen where Bert was trying to find some bread for Ned to eat.

"The way Bert used to tell it, Edwin just stood in the doorway looking at them for what seemed like forever. The first time he told me about it, he said it was like he was doing sums in his head – but that he'd had to move his lips just a little in order to keep track. He was figuring. We none of us could ever have said just *what* he was figuring, but if what Bert said was true, that was just what he was doing."

"The cost of bringing up two boys?" Don wondered.

Charlotte shrugged. "Maybe," she said. "Although given the kind of man Edwin was, I think not, somehow. That may have been part of it, but he was calculating other things, too, I'm sure. Edwin saw opportunity where no one else would."

Given what he had done to Sheila Mackenzie's daughter, I didn't want to think about that – and I certainly didn't want Ashley to have to think about such things, not after everything she'd been through recently. I thought of how she had been with her mother, the last time the two of them had been together, and I saw again that encroaching need within her – the inevitable bleakness that drove her to hang on to me and those she loved for dear life. Ashley was not the child. I doubted she ever had been. With her mother, as with me, she did not regress; she did not suck her thumb and, at least not all of the time, weep inconsolably. Instead... it was as though a black calm overcame her. She reminded me of that moment just before the storm broke – together, poised and, yet, loaded with the weight of a sorrow she could not hold. I'd considered her, for quite some time, now, someone unwilling (or possibly unable) to commit to anything wholeheartedly. Her depressions, if that's what they had been, had merely been reactions to her lack of direction and goals. But I had been wrong. I had been wrong *in so many ways.* The times I had said to her, "Your problem is...", I had been totally missing the point. There was nothing wrong with Ashley, there never had been. That she occasionally made mistakes was undeniable, but she was intrinsically good and right. She had strengths I could only begin to imagine, depths that I hoped would never be revealed to me – afraid of the implication that would carry with it. Yes, she needed my arms around her. Yes, my willingness and wish to protect would always be welcomed. But Ashley was most assuredly not the child her mother had once believed her to be.

As Charlotte continued talking, I felt Oliver's eyes on me. We had come so far, the two of us – from those early, tentative discussions, the drunken examinations and hypnagogic dismissals to this flat-out acceptance. It hardly seemed possible. Charlotte told us how Edwin had taken Ned away and treated him like a skivvy and I thought back to that day in Asda, again – Oliver going on about the different ways in which a bar code could be interpreted. So far removed from where we now were, and yet somehow connected – events and themes carrying through in only the most barely perceptible of ways.

Ashley and I had wanted another child. Just as Sheila Mackenzie had. Little playmates for the daughters we already had. Her hunger and need had been satisfied, whilst ours had been exacerbated. It was cruel, and, yet, so finally balanced that I couldn't help but admire it. There was no perfection in this ungodly narrative, but there was a subtlety I couldn't fail to see.

Ashley looked up at me and smiled. There was nothing in the least bit forced about this. It came as naturally as the tears when, yet again, we realised our beautiful daughter was no longer with us. She smiled and I moved to her side, holding her hand – soothed as she rolled the ball of her thumb over my fingers.

"We don't know the half of it," Charlotte was saying. "That's what our Bert always used to say. Bert saw Ned change in a matter of weeks after he went off with Edwin. He got quieter and more self-reliant, but also got physically stronger. All the food and hard work, I suppose. Edwin made him graft, all right, but he knew you only got out what you put in – so Ned never went without, which was a blessing, I suppose."

Charlotte picked up the secateurs and turned her back to us, snipping away at the tips of some of her unrecognisable plants. I thought, initially, that we were being dismissed – but then she started speaking again, still keeping her back to us.

"It was more of a blessing when that woman did for Edwin, though," she said. "Ned had been with him for about a year – a year of hard work and God alone knows what else. Grandmother was little more than a shade haunting the far corner of the parlour, as our Bert used to have it. She had no real influence, not when Edwin was around, and Ned was virtually totally dependent on Edwin, which is just how the man wanted it. But when he died... everything changed. For the better, too. Dad came home for his father's funeral and never went away again. Mam got back on track and the two of them started afresh. The only tough part, Bert always used to say, was the nightmares our Ned used to have. He had them for a couple of years, starting about a year after Edwin's death, and then they stopped – either that or he learned to keep them from his brother. They shared a bedroom, you see, and Bert used to say that it was horrible to see. Ned used to gasp and blub, white faced and staring at the corner of the room. Ned would never talk about it but Bert figured he must have been dreaming of Edwin. That man was enough to give anyone nightmares, I suppose."

I wasn't sure I agreed with Bert's assessment, but it was too late to get into all that, now. Instead, I simply asked, "And you have no idea where Ned might be now?"

Charlotte still had her back to us. She looked over her shoulder, eyebrows raised. "Oh," she said, facing us. "I know *exactly* where he is, pet."

The wind had picked up and was coming off the sea in icy gusts that made me wonder just where the summer had gone and, more to the point, what the hell we were doing here. This could have waited until daylight. There was no need for the six of us to be out on the beach in the dead of night looking for an old man and his hut.

Charlotte had told us, before wishing us luck and sending us on our way, that Edwin had always kept an old fishing hut down on the beach. Apparently it had been his refuge – the place he had always returned to when trouble started catching him up. Few people had known about it, and those that did weren't especially inclined to mention it to anyone else. Charlotte had said Edwin had used it more and more as the years had rolled on, taking Ned along with him in that final year and, ultimately, leaving the place to him in his will. As she told it, Ned now only used the place when all else failed. It had fallen into disrepair, torn apart by the elements, but she had nevertheless been sure that there was enough of it left to give Ned the shelter he required and that that was where he would be.

We weren't kids anymore. The sand was heavy going, especially with the cold wind and the creeping fatigue – and when Ashley paused, I thought she was simply taking a breather. Don, Oliver, Maggie and I stopped – Don carrying Wee Mark, now, in order to give Mags a break. I put a hand on Ashley's back, moving in close to see that she was all right. The only light we had to see by was the moon, the lights from nearby factories and the roaring, dragon-like flare-stacks. It was nevertheless enough to see that Ashley was crying.

"What is it?" I tenderly asked.

She pointed at the valley between two dunes and I thought I understood.

"Conceived," she mumbled – all she could manage right now. I remembered the dream she had had, and that day all those years ago when we had made a place for ourselves and reshaped our futures in a haven certainly very similar to the one we now saw before us. Nadine had not truly been conceived here and, in fact, since dunes have a tendency to shift and evolve over time, I doubted it was the same

363

place, at all. The associations were nevertheless strong. As Ashley quietly wept, I felt my own tears start to fall – a curiously soothing sensation, one I suspected I could have grown to like a little too much. Oliver took a step towards us but I waved him away, putting my arms around Ashley as we both crumbled and slumped onto our knees in the sand.

"Is it the same place?" Ashley asked me – her sobbing coming under control. "It is, isn't it? This is where we were all those years ago, right?"

Dunes relocate. I thought of telling her this – of what it would be like to just rip whatever there was left of her world right out from under her. But I couldn't. She deserved something to cling onto. It was the least I could do for her – even in the state I was in, I saw that much.

"I think so, sweetheart." I hiccupped. "Yes. Yes, it is. I'm sure of it."

"Then it's good, then, right?"

"What do you mean, love?"

She shivered and I felt it pass through me, instinctively holding her more tightly. "I mean... we should be here, shouldn't we?" she said. "Nadine wants us to be here. That's why she came to me in that dream."

I didn't know how to answer her. I was suffering too much myself to even begin to know how best to make sense of this for her. And so I did all that I suppose anyone could do under the circumstances and agreed with her. "Yes, sweetheart," I said, my own tears falling steadily now. "Yes, that's exactly it."

Right or wrong, it seemed to do the trick. She found the strength to stand up – brushing the sand from the knees of her jeans before helping me to my feet. Together, we again stared at the valley between the two nearest sand dunes, a solemn mark of respect that didn't seem in the least bit out of place, and then Ashley turned to Oliver and the others and said, very calmly, "Let's go. It can't be far, now."

Pinpricks of light on the horizon, out on the frigid North Sea – drawing my eye, making me think of all those lives out there, floating in the blackness, blissfully unaware of their land-bound cousins and their various frictions and puzzles. I could understand what they saw in such a life. To float. To simply lose oneself to the necessary regime that came with the work, the hardship and the constant changing of the world beneath and around them. Their timetable set by port availability, pilots taking them those final few nautical miles, a life on land would be as alien to them as a life at sea would be to me – so altered would they be by the work and the life that inevitably came with it. What would it feel like to slip out of port and know that, for a period of weeks, months, possibly years, you would not have to face your mundane-yet-too-complicated life on land? Was it just a way of making a living, or was it in part a vocation? An escape. As much a calling as the religious life of a nun in an enclosed order.

Ashley and the others stopped. I stopped. In the distance, sitting on the sand a few feet from the edge of the foamy wash of the waves – sepia-tinted in the light from the flare-stacks – was a figure. Thin, back hunched and insubstantial despite the thick fleece jacket he wore, he picked up a handful of sand and let it run through his fingers. The rushing wind blew it back at him, but he didn't seem to notice.

Still unaware of us, he lifted more sand – this time holding it up higher, as if offering it up to those ancient Nordic gods on the far side of the North Sea. The wind caught it more easily, this time, blowing it into his face. Still he didn't flinch.

"Is it him?" Maggie asked in a reverential whisper.

"Yes." This from Ashley – her voice hard-edged and blunt with resolve. She wasn't clinging to me, anymore. If she was still struggling with all of this (I had no doubt that she was), she was hiding it well – hiding it or merely masking it behind this need to accomplish and face off, her determination to do whatever it would take to fulfil the promise, as she possibly saw it, that Nadine's conception had brought with it. I wanted her to know that she didn't have to be like this – she didn't have to be strong and vengeful – but there was no way of me telling her without potentially making matters ten times worse.

Unlike Maggie, Ashley had not whispered. Ned turned his head to look at us – hearing her above the steady, ponderous frequency of the waves. He stiffened and vainly tried to push himself to his feet – giving up almost immediately and sagging back down onto the sand.

"She wants me dead," he said, hopelessly – looking out to sea, again. "I thought she just wanted another wee bairn for her little lass to play with, but I was wrong." Glancing over his shoulder, he spoke directly to Ashley. "You're supposed to kill me, now," he said.

Ashley started walking slowly towards Ned. Her hands gradually unclenched at her sides, and I knew that if I didn't stop her now, it would be too late. Even Oliver would not be able to restrain her. She would lash out, scratch and bite, kick and thump – and however insubstantial her blows might be, it would be enough. Sheila Mackenzie would work through her and Old Man Ned would fast become Dead Man Ned.

I quickly grabbed her arm, and it was enough.

Looking at me, she asked, "No?"

I shook my head. "No, love," I said. "It's what she wants. You heard him. She wants him dead."

"Because of Edwin?"

"Ah." Ned shuddered. He might have been laughing, but I wouldn't have bet the house on it. "So you worked that out. Yes, because of Edwin – but also because... because it's in her nature. She can't get enough of misery, that lass. Maybe Granddad Edwin made it worse, I don't know, but I still find it hard to believe that it was just that what made her do what she did to your little lass."

I was still holding on to Ashley's arm. She had not yet stepped back, but she was no longer pulling against me.

"Why didn't you try to stop it?" she asked.

The wind direction changed, carrying the roar of the flare stacks to us. Coupled with the persistently monotonous sound of the sea, this made it difficult to hear Ned's response. I believed he said something along the lines of, "It was just too difficult, lass," but when Ashley looked at me questioningly, all I could do with any certainty was shrug my shoulders.

We all moved closer as he continued, the sound of the flaring blessedly dying down.

"You have to understand," he said. "I've had this for years. Since I was a lad. She's always been there, at my shoulder – putting me through every kind of hell imaginable. My marriage broke up because of that woman. She mocked me, continually told me that I was just

366

like Edwin – that in time I, too, would rape and kill little girls. I stayed with Edwin for a while when I was a boy. Family trouble. And that was bad enough. That man was no friend to me. He worked me in every way possible and... like I say, he was no friend to me. But her – *Sheila Mackenzie* – she didn't see it like that and a year or so after she'd killed Edwin, she started 'visiting' me, and hasn't stopped since. I suppose that must have been when she died herself. She died resenting and hating, and, for whatever reason, I was the one she chose to punish. Not Dad or Mam, or our Bert, me brother. Me. Little ineffectual Ned." He turned and looked me in the eye. When he spoke again, he lifted his voice to be sure I heard him clearly. "You'd be dead now, were it not for me," he told me. "That's something else you have to understand. She wanted you. Or that was what she led me to believe. Long before that lovely little lass of yours was ever a possibility, she wanted you. Your dad used to see her for a while – I told you that, didn't I?"

I nodded slowly, not in the least liking what I was hearing.

"Yes," he said, as if to himself. "Yes, I told you. She wanted you, you see, lad. That was how it was – or that was how she made me *think* it was. But I wouldn't help her. I was younger, you see. I was stronger than I am now. So I said 'no' and willingly faced the consequences. – And I wanted to do that again for your little lass, I really did, but I just couldn't. It was just too much, lad."

The father lives that the daughter might die, I thought, shuddering and moving closer to Ashley. I could hear Oliver breathing heavily at my right shoulder – his bulk reassuring as I felt the uncertain sand beneath my feet, listened to the sagacious sea as it uttered its coded words of wisdom. It was a natural law, I saw that now. If a daughter was to die, the father must, of course, live. A change of state cannot be affected on something that has not at first been created. But it was more than just a generalised philosophical principle. It spoke of specifics, it implied that, among other things, Ashley and I should never have met – Nadine Verity should never have been born. My father had seen her. He had seen her and said nothing, that I knew of, about it. He had seen her and Ned... Ned had made sacrifices that I might live.

I looked down at him. Such a pitiful sight. In the few days since I had seen him last he had lost even more weight. The fleece jacket bagged beneath his arms and caved in where fat and muscle should have given it form and dignity. His legs in the filthy, stained jeans made me think of flamingos – the only difference being that the knot of his knee bent the opposite way. Ashley would never have killed him, I realised that, now. She would have laid one hand on him and felt his loss and struggle, saw him for the failed hero he truly was.

"It's cold out here," he said, struggling to get to his feet. He stumbled and Ashley quickly stepped in, taking his arm and helping him. In that moment, I was more proud of her than I had ever been of anyone in my life.

"It's okay," I heard her say as he leant against her and I thought that, however much of an exaggeration that might be, it was a brand of optimism wholly required by the circumstances.

Later that evening (the early hours of the following morning, to be accurate), Oliver would say to me as we all drank together and tried to figure out just what the fuck should come next, "We at least have unity. Let's make sure we keep it that way, eh?"

Ned staggered and Ashley called my name. Together with Oliver, I grabbed Ned as all his energy seeped away – the faint total and about as undramatic as a faint could be. We carried him easily in the direction he had been leading us, and ultimately found what was left of Edwin's hut.

I'd known places like this when I'd been a kid. Such huts and shelters, I thought as I stepped over the threshold carrying Ned's legs, were the forgotten places where innocence was lost and miserable obligations were forestalled. It wasn't merely that this was a place so often used for the taking of booze, drugs and virginity – it seemed to me to go deeper than that. In the Tour Guide of Life, these shitholes slipped off the edge of the page and allowed their inhabitants, itinerants and chavs alike, to find a soulful oblivion that transcended the discarded prophylactics and the stink of piss. Here they were alone. Here they were safe. Here they could do whatever they so wished without having to first judge the strength of social mores.

We set Ned down on a mattress in the corner of the room. He looked every bit the old man. His hair seemed even thinner and certainly filthier, and his skin was parchment-like and dehydrated, lacking elasticity and healthy colour. When we moved him on the mattress, centring him and trying to bring him round, I smelt rotten fruit and human faeces and knew instinctively that it did not come from the foam and rusting springs beneath him. Whatever Sheila Mackenzie wanted of him or had planned for him, it was obvious that Ned Mortimer was not going to be around for much longer.

Maggie had remained outside, by the doorway with the now awake and alert Wee Mark. We joined her in the open doorway, glancing over at Ned as we discussed what should be done.

"We can't put him through anything else," Ashley said. "I don't know how much of what happened was his fault. I just can't think about that, now. But I do know we have to look after him. That's why we're here. She wanted us – *me* – to *kill* him."

"He needs a doctor," Oliver said.

"You can put that right out of your head, for a start." Ned had pushed himself up on his elbows and was looking at us. He rubbed his eyes roughly and squinted at me. "No doctors, no hospitals. I'm staying here, and that's all there is to it."

"You can't stay here, Ned," Ashley said. Such a contrast to the woman who had barely acknowledged him as she'd sunbathed on the patio earlier in the summer. Seeing Sheila Mackenzie "manifest" before me, naked and nasty, was nothing in comparison to the stark disparity now provided by Ashley's clearly sincere show of compassion.

"I think you'll find I can stay wherever I want to stay," he said, chin stubbornly raised. "No doctors, pet. No doctors or hospitals. I can't be doing with owt like that. Not now."

"Well we're not just going to leave you here to fend for yourself. Not when you're in a state like this."

"A state?" Ned asked.

Ashley walked over to him and squatted down at the side of the mattress. I no longer had to worry that she was going to claw his eyes out or beat him to a pulp.

When she took hold of his hand, Ned gasped. I wondered how long it had been since a woman had touched him. He lay back, resting his head but never taking his eyes off her. "Look at yourself," Ashley said, kindly. "You need a wash, shave and a good feed. Maybe you aren't ill. I don't know. I'm no doctor. But if you aren't already, you soon bloody will be."

"No doctors or hospitals," he reiterated.

Ashley nodded – slowly and patiently. Behind me, I heard Wee Mark whisper something to his mother. It sounded like "home".

"Okay," Ashley was saying. "How does this sound to you, then? We get you home, get you cleaned up and some food and drink inside you, and take it from there. How does that strike you?"

"I can't let you take me home," he said. Ned, as far as he was concerned, had found his place to die – and he wasn't going to be so easily talked into abandoning his hut and whatever fate awaited him here. He had made it this way. He had chosen to return to this place just as surely as Richard had chosen to enter Maggie Sutherland's/Sheila Mackenzie's garden shed – and in so doing, he believed he had marked out his future; scratched it, ineffaceable and deep. "I can't." He shook his head. "It's not going to happen. I couldn't do that to you."

"You wouldn't be doing anything to us," she said softly.

"Oh but I would." His voice broke and he struggled to clear his throat. I looked around for water, a can of coke or something, but found nothing. "You were supposed to kill me," he finally continued. "If you take me back, she'll be angry. More angry than she's ever been. I can't do that to you."

Given the compassionate mood she was in, I thought that she would merely tell him not to be so silly. It was decided. We were taking him home and we would face the consequences together. But that wasn't what happened. Instead, Ashley patted his hand, got to her feet and walked back over to us.

"What do you think?" she asked.

"We can't leave him here," Oliver whispered.

"I know but..." Ash had something on her mind.

"What is it, love?"

Those eyes so like our daughter's held me. "Nadine," she said. "She's... what if we take Ned back and... what if she hurts her, Sonny? What if she hurts her to punish us?"

Ashley understood this in a different way to me. Whereas I

thought of Nadine as somehow no longer with us, a part of our lives but nevertheless very forcefully absent, Ashley found it far easier to imagine Nadine as more fixedly "somewhere else".

I, however, had had the luxury of "seeing" Jim as our daughter had died – of having his reassurances that he would let nothing hurt Nadine and of having this confirmed by Oliver. Sheila Mackenzie was not one to play by the rules, Ned could more than testify to that, but some things were beyond her, of that I was sure. Jim would take care of her. And if not Jim, my parents would. The more I thought about it, the more sense it made – and as I told Ashley all this, I felt myself lifted. I felt taller and stronger, more resolute and certain of myself. Sheila Mackenzie could not hurt our daughter because there were simply too many people who were prepared to protect her. I saw the sense of this. We all did. Even Ashley.

And so it was decided. However much he argued and contradicted, whatever obstacles he placed in the way, Ned was coming home with us.

Sorrow Street waited for him.

Sorrow Street waited for us all.

Chapter Eighteen

It was after midnight when we pulled up outside our house on Sorrow Street. As might have been expected, the road was deserted and still – preternaturally quiet. Sitting in the passenger seat beside Don, I felt the fears and expectations of my fellow passengers crowding at my back.

Ned had started coughing the minute we got him in the car and hadn't stopped since, and as I worried that his health might affect the rest of us, that we might catch something, I found myself turning in my seat to regard Wee Mark, sitting on his mother's lap. What must he be making of all this? I wondered. All these strange adults keeping him out until the early hours of the morning. Finding him asleep again, I envied him that ability.

He stirred as the engine stopped and Old Man Ned, in the next seat to Wee Mark and Mags, put his skeletal hand on the boy's leg – gently patting. The action had an unexpected, soothing effect on Wee Mark; he snuggled into his mam, holding on more tightly, and whispered sleepily. I didn't hear what, if anything, he said, but I imagined that he was talking to his best friend – the little girl that had inexplicably disappeared from his life.

Outside the car, Maggie drew me aside – Wee Mark still hanging from her neck. She appeared concerned, but I didn't find this unduly alarming; we all looked concerned.

"Don't be fooled," she whispered. "She's not coping as well as you think, love. She's not coping as well as *she* thinks, for that matter."

"Ashley?" I was exhausted.

"Yes, Ashley," she said – a little impatiently. The others were getting out of the car, too, now, so she had to hurry. "Take my word for it," she told me. "I recognise the signs. She's struggling but she's trying to keep it all together. We need to keep our eye on her, Sonny, we really do."

Ashley was watching us. She walked around to where Maggie and I were and put a hand on Maggie's arm. She'd apparently heard – understandable, really, since the street and our Merry Band of Adventurers were so impeccably silent. Given her dislike of being talked about – of being left out of discussions that directly affected or concerned her – I wasn't sure how she would react.

I needn't have worried. She smiled at Mags and gently squeezed her arm. A tear broke free as she said, "I'm okay, honestly. It's hard, but I'm... it's better now that I know what we have to do."

Looking at her quizzically, I asked, "What do you mean?"

She nodded in Oliver's direction. He was helping Ned out of the car. "It's what Nadine would have wanted," she said. "She liked Ned. She would have wanted us to make sure he was all right."

I wasn't entirely sure quite where she got this notion that Nadine had liked Ned. It was certainly true that she hadn't *dis*liked him. She had never run from him or hidden whenever he was around – but the same could have been said of just about anyone she'd encountered. This was the little girl who had run giggling to Sheila Mackenzie, after all. Our daughter had not been fussy, but that in and of itself did not express an opinion, one way or the other.

Nevertheless, I said nothing – merely nodded along with Maggie and tried not to think what would happen once the responsibility that Ned embodied was taken from us.

"We need to get him inside," Oliver said when I went round to help him with Ned. Oliver was anxiously sucking his lips. Ned was barely conscious.

Ned insisted we enter by the front door – and I have to admit that I was relieved. The thought of having to again walk along that tenebrous passageway to the malodorous back garden was certainly not one that appealed to me. Oliver held him whilst he searched in his jacket pockets and found his keys, and something suddenly occurred to me.

"Your cases," I said, and Ned turned to look at me. "What happened to your cases?"

He smiled sadly and shrugged. "I figured I didn't have much use for anything like that, anymore," he said. "Had a right bugger of a time trying to get them down to the hut so I ditched them in the dunes."

"You should have said," I told him as Oliver took the key off him and opened the front door. "We could have got them for you."

"Can't say I'm that bothered, lad. A few old clothes, that's all we're talking about. I think we've got more important things to think about, don't you?"

Ned hadn't wanted to return to Sorrow Street. He'd continued to insist, even after it had been decided, that it was the wrong thing to do – that sometimes you just had to give it up as a bad job and know when it was time to quit. But now he was impatient. Now he saw, even if I didn't recognise it myself, that I was once again stalling. Ashley, Mags and Wee Mark were being accompanied by Don and here we were standing on Ned's doorstep, talking about what in essence added up to lost luggage. It was a ludicrous and graceless attempt.

At his insistence, Ned entered first. Oliver and I followed quickly – Oliver keeping a steadying hand at Ned's waist, me closing the door firmly behind us and reaching out for the light switch. I clicked it on and nothing happened.

"Bulb's gone," Ned said, without looking back at me. "There's some under the kitchen sink."

"I'll go and get one," Oliver said. He started to step around Ned – careful not to bump him – but stopped when I put a hand on his arm.

"Wait," I said.

It was barely audible. Holding my breath, my heart thumping in my ears, I tried to pinpoint the noise – tried in vain to work out just what it was and where it was coming from. Oliver and Ned could hear it, too, now that they were as still and silent as me. The delicate brushing sound of rough fabric against rough fabric, coarse starched, or, perhaps, paper against paper – moving slowly, back and forth, lost in its own lack of purpose or meaning.

"What is it?" Oliver whispered. He turned to face me, the question hanging.

He saw the answer before me.

Drawing Ned and me towards him, the two of us turning to look at the source of the noise, Oliver swore under his breath. He'd never seen her before, I realised. It seemed absurd.

Until I had turned and moved away, Sheila Mackenzie had been standing directly behind me. Leaning back against the wall, she swayed from side to side – slowly rubbing her bare shoulders against the heavy wallpaper. She kept her eyes downcast and to one side, chewing her lip as she again masturbated. Her fingers worked deliberately and monotonously, a displeasing act and one, it suddenly occurred to me, that was endless in its constant, vain pursuit of satisfaction.

"Enough to make you want to rip your eyes out, isn't it?" Ned said – his voice hard with fear and abhorrence. "I was just a boy when I first saw her do that. I thought she'd lost summat up there and was trying to fish it out."

It was an almost casual observation – as if he were speaking of a particularly tiresome exhibit in a museum – but I don't think any of us were under any illusions that Sheila Mackenzie showing herself to us like this was an especially good sign. She might not have been looking at us, but she certainly knew we were there.

Her fingers worked harder. She moved her feet apart and crouched lower – shoulders still pressed hard against the wall as she spread herself, using both hands, now... attacking the problem from every conceivable angle. The harder she worked, the less fulfilling it seemed.

She stopped quite suddenly, her head snapping up to look at us. I had read her journal. I had grown to know her in a way that no one else had. She had at once repelled and attracted me, but more than anything I had been touched by, however perverse, her depth and intellect. I had wished her out of that asylum – away from the Warty Nurse and all her humiliating ministrations. In part I had sympathised. But what I had seen in the pages of that journal bore no resemblance to the woman I now saw before me.

Feral and crude, Sheila Mackenzie's face twisted with all the force of her spite and madness. She brought her legs together and stood up straighter, but still kept her head low – looking at us from beneath her frowning brow, as if considering the best time to pounce.

I thought she was going to speak, or start again that annoying, shoulder-scratching rocking from side to side. But she only stared at us, daring us to make the first move – smiling knowingly, the stench from her rotting teeth reaching across a space both physical and metaphysical. A quick glance in Oliver's direction informed me that he was at as much of a loss as me, and Ned, contemptuous through more than mere familiarity, most assuredly had nothing left to offer.

Minutes passed and none of us moved. To do so would be to risk triggering some possibly threatening response from Sheila Mackenzie. She should be humoured, and this was the only way we could see to do that.

And then she lifted her right arm and pointed at Ned.

Again I thought she was going to speak – but she merely continued standing there, her arm outstretched, staring at Ned intently. The hallway had that difficult to define Old Man Ned smell about it, and as it grew stronger, I wondered if, perhaps, that smell had (and had always had) more to do with Sheila Mackenzie. She sweated bitterness and loathing. The love she had had for her daughter – perhaps the only love she had ever truly known – had been poisoned by the admittedly horrific way the child had died, and now that poison leaked from her, *bled* from her, into this world she should no longer inhabit. I took a step back, my heels thudding against the skirting board as this smell was joined by another – that unmistakable smell of ozone, of thunderstorms and childhood train sets.

Oliver and Ned clearly smelt it, too – and it was enough of a harbinger for the three of us to start thinking of escape. I looked at the front door, about to make my move, but Oliver and Ned were already on their way along the hallway, heading deeper into the house. Surely not the smartest of moves, but, from their points of view, at least, the most logical – given that they didn't have to pass Sheila Mackenzie this way. After a brief hesitation, I followed – doing my best to keep an eye on her as I did so.

In the kitchen, Oliver slammed the door shut behind me. He was so enthusiastic in his efforts to shut Sheila Mackenzie out that he caught my shoulder with the door as he did so – giving it one hell of a whack. I stepped away quickly, cursing and pointing out that a closed door probably wasn't going to make a whole lot of difference. "She walked through me," I told him. "I'm sure she can manage a little thing like that."

Ned was propped against the units in the corner of the room. The excitement had animated him, somewhat – his cheeks flushed, his glassy eyes positively dancing – but he still looked as if he could keel over at any minute. Oliver joined him, putting a big hand on his shoulder and asking him if he was all right. When Ned had answered, saying he was just fine – "as right as rain" – Oliver said, "We need the back door keys, mate. Where do you keep them?"

Ned pointed to a drawer just to the left of the sink. "It's the one with the green key ring," he said. "You can't miss it."

I was looking at the door to the hallway. Sheila Mackenzie was still with us, still waiting for whatever cue she felt necessary. I imagined I could hear her breathing, but then dismissed this as ridiculous. Ghosts do not breathe, I insisted. They were beyond our needs and appetites – lost to them and adrift in... in what? An eternity of bliss? Fluffy fucking clouds and angels with duelling harps? That clearly was not the case. Sheila Mackenzie had carried her need and spite beyond life. Her anger burned as strongly as it ever had, and her discontented, driven urge to punish was just as ingrained. Nothing had really changed for her – except, perhaps, her chances of redemption.

So maybe she did breathe. If only for my benefit.

Oliver clattered about in the drawer for a second or two, and then held up a key for Ned to see. "That's the fella," Ned told him, but it was too late.

She moved quickly. This time there was no melodramatic pointing, certainly no unfulfilling autoeroticism. Instead, Sheila Mackenzie fixed her blood-baked eyes on Ned and made a move for him. To say she lunged is to overstate it. Sheila Mackenzie, ghost or otherwise, had more grace than that. She didn't glide. She didn't fly like some Hammer Horror banshee. She simply walked with elegant threat and purpose in Ned's direction, seemingly growing taller with each step – her body suddenly more beautiful than I'd ever imagined it could be.

"You should be dead," she said – and then Oliver stepped between them.

It was a brave, selfless thing to do, and not something I could have easily imagined myself doing. Maybe I saw her as more of a threat than Oliver ever could – her power somehow tied in with her very obvious sexuality. I don't know. But one thing was for certain; Oliver was not in the least bit intimidated by her. My friend took the room from her. A good couple of inches taller, he looked down on her, his tensed neck as broad as the trunk of a Giant Redwood, and said, "Enough."

Sheila Mackenzie took a step back. She didn't smile. Her face remained unreadable and distant, but as she raised her right hand and placed it against Oliver's brow, I thought I saw her lips tense ever so slightly – the faintest film of self-doubt pass before her eyes. Oliver didn't flinch or try to slap her hand away. She touched him and, more to the point, he let her. A vein stood out on the side of his neck and her fingers pressed against him, passing through his flesh and bone as if they were simply breaking a fine membrane on the surface of a lake. I thought I'd see ripples, but I didn't.

"You will never have a child of your own," she told him. A private regret once again brought to the surface – a sickening echo of what Maggie's mother had said to him in the hospital waiting room.

Oliver was not a man who was easily riled – but it was plain to see that this had really got to him. I'd never really thought about it before, but children were important to all of us. As gay as he was, Oliver had a natural, paternal ability that, on those occasions when I'd watched him with Nadine, Wee Mark or even poor, stifled Veronique, had shone through everything else he was. Don had told me only the week before how good Oliver was with his kids – how they were already growing to love him, in spite of the "difficult" circumstances, and I now wondered how he would react to this echoed affront. Would he lose it and rail against the unfairness of it all, vainly throwing his arms against this phantom representation of his deepest regret – or would he simply fall under the weight, beaten, never to rise again? I couldn't really imagine either scenario. I believed Oliver was above all that and, true to form, he proved me right.

Very calmly, he lifted his right hand – a cold smile creeping. Sheila Mackenzie's hand remained docked to his forehead, but this didn't seem to trouble him in the least. He reminded me of an old friend of my father. We'd once visited his allotment and during the afternoon, a bee had stung him on the back of his hand. Instead of reflexively knocking it off, however, he had sat down with me and explained about the bee's "corkscrew" sting – and as he'd talked, we'd watched the bee unscrew itself and, ultimately, fly away to pollinate another day. He had possessed that same calm that I now saw in Oliver – and as his arm lifted higher, I quickly dismissed the notion that he was going to swat her away. He had something far subtler than that in mind.

Oliver, ever a slave to symbolism, placed his own hand on Sheila Mackenzie's forehead. Ned and I watched as it, also, sank slowly into her – through the appearance of flesh and bone, to the very core of who and what she was.

Sheila Mackenzie's face showed no emotion. If she felt any pain or discomfort, we did not see it reflected there. Her own hand still on – in – Oliver's head, it almost seemed that she were lost, that his thoughts had ensnared her.

As his cold smile faded, the vein in the side of his neck became further engorged – swelling and pulsing. His arm straightened, as if he were holding her back, and, surely enough, the smile returned – this time victorious and full-faced, his eyes wide and accomplished.

"Well," he said, *sotto voce* and measured, "I guess I'll just have to learn to live with that, won't I?"

It was as effective as a slap in the face. Sheila Mackenzie snatched her hand away from him, clutching it in her other hand at her chest – stepping back and releasing herself from Oliver's grip. Oliver's arm dropped to his side, and he staggered a little. I placed a hand at the small of his back, but he nodded that he was all right and pointed at Sheila Mackenzie.

If anger has its outer limits, she had reached them. She clawed at herself in frustration and then screamed silently – hands writhing between her breasts, glowering at Oliver as if he'd just visited the worst possible humiliation on her. She took a step towards him, pointing with something akin to indecision, and then, her hands over her head, turned from us and was gone.

Her departure had been silent. The stillness that followed, however, was of a different cast entirely. Heavy and total – a physical force – it pressed down on us, muffling the sound of our breathing, filling our ears and caressing us with a sibling lethargy. Ned grasped at my arm, close to going down, and I put a still, supportive arm around him. He weighed nothing at all. The smell I had now learned to associate with Sheila Mackenzie was finally fading, replaced by what was more certainly Ned's smell. Stale sweat and lemon drops, faeces and the clinging must of the cold night air.

"That turned out a lot better than I might have expected," Oliver finally said, laughing nervously.

Ned smiled and shook his head. "Don't make the mistake of feeling too pleased with yourself," he said. "If it were that simple, mate, I'd have seen her off a right long time ago."

"You don't think we've seen the last of her, then?" I asked.

"Nope, I don't. This is a long way from being over. She'll not rest until she's got whatever it is she wants."

"Which is?"

"Me. Dead, I suppose."

As we walked through the rest of the house with Ned, collecting a few toiletries and a change of clothes for him – no longer prepared to let him stay here – we saw just how much Sheila Mackenzie's presence had impacted on his home. The rooms looked as if a horde of yobs had been squatting there – tables, televisions and beds overturned and destroyed. The wallpaper had been torn from the wall in places, as if Sheila Mackenzie had been frantically trying to claw her way out, much as she at one time might have in the Sorrow Street Asylum. None of it seemed to come as much of a surprise to Ned, and it occurred to me that it could well have been like this before he had left. There was simply no way that he himself could have been capable of destruction on this scale – so had he witnessed Sheila Mackenzie in the act, or had that come later?

"This is much worse than I ever imagined it could be," Oliver said to me on the landing. Ned was in his room, grabbing some underwear out of an old Mahogany chest of drawers. Oliver spoke quietly. "If she can wreck furniture and belongings, now, what else is she capable of?"

"She's getting stronger," I said, by way of an agreement.

"She wasn't this strong before?"

I shook my head. "I don't think so. Taking Nadine from us would have been simpler if she'd been able to create this kind of havoc."

He nodded dubiously and looked in on Old Man Ned. I could tell that Oliver didn't want to remain here any longer than was absolutely necessary – and, yet, given what had just happened downstairs, he was remarkably calm. I considered telling him that she was wrong – that Sheila Mackenzie and Francesca were *both* wrong – but decided that now was maybe not the right time.

When the three of us left Ned's, we did so by the front door. We paused on the pavement outside and looked back – Ned between Oliver and me for support. The house seemed melancholic and plaintive, separate from the rest of Sorrow Street. I knew hardly anything of the life that Ned had lived there – and I wondered if I ever would... if I would ever *want* to, for that matter. What must it have been like for him for all those years? His wife had left him and then it was just the two of them. Ned and Sheila Mackenzie.

"I just want to rest," Ned said. "Is that too much to ask?"

I didn't think it was, and told him so. "We'll work this out," I said, a little unrealistically.

Oliver looked over Ned's head at me. His face said all that needed to be said, but, just to be sure, he told me, "Stephen fucking Hawking couldn't work this one out, mate."

Not one of us felt safe. We huddled around the fire in our living room, Wee Mark asleep on the settee – no one comfortable with the idea of him sleeping upstairs alone – a cleaned-up and fed Ned sitting in the armchair near the window, holding on to ourselves and each other as we yet again tried to talk our way to a solution.

Don was on the floor with Oliver and me. His intelligence could occasionally be put in the shade by Oliver's altogether bigger personality and self-assuredness, but I was beginning to see much more clearly just what it was that Oliver saw in him. He came to the fore in a crisis. Precise and logical, he took the problem apart in much the same way that Oliver might, but with a greater calm and a distinct and welcome lack of creative flourish.

"Let's look at what we know," he said. "Sonny found a journal belonging to the woman we now know to be Sheila Mackenzie. Sheila Mackenzie was a confidence artist and murderer, among other things. Her daughter was raped and killed by Ned's grandfather, whom she in turn killed herself. We know this, yes, Ned?"

Now that he'd eaten and had a bit of a wash, Ned was looking a little better – more like his old self, anyway. Nevertheless, his voice was still weak and laboured. I noticed that he'd started breaking his sentences in the most unexpected of places, drawing breath as if it had a lead weight tied to the end of it.

"Aye," he said, "we know this. There was never any doubt."

"And it isn't possible that Sheila Mackenzie killed her daughter and made it look like it was Edwin that did it?"

This hadn't occurred to me – or the others, judging by their expressions. I couldn't see how it might change our predicament, but I was nevertheless interested in hearing Ned's answer.

He clasped his bony hands together in his lap, elbows jutting as he lowered his head and thought about it. "I suppose... it's possible," he said. "She was a strong and... creative woman. It would have been easy for her to... make it look as if he'd raped and killed the little lass... especially as he'd just... forgive my crudeness... especially as he'd just emptied himself in her. But I don't see why she would do that. And, more to the point, I don't see how it would help us if she had."

"Me neither," I said. "It seems to me that what happened then isn't as important as we're inclined to believe. We think it is, but that's because we've been conditioned to think like that. What's important is what she wants now."

"You're right, of course," Don said. "I'm just trying to get a clear picture – in case there's an obvious causal link that we've overlooked."

"I tend to think we're all missing the point," Ned said. He was morose and unwilling to look at any of us. He stared at his knees, still breathing with difficulty. "What she wants, causal links – it's all by the by. Sheila Mackenzie's a fickle lass. She's as... dissatisfied with her lot as the rest of us... and if she wants something today... chances are she won't much want it tomorrow."

"Then why keep up such a sustained assault on you for all these years?" Ashley wondered.

"Habit?" Ned ventured.

This didn't strike me as a credible answer. Maybe there *was* an element of habit to Sheila Mackenzie's behaviour. It would be ludicrous to think otherwise, given that she'd existed in this "state" for so long. But there had to be more to it than that.

"Maybe we should just forget the whys and wherefores," I said, "and focus on the problem of how to get rid of her."

Oliver had been oddly silent through most of our discussion. I knew him well enough to appreciate that he was working through something. I also knew him well enough to recognise that to interrupt his thought process would not prove fruitful. On the floor, his back resting against the settee just to the right of Maggie's legs, I watched him as Don wondered aloud if the two could ever be separated. Oliver wasn't listening; the conversation was quickly becoming repetitive and self-defeating – the conundrum growing ever more complicated as we tried, and failed, to pinpoint just what was the central issue.

"The journal isn't the key," Old Man Ned was insisting. "You digging that up... didn't start all this. She was... around long before that... long before I even moved here, for that matter."

"It started it for me," I insisted.

"No, it didn't," Ned said. "Your father saw her, too. I've told you that."

"Why *did* you move here, Ned?" Ashley asked.

"Good question, love," he said. "I knew Sheila Mackenzie died in the Sorrow Street Asylum... so why would I want... to move nearer to the problem? It just seemed like the right thing to do, at the time, I reckon. I'd travelled around a fair bit by this time, you see – and... and no matter how far I went, she was always with me. No escaping her. So I just figured that moving here, where the asylum used to be... might somehow placate her."

"Didn't work, did it?" I said.

Ned smiled ruefully. "You could say that, I suppose. If I had the chance, I'd do a lot... of things differently, lad. Moving here... was..." he trailed off, blinking rapidly and trying to find the right words. A tear broke free as he said, "You have to bear in mind that... Sheila Mackenzie wasn't the only one to suffer and die here. This place... is not a good place, even without her. It's easy to... get confused and... lost in a place like this."

The Sorrow Street Asylum. I'd thought about it so many times but, since the discovery of the journal, always in the context of Sheila Mackenzie's experience of it. The Warty Nurse had been the only other person I'd ever considered when thinking of it, and, yet, as Ned had pointed out, this had in reality been a place brimming with delusion and paranoia, a simple plot of land that had eventually become council owned – broken with sad stories and psychotic perspective.

Oliver looked on the verge of saying something. He sat forward, straightening his right leg, and then stopped – looking at the curtained window behind Ned. I was almost too afraid to look. We all stopped talking and turned to see...

... nothing. The curtained window was just that, the space between it and the back of the armchair empty and still. And then I understood. We weren't actually *looking* – we were *listening*. Shouting, distant and yet near enough for it to matter. The ululation of sirens, still a fair way away, but definitely getting closer.

I glanced at Oliver and he gave me a weary, forlorn look as he pushed himself to his feet and walked to the window. As he eased aside the curtain, the emergency vehicles turned onto Sorrow Street and the flashing blue lights strobed through the room, cold and regular – otherworldly.

We ran out onto the street – even Ned, surprisingly, finding the strength and motivation to move at a pretty impressive pace. Ashley clung to me and I put my arm around her, protecting her from the cold night air and, I hoped, giving her the strength she needed to cope with the added complication of what we were seeing.

"Oh, for fuck's sake," Maggie gasped. "This can't be happening."

"I'm afraid it is, pet," Ned said.

I'd never seen a house burn before, so I had nothing to compare it to. It seemed to me, however, that Ned's house burned with an especially poignant ferocity – a unique energy that, to my mind, could mean only one thing. We stood and watched as the fire fighters extended their hoses and got themselves organised, shouting and the squelching of radio communications echoing off the buildings around us, and I saw immediately the futility of it all. This was no normal fire. It raged with an anger never before seen by the men now faced with the job of quelling it, I was sure – and as Ashley took my hand, I felt the inevitability of it all. This was how it had always been meant to end for Ned.

Something within Ned's house cracked and gave way. The splintering sound was painful to hear – the crash that followed oddly heartbreaking. I looked at Ned to see how he was dealing with this, and as I did so, I noticed that Mags had her arms folded. She watched the fire and hugged herself. Some of our neighbours were now also coming out onto the street to watch and see if there was anything they could do – and as she looked around at them, I realised something was missing from this quaint little picture of tragic recognition, and as I realised, I instinctively looked to the front door of our house.

Oliver spotted that something was wrong before the rest of us. He followed my gaze and immediately started moving. For a man of his size, he was quick – but he just wasn't quick enough. I passed him easily, vaulting the wall as I had on that day when Sheila Mackenzie had taken Nadine Verity from us. This time the danger was a direct reversal of what it had been that day. Wee Mark came toddling out, waving his arms about gleefully as he headed around the side of the house towards the back garden, and I wanted him there with us in the middle of the road. The back garden wasn't safe. Anything might happen there. Children should be seen *and* heard and watched and cared for and that fucking bitch had done it again – like that silly fakir sending that poor fucking boy up that rope, it was all about misdirection. It was all about making us look one place so that we'd miss the obvious and lose, always lose, that which was most precious to us.

I could hear Oliver behind me, but his actions no longer sounded quite so urgent. He thought Wee Mark was safe. He didn't get it. Even now, after everything that had happened, he still didn't understand that the garden was the most dangerous place of all. Ned's house burned and my wife and friends stood in the middle of the road with the rest of the neighbours – watching, no doubt feeling vulnerable to the more obvious dangers, as Wee Mark ran away from me down the side of the house, laughing and calling my name, his echoes stretching out into the miraculously calm distance.

I couldn't see him anymore. I could hear his bedroom slippers scuffing and pattering, hear his babbling and laughter – but the darkness closed in on me the minute I stepped around the side of the house and before I could get a proper visual fix on him, he was gone. I jogged forward, touching the wall occasionally in order that my sense of "place" might be preserved, and the world slipped away from me – the walls closing in overhead, the deep, orange glow of the night sky obliterated.

"Sonny!" Wee Mark shouted, laughing, and I desperately followed the sound of his voice – knowing there was only one way he could go, but suddenly quite certain that I was going to lose him. "Come get *meeee*, Sonn-*eeee*."

I stopped when I got to the place where the back garden gate should have been. Breathing heavily, more afraid than I'd been since *that* day, I put my hand flat against the wall to steady myself as I tried to assimilate just what it was I was seeing.

As far as I knew, there had never been a topiary arch where our back gate had been. My father had always opted for order and beauty in his garden, tempered cleverly with simplicity, and I had leant towards low maintenance and the self-perpetuating. Topiary archways took work and the kind of aesthetic tendencies that, in one way or another, neither of us had had. And, yet, here was one such arch – beautifully crafted and tended, the central base of the arch approximately seven feet from the ground, bottle green with shadow and vitality. I touched it, in awe not only of the patient care its creation must have taken, but also its remarkable, unquestionable solidity. It was real. As real as the wall I had only moments before rested my hand against. As real as the path beneath my feet. As real as the little boy who had passed through it, and who I now had to follow.

I understood the arch's significance, of course. It was a familiar motif and, that apart, I remembered the story Ned had told me earlier in the summer of those two boys who had trespassed in the grounds of the asylum. That I wouldn't find my own garden waiting on the other side when I passed beneath it seemed logical enough. What I wasn't prepared for, however, was the complete eradication of everything with which I was familiar.

The sound of the fire fighters and the splintering, roaring anger of the fire itself dropped away. And I was there.

***

It was a place tinged with sorrow. This was the first thing that struck me. Dark to the point of obliterating my otherwise visible surroundings, it was a place textured and expressed not in colour and shade but, rather, in feeling and, perhaps, need. I experienced emotion the like of which I had never before known – overcome not, as might have been expected, by my own grief for my dead daughter but instead by an overpowering sense of this world I was in as somehow *internal*. I existed within an idea, and just what that idea was felt beyond me. I was shaped and inspired by things over which I had no power, and as I stood there in the darkness it seemed as if this had always been the case.

I had striven to keep control – to *take* control – of my life, my work and, to one degree or another, of Ashley. I had lived with ideas, worked with them in such a way that they could only ever grow in unjustifiable importance. Fashioning worlds and characters, I stole from those around me... and became indignant and heartbroken when I in turn was stolen from. And the harder I tried, the quicker it all seemed to elude me. The story slipped ludicrously away, my wife had very nearly become a stranger – and only something so tragic and irreversible as the death of a daughter could go at least halfway towards setting me back on track.

"Irreversible," I heard Sheila Mackenzie say – out there in the darkness and, yet, so close... close enough to brush a kiss against my cheek, to breathe her foul but not unwelcome breath in my ear. "Irreversible, irreversible... irreversible." She was mocking me – that much was obvious. She saw my truth as well as I, and she knew just how ridiculous I truly was. Insect-like and panicked, I scuttled from one desperate scene to another – looking for meaning, looking for explanation, looking for solutions – and she calmly looked on, grinning sardonically and waiting, waiting... waiting.

But for what?

I pushed this thought to the back of my mind. It was just another insect-like attempt at escape – unworthy of me, not valid when there were more important things to consider. Wee Mark. He had come through the archway. There had been nowhere else for him to go... and, yet, I couldn't see him. He could not have gone far. He had to be nearby. But the darkness closed in, as if sensing my need to find the little boy and determining to thwart me, and the best I could do was stumble about, tripping and calling his name – suddenly quite sure that it was too late, that Wee Mark was now with Nadine, the two of them irreversibly lost.

Irreversible.

Something was blocking my way. I couldn't see what it was. Holding out my hands, I tentatively touched this new obstacle – feeling a warmth I didn't initially recognise. The shape gave more away, however. Evidently a woman, clearly comfortable with my touching her, searching, looking to understand. My hand brushed a warm, soft breast and I stepped back. Sheila Mackenzie. It had to be. It could be no one else... but... such *warmth*. Was that even possible? She was before me, concealed within convenient and now total darkness and she was *warm to the touch*. She had been dead all these years and she was *warm to the touch*.

It didn't make any sense, but as I took another step away from her I felt the fingers of her right hand curl around mine. She held me there – in that place, in that moment – and I couldn't pull away from her... I didn't want to. Such warmth. Complete and, or so it at first seemed, unconditional. Rather than move further away, I took an involuntary (or was it?) step towards her.

"The father lives that the daughter might die," she whispered in my ear – and then she was gone.

It was bright. Too bright. Sunlight streamed into the room and I flinched, putting an arm across my eyes and looking cautiously at the shadowy form that was now leaning over me... the shadowy form that had a warm, shaky hand pressed against my bare chest. It hurt to look at her, but I knew that I had to. It just wasn't good enough for me to lie here and blithely accept whatever it was she intended to inflict on me. Wee Mark was still lost and now there was light to see by – too much light – and I had to fight this. I had to push against it. I couldn't just –

Before I could act on that primary impulse, however, Ashley spoke.

"Hey, love," she said, sitting on the bed beside me and smiling. Her hand moved from my chest and instead rested, a little uncertainly, on my upper arm. Her eyes where more like Nadine's than ever, and I once more felt grief's fingers squeezing at my larynx. "Welcome back," she said, smiling and rubbing my arm.

"What happened?" My throat was dry and clogged with emotion, but she understood me easily enough.

"We're not sure, exactly," she said. "Mags and I followed you round to the back garden when you went after Wee Mark. Oliver and Don stayed with poor old Ned. We found you..." The emotion started to get the better of her, too; she hiccupped and swallowed hard, blinking back the tears as she rubbed my arm more rapidly. "... We found you unconscious on the ground, where the hole used to be, with Wee Mark sitting cross-legged on the grass beside you, calm as you like. I thought I'd lost you, again, Sonny. It was just like last time only this time it was worse... I would have had no one. It would have just been me, Sonny, and I don't ever want that."

I still wasn't completely with her. Wee Mark had been sitting on the floor beside me. He was quite clearly all right otherwise Ash would have told me and, yet, I couldn't help wondering what it must have been like for him – what he must have witnessed. Sitting cross-legged on the grass beside me, had it all been just another game to him? I wondered. Or had it frightened him to such a degree that he would hold the horror of what he had seen deep within for years to come? Wee Mark was a wee bruiser – of that there could be no doubt. He was the kind of kid who could keep himself entertained head-butting walls for hours on end. And the walls would undoubtedly come off worse. But if he had encountered the kind of total, impenetrable darkness that I had, what might he have made of it – how would he deal with it? And if he hadn't, I wondered... if it had been different for him and he had *actually seen* the things that I had only felt... what then? The thought of Wee Mark seeing me reach out like that – reach out and touch the strange woman's breast, however unwittingly – made me feel unusually guilty. He wouldn't understand. He could *never* understand. With time, as he grew older, he would form him own conclusions and revise appropriately, as we all do, and that more than anything made me afraid for him.

Sometimes answering our own questions is the worst thing we can do.

"You looked so peaceful," Ashley was saying. "I was... you had to be dead. That's what I thought. Nobody could look so calm and content and still be alive, not after everything that we've been through. It just didn't seem possible."

"I'm not dead," I told her, placing a hand on her thigh and giving it a hopefully reassuring squeeze – but I had to wonder. Something had changed. I felt Ashley's warmth through the loose cream skirt she wore and desperately wanted to be with her. It was the most primitive and natural of impulses – to cover her and enter her, make her mine as I became hers – but it was also a refusal to accept that which I now knew to be true. I reached under her skirt, slipping my fingers beneath the elastic of her knickers and said again, "I'm not dead." Ashley moved for me, smiling a puzzled smile as she brushed a tear away, and I caressed her, stroked her – lost myself, however momentarily, in this simple act, in touch and memory and uncluttered physical need.

"I know, sweetheart," she said. "Sonny... love?" I looked at her. "I want to. But we can't. Not now. We need to talk."

"I'm not dead." I couldn't stop myself repeating this. It had to be said and then it had to be said again – because that was the point. That was the one thing that none of us had acknowledged, not in any meaningful way.

"What happened, Sonny?" She was so beautiful. My wife. Ashley Moore. I saw her every day. I lived with her. I *breathed* her, for fuck's sake. But I hadn't known her beauty until then – or that was at least how it felt. She shone through her grief, pain and confusion. Yes, there were flaws. Yes, in time she might crumble into the sea with the rest of us. But at that moment I saw within her an understanding that – for all our years together – I had previously missed. My wife understood that everything had its limit, that sometimes the happiness just wouldn't come because our need would always be greater. On some level, I believed she had learned to reluctantly accept that – and it was this that made her so beautiful.

It was true that I wanted her so that I wouldn't have to confront the now undeniable truth with which I was faced – but I also wanted her because of this. In that moment, Ashley's beauty sang of redemption. And right then, redemption was something I most assuredly wished for.

"Talk to me, love." She moved again and my fingers slipped out of her. I let my hand rest against the warmth of her thigh, still beneath her skirt. The flesh beneath her eyes seemed recessed and shadowy, perhaps the only physical sign that hinted at her condition and made me question whether or not she was ready for what I had to tell her. She brushed something from my cheek and then let her hand rest against my neck. "You saw her, again, didn't you?"

I shook my head. "No," I said. "I'm not sure what happened but, no, I didn't see her." It wasn't exactly a lie, but Ashley saw through it, anyway.

"But she was there, wasn't she?"

Nodding slowly, I said, "Yes, I think so. It was dark. It was hard to tell."

"It couldn't have been that dark, love – there was a house fire raging a few doors down the street."

"I know, but it was still dark. Dark like you wouldn't believe."

She frowned. "I don't understand."

"Neither do I, love. I just know... I need to think it through, Ash. Is that okay? I... I just need a few minutes to wake up and work out what actually happened and what I dreamt. Do you mind?"

She smiled and it hurt. It was time to savour everything. "No," she said. "I don't mind. But I want to know about everything when you feel you're ready, yes?"

"Of course."

"You can even tell me about Mags, if you want."

It came so softly and unexpectedly that I almost missed it. Nodding sincerely, I again started to say "of course", but stopped myself as I realised just what it was she had in fact said.

"Mags." It wasn't a question.

"I know, Sonny. I've always known." There was nothing accusatory in her tone. If anything, she seemed amused – as if the look on my face had been just what she had expected and which, perversely, perhaps, made her love me all the more.

"Ash – look, it – "

She put a finger to my lips and closed her eyes, shaking her head. "Don't," she said. "It happened, Sonny, and I know nothing like it has happened since. It's not an issue but... well, we need it out of the way, now."

"That simple."

"Yes, I think so. You still married me, didn't you?"

"Yes."

"Well there you go, then." She smiled and then lowered her eyes. "I'm not saying we don't have to talk about why it happened and why you never told me, I just... it can only be a beginning, I think that's what I mean."

"I can't believe you're being so calm about it."

"I've never felt threatened by it," she said. "Mags was never going to take you away from me. Neither of you wanted it. Then... last night, when I saw you there and I thought you were dead..." She swallowed hard.

"What, love?"

"I know what she said to you, Sonny. I know what she said to you and I know what you think it means. And it's not going to happen. I won't let it. I won't let Sheila Mackenzie take you away from me."

I closed the bathroom door behind me and sat down on the toilet – my face in my hands, eyes closed and gritty with fatigue. I hadn't known what to say to Ashley. So many different things were battling away inside me that the only option was to get away from her – run to the bathroom with the lame and obvious excuse of needing to pee. It bought me time. That was my only real consideration. That it also meant that Ashley was left alone with the horror of what she so clearly knew crept in later – the guilt at my "deserting" her at this pivotal time intense and unremitting – but for the time being I wanted only to think, to find this space for myself and dig in until I could finally make sense of the dilemma I now faced.

Irreversible, I thought – rocking a little against the clarity and cruelty of what Sheila Mackenzie had said. From my now vertiginous vantage point it all seemed so simple and predictable. With a twisted, seemingly unfathomable methodology, she had worked us – patiently arranging each part, counting the minutes and the missteps. There'd been a crudeness to it all. Her lack of grace had at times been overwhelming but I had to admit that, yes, she had worked us all and done so with a crafty skill that made me want to throw up. Every part of her little Mystery Play had been intended to serve a purpose, and I suspected that the dead – in the form of the mourning Jim – had been equally manipulated. *The dead have needs, too,* I thought grimly. *A dissatisfied lot.*

I heard a noise. Movement downstairs. Raised voices. Someone (Ashley, I assumed) stepping from the landing and quickly descending. It all seemed so inconsequential. We'd been running about for days, endlessly talking. And the harder we had tried, the more futile it became. Pointless. An exercise in butting our heads against a wall.

And all it had finally taken had been for a wee bruiser to show me the way. Wee Mark had led me through that archway and... how could I have not already known? I was a writer. A novelist, to be more specific. It was my job to take life – the tragic and mundane – and give it order and meaning, an unbroken form that teetered on the brink of epiphany. So how in the name of all that was sacred could I have not seen just how simple it was?

She had wanted me. Ned had said as much, even if he hadn't understood it as precisely as I now did. She had wanted Sonuel Moore, but she had wanted the man, not the boy – the man rich with sensual pain, fashioned from grief and insight. She didn't want Ned dead and she most assuredly didn't want Nadine. One was merely the amusing possibility for a subplot whilst the other was nothing more to Sheila Mackenzie than a bargaining tool.

Irreversible.

There was nothing irreversible about any of this. That was what I now saw she had been trying to tell me. Nadine... it didn't have to be the way it was. She didn't have to miss out; she could be the young woman Ashley had dreamed of. All it would take would be for me to accede to Sheila Mackenzie's wishes.

If the father lives that the daughter might die, I thought, *then the logical inversion of that is that the father dies that the daughter might live.* A natural sacrifice – one that any right minded parent wouldn't hesitate to make – but there was so much to consider. If Sheila Mackenzie wanted me in exchange for my daughter then as far as I was concerned, she could have me. If it were just about me, then that was exactly how it would be. But what of Ashley? She would lose her husband and miraculously have her daughter returned to her. A single mother under the most bizarre and inexplicable of circumstances. How would she deal with that? What would she tell people? Would it slip under the radar, somehow, or would she be looked upon with suspicion?...

I couldn't *see* any of it. The images and ideas were blurred and weary. For all I knew, none of this was possible. We had assumed that Sheila Mackenzie had had a forceful and physical effect on Old Man Ned's house, but was she, a ghost herself, capable of resurrecting the dead? And if she were, who was to say that she wouldn't renege on the deal?

Thinking about what it would be like to make that decision – to face the finality of it without actually knowing that there were any guarantees – I got to my feet when I heard what sounded like a rather urgent knock at the door, removing the latch and letting Ashley in.

Now that the door was open, I could hear the voices downstairs more clearly. I frowned at Ashley questioningly and she said, "It's Ned. We're having a bit of bother with him."

"What kind of bother?"

She ignored my question. "Can you come down?"

Insisting that she answer me first seemed futile – and not a little childish – and so I merely nodded and left the bathroom with her.

"I know you don't like the idea, lad," I heard Ned say as I entered the living room. "But this isn't just about what you do or don't like. I need to do this. It's the right thing."

"It was a shit hole, Ned," Oliver was saying. Ned was sitting in the far corner of the settee looking remarkably like a ventriloquist's dummy – his hands hanging loosely against his thighs. Oliver stood over him in a manner that, to those who didn't know him, might have appeared threatening. "It was a *freezing* shit hole and if you go back there we *all* know what's going to happen to you."

"And your point is?"

Don was by the window, elbow resting on the sill. He looked at Mags – sitting in the armchair opposite with a sleepy, sulky Wee Mark on her knee – and rolled his eyes.

"My point?" Oliver was beginning to sound just a little exasperated. I got the impression that this conversation had been going on in one form or another for quite some time. "My point is that you'll die if you go back there, Ned. You'll die and we none of us want that."

"We all have to die sometime," Ned insisted. "And I'm ready. Whether she wants it or not, I can't say no more – but it's what I want. I need the peace, lad. It's time for me to just accept what I have ahead of me and stop trying to fight it. Whatever you say, I'm going back there."

Oliver glanced up at me. "Sonny," he said. "Have a word with him, would you? See if you can talk some sense into him." Oliver turned away and joined Don by the window, leaving me the stage.

"Going back where, Ned?" I asked.

"Back where I belong," he said, begrudgingly.

"And that would be?"

"You're a bright lad. Given that my home's burned to the ground, I'm sure that's got to narrow it down a fair bit for you."

"Edwin's hut."

"Well done. Go to the top of the class and sharpen the rubbers." He spoke flatly – with all the energy of a deflated party balloon. I could already understand Oliver's exasperation.

"Why on earth would you want to go back there?" I came round and stood with my back to the fire, so that I could get a better look at him. In spite of the food and care he'd been given, last night had clearly taken its toll. His body looked on the verge of caving in on itself, his eyes and mouth too large for his oh so tiny face – skull-like and shrunken, totemic and oddly endearing.

"Why on earth *wouldn't* I want to go back there?" he asked. "I've got nowhere else, Sonny. As I see it, it's the most sensible decision I can make."

"You want to make like an elephant and go off to die?" Trying a different tack seemed like a good enough idea. No other approach had worked. "Very noble, I'm sure – but aren't you forgetting one thing?"

"I very much doubt it," he mumbled.

"How's it going to look, Ned?" I said. "Your house burns to the ground. You're staying with us. Next thing everyone knows is we've let you bugger off to die in some shitty old hut by the sea. They're going to love us. Can you imagine what the Gazzette'll make of it?"

Ned sniffed and refused to meet my eyes. Staring at Maggie's bare feet, he rubbed his neck, thinking, and finally said, "You don't get it, do you, Sonny? I don't have any choice. Not really. If I don't do this... if I don't just hold up my hands and accept my fate... it'll just keep going and keep going and keep going. She won't stop until I'm out of the way. That's the way she is. She'll keep persecuting all of you and it'll all be my fault." He choked back a sob and wiped his eyes with his sleeve, and then continued. "I don't want to do this," he said. "I really don't. But I have to do it. It's the only way."

Except it wasn't. Ned was torturing himself, believing that this was his fault – that somehow he could put everything right by dying when, in fact, I knew that I was the one who had to die. Perhaps ever since he had been a boy, Ned had borne his cross of supposed responsibility, only now truly prepared to face his martyrdom. And I couldn't let him do it – because it was wrong in so many ways.

"No," I said, looking at Ashley – her mouth trembling as she slowly shook her head. "No, it's not the only way."

We sat on the stalker wall – just the two of us – our arms around each other as we stared at the lawn where our daughter had once played, and where she might one day play again. The sun, as bright as it was, seemed weak and unnaturally low in the sky. The chill air, or more probably the subject of our impending conversation, made Ashley shiver.

I tried to find a way in – some opening that would help her see the sense of what I was about to propose. Any argument she would have to the contrary was easily predicted (I'd already considered them myself any number of times), and, yet, I didn't feel confident in my ability to counter them. She would talk rings around me, unless I could find that one thing that would provide the necessary leverage. The reality that Sheila Mackenzie had, however subtly, made known to me would be wholly wasted on her unless I could somehow evoke a sense of what I had felt upon waking that morning. I listened to the others whispering in the kitchen and it occurred to me that maybe there wasn't a right way to do this. Maybe there would never be a right way in because Ashley would always disagree with the decision I believed I had already made. It was the way it was no doubt meant to be, I thought.

It was Ashley who finally broke the silence.

"I know what you think you've got to do," she said. "I know and I think it's ridiculous that you're even considering such a thing, Sonny."

"You think it's ridiculous that I can get our daughter back?"

"I think it's ridiculous that you're willing to risk an actuality for a highly doubtful potentiality." She'd been spending far too much time around Oliver. I thought of telling her that this was not the time for philosophical argument, but instead took a breath and considered my reply more carefully.

"That 'highly doubtful potentiality' happens to be our daughter's only chance of living a full, happy life, love," I said, holding more tightly against her increasing rigidity. "Maybe it's wrong. I really don't know. But that's what this is all about. It's a trade off. That's what life *is*. My parents died that I might live and now – "

"You don't really believe that?"

"I think I do, yes." It had a kind of logic to it. It made sense and provided *meaning*. I couldn't really see a good reason to simply dismiss it out of hand.

"They somehow sacrificed themselves?" she asked.

"Yes... no, I don't know, Ash."

"It was an accident, Sonny. I know you'd like to believe otherwise, but that isn't how it was. It was just a meaningless accident and to make anything more than that of it is... it's not good, Sonny. You can't base anything on that, let alone a decision of this magnitude."

It was all too easy for me to imagine my father applauding her from the kitchen doorway. He would have approved, that much was clear. My assumptions were clumsy, at best, whilst Ashley's impressive handling of the situation was something he would have embraced and encouraged. I had no idea how he had dealt with the problem of Sheila Mackenzie, or even the precise form of the problem as it had been presented to him – maybe it had been his intention to tell me about it one day, when the time was right – but it was not difficult for me to imagine his no-nonsense response to my proposal.

"If you must insist on being so bloody stupid," he would have said, "I've got some fencing posts in the garage. I'll knock you up a cross and bloody well nail you to it."

But, of course, neither Ashley nor my father had ever been in my position. I could not write Ashley out of something so important, but, ultimately, it was my decision – and I was growing increasingly certain that it was the only real choice I had.

"I just can't see any other way, Ash," I said.

She pulled away from me, putting her clenched hands in her lap. I watched them carefully as she struggled to make herself smaller. "So you're going to kill yourself?" she said coldly. "No matter what I say."

"That wasn't what I said."

"Wasn't it?"

"No."

"Then what were you saying, Sonny? Because that's what it sounded like to me."

"I just can't... I don't know how to live with something like that, love. Knowing... knowing there was a chance and – "

"*A chance?*" she erupted. Her hands were still clenched. *Can't rely on anything anymore,* I thought. It could almost have been funny. "*A chance*? That's what it all comes down to? You're willing to risk everything we've got on a *fucking chance?*"

She was up on her feet, now – pacing back and forth on the lawn, ranting on about how irresponsible it was of me to even consider something so final and *disrespectful*. I stood, too, trying to calm her, insisting that this wasn't what I wanted and that I'd just been looking for a way to get our daughter back. Desperately, I tried to hold her but she only pushed me away – turning her back on me as the others came out to see what all the commotion was about. When she heard Oliver ask uncertainly if everything was all right, she spun quickly on her heel, marching past me and addressing Oliver, her face streaked with tears and snot, her arms waving about exaggeratedly.

"He wants to kill himself," she said, pulling her chin in against the sheer absurdity of it all. "What do you think of that? He thinks she wants him, this Sheila Mackenzie. He thinks that by giving himself to her we'll get our daughter back. Sorry. Sorry, *I'll* get our daughter back – because Daddy won't be here, will he? Oh, no. He'll be off doing the fucking bump and grind with his dead *friend*."

"Ashley."

"*Don't* Ashley me, Sonny! Just don't, okay? This is so easy for you, isn't it? And don't say it isn't because I know. *I know.* All you have to do is leave. All that's required of you is that you let this world go and step over the threshold into another. Piss easy, right? You do that just about every bloody day of the week. But what about me, Sonny? What about *me*? What happens to the selfish bitch when dear, darling hubby buggers off and never comes back? What happens when Nadine doesn't come back?" The rage was beginning to leave her, now. Her fingers unfurled like petals and I realised just how little I really knew her. "We have to accept that she's gone, Sonny," she told me, sitting back on the wall, shoulders slumped. She was crying quietly, now. "If we're to get through this we just have to understand that there's nothing... there's *nothing* we could have done to prevent this, and there's nothing we can do to change it. We can't go on looking for ways..." she trailed off. "I don't know," she said. "Maybe that's how all this ends."

"What do you mean?" I asked. It seemed like a lifetime since last I'd spoken. My voice sounded alien and untutored.

Everyone watched her expectantly – Old Man Ned squinting against the sun, Mags putting Wee Mark down so that he could cling to her leg and suspiciously eye the goings on. Contrary to what Ashley seemed to believe, I didn't want to die. The thought of leaving her was painful and repellent. Whatever she had to say, however, needed to be convincing. It was all so logical, now. It made sense that Sheila Mackenzie would want the kind of fulfilment that she had once taken for granted. And if Ashley were to dissuade me, her case would have to be watertight.

She shrugged. "God, Sonny, I don't know," she said. "It's just that... we're constantly... it's never enough. We're always looking for more and now's no different. Maybe that's what she wants. Maybe she wants everyone to be as dissatisfied as her. By accepting that we'll never have Nadine back, maybe we somehow rob her of her power."

"I'll just have to learn to live with it," Oliver said, looking at me. "She has a point, Sonny. Look how Sheila Mackenzie reacted when I said that to her."

"She came back and burned Ned's house to the ground," I reminded him. "It made her stronger."

Ned sniffed derisively. "Nah, the little lass dying made her stronger. I watched her trash my house before I went off to try to get that sister of mine to take me in. She'd never been capable of owt like that before, as far as I recall. My bet is, if you top yourself you'll make matters ten times worse."

"This from the man who wants to go off to his grandfather's hut to die," I said.

"I don't have a pretty wife to watch out for," he told me. "Listen to her, Sonny. She's talking sense."

Sense. It suddenly seemed so ludicrous that all I could think of was how, the night before, I had been in this very garden with Wee Mark and known only darkness and Sheila Mackenzie's touch. The familiar had been taken from me. Everything of value had fallen away and I was instead presented with something from another time, an idea of loneliness and possible recovery. Ashley had not been there. Whatever she claimed to know was of no real value; *she had not experienced what I had experienced.* I had walked through a topiary archway, Ashley had walked through a gate – the same gate we had walked through a million times, solid and real, as ordinary as the wall on which she now sat. And, yet, I owed her. She was my wife and I loved her – two things that, even through our most difficult of times, I'd never found it hard to acknowledge. That she had known about Maggie and me all this time, known and quietly accepted it as a minor flaw that would never truly test the fabric of what we had made together, underscored just how important I was to her. That we occasionally lost our way did not truly worry her. That was merely nature's way of reinforcing the good – of letting us see that nothing should be taken for granted. And whilst it was true that it had taken our daughter's death to fully bring that home to us, we had clearly learned enough as a couple to withstand such faithless tragedy. Nevertheless, I believed my understanding of our current circumstances was unique. Our friends stood around us, sharing their interpretation of events – and whilst I understood the logic of what they and Ashley were proposing, I couldn't help but feel that their arguments were flawed, simply because they were not me, they had not lived through it as I lived through it. It seemed presumptuous that they could even begin to contradict what I believed I knew, and right then, the fact of whether I was right or wrong no longer seemed the issue. This was my experience. I wanted to embrace Ashley. I needed her close to me and she *had* to be involved. But, for this one, last time, I knew I had to follow my own course.

And in order to do that, I needed room to consider... room to breathe.

I nodded at Ned and sat down beside Ashley, putting my arm around her. "I'm sorry," I said. "I don't know what I was thinking."

When I stepped out into the back garden later that night – a light rain falling, the house dark and silent behind me – I didn't think of myself in heroic or even cowardly terms. I felt adrift, no longer my own master. Tilting my head back and letting the drizzle fall onto my face, it occurred to me that this had perhaps been how it had always been. I'd unknowingly struggled for form, striven to give my life (and that of my wife) meaning, but life had a current all of its own. It dictated to us and the best we could do was go with it. I was a man. I was a husband. I was a father. And, yet, were I asked to define myself, I would have in the past always answered, "A writer." Fighting the current. Pushing against the inevitable. Unwilling to accept, I had tried to improve on something that was already pretty special.

Before coming down, I had stopped off by my study. Taking Sheila Mackenzie's journal from its locked drawer, I'd opened it and flicked through the now blank pages. I'd wondered if there had ever been anything written there – and then remembered that Ashley had seen that cramped, occasionally indecipherable handwriting, too. It had been real. It had been real but now, having served its purpose, it had faded away to nothing, leaving only memory and heartache and regret.

Looking up into the fine, hazy rain, I now held the journal in my left hand. Flesh-like and warm, it was a sharp contrast to the kitchen knife in my right. I was prepared. I would do what needed to be done.

Summoning the courage I walked along the garden path and onto the patch of ground where the hole had been. Kneeling down, my throat and temples throbbing my heart's frantic objection, I set the journal on the ground before me – turning the knife in my hand, its sharp, serrated titanium edge the cruelest of invitations. The journal should not be reburied. This much seemed obvious. That would be cowardly. It would achieve nothing. Our world would continue to spin through its lamentable orbit and loss and suffering would be and would still be and would always be. Nadine would still be dead. Sheila Mackenzie would still torment us.

I held the journal in my left hand again, letting it fall open – its pages fluttering in the breeze as the light rain pattered down onto it. The knife blade suspended over my left wrist, I closed my eyes, desperately struggling to find the remaining courage I needed to finish this.

And then she moved.

I didn't know how long she'd been standing there, but when she started walking hurriedly towards me I opened my eyes and turned to look at her. I couldn't see her face clearly, but as I started slicing away with the kitchen knife, she called my name and stopped dead in her tracks.

It was a clumsy effort. The paper and binding cut and shredded, but the knife was not the best tool for the job. Nevertheless, with Ashley's help I made a fairly good job of destroying it. Its broken pages and binding scattered and grew sodden, and I felt Ashley's relief overtake the moment – reassuring in its faith.

"There's more to it than ripping the shit out of an old journal," she told me.

"I know," I said.

"She's not coming back." She meant Nadine. She meant Sheila Mackenzie.

"I know," I repeated.

Postscript

Watching them from my study window as they worked with patience and evident glee on the building of their snowman, I marvelled at our resilience and wondered distantly if it could ever have turned out differently.

It was a question I had asked myself a thousand times since that night four months before when Ashley and I had successfully rid ourselves of Sheila Mackenzie, and if not all of the pain and heartache she had brought with her, then at least a substantial part of it. And whilst that question persisted, with each asking it lost a little more of its power over me. I would not exactly have said that it no longer pulled me from sleep sweating and shaking but I had at least learned to understand the nature of acceptance and gone a good way towards developing the skills I would need to see Ashley and I through the remainder of our life together. How it might have turned out, I now saw, was of no consequence. To dwell on such imponderables was to serve oneself a meal that could never be eaten – that would never satisfy and always mock. Like Ashley, I still mourned the loss of our daughter – I still cried for her and wished for the chance to defend her. I wanted to hold her in my arms and breathe in her sweet, talcum powder smell. When I came in from visiting Oliver and Don, I wanted her there, waiting for me, excited by my return. But I saw that that could never have been, that, maybe, it *should* never have been – and whilst I knew that this was a wound that would always ache and burn, I was learning quite ably to live with it.

That Sheila Mackenzie had not returned validated, as we saw it, the decision we had made... the decision *I* had made. It answered questions and confirmed suspicions, and we took some strength and consolation from that. I still expected to see her, of course. Even now, watching Oliver and Don with Wee Mark and a remarkably animated

Veronique, the four of them putting the finishing touches to their precariously lopsided snowman, I couldn't help but imagine Sheila Mackenzie stepping out from within its icy midst – showing herself for just a moment before stepping back.

It didn't help that the snowman was on the patch of ground where the hole had been.

Wee Mark appeared to be growing typically hyper. Earlier that day, over lunch, I'd braced myself as Molly had tactlessly asked Mags if she had ever considered that Wee Mark might have ADHD – "Or maybe he's on the Autism Spectrum," she had added. "Asperger's or something." It had been a tense moment. Glances had been exchanged and Ashley had looked about ready to jump in to defuse the situation. Finally, Maggie had replied. Her drinking a lot more under control these days, she set down her half full wine glass and said, "He's a boy, Molly. He's got Healthy Little Boy Syndrome. Get used to it, pet." Molly had taken it quite well, accepting this with a little nod that suggested a willingness to embrace new ideas that I hadn't seen in her before – and as I watched Wee Mark now, I realised that nobody could have argued with Maggie's diagnosis. Healthy Little Boy Syndrome. An apparently contagious disorder, if Veronique's increasingly boisterous behaviour was anything to go by.

Oliver face down in the snow after what looked like a far from accidental slip and fall, Veronique and Wee Mark jumped on his back – rubbing snow into his hair and doing their damnedest to get some of it down the inside of his jacket. Don stood by, laughing and encouraging the kids to do their worst, and then looked up, catching me watching them. He smiled and beckoned, and I held up a hand. Five minutes. Nodding and giving me a thumbs up, he turned his attention back to the Smackdown Snow Wrestling Bout – grabbing Veronique under the arms and spinning her in the air. The toe of one of her wellies clipped the snowman's head, showering Oliver and Wee Mark with what Wee Mark would later refer to as "snowman brains".

I made a mental note to tell Don that he really must bring his kids to our next gathering and sat down before my PC. I had new email. More special offers from Amazon.co.uk, a fraudulent phishing scam that my privacy protection software auto-filed for me and a message from my old mate, Ned.

Three lines. A blessing, since he had a tendency to email two or three times a day, now. He'd grown oddly paternal towards Ashley and me. Even Ash seemed to welcome this.

"I'm grateful," he had written – using, I knew, the laptop Oliver and I had rescued. "But she's driving me bonkers. Why do the women in my life always feel the bloody need to haunt me?!"

I knew who he meant, of course, and couldn't help but smile to myself.

It had taken Ashley close on two hours to persuade Charlotte Mortimer to take in her brother– and when I had visited him a couple of weeks before, he had described Ashley's skilful intervention as generous and welcome, something for which he would never be able to thank her enough.

"But it's hard," he had said as we strolled along the Esplanade together. "Don't get me wrong, I'm not complaining... well, I suppose I am, but that doesn't mean that I don't know how bleeding lucky I am. It's just that that sister of mine can be... well, let's just say she hovers. It's like she watches me all the time. I daren't put a foot out of place."

"It won't be for much longer," I remembered telling him. "They'll be starting rebuilding soon and then – "

"I'll be selling up," he had said. "I don't really see myself going back there, lad. However much the neighbourhood might have improved recently."

It made sense, of course. My own instinct had been to get away from Sorrow Street as soon as possible – but Ashley had insisted that that wasn't the way. We had to reclaim our lives, she believed, and a significant part of that had to begin with us first reclaiming our family home. I hadn't argued. The truth was, whatever my instinct, Sorrow Street was a place of happy memories as well as sad – and I certainly didn't want to simply walk away from all that, however much I felt I should. So I could understand Ned's decision, even as I recognised that it was one that I myself would never choose to make.

"There's something I want to show you," Ned had then said – leading me down an all too familiar concrete ramp and onto the beach.

"What is it?"

"Wait and see."

I walked beside him along the beach, in the same northerly direction we had taken that night all those months before. It was hard going, even for me. The wind had bitten into us, burning our faces as it gusted in from the sea and whipped up the sand. Squinting against this unwelcome assault, I remembered glancing at Ned; still the frail old man, he nevertheless seemed to be coping admirably with the exertion. He had stridden along purposefully, whistling the Colonel Bogey March between his teeth and swinging those arms. It had been good to see, for not only did it tell me that Ned was once again thriving (whatever he might say to the contrary regarding his sister's influence), but it also strongly suggested that whatever he was about to show me might not be as bad as it could have been.

Predictably, our walk had brought us to Edwin's hut – or what remained of it. Standing with his hands buried deep in the pockets of his coat, chin pulled in against the icy wind, Ned had nodded a satisfied nod. Burned to the ground, it was clearly how he thought the hut should be. It was not a sacred place, not a place of virtuous memory. When we walked through the hut's charred remains, kicking over the occasional blackened piece of wood, I felt a sadness that I couldn't understand until Ned said, "He abused me, you know, lad. Never told anyone that in my life, but he did. That's why I never found it hard to believe that he did what he did to Sheila Mackenzie's little lass."

Sitting before my PC and jotting a quick reply to his email, I remembered that he'd had his back to me. It had made discussing such a personal subject easier.

"He did it here, didn't he?" I'd asked.

Ned had nodded. "He did it other places, too, but this was his favourite place. This was where he was at his most inventive."

"And so you torched the place."

Looking over his shoulder at me, he smiled. "Oh, I didn't do it," he'd said. I had started to question this, thinking the worst, but Ned turned and walked back to me through the debris, laughing. "No, not her, either. Yobs. A bloke I've got pally with comes down here fishing. He saw them at it. About twenty of the buggers, drunk as skunks and shagging each other senseless in the sand dunes. When they got bored with that..." he'd gesture at the mess around us. I could still smell the smoke. It reminded me again of the night his house had burned down. "They saved me a job, as I see it. It needed doing."

Walking back to Charlotte's, I'd experienced a degree of contentment I hadn't felt in a long while. I had strength and love in my life, a way of moving forward in spite of all the things that could so easily have held me back. Ned, I now saw, had had so much more stolen from him and, yet, here he was, still bitching and moaning about Charlotte, still making new friends.

"How's that pretty lass of yours," he'd asked before saying goodbye, and I'd replied with what was fast becoming my pat response.

"She's getting there, mate," I'd said. "She's getting there."

This had not been a lie. Ashley was indeed "getting there". But if I had found the going difficult then it had been doubly so for her. Shortly after we had rid ourselves of Sheila Mackenzie, the acceptance we had opted to struggle for gradually finding its place within our world, realisation had hit her with newfound force and for a while I was certain that I had lost her. It was more than grief and more than a clinical, reactive depression. There was rage and a spiritual *sinking* that I just couldn't do anything about. I watched her, begged her to see a doctor, but she merely continued to retreat from me, growing smaller and angrier with each passing day.

"She blames me," I'd said to Maggie and Oliver one day – and Mags had been indignant, more forceful in her response than I ever remembered her being.

"No, Sonny," she said. "She *doesn't* blame you. She blames herself. She blames herself because *that's what we do*... and it's got to stop now, before this goes too far."

Maybe Maggie was the only one who could have achieved what she did that day, I don't know, but as I waited downstairs with Oliver, Don and Wee Mark, listening to the rise and fall of the three hour "conversation" she had with Ashley in our bedroom, I wished it could have been me. I needed to be Ashley's hero, her saviour and the one who understood her like no one else could. But when Oliver pointed out that Mags was more ideally placed than any of us to talk to Ashley, regarding this matter, at least, I saw the sense in this and accepted the scotch he'd poured me.

The Realm of the Hungry Ghosts

Christmas had been different. Just the two of us, Ashley working hard at finding a way through all the seemingly forced revelry going on around us – designed with the sole purpose of making our loss, we were both convinced, all the more painful – we felt an admittedly gloomy but nevertheless total connection. We hadn't needed to talk. We hadn't needed to "externalise" our "innermost feelings". All that we'd truly required had been the generosity of the other's warmth – the only yardstick by which a successful life could truly be measured. Sitting side by side on the settee – the heat from the gas fire making my eyelids itch, the television silently flickering its Christmas Day nonsense in the corner of the room – we had held each other close, lost in memories and forlorn wishes. It had been a solemn time but I now saw that it had also been a positive period of almost complete acceptance, something that had been required... the final insult to the intrusive memory of Sheila Mackenzie... the final compliment to the beautiful memory of our sweet, precious daughter, Nadine Verity Moore.

When we had felt it necessary to speak, it had been with purpose – a way to move, a method by which to create rather than destroy.

"It was the right thing to do," Ashley had said as we fell into each other, the afternoon becoming evening, our positions hardly changing at all during the intervening hours. "We made the right decision."

"I know." Those two words had developed the feeling of a mantra – or perhaps the response part of a catechism. I'd wanted to say more, but it was unnecessary. I'd spoken the truth. What else was there for me to say? *I knew*. Sheila Mackenzie was gone from our lives. Denying her, refusing the cruel offer she had made us, had disempowered her, just as Ashley, Oliver and the others had argued. But knowing didn't make it an easier. Whatever peace I was on the way to discovering, I'd still believed that a part of me would always wonder if there had been something we had missed, a way of turning back the clock and recreating all that we had lost.

"I don't want another baby," Ashley had said later that evening. Nothing either of us had said, that I could see, had prompted this – but I couldn't help feeling that my thoughts had somehow betrayed me and that she had seen in my body language that underlying need to "recreate"... a need that even I was not wholly convinced by. "Not yet, anyway. It would be wrong... for so many reasons."

"We'd be trying to replace her," I'd agreed. "And we never can."

"No."

"I miss her, Ash."

"Me, too, love." She moved in closer. I hadn't thought this possible. "We'll always miss her, but... we'll see her again – when the time's right."

"You believe that?"

"I have to."

I could hear Wee Mark shouting outside. His enthusiasm brought a smile to my face – especially when I heard his mother shouting a warning to him from the kitchen. Maggie. Sweet Maggie who had lost just as we had lost, who had shared a similar need for self-destruction as my own and had perhaps been the only one brave enough to stand on the brink with Ashley and skilfully bring her back in one piece. We had discussed her, too, Ashley and me – that solemn Christmas Day.

Some sickeningly twee retrospective television show had been playing Johnny Mathis singing *When a Child Is Born* and we were still on the settee. We'd made an effort to eat the food Mags had brought round for us – two plates of turkey, veg, roast potatoes, Yorkshire Puddings, stuffing and gravy that we'd heated up in the microwave – but most of it was still on the plates on the floor by our feet. Maggie had again tried to get us to join her round at Oliver and Don's, but we'd once more declined, telling her that we couldn't do it any other way right now and that however unhealthy it might seem from the outside, it was right for us.

"You haven't said anything to her, have you?" I'd asked Ashley after Mags had gone.

"About?"

"What happened in Wales."

She'd shaken her head. "No, Sonny," she said. "That stays where it belongs. It has no place here, now. It never will. We all know that."

"I'm not sure I could be so forgiving," I'd told her. This wasn't quite true. I think a part of me wanted to test her commitment to this philosophy... or maybe I just wanted punishing.

"I was taught by an expert," she'd said, smiling. It was one of only a few times she'd smiled that day.

"An expert?" I didn't have a clue what she was talking about.

"Molly. Our Christian Friend."

"Molly. Yes. Of course. But she said she wouldn't tell you."

Ashley had smiled again. I saw our daughter there. "She didn't," she'd said. "I told her. Many moons ago."

"I don't understand."

"I needed someone to talk to. That bitch Francesca had somehow found out what you and Mags had been up to in her cottage and she took great pleasure in telling me all about it. I had no one else to talk to, love. Molly was... for all her faults, she was wonderful. She didn't preach, she just talked good old-fashioned sense. We might not be together today had it not been for her."

There had been more I had needed to know, but I'd understood that that would have to wait for another time. The evening had stretched out and we had found a kind of comfort in the oddly uplifting realisation that we had once come close to losing even the hope of the things we now had, and with the unexpected help of a friend, it had been avoided.

It was meagre consolation, but consolation nonetheless.

The noise from the garden had lessened, now, and I realised that I'd probably missed my opportunity to play in the snow with the kids – something that, I promised myself, would never happen again. I started to get to my feet, and then sat back down, remembering something. Hand lightly on my mouse, I pointed and clicked my way through a series of sub-directories until I found what I was looking for; the final section I had written to the *Ma Boy, Ma Boy* story.

Reading through it, I finally acknowledged what I had probably known all along. It was unpublishable. If I'd chosen to do so, I could have quite easily worked it into something worthy of being a Sonuel Moore long short story – but, as it was, it had served its purpose, and as such, I had no further need of it. When Richard had stepped from the garden shed, turning and walking away from the woman that had become Sheila Mackenzie, he had done the one thing I had not expected – the one thing that had not been foreshadowed within the confused lines of that story. And it had been right.

Dragging the story to the recycle bin, which I then very deliberately emptied, I felt another kind of peace entirely. I still had a copy of the story, within the project I was currently working on (the book you are now holding in your hands), but deleting the original was somehow liberating. I no longer felt tempted to go back and rework it. I no longer pondered the ways in which I could tighten up the theme of rebirth... the theme that had become so diluted in the writing.

It was gone.

It was as it should be.

A further twenty minutes had passed since I had last considered going downstairs. I didn't want to linger. I wanted to be with my wife and friends.

My study door was open.

I distinctly remembered closing it. Feeling that old, all too familiar dread, I glanced around, looking over my shoulder before tentatively walking to the door. I expected to see Sheila Mackenzie waiting for me on the landing. It would be just like it had been all those times before. She would masturbate and walk towards me, and there would never be any peace – not for me, not for Ashley... possibly not for Ned and the rest of our friends. It would all start again and this time we would know from the outset that there could be no end.

But the landing was empty. Neither Sheila Mackenzie nor anyone else awaited me, and after a cursory examination of the door jamb (maybe there was something wrong with the latch, after all) I went downstairs – doing my best to put it from my mind.

Wee Mark greeted me in the living room... I say "greeted", he actually launched himself at me from the back of the settee. If I hadn't had my wits about me, he would have landed with a sorry but very expressive thud on the living room carpet. I caught him easily enough, even though he was quite a weight for a lad his age, and walked through to the kitchen – where I could hear the others talking, Veronique giggling as Oliver casually held her upside-down by her legs.

Ashley smiled at me and started making me a coffee, whilst Molly cautioned Olly not to get Veronique too excited. "I'm warning you," she said, "much more silliness and she'll vomit on your shoes."

"You missed out on the fun," Don said.

411

"I saw more than enough from upstairs," I said. I couldn't get that open door out of my mind, however. It should have been closed. There was no way that it could have opened by itself, even with a faulty latch.

Don seemed to sense that there was something on my mind, but before he could ask if everything was all right, I said, "Did any of you look in on me while I was in my room?"

Ashley stopped stirring my coffee. They all looked at me, shaking their heads – Molly and Don seeming a little confused. Oliver put Veronique down and helped her to her feet. "No," he said. "Why?"

Ashley knew what was coming next. She dreaded hearing it almost as much as I dreaded saying it. She started to shake her head – closing her eyes as if this could somehow block out what I was about to say.

"My door was open," I said. "My door was open and... and I know I closed it."

I'd thought that telling them would make it better, but it didn't. Their confused faces, bereft of the hope I had seen there only moments before, stared back at me and I felt removed from them – pulled away even as I struggled to remain. We belonged to each other. We knew the same pain. And, yet, we were all so alone.

I started to dismiss it, my rationalisation crude and clearly desperate.

And then Wee Mark spoke.

He leant in to me – giggling as he pressed his lips against my ear. His breath was warm, his words barely a whisper.

"It was me," he said.

Acknowledgements

The Realm of the Hungry Ghosts was written in a ten month period prior to my writing my first two published novels, *If I Never* and *Children of the Resolution* – and whilst it was very much a novel that I intended to write in my own way, adopting a style and approach that I would further develop with *If I Never*, it is nonetheless fair to say that it would not be the book it is today without input I received along the way.

I would therefore like to thank a handful of the many people who contributed in some way towards the creation of the novel you are now holding.

A big thank you to Elaine Pettigrew, who was kind enough to proof read the final manuscript – spotting a few potentially embarrassing errors – and also offered much support along the way, discussing possible ideas for cover artwork and marketing approach. Her humour and keen eye was much appreciated.

Special thanks also go to Desmond Greene, who offered numerous helpful thoughts on the manuscript and, though he may not realise it, helped considerably towards my decision to bring this novel out through my own publishing company, GWM Publications. Cheers, mate.

Ruth Dugdall, in her enthusiasm for my writing, also helped me see that Hungry Ghosts is a novel that deserves its chance. Thank you, Ruth.

Early in the novel's development I was much indebted to my dear friend Jane Adams. Her encouragement and initial incredulity helped greatly. As has so often been the case.

Thanks must go (though they will insist they aren't required) to my ever tolerant and supportive parents, Bill and Sandra. In this case, special thanks must go to Dad for reading the manuscript numerous times, and to Mam for having to endure listening to the two of us talk about the various themes and developments within the novel.

Finally, a huge thank you to you, Dear Reader, for spending your hard earned cash on my little effort. I hope you consider it money well spent.

Lightning Source UK Ltd.
Milton Keynes UK
UKOW051649190612

194705UK00002B/2/P